D0779852

The
SLEEPWALKERS

The
SLEEPWALKERS

J. GABRIEL GATES

Health Communications, Inc.
Deerfield Beach, Florida
www.hcibooks.com

Library of Congress Cataloging-in-Publication Data

Gates, J. Gabriel.
The sleepwalkers / J. Gabriel Gates.
    p. cm.
    Summary: When he receives a mysterious, disturbing letter from his long-lost
childhood playmate Christine, privileged and popular Caleb, celebrating his high
school graduation, travels to his tiny hometown of Hudsonville, Florida, to find
her, uncovering terrifying prophecies of the spirits.
    ISBN-13: 978-0-7573-1588-6 (trade paper)
    ISBN-10: 0-7573-1588-7 (trade paper)
    ISBN-13: 978-0-7573-9173-6 (e-book)
    ISBN-10: 0-7573-9173-7 (e-book)
    [1. Horror stories.   2. Mystery and detective stories.   3. Supernatural—Fiction.
4. Florida—Fiction.]   I. Title.
PZ7.G222Sl 2011
[Fic]—dc23

                                                                    2011011959

©2011 J. Gabriel Gates

All rights reserved. Printed in the United States of America. No part of this publica-
tion may be reproduced, stored in a retrieval system, or transmitted in any form or by
any means, electronic, mechanical, photocopying, recording, or otherwise, without
the written permission of the publisher.

HCI, its logos, and marks are trademarks of Health Communications, Inc.

Publisher: Health Communications, Inc.
            3201 S.W. 15th Street
            Deerfield Beach, FL 33442–8190

Cover design by Larissa Hise Henoch
Interior design by Lawna Patterson Oldfield
Interior formatting by Dawn Von Strolley Grove

This book is dedicated to my mother,
Cynthia Walker, a wonderful mom,
an extraordinary teacher,
and my first reader.
Thank you.

⇥ Chapter One ⇤

Something in the ruins waits.

A daydreamy, hot Southern summer, the sky above like a great blue eye. Watching. Two little girls with laughter in their smiles. Two same smiles, giggling. They hug. They hit one another. Two sisters, and me. High, dry weeds, brown and scraping. We fight through them together. The forest behind is black liquid. Pathways through the weeds, a thousand pathways, a game of chase. Now lying amongst the long grasses, giggles give way to sighing.

Something waits.

I get up. I whisper to one of the girls. (This has happened before.) Her hair is long and straight. Eyes glitter. There are no sounds, as if this were a silent movie or something, but there is one word that bleeds through like a subliminal message: dare. *Eyes glittering, this is a childish contest of pride. I smile my dare to her—I feel the smile on my face. She swallows once in fear, then giggles it away. The other sister says nothing, watches with sad, distant eyes. Long, straight hair. Through the weeds again now. Shuffling, we three. Biting burrs on white socks. A little hill. We reach the top and the air stops. There it is. Edifice. Eclipsing all. Empty. A thousand windows stare through us like blind eyes, black and shattered, the lights that once waited inside them now betrayed to darkness. Another word bleeds through:* hospital.

Their momma told them not to go.

The dare hangs all around us. Two little girls, just alike. Dirty dresses and dimples. One stands still and scratches her leg.

The other, the Dared, has half crossed the clearing already. She's passing the swimming pond, sleeping mirror. Tiny girl, she blazes through the weeds on scabbed, bruised legs.

She keeps walking.

She'll show us she isn't afraid. But she's very afraid. She walks slowly. Keeps looking back. Acting brave. I look up at the too-many windows, and they gape at me like gnawing, starving maws. Suddenly, I want to call her back. My stomach aches, I want to call her back so bad. But I don't. I watch her. She sneaks under the chain-link fence, little dared one, catches her dress as she wriggles through but tears herself free. Crosses a patch of cracked, scarred cement; the heat waves from it dilute her for an instant; for an instant she seems almost to melt away, but she walks on, over old beer cans and fallen bricks, patches of grass poking through the cement. Up to the stoop. Up to the door.

The back door. A black hole. Her tiny feet follow each other forward, one after another, closer and closer, and she pauses at the threshold, looks back at us. Even from so far away there's no mistaking, no denying the meaning in her pleading silence: "Take back the dare." But she's already there.

Then it happens, too fast to be real. The little girl next to me screams, only her breath goes in instead of out and makes the words:

"Something in the ruins waits!"

And in the black square of the doorway, something jerks the other little girl backwards into the dark.

Forever gone.

THE CEILING IS BLUE. His first thought is that nothing is real. Nothing is to be trusted. He pushes himself up against the headboard and stares at the knob on his closet door, waiting for the feeling to drain out of him. The knob is glass. Antique. He half expects it to move, but it does not. Nothing moves. The room is saturated in stillness. When there's no sound, no motion, it's easy to see how flimsy everything is. Reality seems mushy. Liquid, almost, in this half-light. The little illumination leaking through the curtains is tinted with blue. It must be late. The clock says six o'clock exactly.

The hum of the silence is disconcerting. He keeps thinking he hears something. Somehow, the sound of the non-noise has the same quality of a real sound. It sounds like . . . what? He can't put his finger on it, but it doesn't go away.

He gets out of bed, twists his boxers, straightening them, and walks across the rug and onto the hardwood floor. It creaks under his weight and he's grateful; it chases away the non-sound for a moment. He opens his door, steps into the hall. Here, the stagnant air is filled with the same timid light as his room. Twilight. He walks over to the stairs and leans over the rail.

"Hey, what's for dinner?"

No answer, except for a barely perceptible echo. He walks back up the hall. His legs hurt. Shin splints. He walks into the bathroom, blows his nose on some toilet paper, pulls on a pair of jeans—the belt is conveniently waiting in the loops from the last time he wore them—and walks back down the hall, thinking about the dream. Trying not to think about it, actually, but reliving it in spite of himself. It won't leave. Even now, as he's going through the motions of life, performing all these normal actions, the fear still aches in his bones. He acts like he's ignoring it, but he cannot.

He crosses back down the hall, listening intently for some familiar sound—the chopping of vegetables for dinner, the mindless, chattering drone of the TV, the moan of the garage door as one of the parents makes an early appearance home from work. There are no sounds. The ache in his bones won't stop. He can't shake the dream. Hell, maybe he's still asleep; maybe this is just another hallway in the labyrinth of his subconscious. Maybe he woke to a world where he's the only survivor of a terrible cataclysm; maybe he's the last person left alive on earth.

Or maybe—and this thought really chills him—maybe this is where the door the little girl was pulled into so many years ago led—maybe, in some terrible metaphysical contortion, that black doorway leads here, to the shadowed foyer of his own empty house.

As that thought seeps through his mind, dripping from the land of fleeting fancy into more primal regions, it almost freezes him in his tracks. It's a horrible idea, the kind that keeps coming back to you, like the image from a video he saw in history class of the Buddhist monks who burned themselves to protest the war in Vietnam. When you turned away, when you closed your eyes, the sight remained.

He's made his way downstairs now. He passes the coatrack in the hall, trips over the shoes he shuffled off an hour earlier, before his nap, and continues toward the kitchen. It's getting deeply dark outside and here, away from any windows that might leak in the last residual rays of the dying sun, the blackness is almost total. He fumbles with his hand—here's the table, here's one of the doilies his mom insists on draping over everything, even though it looks archaic and lame—and here's the lamp. He traces his hand up the smooth brass shaft of its neck, without seeing it, bumps the shade with his elbow, finds the switch with his clumsy, still-waking fingertips, and twists. There's a click and a flash. He gasps.

Eyes.

Someone there? The hairs on the back of his neck are standing up.

It's dark again—the light has burned out. His body is tense, his back pressed against the hallway wall.

Then he smiles, realizing. There's no one there: he just saw himself in the hall mirror. He exhales a snorted laugh. What a jackass. What a baby. The lightbulb popped and he saw himself. Good ol' scary Caleb, a skinny eighteen-year-old guy. He probably couldn't scare a 7-Eleven cashier with a ski mask on. His body relaxes. A car approaches outside, its headlights shining through the stained glass windows flanking the front door, casting everything, fleetingly, in an eerie glow. Then it passes. He snorts again, laughing at himself. What a baby. . . . Can't shake a wittow scawy dweam. He takes a step forward, toward the kitchen door, then stops dead.

Something behind the door moved.

A scraping sound. Tiny. Real. No light shines around the doorjamb. The room beyond is dark. He realizes he's shaking. He tries to breathe, tries to still his limbs, but cannot. Something is really there.

Courage . . . this is your house, right? Not a dream, right? And you're eighteen now—supposed to be a man.

His teeth clamp together, eyes narrow, fists clench. His hand rises up from his side and tentatively rests on the wood of the swinging door. Only a push now. Why's he so scared? Why can't he shake that dream? Okay, one . . . two . . .

Another sound, almost too faint hear at first. But there. His mouth falls open and he shivers, leaning closer. Voices. A thousand, whispering, clamoring, lisps mingle and seethe over one another, creating a sound that is almost like silence—but isn't.

He feels his heart pounding, man or not, but steels himself against the rising tide of his fear.

The door. Open it. He's a man now; it's just the *kitchen,* for Christ's sake.

One.

Something behind the door.

Two.

Something waits.

Three.

He shoves open the door—to the sound of a thousand screams, a blast of light, and gigantic sign that reads:

Happy Graduation, Caleb!

"Surprise!" a chorus of familiar faces sings.

"So, you were really surprised, right? Not just blowin' smoke up my tush?"

It's Bean who speaks. His real name is Benjamin Friedman—Ben—but no one remembers the last time anyone called him that.

Bean. God bless him, the kid is all curly black hair and dimples. Round face. Stocky guy, about five seven or something. The kind of guy you end up drinking with, laughing with, running naked laps around the block with, stealing people's garden gnomes with until seven in the morning—when you had no intention of drinking in the first place. Bean is that guy.

"I actually crapped myself a little," Caleb says with a grin.

"Yeah, I noticed that," Bean says. "You had that look of 'yes, although I have just soiled myself in front of my chemistry teacher, my girlfriend, and my Nana, I shall maintain my composure and eventually sneak out and change my Fruit of the Looms at a more opportune time."

"That was my thought process, yes. Astute of you to pick up on that," Caleb says.

This is their shtick. Caleb isn't sure if all best buddies have a shtick, but he and Bean certainly have theirs, and it could land them in prime time any day of the week. Caleb plays the straight man, Bean is the comedian, and it works. It's made them the envy of most everyone else in school, actually, although they aren't even consciously aware of the fact. But why not? Girls love a good laugh, guys love a good time. And with Caleb and Bean around, neither are in short supply. Fun breeds popularity, a coveted prize amongst the high-school ranks, and this evening is certainly a good example of that—almost a hundred people are probably here in all—though it's hard to tell for sure, since they're scattered all through the kitchen, across the patio, and downstairs in the game room, too. Of course, neither Bean nor Caleb thinks much about things like social status or peer acceptance. They just have fun together. And it's magnetic.

A little swarm of people ring the guest of honor and his comedian friend, and one of these, a girl named Brittanee, pipes up now.

"So, Bean, what are you doing after graduation?"

Bean clears his throat. "I got a gig shovelin' bird shit outta cuckoo clocks. Union. Good pay." He glances at Caleb with a wink.

Everyone laughs except Brittanee, who isn't quite sure if she's being made fun of or not. Bean smiles and puts her at ease (Bean puts everyone at ease).

"Naw," he says. "I'm going to Pepperdine. I figure it's right up the road, so I can live with the parents. I'll stay shacked up with them as long as I can, man. I never want to pay bills. I might even stay there for my doctorate. Maybe I'll even get lucky and my parents will die in a plane crash or something and I'll inherit the pad after that. I'm all about never having a real job, ever."

"What about you, Caleb?" asks Dan, a guy from Caleb's track team.

"Oh, don't get him started," Bean says. "This guy is going to go live in elephant dung for six weeks, then die of malaria, probably. Please tell him he's nuts."

"I'm going to Africa to write about the AIDS crisis," Caleb says. "Everybody says if I can write a good piece and get it published, with my grades and everything I should be able to get into any school in the country. I want to do investigative journalism, go to Yale or maybe Stanford, become the editor of a big newspaper someday—or maybe a magazine like *Time* or *Newsweek*."

Everyone just nods. No one really knows what to say about that, and nobody's willing to follow Caleb's impressive goals with their relatively lame plans for the future.

"Yeah," says Bean sarcastically, "you know how much tail those newspaper editors get."

Everybody laughs.

Caleb rolls with it; this is all just part of the shtick.

"If I can save one life while you're busy roofieing sorority girls, I think it will be pretty worthwhile."

"How ya gonna save any lives," says Bean, "unless you're packing a suitcase full of condoms and anti-AIDS drugs?"

"When people know what's going on, they'll do something. Did you know a child in Africa is orphaned every fourteen seconds?"

Bean makes a snoring sound then feigns waking up. "Sorry, did you say something? Seriously, man, nobody cares about people right next to them; they sure aren't gonna start caring about people on the other side of the planet just because Caleb tells them to. A million newspaper articles won't change human nature. Sure, people might donate a buck or two as a tax write-off, but the fact remains, my friend: nobody really cares."

"I do," says Caleb.

"Well, you get a gold freakin' star then, buddy." Bean makes a toasting motion with his cup and downs half of it. "Usually when Americans try to help people, all that seems to happen is a lot of people get blown up and some company makes a crapload of cash. That's how we save the world around here," he says. "Things never turn out how you expect them to." Then he laughs, leaning a little too close to Brittanee, and confides: "This jackhole thinks he's gonna run off to some hoity-toity Ivy League college and leave me here holding my twig and berries all by my lonesome. Not happening."

"We'll see," says Caleb with a shrug.

"I agree with Bean," someone says. It's a girl's voice, even and smooth. Amber.

This, for the record, is the first time Amber has ever agreed with Bean about anything.

"Hey, baby," Caleb says.

Amber walks over and presents her cheek, not her lips, to Caleb for a kiss. He gives it to her and she takes his hand, displacing Bean.

Brittanee says, "Hi, Amber. Bean was just telling us how Caleb is going to Africa. That is sooo amazing. I would love to go."

"Well," Amber says, "you kind of need to be savvy. When I was in Niger, a chimpanzee stole a baby from a village and tore it apart. There are a lot of native customs and wildlife issues to get used to. Plus, you have to get a lot of uncomfortable shots and stuff before you go."

Brittanee says, "Oh my God. That poor baby! That's . . . awful."

"Yep," Amber says with a flippant smile. Then, to Caleb: "Hey, honey, can I talk to you in private for a minute?"

Caleb glances at his friends, reluctant to leave.

"Uh, okay," he says and, throwing a final smile to his guests, allows himself be led away by Amber's tugging hand.

Bean snorts. "Leave it to good old Amber to bring the mood down." And he takes a sip of a Coke that may or may not be 40 percent Jack Daniels. He squints at Brittanee. "Hey, Brit, you look a little Hebrew. I always meant to ask you, do you have any Jew in you?"

Brittanee smiles, "No, and I don't want any, thanks very much."

"Oh," says Bean, "I already tried that one on you, eh? I gotta find some fresh meat. . . . " He turns on his heel and heads for the game room, leaving Brittanee laughing and shaking her head in his wake.

Outside on the deck, the wind is fitful. Far away, a single light, like an earthbound star, heralds the passing of a ship.

The break of the surf is incessant and, to Caleb, unnerving. When he first moved into this house with his mother and Bob six (or seven?) years ago, he had been sure he would love it. He did not. At first, he had figured he would get used to the rush of the ocean. But in fact, it seemed to grow more prominent over time. More *insistent*. The problem, he figured, was that it never stopped. When he was trying to sleep, it was there. When he was studying, it crept into his ears. Even over dinner, when his mother had one of those fancy dinner parties that she insisted he attend, and Yanni or Enya or some other aural barbiturate was playing in the background, he would sometimes get distracted from the conversation by the barely discernable (but there) roar of the surf. The sea. Always reaching for you, wave upon wave, like some liquid creature trying to clamber ashore. He takes the last sip of his punch as Amber comes to a stop and steers him, using his hand as her rudder, until he's facing her.

"What's different?" she asks. Caleb knows this is a test. She changes her appearance daily, and if he doesn't get this question right . . . bad stuff happens.

Time to buy a little time. He leans against the cool steel of the rail. The house is on stilts, so standing out here on the deck one can look almost directly down at the water. There it is. The sea. Powerful. Scary powerful. . . .

"Well?"

Amber stands a good three inches taller than Caleb. She won the state debate title three years running, and was the number-one seed in the USTA women's junior tennis championship for the last two years (though she was eliminated in the quarter finals both times). She expects things. To be engaged to Caleb by their junior year of college is one of them. To have one child is another. Only one, no more. She believes having more than one child is grossly irresponsible, and although she is a card-carrying member of the ACLU, she believes the government should limit the number of children people can have—to prevent overpopulation. She is also a staunch pro-life activist.

Despite her dizzying inconsistencies, she is Caleb's girl. After all, she is devastatingly attractive. And she fits into his plan perfectly: Amber will be a senator and Caleb will be an editor at the *New York Times*. They'll be in the middle of everything, able to really make a difference. And that's all Caleb really wants; or thinks he wants. But lately . . .

"Well?" Amber's demeanor is quickly deteriorating from "flirty" to "glowering." Not a good sign. He has to act fast.

He rubs his nose, not because it itches, but because somewhere in his brain, it seems like a good ploy to buy an extra second. It doesn't work.

"My hair is red, Caleb. Jesus."

Since Amber lives up in Santa Barbara and Caleb lives down here in Malibu, that means he doesn't get to see her much. And she changes her hair color just about every week, so how could he possibly know what color it was last time he saw her? Hell, she might have already cycled through every color of the rainbow since last time they hung out. For all he knows, her hair *was* red the last time he saw her, and she's dyed it three times since then and landed back on red again. One thing's for sure: he doesn't remember.

"It looks great, babe," he says.

"What else?" she asks, and his heart sinks. Now he's really screwed.

He squeezes the plastic cup in his hand, making an annoying clicking noise. Dent in, dent out. Dent in, dent out.

"Well?" Amber asks, then before he can respond, she says, "Hair extensions and a French manicure. Not a very observant boyfriend, now are we?"

Caleb wonders, suddenly, when this became his life. It almost seems, in this strange moment, as if he's been sleepwalking for years. As if he's gone through these grueling years of study and romance and sports and life without even being truly aware, without being really present. It's as if it were all hardly real at all. Now, on this deck overlooking the black, endless ocean, he's suddenly, disconcertingly awake. And for some reason, he thinks of the dream again, of when he was a kid.

"Cake time!" someone calls from inside. Caleb sees his mom bringing out a cake, lit with a bunch of candles as if it were somebody's birthday. He stands there for a moment, wondering if there is any precedent for blowing out birthday candles at a graduation party, but Amber is already leading him back through the French doors with one of her newly manicured hands.

Everyone is gathered. Someone seems to have put the word out with the partygoers downstairs that the culmination of the festivities is approaching, because people are filing up the steps in droves. There's Bean, hooting as if he were at a strip club. There are the guys from the track team, their girlfriends, his whole group of friends from school; even a few teachers. Caleb's stepfather, Bob, and some of his stiff buddies from the glorious airline catering industry, of which he is a mogul, stand in the corner, and, of course, Mom, holding the cake, waits by the fireplace, still dressed in her suit from work, her hair a mess but her face beaming.

"Thanks," he says as he approaches her.

"Happy graduation, hon," she says. "Now blow out these candles. This thing weighs a ton."

"Is it customary to have candles on a—?" Caleb begins, but he's rejoined with a chorus of "blow out the candles!" so he says, "Okay, okay," and blows them out. Everyone claps. As he looks around him, all the smiling faces seem at once familiar (because they *are* familiar, after all) and strangely, disturbingly foreign. It's the dream. He knows it. The dream still hasn't quite let go of him.

"Speech!" Mom cries, and everyone else joins in, "Speech, speech, speech."

Caleb blushes in spite of himself (which, he thinks, is not like him at all) and waves them off with one hand.

"Later, guys. Cake first, speech later. I promise."

Everyone accepts that, mostly because it's a tasty-looking cake: chocolate marble layer cake with buttercream frosting, Caleb discovers as he takes the first bite.

"Mmm," he says loudly. He feels like he's in a TV commercial, but he can't help it, it's that good.

"I'm going to powder my nose," says Amber.

"You don't want cake?" Caleb asks.

"No," she says, wrinkling her nose up as if he had just said, "Don't you want Ebola?" She squeezes his hand once and lets go, heading off down the hall with her long-legged, strangely cocky but sexy gait. Caleb goes back to work eating. He has a method—cake first, then the frosting.

Bean saunters up, his mouth brimming with chocolate.

"Wats da eel, aam?" he asks.

"Did you come here on the short bus or what? Chew your food." Caleb laughs. It's good to have a friend you can say anything to.

"This cake is so rad," says Bean.

"That's not what you said, man."

"No," says Bean, a little reluctant, "I said: 'What's the deal?' With Amber."

"What do you mean?"

"Dude, she's like the queen from *Alice in Wonderland*. Every time she comes around, my balls shrink up like they're trying to hide. It's uncomfortable."

Caleb nods. "She can be a little . . . direct."

"Yah. But, hey, dude. She's your girlfriend; you guys have been together for a long time—God knows how—and I respect that. If you're happy, more power to you."

"Thanks, Bean."

"Just between you and me, though, the Little Man's making your decisions for you, isn't he?"

"Oh," says Caleb, "you must mean the Big Man. I don't know, you'll have to set up an appointment and ask him. He's a busy guy, though."

"Yeah," says Bean, "busy getting smaller. I'm going to go flirt with your mom and see if I can make Bob jealous. Wanna come?"

"Yeah," Caleb says, "right after I get some more of this bomb-ass cake."

Caleb fights off the pang of guilt he feels at the thought of having seconds. Why shouldn't he have more? Track is over forever unless he decides to pursue it in college. Still, to have seconds seems foreign. He's used to walking a very narrow path.

He looks around the room for a moment before spying the cake's resting place. It sits at the end of the dining room table. The table is covered for the occasion with a fancy white tablecloth and also seems to be serving as the gift repository. He walks down its length, surveying his spoils. There are only a few gifts, actually. Mostly, the table is littered with cards. The cards are full of money, of course— and that's a beautiful thing because there are a lot of them.

He cuts himself another piece of cake then balances it between his finger and the knife in an attempt to transport it to his plate without getting too much frosting on his fingers. The attempt proves futile. He drops cake and gets frosting all over his hand anyway.

"Aw, son of a . . . "

Using the knife and slipping the paper plate underneath, he manages to get the piece of cake to safety. As for the tablecloth, it's pretty screwed . . . But it's his special night, Caleb figures, so if he tells her right away, his mom won't be able to get mad at him . . . And it's actually not as bad as he was thinking because the cake landed mostly on one of the cards. He picks up the frosting-laden envelope, licking the sugary goodness off his finger at the same time. The envelope doesn't look like it would contain a greeting card—it's plain white, and letter sized. He turns it over. No writing on the back, and no return address on the front. There is a stamp on it, though, so it apparently isn't from anyone at the party. Heck, maybe it's not even for him at all—but he can't tell; the address is covered in frosting. He glances at his mom—thinking he could ask her about it, but she's rapt in a conversation with Bob and his terminally boring friends.

There's only one way to find out who this particular piece of mail is addressed to, and if it involves eating more frosting, then so be it. He licks where the address should be. Delicious. But the writing is still illegible, which calls for one more lick and . . . there—it's the correct address, all right, but as for who the letter is addressed to . . . He licks once more. And the revelation is: the letter is addressed to—"Billy."

Caleb stares at the envelope for a minute, perfectly still. Billy. His first thought is that this letter was simply sent there by mistake. No Billy lives here.

He studies the handwriting on the envelope. It's cursive. Almost childlike. He doesn't recognize it.

Billy.

Of course, Caleb's full name is William Caleb Mason, but no one calls him "Billy." Not since he was a kid. Not since he moved to California.

His brow is knotted up and his forehead begins to feel heavy. He sits down, staring at the envelope. He hesitates, that weird foreboding washing over him again, then tears it open.

"Speech, speech, speech!" everyone calls—but the laughter, the clink of glasses, the music are all muted. There's Bean, winking at him. There's Amber, expectant. Everyone is waiting for him, everyone is listening.

Now Mom speaks: "Thanks for coming, everybody! I just wanted to say how proud we all are of you, Caleb. Valedictorian is a great honor, and I know great things are ahead of you. But you'd better be careful in Africa. If you get eaten by lions, you're totally grounded, young man." She laughs. To Caleb's mom, that constitutes a joke.

". . . And here's a little something to help you on your trip into the heart of darkness." She hands him an envelope. Now, he clutches two, because he still has the one from the table clenched in his trembling fist. He looks at the new envelope, dumbly. Everyone falls silent now, watching him. It occurs to him that this is another part of the dream—he still hasn't woken up yet. This is the part where everyone's looking at him, and he looks down and finds himself naked . . . or covered in blood. Out the window, he hears the sound of the ocean, unending.

"Well, open it," his mother urges.

Fumbling, he crams a thumb under the flap and tears. It's a cheesy card and a check for two thousand dollars. Mom is smiling at him. He tries to smile back and can't. Everyone waits for him. Suddenly, his head feels light, unright. He puts the check in his pocket and looks at the other envelope, the one addressed to "Billy." Awareness washes over him. Everyone's watching him, everyone's waiting.

Someone—Bean, probably—yells, "Speech!"

Caleb clears his throat, still looking at the envelope.

Silence swirls around him maddeningly. Except it's not really silence.

Finally, he speaks: "I'm not going to Africa anymore," he hears himself say. He hardly knows why he said it, but it occurs to him in that instant that it's already said. It's already in the air, too late to take back.

Now everyone's going to ask him why. That's the question percolating upon all of their lips, even now. And as he looks at the envelope in his trembling hand, he knows he will never be able to tell them the truth.

⊰ Chapter Two ⊱

Dear Billy,

I have been erased. The world doesn't spin right anymore. Colors run away from me. I know why the caged bird sings. His song means "help me."

Do you remember my sister? She was a beautiful singer. Much better than me. She sang the same song. She still sings it, only very, very softly now. You must remember my sister. My greatest fear of all is that you don't remember me anymore because there's no one else who will. I have only been here six months, and already the world is washed clean of the faintest shadow of me.

I live in the House of White Walls now. You will be glad to know I am making excellent progress. They send my mother letters every day, detailing my fantastic advances. I am erased from the world. I exist only in a one-paragraph report, biweekly delivered.

Horrible things unravel me more and more. Every night, it steals my breath from me. My soul has grown dangerously thin.

I was just writing to let you know THE WORLD IS ENDING AND THE DROWNED CHILDREN WHISPER TO ME EVERY NIGHT, and it's HORRIBLE. You Don't Know. I hear them GASPING.

They are coming now. They come at night and steal pieces of me. Save me, Billy

Billy, I love you

I love billy. Lovely billy. SAVE ME!!

Love, Christine

xoxox

→

BEAN FOLDS UP THE LETTER SLOWLY, carefully, and places it on the little foldout tray next to a half-spilled bag of airline peanuts. He picks up two peanuts delicately, tosses them into his mouth and starts chewing, staring all the while at the back of the seat in front of him. Caleb waits for the joke, for the wiseass comment—he longs for it, in fact, needs it to steady his nerves, to know that at least *some* things never change: no matter what, Bean takes nothing seriously. But Bean doesn't say anything. He just takes a sip of his Coke and looks at the letter distrustfully, as if he expects it to sprout arms and slap him upside the head.

"So . . . ?" Caleb says, and even this prompts no response. "What do you think?"

"Dude, it got into my head," Bean says, cracking an ice cube between his teeth and glancing sidelong at his friend.

"Yeah," says Caleb. Out of all possible responses, this is perhaps the worst he could have received. "Dude, you're stupid," "Dude, you're gay," "Dude, this person is just some wacko; pull your head out of your ass"—these would have all been acceptable, if embarrassing, quips from his best friend. They would have been comforting. This is not comforting. This is bad.

Ever since he made an early exit from his graduation party, feigning stomach flu, he has been waiting for someone to tell him he's crazy, waiting to come to that conclusion himself. He read the letter over and over, in a display that could only be considered obsessive in the extreme, trying to find some flaw, some hint of a joke or a hoax, anything that might discredit the piece of dread correspondence. He found none. Worse, he found the letter to be spotted with dried tear marks. He observed how the handwriting became sloppier at the end, as the writer's perceived threat drew near. It only proved what his heart had known all along—the letter was real.

"So," Bean says, "who's Christine?"

"This girl I knew," says Caleb. His voice sounds hollow in his own ears. "She was my friend when I was a kid in Florida. That's where the letter is postmarked from—Hudsonville."

"Right," says Bean, "where your dad lives."

"Yep. She was poor. She had a twin sister who got kidnapped and they never found her. We were all best friends."

Bean pauses, thinking. "So if you haven't seen this Christine girl since you were a kid, why would she send you this?"

Caleb shrugs, not trusting his voice this time.

"And why all the secrecy?" Bean asks. "I've never seen you lie to your mom. I mean, you're a total sissy momma's boy. And you didn't even tell Amber the real deal, and she's like the puppet master holding your freakin' strings."

"Bite me," says Caleb.

"I don't mean it as a bad thing. I mean, damn. Most guys would be more than happy to be pussy-whipped by her. But it's just weird that you told both of them we were just going on a little trip to visit your dad, when we're actually—wait, what *are* we doing?"

"I don't know. I don't even know where Christine is. I don't know if I'd recognize her if she were sitting right next to me."

"I just can't believe you actually lied to your mom."

"I'm not that much of a momma's boy. I had to lie to her because she hates my dad completely. If she knew we were staying with him, she'd crap herself."

"You ever get a hold of him?"

"Dad? Nah. He must've changed his phone number. We had to do that sometimes. He's a lawyer. He represents a lot of controversial cases. We'll just surprise him."

"Sweet," says Bean. "Now leave me alone. I gotta get my beauty sleep. But first, take that letter back. It creeps me out. Seriously."

Caleb puts the letter back in his pocket, and Bean leans his head against the airplane window.

Caleb stares past him, out at the infinite blue. He told everyone that he had become overwhelmed with the exertion of finishing the school year, going through graduation, writing college essays, and all the other crap that came with being an eighteen-year-old. Total bullshit. Still, his mom and Bob bought it and sprung for a "vacation" to Florida for him and Bean. After all, "breakdowns" are par for the course for teenagers growing up in Malibu, so, if anything, this lapse made him seem more normal in the eyes of his peers and maybe even his family. It made him wince to imagine himself as one of those lame kids who were always paging their therapists and popping handfuls of Xanax.

But the lies will all be worth it if Christine really is in trouble and they're able to help her.

"This trip's gonna be cool," Caleb says, but somehow he doesn't believe it. He's racking up the lies.

"Shut up," Bean mumbles. "You're screwing up my beauty sleep."

The humidity is dizzying as they step out onto the tarmac. Waves of heat rise off the blacktop and the sun seems to bore through the top of Caleb's baseball cap and into his brain.

"Thank Jesus," says Bean, "I thought we were dead, man. I swear to God, I did. That turbulence was crazy. We like, fell. We should sue for emotional distress, I'm telling you."

The plane had hit a tiny bit of turbulence on the way to land, and Bean had started freaking out. It was funny to Caleb, who had never seen that side of his friend, but Bean had recovered quickly and had spent the rest of the landing in macho talk about how they should kick the pilot's ass and sue the airline and use the money to buy a giant RV so they could travel the country in real comfort and never have to fly again. All through his tirade his eyes were big and scared, and a sheen of sweat sparkled on his forehead, giving him away. Caleb had been tempted to make fun of him, since that's certainly what Bean would have done to him, but decided against it.

"Come on," Caleb says now, heading off the lingering urge to crack a joke by changing the subject. "Let's get our bags and find a rental car. I don't know if I can find my dad's house in the daylight, much less in the dark."

They hustle through the airport, which is decked out in pastel pinks and greenish blues, Florida colors, and head for the baggage claim. In no time, they reach the rental-car place where, thanks to Bean's trusty fake ID (which lists him as a twenty-seven-year-old bearded guy named "Dirk Stephens"), they soon secure a car and hit the road.

The windows are down, the sun is bright (though it's past its zenith now; four o'clock has come and gone). In the air, the sickly-sweet smell of a paper mill makes the humidity seem even thicker, even more intoxicating, and Caleb keeps thinking how much difference a few days can make, how the course of everything can reverse like the changing of the tide and pull you in the opposite direction with frightening force.

But somehow, in this moment, that's okay. After all, the ability to change direction is freedom, and on a beautiful afternoon like this, with his best friend at his side and all the demands of his life thousands of miles away, freedom has never felt so nice. The sense of foreboding that haunted him since the moment he read Christine's letter has dissipated, leaving in its place only the road and the sun and the warm, sweet-smelling wind. Bean, who's been looking out the window, lost in his own thoughts, reaches down and turns on the radio. He scans for a minute and finally comes up with some old-school rock song and blasts it, singing along at the top of his lungs.

Caleb joins in, and they laugh and mock head-bang for a minute.

The adventure has begun. Still fifty miles to go to make Hudson-ville, they race along an empty two-lane road, skirted by endless pine trees and punctuated with the occasional run-down gas station or grapefruit stand. They're the only car in sight; they're free of parents and tests and stress and girls and everything complicated and bad. In this moment, there's only the wind and the sun and the radio and the possibility of great times ahead.

Around a turn in the road, a sign: THE ROTARY CLUB WELCOMES YOU TO THE VILLAGE OF HUDSONVILLE, POPULATION 123.

Bean has been talking excitedly for the last hour. ". . . Dude, I wonder if this chick Christine's a hottie. After we rescue her, maybe she'll, like, rescue us a little bit, you know what I'm sayin'? Oh, yeah, forgot about your ball and chain. My bad. All I'm saying is we have to get to the beach while we're here. I hear the beaches here are sweet.

Of course, we live on the beach—but still I've never been to a *Florida* beach."

Bean sees the sign and falls silent for a second. "A hundred and twenty-three people? I've see that many people in one bathroom at LAX."

They pass a sandy driveway. There's a half-collapsed green and white motor home squatting in a field of sand with tufts of scraggly grass protruding everywhere. A skinny old man wearing overalls, with close-set, beady eyes, watches them pass. The air is still and hot as it rushes through their windows, but its sound falls to a whisper as Caleb slows the car down. There's a gas station called Pete's Gas and Store, covered in peeling white paint. The parking lot is gravel and the pumps are antique. The place is silent. They pass a few boarded-up stores, maybe three on either side of the road. On one side they see a hardware store that seems to be open for business and on the other side they see a diner with a few patrons sitting by the window, eating. That's the whole downtown strip. They pass a few more drive-ways, marked by listing mailboxes, that curve and disappear from sight amidst dense vegetation, then nothing but woods.

"Damn," Bean says. "That's it, that's the town?"

"Yeah," says Caleb, "this is where I grew up."

They pass another driveway or two, but they're coming less frequently now. Caleb squints out the windshield, concerned. It'll be dark soon. The red sun skates on the edge of the horizon. Caleb glimpses it fleetingly through breaks in the trees. Soon, he won't see it at all. And he knows he won't be able to find his way after the light is gone.

"Shit," he mumbles.

"What?" says Bean, concerned. "You know where we're going, right?"

"Well, I remember the old address was Walnut Road, but I haven't seen it. Maybe we passed it."

"Dude, you used to live here, right? Come on, we can't be lost."

"I moved away when I was, like, seven," Caleb says, defensively.

"Great," Bean says. "We're lost in the Land of Rednecks. I mean, that's fine for you, you're cousins with everybody here, but what about me?"

"Walnut Road," Caleb says, spotting the sign. He swings the car around the corner. The wheels squeal and Bean almost falls out of his seat, across the arm rest, and over onto Caleb's lap.

"Jesus, Knight Rider," says Bean, "give KITT a rest."

The road is gravel. The grind of the tires eats up the silence all around them. One driveway, another driveway—Caleb leans forward. The sun is going fast now, and here, under a thick canopy of trees, night is already closing its fist on sight. The car rolls a little farther, and Caleb sees what he's looking for.

"Bean, what does it say on that mailbox?"

Bean squints. "Mason."

The mailbox was once white, but mold and dirt have stained it a streaked greenish brown. The reflective letters stuck to the side, however, are still legible.

The roar of gravel on tires gives way to a gentle hushing sound as they turn into the sandy driveway.

"We're here," Caleb says.

Bean thinks he hears a slight tremble in his friend's voice. He almost makes a joke about it, but what he sees out the front windshield causes words to evaporate in his throat.

It's like nothing Bean has ever seen.

Massively girthed live oak trees line the sides of the drive like huge,

ancient sentries. Their arms reach out over the rutted dirt path, inter-
locking, forming a thick canopy above. It's like passing through a tunnel, except this tunnel is *alive*. Tendrils of wispy Spanish moss hang
from the gnarled branches above, floating above their passing car like a
host of drifting ghosts. The air is very still all around. Bean wants to say
something, but when he breathes in, it doesn't feel like there's enough
air to fuel his words, so he closes his mouth again. One thing's for
sure: this place is weird. There's something creepy about the trees. Like
they're *watching*. And Bean is not a superstitious guy. Hell, he never
worries about anything. When any normal person would be in a panic,
Bean is chill. Gonna fail history, no problem. Find out your girlfriend
blew the captain of the wrestling team, well, it was time for a change
anyway. But this, this is weird. As he looks down the drive, it feels like
he's looking into a hole. Like staring down a well. And now the house
comes into view at the bottom of the well, small and distant but growing larger, coming nearer. Like they're falling toward it. Bean feels a
sense of vertigo. A finger of nausea worms its way into his stomach and
won't leave. The house comes closer and closer, growing impossibly
large. The driveway splits into a circle, which rings another gigantic live
oak. They orbit its trunk and slow down in front of a set of crumbling
front steps. Caleb stops the car with a jerk and turns off the key. They
both sit listening to the ticking of the cooling engine and looking up
at the house. Already, Bean has never hated a place so much in his life.

It's an old, plantation-style mansion with huge, towering columns.
The paint is coming off in sheets. Shingles, fallen from the roof, now
litter the mossy brick walkway. One section of the eaves trough hangs
almost to the ground. The windows are all black and lifeless. A few
errant shafts of light still break through the foliage—apparently the
sun isn't quite gone yet—and their glow reveals air thick with still,

choking dust particles. A thought creeps into Bean's head, and the more he tries to block it out, the more insistently it blares in his mind:

The place is dead.

He hears a click. Caleb is out of the car.

"Hey, buddy," Bean says, trying to sound jovial, but knowing his desperation is coming through. "This isn't the place, is it?"

Standing next to the car, Caleb stares at the front door blankly, as if lost in thought. For an instant, an irrational fear shoots into Bean's head that his best friend has suddenly become a zombie.

"Yeah," Caleb says finally. "This is where I grew up."

And Bean suddenly wonders: if Caleb grew up in a place this strange, this different from what Bean imagined it would be, does he really know his friend at all?

Caleb begins striding forward, toward the door. Bean is out of the car and lurches forward to stop him.

"Hey, man, it doesn't look like your dad lives here anymore. I mean, didn't you say he's a lawyer or something? This joint is a rat condo. Let's dip, find a hotel, and call him in the morning."

Though Bean places himself squarely in Caleb's path, his friend brushes past him and up onto the wood of the porch, which whines in protest at each footfall.

Bean is getting desperate. He doesn't know why, but he is. "Hello? Earth to Caleb. There's no one home!"

But Caleb is already inside.

Bean swears under his breath and follows.

Inside, the light isn't to be trusted. It's corrupted by shadows, especially now, at dusk, when reality is almost liquid, and especially here, in this place, which seems alive with a strange energy that makes everything . . .

"Empty," says Bean from the doorway, making Caleb jump. "See, I told you. Now let's get the hell outta here and find a Days Inn or something."

But the place isn't empty. It's full. Full of furniture, covered with a thick coating of dust, full of rotting books and musty rugs, oil paintings so dusty they are only shadows of themselves, and the old grandfather clock, long since silenced mid-tock.

"It's not empty," Caleb says absently.

Bean shivers. That's exactly what he's afraid of.

"It's all here. Just like when I was a kid . . . This is my dad's stuff." Caleb presses further inside, past foyer and into the hallway.

"Dude," Bean protests—but his friend has already gone ahead.

The kitchen. Pots and pans hang from a rack over a central island, woven to one another with thick cobwebs. Over Caleb's shoulder, Bean sees the biggest spider he's ever seen, sitting very still in the center of his web. *Not sitting*, Bean thinks, *waiting*. Caleb crosses over to the fridge and opens up the door. The reek is horrendous.

"Oh, Jesus," says Bean. "Just shut it and let's get the hell out of here."

"It's still full of food . . . " says Caleb. He crosses into the dining room. Not much to see there. A wooden table, a china cabinet. The scurrying of mice.

Caleb crosses out of the room, down the hall, up the stairs. Bean follows as he pokes his head into the master bedroom. The bed is unmade, clothes litter the floor. One window is broken out and the wall is stained yellow with water damage. Another room, this one a guest bedroom. The bed is made, and next to it on the nightstand are the husks of what must once have been fresh flowers. There's something crunching on the floor here—leaves maybe. There might be a hole in the ceiling above, but it's too dark to see for sure. It's getting really dark now, especially in the hallway. The whole place smells like something. Sweet, rotting something. Not a dead animal, or rotten eggs, but *something*.

Bean can barely keep up as Caleb swings into another room. This one is a study, with a heavy wooden desk, filing cabinets along one side, and a big, empty leather chair. The window across the room is a pale, glowing rectangle. They're almost out of light.

"Look, man, I think we've established that no one lives here, so let's just grab a phone book in the morning and look him up." Bean is barely holding it together. "Come on."

"Look at this," says Caleb. He's holding a file in this hand, rifling through papers.

Bean wishes he had a rifle right now—he'd march Caleb out of this crazy, abandoned place this minute, at gunpoint, since it seems he won't go willingly, and never look back. He'd hop the first flight to LAX, grab a soy latté from Coffee Bean, and catch a flick at the ArcLight. And forget about this place, if he ever could.

"This is one of my dad's case files. There's no way he'd move and just leave this here."

"What kind of case is it?" asks Bean. Maybe if he humors his friend, he can speed up the process.

"Just a routine DUI defense it looks like," Caleb says, shrugging. "But he wouldn't move and leave it here."

Caleb crosses to the filing cabinets and opens one.

"See, these are all case files. There's no way he'd leave them here and move away. There's no way he'd leave any of this."

"Well," says Bean, getting irritated now, "looks like he did."

"I know, it's just so . . . "

Bean says: "Hello, your dad isn't home right now, but if you'd like to leave him a message, please wait for the beep and *let's get the hell out of here!*"

→

Spanish moss, reaching for them, trees watching, an abandoned house now waiting in darkness. This is some bad, trippy shit. Bean has been trying to have fun all day, cracking jokes, talking about adventures and beaches and women—but the truth is, from the moment he read that letter, something hasn't been right with him. And it isn't just the fact that his best friend wasn't honest with him about the reason for their trip when he first invited him—in fact, he blatantly lied about it, saying they'd just chill out at the beach—it's that something is deeply, profoundly wrong about all this. The letter, the house, this town. Where the hell are they, anyway? Somewhere in the Podunk panhandle of Florida. This is no place for a kid who lived most of his life in Beverly Hills until he moved to Malibu at the age of ten. This is no vacation. A cruise is a vacation. Cancun is a vacation. This is some goddamned Hardy Boys shit.

Now that they're back in the car, rolling away from the house, Bean feels a little better, but not much. The trees still make a weird tunnel, but the sense of vertigo is gone, replaced by hunger and that deep, nagging unease.

"I need a frigging joint," says Bean.

This is one way in which the two friends were very different. Caleb is straight as an arrow, while Bean is a fan of intoxication. It isn't like he's a fiend or anything. Such things just facilitate having a good time, and Bean's a big fan of good times. Plus, there's nothing to steady your nerves like a bowl, and damn are his nerves unsteady now.

"I told you, I could have worn some tightie-whities on the plane and stuffed some weed in there and they'd have never caught me," Bean says. "They didn't even check me over that well."

"You need all the brain cells you can get," says Caleb.

"So what's the deal?" Bean says, still trying to shake off the jitters. "What now?"

"Now," says Caleb, "we're going to go visit a neighbor and find out if they know anything about Dad."

"Dude! It's dark out. The people around here might be cannibals, for all we know! We can't just go to someone's door in the middle of the night."

"It's not the middle of the night."

"Even worse," Bean says. "It's dinner time. Do you know what rednecks do to people who interrupt their dinner? One word: *buckshot*."

"Don't worry about it," Caleb says. "I grew up around here. I know these people."

"Yeah, but you haven't been back in ten years! A lot can change."

But Caleb is already turning down the neighbor's driveway. The headlights reveal forest all around and another rutted, sandy driveway just like the one at Caleb's father's place. There's a "whoo, whoo" sound, deep and throaty, and a big, brown hound dog runs into the light of their headlights, dragging a thick chain from its neck. It barks fiercely enough, but it doesn't look too healthy.

That thing's bonier than the last model Caleb dated, thinks Bean, and he almost laughs out loud.

Ahead, the headlights blaze upon the side of a mobile home. It appears to be better kept up than the one they saw earlier, but not by much. An old Dodge Diplomat sits near the doorway, with four flat tires and several potted plants adorning its hood. The dog is still barking.

"Shit," says Caleb as the screen door opens. A fat man with a rifle, no shirt, and a big red mustache steps out, glaring at them, and starts walking toward the car.

"You might be a redneck if . . . " says Bean.

"Just shut up," says Caleb. "I'll do the talking."

The man with the gun steps up to the window. The gun isn't pointing at them, but it's not exactly pointed away from them either.

"Yer trespassin'."

"I'm sorry, sir," says Caleb. "I just had a question for you, and I thought you might be able to—"

"Askit."

"Alright," he says, with a glance at Bean. "Do you know what happened to your neighbor?"

"Jim? Hurt his back at the lumberyard."

"No," says Caleb. "The other neighbor. In the big house over there?"

"Oh," the man grunts and nods. "The law-yer. Yeah. He's gone, alright."

"Do you know where he moved to?"

"Didn't move. Didn't take any of his stuff, anyway. Was going to go over there and see if there was anything useful in the place, but I didn't want to be stealin'. If ya ain't got yer honesty, ya got nothin'."

"So you don't know where he is?"

"Nope."

Bean leans over, impatient, and whispers to Caleb, "This redneck doesn't know anything—he's too stoned. Let's get out of here."

"Shut up," says Caleb, shoving Bean back to his side of the car.

"Excuse me, sir?" says Bean. "Do you know where we might be able to score some crippie?"

"Beg yer pardon?"

"Shut up, Bean."

"You know," says Bean, "mar-i-juana?"

"I don't use no dope, and I don't want no druggies on my property. Now you boys had better get on outta here."

"Sir, I'm sorry for my friend," says Caleb. "I just wanted to know—"

"You boys git. I'm within my rights to shoot ye, you know that? And with all that's been goin' on around here, ya'd be smart not to poke yer nose around."

"Please, the lawyer next door was my father. Do you have any idea where he might be?"

This seems to soften the man. He sucks his teeth for a second, nodding to himself. "Ya ain't from around here, are ya?"

"Well, I grew up here, but no. I haven't been back in a long time."

The man nods again. The reflection of the headlights off the trees casts a strange shadow on his face. He spits.

"People 'round these parts just disappear sometimes. I was you, I'd go and ask the witch."

⤙ Chapter Three ⤚

TRANSCRIPT—Patient #62, SESSION #76

(In this session, the patient discusses her ongoing delusions regarding the staff of the DREAM CENTER.)

DIRECTOR: *Well, it's very nice to see you again.*

PATIENT #62: *Thank you, Director.*

DIRECTOR: *So, let's pick up where we left off, shall we? Do you remember?*

PATIENT #62: *Yes. I was telling you about the lump on the side of my head.*

DIRECTOR: *That's right. And didn't I and two other doctors examine you and confirm for you that there WAS no lump on the side of your head?*

PATIENT #62: *Yes, Director.*

DIRECTOR: *Good. So what shall we talk about today? Any more dreams?*

PATIENT #62: *But there IS a lump on the side of my head.*

(The patient is touching her temple.)

PATIENT #62: *I can still feel it right now. It's a little smaller, but . . . And I looked at it—*

DIRECTOR: *How could you have looked at it? There are no mirrors in your room.*

PATIENT #62: *I used a spoon. And I saw stitches. It's an incision. You cut me open and did something to me. I know you did. And I know you're not really a doctor.*

DIRECTOR: *How have the nightmares been?*

PATIENT #62: *What?*

DIRECTOR: *Your mother sent you here because you were having terrible nightmares. You were clawing your face in your sleep. Getting blood all over your pillow. Do you remember?*

PATIENT #62: *Yes.*

DIRECTOR: *Have you been having nightmares?*

PATIENT #62: *No.*

DIRECTOR: *Then it would appear our sessions are having some effect.*

PATIENT #62: *But the incision—*

DIRECTOR: *There is no incision. Let's talk about something else. What about the voices? Are you still hearing them?*

PATIENT #62: *I've always heard them. I'm not schizophrenic.*

DIRECTOR: *No one said you were. Who is it that speaks to you? You said last time you think they're spirits?*

PATIENT #62: *Yes. Most of them are just, like, whispers and shrieks, but there's one of them I can understand. But just in little pieces.*

DIRECTOR: *And what does this "spirit" say to you?*

PATIENT #62: *This morning, it said that the clock—no, the clocks—clocks, clocks, the clocks are ticking.*

DIRECTOR: *That's very interesting.*

PATIENT #62: *I'm not schizophrenic.*

DIRECTOR: *No one's saying you are. So who is this "spirit"? Does she have a name?*

PATIENT #62: *How did you know it was a she? I didn't say it was a she.*

DIRECTOR: *Yes, you did. You just did. What's her name?*

PATIENT #62: *I don't want to talk about it.*

(The director makes a note on his pad.)

DIRECTOR: *You may actually have what's called paranoid schizo-phrenia. It's very treatable with modern medications, so you have nothing to be afraid of, alright? Okay?*

PATIENT #62: *You'll never let me out of here.*

DIRECTOR: *Of course we will. Once we get you healthy.*

PATIENT #62: *No, no, no, no, no. . . .*

(At this point, the patient begins crying inconsolably. The director's remaining questions are unintelligible, and he ends the session.)

→

THE WINDSHIELD IS FROSTED OVER with tiny buds of dew. Outside, the sounds of a forest waking up fill the air—scuffling of leaves, calling of birds. Somewhere a dog is barking low and long. It's still cold in the car, but stripes of yellow sun are starting to fall across the side windows, evaporating away the spots of moisture, burning clarity out of a translucent blur. Something shoots past outside—probably a big eighteen-wheeler stacked high with pine lumber. The car rocks in its aftermath and a great, roaring "whoosh" washes out all other sounds before dying away into the wind.

"We could have gone to Vegas. Cancun. Fiji. The Cayman Islands. The Grand Canyon—I've never even been there, isn't that crazy? We could've gone to Australia—done some surfing, adopted a pet kangaroo, learned how to use a boomerang. But no. My best buddy would rather go to Podunk, USA, and now—ouch, shit—I have the worst kink in my neck. Dude, we could've gone to—"

"I get it," Caleb interrupts. "I didn't sleep much either, alright?"

Caleb is scrunched in the backseat, huddled under one of his dress shirts. His eyes feel dry and swollen. Bean is slouched in the passenger seat, which is reclined almost far enough to rest on Caleb's restless, cramped legs.

"So what do we do now?" Bean asks. "What's the plan?"

"I don't know," Caleb says, thinking. "But I'm not really cool with the fact that my dad is just *gone*. I think we should try to . . . I don't know . . . find him." He looks at his friend, trying to gauge his willingness for such an undertaking—after all, Bean only signed up for a trip to the beach and a week of Southern-fried cooking, and so far he's already been threatened with a rifle and forced to sleep in a car.

Bean begins to nod, but is instantly stopped by the pain in his neck. He curses under his breath, then says, "Alright. Where do we begin?"

It takes two passes through town to find the sheriff's station. It's a trailer set back from the road with a little green sign next to the entrance that reads HUDSONVILLE SHERIFF, PROTECTING YOUR PEACE. They pull in the driveway, (it's dirt again, and Bean wonders to himself if anyone in this town can afford pavement). There are two squad cars in the driveway. The young men head up to the door. Though it can't be later than eight in the morning, already the chill has burned out of the air and a heat so thick it's almost palpable radiates through everything. As the old folks say, "It's gonna be a hot one."

They get out and head up the drive, Bean in one tire rut and Caleb in the other.

"Okay," Caleb says, "just stand there, look pretty, and shut up this time, please. I like you and everything, but I really don't want us to have the intimate type of relationship that develops between two dudes in jail."

"Point taken," says Bean. "Mum's the word."

They tromp up the unpainted wooden steps and hear a faint sound coming from within, a low rumble of a voice, saying ". . . can't make a goddamn cup of coffee. . . . "

They glance at one another. Knock or walk right in? They don't want to interrupt anything, but standing on the stoop all day doesn't have much appeal either. Caleb knocks—he's always one to err on the side of caution. As he does, Bean twists the little steel knob and pushes the door open and enters. Caleb follows him.

The place is small, of course. A counter faced with wood paneling runs along the front. There's a large map hanging on the wall to the right and a row of plaques leading back to the area behind the counter, which is populated by a couple of desks, each boasting an outdated, yellowing computer and a messy stack of files. The place smells like mildew and cigarette smoke.

The friends exchange another glance and step up to the counter, which is when they see the sheriff and his deputy. They're both near the back of the office, standing over a table laden with a coffeemaker and its accoutrements. The deputy is a woman, in her late thirties, with massive thighs and coppery-colored hair, which is feathered and hair-sprayed up in front into something like a rooster's crest. The man is barrel-chested, bowlegged, maybe fifty years old. He has a bushy, salt-and-pepper mustache and eyes that blink too much. The two must've been arguing, because Caleb can still feel it hanging in the air, but now they're staring blankly at their two visitors.

The woman looks from them back to the sheriff. He gestures impatiently with a gruff "Well?" and gives her a little shove in the direction of the counter.

She marches up to the desk, a little flushed from anger or something else, and drawls, "Hello, boys. What brings you to these parts?"

"Well," Caleb and Bean say at once. Bean laughs and shuts up, deferring to his friend, but his laugh seems to hang in the air for a second, like a voice in a cave. Caleb imagines there isn't much laughter in this office—especially if the way Sheriff over there is glaring at them now is any indication. He clears his throat.

"My name's Caleb Mason, and I just had a question—or something to report, maybe. My father is missing, I guess, or he's not at home, anyway, and—"

"You check the bar?" the lady asks. There's a boredom in her voice that's no accident. An attitude of such complete disinterest can only be achieved through years of practice.

"No," Caleb concedes, "but—"

"Check the bar," the woman says, and turns away from the counter.

"No, it's not like that. I mean, he's been gone for a long time. Like, for probably a year."

"At least," Bean agrees.

The woman sits back at her desk and shrugs. "There's a lotta bars," she says, "First thing to do is always to check them all."

"My dad isn't a drunk," says Caleb evenly. "He's an attorney. Michael Mason."

The woman opens her mouth to speak, then doesn't. She looks over to the barrel-chested man, who has been sitting at his desk reading the paper. At this, he looks up, folding the paper in half.

He squints at the boys from behind his counter and blinks. "You Mike Mason's boy?" he asks.

"Yes, sir."

"You haven't been around these parts in a long time, have ya?"

"No, sir," says Caleb.

The man lights a cigarette, staring at them, blinking at them. He blows the smoke out his nose in a snort.

"Well, he ain't here, I'll tell ya that much. When was the last time you heard from him?"

"About . . . " Caleb begins—and he falters, because he doesn't know. He doesn't remember. But it's been a long time.

"You two were estranged, were ya?" the sheriff asks.

"I guess so," says Caleb, looking down at his hands on the counter.

"Well, I heard some folks say he went up to Georgia for some big, fancy job. Some people said he went to Arkansas for something, to teach at a college or something like that. Your father was a book man, wasn't he?"

"I guess so," says Caleb.

"Yep, well," the sheriff says. "Book folks don't usually stay around here for too long. Only thing for sure is he ain't here and he ain't been here in a long time." His demeanor is becoming downright jovial now, amused.

"Do you know how long he's been gone?" Bean asks.

"Nope," says the sheriff, smiling. "Long time."

"And nobody knows where he went?" Bean says. "Shouldn't you investigate something like that? I mean, he didn't even call his own kid and tell him where he went—don't you think that's strange?"

The sheriff shrugs. "Round here we investigate crimes," he says. "*Strange* ain't a crime."

"Maybe a crime *was* committed!" Bean presses. "The guy disappeared and left all his stuff at the house. Who moves and doesn't take anything with him?"

"Bean—" Caleb says.

"No, no," says Bean, "I just think they should do their friggin' job and investigate. And if they don't want to, that's fine. We can just get someone else to come out and investigate for them. My dad knows a bunch of private investigators."

The barrel-chested sheriff's grin melts into a frown, then to a fierce scowl.

"Boy, you gonna come in here and tell me what my job is?" He rises from his chair and sidles up to the counter. Now that he's this close, it's pretty easy to tell that he's huge, much bigger than either of the boys.

"No," says Bean, with a voice still full of righteous defiance. "I'm just saying, when someone goes missing, one way or another you have to find out the truth."

The sheriff takes another drag off his cigarette. "Nobody knows the truth. The truth is unknowable. All you can know is what folks tell ya. And I'm tellin' you, Mike Mason moved up to Georgia. Everybody knows that. I suggest you look for him up there."

"Okay," says Caleb before Bean has a chance for another outburst. "We'll look up there. Thanks for your help."

He takes Bean by the shoulders and steers him out the door.

"Hey, Billy," the cop says. Bean is already halfway down the steps, but Caleb pauses in the doorway. "Watch out for your friend. This ain't a good town to have a loud mouth in."

Caleb tries to smile, but something in the sheriff's blinking, serious-as-granite stare squelches it, so he just nods and ducks out into the mounting Southern heat, shutting the door behind him.

"God, I hate pigs!" Bean says, too loud.

"Be quiet, man."

"No, they're so smug. And they don't even give a crap about people. I mean, obviously there's something going on, right? I mean, your dad is missing. Like, *missing*. Like, disappeared off the face of the earth, and they won't even get up off their porky, doughnut-munching asses to check it out! I mean, obviously *something* is going on."

They're standing at the car now, Bean on one side, Caleb on the other.

"Maybe he just left, Bean. Maybe he just moved to Georgia. People move all the time."

"But he didn't even *tell* you, man," says Bean, with a slap to the roof of the car for emphasis. "I mean, he'd tell you, right?"

Caleb's arms are folded and he stares up the driveway. He sighs.

"Right?" says Bean.

Caleb sighs again. "When I was a kid he used to disappear. Sometimes for weeks. His law practice would shut down, I guess, and our lives would shut down and we'd just wait for him to come back. A few days or weeks would go by and he'd come back. No explanation, no 'I've got a mistress,' no 'I went on a drinking binge.' He'd just show up and act like everything was okay."

"Maybe he was in the CIA," Bean offers. "Sorry, man," he quickly amends.

"It's alright," Caleb says. "I didn't mean to get all 'After School Special' on ya. My point is just—"

"He might have left and not called you," Bean says. "I get it."

"He could be in Georgia. He could be in Brazil. Who knows, who cares?"

"Yeah," Bean says, "I think this calls for the Universal Problem Solver."

"What's that?"

"Bacon and waffles, on me."

"Amen, brother. Let's roll," Caleb says, his despondence dissipating.

Bean smiles as he gets in the car. As much as he screws things up, he sometimes has a knack for setting them right, too.

→

TRANSCRIPT—Patient #62, SESSION #77

(In this session, the patient attacks the director in an unprovoked episode of violence.)

PATIENT #62: *I know what you're doing and I don't trust you. None of the other patients do either. We all know what you're doing.*

DIRECTOR: *Well, hello. That's quite a greeting. And what do you and the other patients suppose I'm doing, Patient Sixty-two?*

PATIENT #62: *That's not my name.*

DIRECTOR: *I'm aware of that.*

PATIENT #62: *Then why won't you say it? Why won't anyone say it? Why are you trying to make me forget my name?*

DIRECTOR: *You were sent here to rid yourself of your nightmares. Nightmares are a normal phenomenon, of course, but when one exhibits behaviors like yours—self-mutilation, sleepwalking, insomnia—then nightmares pass out of the realm of normal and become a disorder. Natural, or healthy, nightmares grow out of your identity. In my school of thought, unhealthy nightmares, the ones that wind up producing disorders, come from rifts in one's identity. Hence, a temporary break with your identity might be therapeutic. And as you yourself have noticed, your nightmares have all but disappeared. Does that answer your question?*

PATIENT #62: *Yes. But there's another question, Director.*

DIRECTOR: *What's that?*

PATIENT #62: *What do you replace the nightmares with?*

DIRECTOR: *I'm sorry, I don't understand.*

PATIENT #62: *There are no more nightmares. That's true. But there's something else. Something worse.*

DIRECTOR: *And what is that? I'd be very interested to know.*

PATIENT #62: *But you already know. You put it there, through the hole you made in my head.*

Note: *The patient touches the side of her head here. This habit of hers is becoming more pronounced. Watch for this behavior in the future as a possible precursor to violent episodes.*

DIRECTOR: *I thought we agreed last time that no one made any incision in your head.*

PATIENT #62: *But it's there. I'm not crazy. Stop trying to make me think that! I can feel it right now.*

DIRECTOR: *Let me see. No, there's no incision there.*

PATIENT #62: *It's easy to lie. Everyone does it.*

DIRECTOR: *Why do you think I made an incision in your head? Do you have a memory of my doing that?*

PATIENT #62: *No . . .*

DIRECTOR: *Then what makes you think it happened?*

PATIENT #62: *She told me.*

DIRECTOR: *Who told you?*

(The patient appears to be shaking. The director approaches to comfort her.)

DIRECTOR: *Who told you I did that?*

PATIENT #62: *She never lies. She can't lie.*

DIRECTOR: *Who? Whose voice are you hearing? Answer me, Patient Sixty-two.*

PATIENT #62: *MY NAME IS CHRISTINE!*

(Here, the patient attacks the director. She bites his face in several places and causes a wound on his scalp that requires over twenty stitches. This concluded the session.)

➔

Maybe this town isn't so bad after all. Everything looks better after a plate of hash browns and a fluffy omelet the size of a football— not just a junior football either, but something more akin to a big, old, massive NFL pigskin. These plates are heaped with the best stuff Bean has ever tasted. Bacon smoked by a real local farmer (probably in very dubious conditions from a sanitation standpoint, but still . . .), spicy venison sausage, buttermilk pancakes steeped in Tupelo honey. The only thing Bean can't really figure out is the grits. They have all the texture of way overcooked white rice with half the taste. But by the time he gets around to prodding them with his fork, he's so disgustingly stuffed that he's actually relieved not to have to eat anything else, and he pushes his plate away and leans back in the seat. Caleb is still eating, slowly. He hasn't eaten much.

Bean is already restless, needing to burn off the ten pounds of food that's fast congealing into a bowling ball in his gut. So he does what he does best: talks.

"So what's up with Amber? How'd she take your big disappearing act?"

Caleb grunts with a mouthful of French toast. "Mot ell," chew, chew, "not well at all. But in the end, I think she thought it was cute or something that I was having a breakdown. She got me a teddy bear and gave me a card and a picture of her to take with me on the trip, and that was it. And, of course, she dropped about a million hints about coming along."

"Way to be strong, brother," says Bean. "This is a man's mission anyway—saving a damsel in distress and whatnot."

"Yeah," Caleb says, "she might've been a little jealous about that, too. I didn't mention it."

"Probably best." Bean belches softly.

Caleb looks around. There aren't many folks in here—all the working people of Hudsonville ate their morning vittles, drank their coffee, and punched the time clock hours ago, and it's still at least an hour away from lunchtime. The only people here are the shriveled-up old waitress who served them—and miraculously did so without uttering more than three words—and one quiet, middle-aged woman who sits in a corner booth, sipping her coffee and staring at the yellowing wallpaper. Of course, the banging of pans and the sizzle of grease from behind the pass-through window announce the presence of a short-order cook back in the kitchen somewhere, but he's nowhere to be seen. Out here, it's just the waitress, the woman, Caleb, and Bean.

"Ugh," groans Caleb, "I can't eat another bite. This stuff is, like, dipped in lead or something." He pushes his plate back. "Let's pay the bill and get out of here."

"Cool," says Bean. And they sit and stare at each other.

"Oh, right," says Bean. "I was gonna pay."

Bean opens his wallet, scrunches up his forehead, looks in a couple different compartments, takes out a few business cards, sets them on the table, and mumbles, "Man . . . "

"Bean," says Caleb.

"No, no, dude. I said I'd pay for it. I just have to find an ATM or something. It's totally cool."

"Bean," says Caleb.

"No, no, I'll get it. I said I'd get it. But I spent my cash on that travel Yahtzee game at the airport. Yahtzee rocks. I just need an ATM."

Caleb is already halfway to the register. "Forget it, man," he says. "Get it next time."

Caleb weaves around a few chairs, heading up toward the front of the restaurant—but the woman, the only other customer in the place, has beaten him to the cash register, so he waits in line and looks around. The name of the place, "The Blue Crab," is painted on the storefront window. Caleb sees the words backward now, and they look like they say something totally different. He can't come up with what they look like; they just look strange. Somehow it reminds him of everything in this place.

Since his return to Hudsonville, he has seen his childhood home, and he has passed streets where he used to ride his bike and the creek, or *crick*, as the locals call it, where he and Rich Baker used to catch frogs and have contests to see how far they could throw them. He has passed the corner where he used to wait for the bus, where Rusty Brown once unfurled (with much fanfare and rhetoric) the first porno mag Caleb ever laid eyes on. This was home. And it's just as he remembers it. The air still has the same indefinable sweet smell, the wind makes the same sound coming through the tops of the pine trees; even the paper kid's menu at the Blue Crab hasn't changed a bit. He had traced his finger through the maze on the textured paper just as he had done with a crayon a thousand times as a kid. Everything is the same. But nothing is *familiar*. It's all here, every wrinkle of every long-lost memory—real, vivid, unchanged, rendered in perfect detail, but still *not quite right*. Like "The Blue Crab," written across the window, everything is backwards.

The woman from the corner booth is still speaking to the old waitress in a hushed, raspy monotone. It's taking forever. In his boredom, Caleb tries to overhear their conversation but it's tough to make out the words. He takes a small, shuffling step forward and hears:

". . . it ain't what Jesus wanted for 'em. I know that in my heart. Jesus hates what's going on here. It ain't natural. And nobody will do nothing about it. You knew him. You knew Keith. He called you Grandma. He was nine years old. Nine years! Like he was suckin' off my tit yesterday, that's how I remember him. Like my baby. He *was* my baby. Well now the devil's got him, and ain't nobody to stand up, just like nobody stood up for Jesus when he was nailed up. Just like you ain't standin' up now. Margie, come on with me and tell the sheriff that Keith wouldn't run away. He wasn't that kind of boy, and you know he wasn't. He didn't run away." Here, the voice that had until now been as resolute as stone wavers for the first time, withers into a broken falsetto.

"You know he didn't. You know he didn't, Margie."

Margie, the old waitress, has been staring at the counter, never looking up once. Caleb can see her clearly over the other woman's shoulder. Only Margie's lips move as she says: "Five eighty-one."

The woman with her back to Caleb raises a hand up and clubs it down on the Formica counter with a dead thud, so hard that the cash register jumps and the phone belches a tiny dinging sound. She releases the handful of bills locked inside her fist and sniffs. Margie still stares at the counter. She hasn't moved, except for a tiny flinch when the woman's fist fell. Now she moves, but only her lips again, and she says very low: "I'm sorry, Lee. But your son ran away."

The other woman doesn't speak. She shudders as she takes in a breath, turns and strides out of the restaurant, shoving the glass front door wide on its hinges as she departs.

Caleb looks back at the old waitress: Margie. He remembers her now. It was perhaps eleven years ago, but she looked at least twenty years younger back then. She used to laugh so loud you couldn't hear your dinner conversation, and sing Dolly Parton tunes under her breath as she slapped down your plate of steak and eggs. She had watched Caleb sometimes when he was a kid, when his parents would head over to Tallahassee for the drive-in movie. She would make popcorn in a saucepan over the stove and let him sit up late watching scary movies like *Swamp Thing*. As far as babysitters go, Margie had been the best. Now, as she stands there, still staring at the counter, Caleb wonders where that jovial young woman went. And what made her so . . . old.

She gathers up the bills on the counter with trembling hands, puts the money in the register, and utters a lifeless: "Next."

Caleb steps forward, money and check in hand.

"Hi, Margie," he says. She looks up at this, and he can see her eyes are budding with moisture in the corners, but no tears fall. "I bet you don't remember me, but you used to give me free vanilla pudding every Sunday. I'm Billy Mason."

⇥ Chapter Four ⇤

MARGIE DOES REMEMBER BILLY MASON. Now she sits in a booth across from Caleb and Bean, laughing and rattling on in her raspy Southern drawl. Her wispy, whitish-blond permed hair bobs strangely as she seems to nod her head with emphasis on every syllable. The heaviness of her altercation with the corner-booth woman has been shuffled off like a winter coat on a spring day, and as she tells her story, she gestures wildly enough with the fork in her hand to make Caleb lean back in the booth, fearing for his eyeballs. A triangle of key lime pie rests on the table in front of each of them, "on the house." This is the Hudsonville Caleb remembers.

"So the pie-baking contest was down to three finalists; it was Billy's mommy, Jane Pierce, and Genie Barowski, and Billy's daddy is one of the judges. So they bring out the first pie, and they all eat it, and it's good and all. And they bring out the next one and eat that one all up, and now they're fixin' to bring out the last pie. Well, old Billy is—aw hell, not quite two, I guess, and I was watching him for his folks. I look away for a second and Billy's gotten away from me—he was prone to do things like that. And he goes toddling over next to his daddy with a load in his britches, stinkin' to high heaven. And Billy's daddy says . . ." Margie is already gasping for air, holding back laughter. "He says, 'Mmm, something smells good—that must be my wife's pie next.'" Margie erupts into laughter, and so does Bean.

Caleb smiles and chuckles. "Guess that explains the divorce," he says.

Bean, still red with laughter, points to the remaining bite of pie on his plate. "This stuff should have won the blue ribbon. This pie kicks ass, ma'am."

"Why, thank you, young man," says Margie, then to Caleb, "It's a shame you left, Billy. The young ladies of Hudsonville sure missed out on a handsome young man. Everybody knew you was gonna be a good one."

"Thanks," says Caleb.

"You went to California with your ma?"

"Yeah."

"You didn't miss us? You never came back to visit."

"Well, I guess I did miss you all," Caleb says, "but Mom was never too keen on my coming back, and with track and debate and journalism, I was pretty busy, even during summers."

"Well, what a fine young man you turned out to be," says Margie.

"Yeah," says Bean around his last mouthful of pie. "We're hella proud of the little guy." He tries to put an arm around Caleb's neck, but Caleb shoves him away, smiling.

"So, what brings you back now," Margie asks, "after all these years?"

"Well, I was going to see my dad, for one thing."

Margie nods, but keeps her lips pressed tightly together.

"Do you know where he is?"

Margie just looks at him, still as a statue. Little crescents of moisture build up under her eyes, but she still doesn't speak. She looks down at her piece of pie—it's still largely uneaten.

"No," she says. "I ain't seen him in a while."

Caleb studies her. Even Bean is silent.

"What about Christine?"

"The Zikry girl?" Margie asks, looking up again.

Caleb nods. "I got a letter from her. And, uh, thought I'd come visit. Any idea where she is? Does she still live in the same place?"

Margie shakes her head. "Not since the accident."

"What accident? Is she okay?"

Margie shrugs. "I ain't seen her since. It was a while ago, though, I imagine her legs would have healed up by now."

"What happened?" Caleb asks.

"It was at the prom—well over a year ago, I guess. She went with the Davis boy, Zachary, though they wasn't going as boyfriend and girlfriend—there's a lot of folks that think Zach Davis ain't the type who likes girls at all, but I don't believe it. Anyhow, she was sitting in a chair—so they say—I wasn't there, so I don't know nothin' for sure—you know how rumors can run like locusts once they get goin'. Anyway, they held the dance in the gym. They say she fell asleep in a chair above the dance floor, up top of the bleachers, where they keep the punch bowl and where the concessions are during basketball games, and they say she stood up while she was still sleeping and started walking with her eyes still shut, then started running—still sleeping, mind you, not sleepwalking but sleep*running*—and they say she run herself right off the bleachers. Landed on the dance floor, 'bout twenty or so feet down, and broke both her legs. After that, her momma sent her to the Dream Center."

"Dream Center?" Caleb asks.

"Big-shot doctor from Chicago or someplace—I don't know him, I never met the man—came into town a while ago and started it up. He's supposed to be very good. He's got all kinds of new methods, but I guess he's mainly just another kind of shrink. That's what Sheriff Johnson says, anyway. Gets a lot of business, though. You'd be surprised how many folks don't sleep right, especially nowadays. Seems like everything's corrupted now, even folks' dreams. Not like when I was a girl. We used to—"

"Where is this Dream Center?" Caleb interrupts.

Margie looks surprised. "Why, it's right behind your house, Billy. They renovated the old mental hospital."

The sky is a blue canvas, accented by a few huge, billowing, black-laced clouds. The air is still. As they turn down the drive, the hum of insects rises, an infectious clamor. This is not as he remembers it. There are palm trees, for one thing. They line the drive. And flowers stand row upon row in perfect, neat beds where there used to be only tangled weeds and moist clumps of rotting pine needles. The half-grassed-over dirt drive has been replaced by an arc of clean, black pavement, which cuts its way through the vivid green of the neat-trimmed lawn before disappearing amongst the trees. The driveway is long. The day is getting hot, but somehow rolling the windows up and turning on the air-conditioning would dampen the spirit of exploration.

Bean has both of his bare feet up on the dash and is patting one of them at superhuman pace.

"So what do you think the deal is? You think this chick, Christine, is a nut-job, or what?"

"I don't know. From her letter, it sounded like there was something else going on, like she was being held against her will or something," says Caleb.

"Yeah, but that's what everybody who's nuts says," Bean is quick to point out. "They all think the world is out to get them or something. My aunt had a nervous breakdown and she thought my uncle was secretly becoming a Republican behind her back. They almost got divorced because of it. Later on, they did get divorced, but that was because she screwed two sailors and—holy shitburger . . ."

As they pass from the cover of trees into a clearing, the Dream Center rises before them.

It's an imposing place. There are six stories if you count the windows, but that's deceiving—it's much taller than six stories, because it was built in probably the 1920s, with high ceilings. But the height of the building isn't as impressive as its length. It has to be at least six hundred yards long. The windows are simple squares, but there are thousands of them, many of them covered with bars. The façade of the building is painted a stark off-white. It reminds Bean of the *Titanic*. Far away, at either end of the building, there are glass sun porches on every level. A banner is hung from the roof that proclaims DREAM CENTER in red letters. The driveway curves around and they stop near the front entrance. Caleb shuts off the car and they get out, their heads tilted upward, taking the place in.

Bean tries to determine what makes the Dream Center so remarkable. Certainly, he's seen much bigger buildings; when he was a kid his dad had an office in the Transamerica Pyramid in San Francisco, and there are plenty of buildings in Los Angeles that dwarf this one too. But now it comes to him: it's not the size of the place, it's the *stillness*. Nothing moves. There's no lawn mower, no sound of laughter, no dog barking, no radio playing, nobody poking their head out the window to see who's pulled up out front. There's only the stir of insects in the dark of the forest all around, and the huge, silent edifice.

The hairs on the back of Caleb's neck are standing up too. He fights the urge to jump back into the car and lock the door. He had thought when he came back here it would be different, that his child hood fears would have been shed along with the Tonka trucks and the LEGOs. He realizes now, it doesn't always work like that. Looking around, he had thought everything had changed. Flowers supplanted the weeds, pavement smoothed the approach. The gnarled, clawing branches had been trimmed back from the driveway; but now he sees that a fresh coat of paint, like makeup on the face of a whore, changes nothing. This is the asylum, the same as it was when he was a kid. A broken place. A ruined place. Abandoned. Maybe even haunted.

You shouldn't play there, everyone said. They were right.

"Alright, let's go visit your buddy," Bean says.

He's halfway up the walkway, so Caleb has no choice but to follow him.

They pass large pots of pretty flowers stationed on either side of the heavy, polished-wood and glass doors, before stepping into the cool of the foyer. The floor is made of brown and white tiles, alternating, and is polished to such a sheen it seems almost clean enough to eat off of. There's a window to the left of the door, like a ticket booth at a movie theater. A lean, middle-aged man with a shaved head and a white, button-up shirt stands behind the glass and greets them.

"Hello, and welcome to the Dream Center," he chirps.

"Hi," says Bean.

"How can I help you today?" the man asks. His voice sounds a little canned from behind the window.

"Well," says Bean, "my buddy here is looking for a friend of his who we think is being treated here."

"Of course," the man says. "The patient's name?"

"Christine Zikry," says Caleb.

"Of course," says the man behind the glass. He turns and disappears into a back room, emerging a moment later with a file in his hand.

"This isn't really a visiting day," he says apologetically. "Are you a relative of the patient?"

"Yes," says Caleb before Bean can speak. "I'm her brother."

"Okay," says the man, flipping through the file.

"Just tell her Billy's here to see her," Caleb says.

"It . . . doesn't look like she has a brother listed as an authorized visitor, only her mother," the man says.

"What," says Bean in mock bewilderment, "your mom didn't put you on there?"

"I thought she did," says Caleb. "I guess she forgot."

"Huh," says Bean. "You see, ol' Bill here has been off at college—he's a freshman this year—"

"Sophomore," Caleb corrects.

"Right," Bean agrees. "Sorry, sophomore. Anyway, he's been very busy with school and he has to make it back for summer school, so this is the only time he can see her."

"Sorry," the man behind the glass says. "We don't make exceptions."

Caleb has an idea. "Here," he says, "I can prove it. I have a letter from her. See?" He pulls the folded-up envelope out of his back pocket, triumphant.

"Patients here aren't allowed to send correspondence."

"I assure you, it's from her," Caleb says. "It even has a Hudsonville postmark."

The man raises the glass window and nimbly grabs the envelope out of Caleb's hands.

By the time this registers in Caleb's head, it's too late: the man in white has already dropped the window again and is unfolding the letter.

"I don't think—um—that's a private letter. I don't think you should—" Caleb stutters.

The man's eyes are already scanning, line by line.

Caleb casually moves forward to the window and tries to pull it up without being noticed so he can snatch the letter back, but the window is now locked in place and won't budge. He glances at Bean, helpless.

The man in white finishes reading, and his eyes flick back up to Caleb. He folds the letter and puts it in the front pocket of his shirt.

"Please wait here," he says, his voice bleached of any emotion, and he disappears into another room.

"Shit," says Caleb in an explosive whisper.

"What?" asks Bean.

"What? He took the letter!" says Caleb.

"So what?" Bean says, looking confused.

"What if she's telling the truth, and they're doing some twisted things to her? Now they'll know she told somebody. They might do even worse things now," says Caleb.

Bean actually smiles. "Come on, man. All that letter proves is that she's crazy, which they obviously already know, or she wouldn't be in here. Who knows, maybe it'll actually be good. They can talk about it in their next therapy session and break down some walls or something. Chill out."

But the black hole Caleb feels deep in his stomach tells him otherwise. He is about to voice this doubt to Bean when the man in white steps out of a door he hadn't noticed before, to the right of the little booth.

"I'll take you to the visiting room now," the man says, handing Christine's letter back to Caleb. But despite the good news, his words come out flat and bereft of goodwill. "It turns out we were expecting you after all."

They walk down a long hallway amid the echoes of their footfalls, passing door after door after door. Some of the thick wooden slabs have little plaques with labels like JANITORIAL CLOSET, or MEDICINE ROOM, but most only bear numbers. The air is stale, sterile. Occasionally, they pass a hallway running perpendicular to their course. Looking down one of them, to the right, Caleb sees light spilling in from exit doors with frosted-glass windows and heavy bars.

Their walk feels interminable, but finally the walls of the hallway fall away, and they enter a large gallery with a high, vaulted ceiling. The floors are wood, newly refinished (he can still smell the sweet, chemical smell of the varnish) and covered with row upon row of cafeteria-style tables with benches. There is some artwork, childish stuff mostly, taped up along one white-tiled wall. The other wall is plastered with posters bearing messages like:

Perseverance:
The wings on which
dreams soar

It reminds Bean of his days in public elementary school, and the cafeteria/gym/auditorium where they used to hold assemblies. The principal (Jenson was his name; Mr. Jenson) used to raise his hand and everyone was supposed to shut up. Of course, Bean was incapable of doing that. Sometimes, he would just make up stuff to keep rattling on about, to no one in particular, until the other little kids would try to hush him, desperately hissing, terrified he was going to get them all in trouble, as he often did. God, he had hated that school. And those boring antidrug assemblies. And that cafeteria, which was just like this place, an institutional joint with windows too high to look out of and nothing fun to do and lame, colorful crap on the wall, all to distract you from the fact that you were basically in a prison.

"Christine will be down in a moment," says the man in the white shirt. "Please have a seat."

The guys comply, and the man turns and walks away, disappearing through a set of double doors at the far end of the room.

"Well," says Bean, "here we are. Only with you . . . I pack for the beach, expecting a vacation of broads and booze, and we wind up in the loony bin. Good times."

Caleb is about to respond when he hears footsteps coming from the same door he and Bean entered. At first, he thinks several people are coming—probably some burly orderlies arriving to say they know Caleb isn't really anybody's brother and to escort the two young imposters out of the building, Caleb guesses.

But instead only one shadow spills through the doorway, growing larger as the footsteps approach, and only one person enters the room. A little girl.

She comes closer, and Caleb realizes she's not quite a little girl, but not quite a woman either, really. So pale . . .

Closer.

She wears a white gown, like a nightgown. Her long, dark hair is a knotted mess.

Closer.

She's very petite. Her arms are tiny and her breasts barely show through the baggy gown. Her bare feet make a patting sound on the wood floor.

Closer.

She's biting her lip. Her features are small, exquisite, like those of a china doll. Her dark blue eyes are big and arrestingly beautiful, but ringed with unhealthy-looking circles. They flit back and forth between her two visitors.

Caleb rises.

"Christine?" he says. There's a mistake. This isn't the little girl he knew.

Suddenly, so fast that Bean and Caleb both jump, the girl jerks her shaking hands to her face to cover her mouth as tears fill her eyes.

"Billy?" she whispers through trembling lips. Before Caleb can answer, she slowly reaches out to him, her arms spread wide, and takes a few small, uncertain steps forward. She grabs his shirt in her surprisingly strong fists, buries her face in his chest, wraps her arms around him, pressing her body hard against his, and begins sobbing so loud and shaking so hard Caleb is afraid she must be terribly injured. He looks down and sees no blood, only tears and a little snot, so he brushes her hair out of her face and hugs her back.

"It's okay," he says. "I'm here."

And she squeezes him so hard it hurts.

They sit at one of the long cafeteria tables.

"So," says Caleb.

"Shhh," whispers Christine. She points to her ear, then all around the room. She is much calmer now, but to Caleb she still has the aspect of a squirrel that might dart away up a tree at the slightest sound.

He thinks back to the Christine he knew. The memories he has are scattered, but the few he's able to pick out don't seem to correspond with this strange person sitting across from him. Little Christine laughed loud and freely. She could burp at will (this was an impressive trait at the time) and run faster than Caleb. He remembers one event vividly—Dave Kimble, the neighborhood bully, had stolen Caleb's (Billy's) bike, and they, the inseparable three, Billy, Christine, and her sister, Anna, give chase. Anna fell out of the race first; she was prone to bouts of wheezing when she exerted herself too much and was usually the first to give up in such contests. Billy and Christine were neck and neck, until Billy stepped on a sand burr and had to stop instantly and dig the painful little thorn out of his foot. But Christine finished like an Olympic champ. She caught up with Dave and jammed a stick in the spinning front wheel of the bike, sending the bike to the hardware shop for repairs and Dave, who soared impressively over the handlebars, straight home, crying (and, Caleb imagines, to the doctor's office in Bristol). That was the Christine Caleb remembers. She loved dirt and boogers and singing and ice cream. She was loud and happy and fearless.

The girl before him, though bearing a physical resemblance, will hardly raise her eyes to his.

"I've missed you so much, Billy, you have no idea; it's been terrible. But how have you been?" Her voice is a soft Southern drawl.

"I've been pretty good. Just graduated, out in California," he says.

Christine nods. "I'd have graduated—near the top of my class too, if it wasn't for the accident."

"I heard about that," says Caleb. "Seems like you're walking okay now, though."

Christine nods jerkily and adds a distant, "Yeah."

"So what's with this place?" says Bean. "Are you okay here, or what?"

Her eyes become wide and dark, and she shakes her head and keeps shaking it, to the point where she looks like some kind of machine gone haywire.

"Why don't you like it?" says Bean.

Christine snaps an index finger to her lips and shushes him so fiercely that he's instantly brought back to the assembly days again. The sensation is distasteful, and he shuts up.

"So you had the accident," says Caleb, trying to walk the minefield without getting shushed himself. "Why did you end up here?"

"Mom sent me for the nightmares," she says.

"What were they about?"

"Lots of things."

"Like what? Christine, you can tell me. It's okay."

She performs an elaborate ritual of looking all around, up to the rafters, over both shoulders, and under the table. Satisfied no one is there to hear her, she whispers: "The devil is here."

"What do you mean? Where?" Caleb asks.

"Sleeping. Close. In a cold, cold cave very close. And," she says, pointing to her temple, "here."

"The devil is in your head?" Caleb asks with a glance to Bean.

She nods.

"What does he do in your head? Does he say things to you?" asks Caleb.

"He put him there." She points upward.

"God put him there?"

She shakes her head and mouths a word that looks like "arrester." Caleb just nods, uncomprehending.

Footsteps in the hallway, distant and hollow.

Christine looks over her shoulder at the gaping arch of the doorway, then back at Caleb with fearful eyes. She jerks to her feet and clambers frantically around the table to a startled Caleb, cups her hand, and whispers in his ear:

"They're taking me back now, upstairs—you have to get me out, Billy, you have to, he's going to cut me, she told me, he's doing terrible things, I just don't know, I just haven't figured it out, but my dreams are gone out of my head and there's something else there instead, something—they're coming!"

She stands upright. Caleb watches her chest move beneath her gown in shallow, quick breaths.

"Do you have a pen?" she asks, staring at the door.

"Uh . . . " says Caleb, feeling his pockets.

"Do you have a pen?" she hisses desperately.

"Yeah," Bean says, pulling one out and handing it to her.

She grabs Caleb's hand and yanks it toward her with surprising strength, bringing his palm close to her face.

"Anna told me to tell you . . . " she says, writing, pushing the pen into his hand so hard with her shaking fingers that Caleb is afraid she might actually puncture his skin. "The clocks are ticking." She kisses his hand, glancing back at the door with a look of wild determination. The footsteps have stopped, but there's a shadow spilling out of the corridor. She squeezes Caleb's hand, then drops it and walks away on her pale, white feet, across the room, through the arched doorway, and into the hallway beyond, where she's lost from sight.

"Dude, what did she write on your hand?" asks Bean with an amused grin.

Caleb responds only with an absent gesture of negation. "Let's go," he says, and starts for the door.

No one is there to escort the guys back to the exit, and when they reach the little "ticket window" where the man in the white shirt had been, they find it dark and empty. They push through the front doors into the insect songs, bird calls, and blaring light of the world.

Neither of them speaks. They get in the car and drive away, watching the sleeping colossus bearing the DREAM CENTER banner disappear amongst the green boughs of the forest. It isn't until they've reached the street that one of them cracks the silence, and naturally it's Bean.

"Dude, that's messed up," he says with outrage.

"Huh?"

Bean frowns and pats his pockets. "She kept my favorite pen!"

⊰ Chapter Five ⊱

"**F**IVE THIRTY-FIVE AM," CALEB SAYS with a shrug.

He and Bean sit in the living room of the abandoned Mason house. After some major dusting and bringing the sleeping bags and backpacks in from the car, they've managed to set up a fairly cozy campsite in the living room, complete with a roaring fire in the fireplace, thanks to some wood Caleb gathered out back and the can of lighter fluid Bean found under the kitchen sink. The fire pops and sputters, casting strange, dramatic shadows on the far wall. The guys sit in a cocoon of firelight—no streetlight shines through the windows, no electricity burns through the household bulbs. Still, in their pale halo, everything glows orange and feels safe. The fire makes the hot Florida air almost unbearable, but darkness would be even worse.

Caleb slouches in a wing chair and Bean lies on his stomach, sprawled across an ottoman.

"Let me see," says Bean, and positions Caleb's hand so he can read the writing.

"Ow," says Caleb. "I don't really bend that way."

"Oh, you're not double-jointed like your girlfriend, eh?"

"Ha-ha," Caleb says distractedly. He stares at his hand for a moment, then continues: "And she mentioned Anna, but Anna has been missing for years. Everyone but her mom was pretty sure she was dead. But maybe she's not."

Bean squints at Caleb's hand again. "I don't know, man. Maybe an S. Could be S-three-Sam."

"What the hell does that mean?"

"It means, of course that . . . um . . . I don't know! I'm just here for moral support, anyway. This is all you, Sherlock. Maybe it *is* five thirty-five AM. What does that mean? She wants us to rescue her at five thirty in the morning? I don't think so. It's five thirty in the morning and I'm either sleeping or drunk—in which case I'm still probably sleeping."

"I think maybe we should be there then. We can just wait in the woods and watch, see what happens. Just in case," says Caleb.

"Are you out of your friggin' mind?" says Bean. "First of all, she's crazy. Really, obviously, like, whacked-out. And if we actually help her escape, I'm pretty sure that has to be a major, serious crime."

"What are we supposed to do then? She's asking us for help. She's counting on us. And granted, she does seem a little out there, but just hypothetically speaking, what if she is telling the truth? Wouldn't we owe it to her to find out? I could even write a story about it and have it run in the papers and get the place closed down or something."

Bean laughs. "God, here you go again with the journalism bit. Does everything have to be an investigative report for you? This was supposed to be a vacation."

Caleb looks at his friend. "Alright. Tomorrow we'll go to the beach, okay?"

"The beach is cool, but I'm talking about going home, man. This place sucks. It's humid, the people are like redneck zombies, with the exception of your buddy who gave us the pie and . . . let's see, what else? Well, your dad's gone, we're staying in an abandoned, probably condemned, rat-infested shitbox, there are no chicks here who aren't wards of the state, and let's not forget *numero uno*, we live on the beach already! Why are we here? Your friend is nuts, mystery solved."

"But she has no one else to help her," Caleb says.

"What about her mom?" Bean says. "She even said in her letter that her mom gets weekly reports about her progress."

"Her mom got a little weird after Anna went missing . . . I don't know if she'd be much help."

"There you go! Her mom is nuts, she's nuts, case closed."

Caleb looks at his friend. "You really want to get out of here that bad?"

"Yes!" says Bean. "I got places to be, ladies to do, my friend. And while we're in Podunkville, USA, none of that is happening. I vote we go back tomorrow."

The fire pops and a spark shoots up the chimney. There's a scuttling sound from upstairs. Probably a rat. Bean is right. What can they do for Christine anyway? She's already getting professional help.

Still, a tiny voice of protest in Caleb's head won't shut up. He tries to reason with it, he tries to ignore it, but it keeps whispering in his ear as he watches the gyrating, primal dance of the flame. It whispers to him like Christine did earlier. And it won't be ignored.

Bean is humming Whitney Houston's "I Will Always Love You," and putting a marshmallow on a stick to sacrifice to the fire god in that ancient ritual called "s'mores" when Caleb makes his decision.

"Okay," he says. "We'll leave tomorrow. But there's one stop we have to make tonight."

"What's that?" Bean asks warily.

Caleb is staring at the fire again. "Remember when that guy said we should go see the witch?"

The flashlight beams cut through the night like shears through layer after layer of thick, black velvet. It's a long walk. Branches claw and unseen things rustle in the weeds, always just out of the light. The path is uneven, studded with roots and puddles and branches. Sometimes it's not really even a path at all; still, Caleb seems to know his way, leading them onward with step after determined step. Shrouds of Spanish moss hang all around them like wisps of lingering smoke. They pass the huge, deformed stump of a long-rotten tree. Bean's light flashes over it, revealing a nest of crawling bugs—a kind he doesn't recognize. All he knows is they're big. He looks away and keeps walking.

Caleb's thoughts race through his mind like a fire through a meadow: *I don't like this. I don't like it here. This is not my home. This isn't what I remember. There's something about Christine, something in her letter—damn spiderweb.* (He brushes it from his face.) *Nothing worse than walking in the forest and catching a mouth full of spiderwebs. Big-ass spiders in this forest. Remember plucking their legs off, me and Christine. And Anna. Why do I always forget she was there? How awful, to be forgotten. Jesus, Bean sounds like a steam engine back there, out-of-shape bastard. A few more sit-ups and a little less beer maybe, buddy. I'm lucky he's behind me at all. Who else would follow me here? We shouldn't be here. We don't belong here. I don't belong anywhere. But no one belongs here. I don't remember the path angling left here; I remember it angling right. I remember for sure there was a big rose-colored piece of granite. See, this is what I'm talking about—this isn't right.*

And that's when he hears it. He tries to pretend it's nothing—just part of a song he's singing in his mind, maybe, just some atonal notes strung together to drown out the sound of bugs, the sound of fear. He glances at Bean. Bean isn't behind him. For an instant, he feels his heart quicken—then he sees his friend, maybe ten yards back, standing still. Listening. He's standing under one of the rare breaks in the leafy canopy through which moonlight has been able to spill through. And from the look on his face, Caleb knows he hears the singing too.

"What the hell is that?" Bean asks.

"What?"

"It's freakin' eerie," says Bean. He doesn't move.

"Probably just . . ." and Caleb has no platitude to fit this. This is inhuman singing. Chanting.

The devil is close. Her words blow through every synapse in his brain.

But Christine is crazy, isn't she?

They walk on.

This whole thing is screwed. He shouldn't have brought Bean. He has to get his friend out of here.

"Do you want to go back?" asks Caleb suddenly. Bean clearly does. He's sweating badly and keeps looking over his shoulder at nothing.

"Do *you*?" Bean asks.

Caleb does want to go back. And not even just back to his dad's house, but back to Malibu. Back home, to surf and go for runs on the beach every morning, to get ready for college, read some good books, to meet Amber at a hotel in Santa Barbara and screw her and bask in the secret thought that he doesn't really care about her anyway. To do some writing, maybe even finally get something in the *LA Times*. These are all things that Caleb understands. Here, he understands nothing.

The singing starts up again. It's a howl now, chopped up with a few explosive consonants that ring through the woods like gunshots.

Caleb looks in the direction of the sound. He whispers: "Look, I think the witch the guy was talking about is Christine's mother. The kids in school always used to make fun of her, saying her mom was a witch and everything. I only met her a few times, but she seemed okay—and they say kids are the best judges of character, right?"

Bean gives him a wary look.

"Okay, man." Caleb says, "I promise, if everything is cool with Christine's mom, and we still think that Christine is just a crazy girl getting the help she needs, I swear we'll get on a plane tomorrow, deal?"

Bean looks at his friend and exhales heavily. "Deal."

"But we have to talk to her mom tonight," says Caleb.

"Dude, I said 'deal.' Move your ass before I renege."

Caleb turns and takes a step forward to lead the way—and sees that he has come to a fork in the path.

"Whoa . . . " he says, half to himself. "I don't remember a split here."

"Stop trying to scare me, dickhole," says Bean. "Which way?"

"This way," Caleb says, leading his friend down the left fork. What he doesn't mention is that he wasn't trying to frighten Bean at all. In fact, Caleb is the scared one. Because the path is changing.

Above, it looks like a Van Gogh painting. A field of stars. That's how Caleb describes it to himself later. There's a clearing, mowed and empty of everything but a crappy trailer and an old, rusting propane tank. Light spills from the windows of the trailer across the brown, parched lawn—in fact, every light in the place seems to be on, judging by the beacon-like aspect of the little square panes of glass. And above, stars pepper the sky, sloppy traces of a higher power, maybe, like Jesus's breadcrumbs or God's dandruff. There's something in the air. It's heavy. Not just humidity, either. Something humming. Something hissing. Caleb doesn't like it.

The singing is coming from behind the trailer. And it's louder now, a shrill warble. Like some terrible battle cry, it crescendos loud enough to pierce reality before degenerating into barely audible chattering.

"I do not like this," says Bean.

"I do not like it, Sam I am," says Caleb, feigning a grin. He steps into the clearing. Bean follows like his shadow. They make a wide arc around the trailer, passing in and out of the glare from the trailer windows. Caleb is struck for the second time that day by the stillness of a place.

This is what it'll be like on doomsday, he thinks, but he doesn't know where the thought came from. Certainly it isn't his. He isn't a morbid guy. He's a guy who believes in . . . what? He doesn't know how to finish the thought and doesn't have to, because around the corner of the rundown trailer, on the other side of the clearing, underneath the wide-reaching arms of an ancient live oak, a bonfire burns. Caleb hurries toward it.

"Hey, man—I don't think we should . . . " Bean begins, "I don't know if we . . . "

But Caleb is already striding with determination, so fast Bean can hardly keep up. He senses his friend lagging behind, but something, some impulse deeper than will, stronger than desire, pushes him onward. The singing is everything now, as bone-chilling as the roar of a siren but gilded with words of a tongue he doesn't understand, and doesn't want to.

Caleb is getting close now, almost into the ring of firelight, and he can see clearly that all the ear-splitting sounds come from the lips of one woman. She kneels, shirtless, her dark, gray-streaked hair spilling over her face and down to her bare chest, which looks as ashen as the skin of a corpse in the moonlight. She wears a dark skirt, which seems to seep from her waist into the grass around her like liquid. Caleb follows her downturned gaze to a small book, sitting open at her knees. Next to her left hand is what looks like a cowbell, but there's no mistaking what lies next to her right hand, half-obscured in the grass. It's a big, serrated knife.

The woman's song deteriorates into another bout of guttural clicks and snapped, unintelligible phrases, and that's when Caleb does it:

"Ma'am?" he says.

The woman's eyes snap up from the book and her song pinches into a scream—whether it's anger at being interrupted, fright at their sudden appearance, or simply another phrase in the song, he can't tell.

Instantly, the woman snaps her mouth shut. With one groping hand she seizes the cowbell, and with the other hand she scoops something out of the grass. She leaps directly over the probably three-foot-tall bonfire, and stands before the guys, brandishing what now looks to be a bowie-style survival knife in one hand, and ringing the bell violently with the other.

"It's okay," says Caleb to Bean, trying to sound as calm as possible. He takes a step forward.

"Don't break the circle," the woman says fiercely.

Caleb stops and puts his hands up. He glances at his feet and sees there is indeed a circle made of some kind of white powder that stretches around the bonfire.

"There are spirits here that will drag you into the netherworld, where no eyes see and no lips speak," the woman yells with wild wolf's eyes.

"Say your names," she commands. The clangor of the cowbell is maddening.

"Benjamin Michael Friedman," says Bean.

"Billy Mason," says Caleb.

The witch freezes, her bell clanging its last clang. She squints at Caleb, leaning forward as if trying to read some distant word.

"Billy? You're the little boy that was friend to my Annie?"

"Yes," he says, relieved. "You remember me."

"Don't move." She jabs her knife in the air. "My Annie was only a little girl, and you're halfway a man. Yer a liar."

She drops the bell. It lands in the grass with a metallic clank.

"I'm not lying. It's me, Billy. I visited Christine at the Dream Center. I wanted to come and talk to you. This is my friend. I swear to God it's me. I remember you used to make the cookies with the M&M's because Christine used to sneak me some. It's me, Billy."

The witch says nothing. She slowly turns the knife in her hand, as if twisting the blade in the heart of some unseen beast. She stares at Caleb.

"Where's my Annie?" she demands finally.

"I don't know, Mrs. Zikry," says Caleb. "I wish I did."

In the moment that ensues, a strange thing happens. The woman's fearsome scowl melts away and is replaced by a look of childish disappointment. She scratches her head with the knife-blade, almost as if confused, then sniffs and covers her breasts with her arms. Her shoulders hunch over and she seems to collapse in on herself.

"I was hoping you'd know, Billy," she mumbles. "I was really hoping."

"I'm sorry," says Caleb, not knowing what else to say.

The witch looks at the boys and tries a smile. It seems she's putting up a mighty fight to hold back tears. She looks down at her mud-stained bare feet.

"You boys want a Coke?" she asks. The question might be directed to her toes, but Caleb answers:

"Yes, ma'am. Thank you."

"Ahright," she says. "There's a hose over there. You boys put out the fire and come in when you're done. Don't step in the circle. And don't forget to wash yourselves up out here—you know the water don't work inside."

Caleb had no idea the water didn't work inside, but he obeys just the same, walking around to the side of the trailer with Bean in tow, turning on the water, and dragging the dirty green hose across the field of stars. On the way back to the fire, they pass the witch. She's walking to the trailer, taking small steps, her arms full with her hunting knife, cowbell, and the book, on the spine of which Caleb reads the words: *Holy Bible*. As she passes them, the witch gives a little nod and wistfully mumbles:

"Little Billy."

Bean only speaks once during their chore: as the fire gives up the ghost, he looks at Caleb, snorts, and says, "Dude, you owe me big-time."

As they mount the steps to the trailer, Bean pauses behind Caleb. "You hear that?"

"No, what?"

Bean frowns. "Nothing, I guess. Sounded like a crackly whisper or something. I thought it was coming from under the steps. Never mind, I'm just cracking up. Let's get this over with."

The screen door moans as Caleb pulls it wide and sticks his head inside the trailer. A wave of nausea twists his gut instantly; the place stinks so bad he turns his head away.

"Billy? Billy, come in," the woman says. Her tone is pleasant, matronly.

Caleb takes a deep breath and steps into the trailer. The reeking, stagnant air is so pungent he can almost taste it. Flies are everywhere, zipping into his ears and bouncing off his arms, tangling themselves in his hair. What must be the remains of fifty TV dinners lie stacked, one upon the other, on a flimsy-looking dining table. The carpet crunches with crumbs, and its stickiness tugs at the soles of his shoes with every step.

He hears Bean exhale sharply behind him. Caleb figures his friend's reaction is probably to the filth of the place, but there is plenty else to be shocked about. Both guys are forced to duck, because what must be thousands of Native American dream catchers hang by little threads from the ceiling. Some are wound together with dusty old cobwebs. A stack of yellowing newspapers as high as Bean is tall sits in one corner, behind a plastic-covered recliner. Caleb presses deeper into the living room. In front of a worn, brown couch, on a badly scratched coffee table, sit a Ouija board, what must be six or seven decks of tarot cards, a book entitled *Hearing Ghosts: A Guide to Communicating with the Spirit World* by someone named Chuck Macomb, and several old bottles of whiskey, most of them long since cashed.

"Seriously," whispers Bean, "if we don't get out of here, I'm going to puke."

They hear the familiar slam of a fridge door, and the witch appears from a doorway veiled by strings of clicking beads. She has a can of Coke in each hand.

"Here, here, take them. Sit down. Let's talk about my Annie," she says, settling into the recliner and gesturing to the couch.

Despite its dark color and the dim light (the only illumination is provided by a lamp made in the shape of a horse head in the far end of the room), they can clearly see that the couch is badly stained and littered with crumbs. Caleb sits anyway, setting his dusty Coke can next to one of the tarot decks. Bean brushes a crushed beer can, a wadded-up paper towel, and several pieces of candy corn onto the floor and, wincing, sits next to Caleb.

"Here are pictures of my Annie," the witch says, producing a huge stack of photos. "Yes, here she is. She's only four here. Look at these pretty barrettes. She was going to be a great dancer. Ballerina. Look, here she is with her cute little ballet shoes. This was her birthday, I forget which year. Isn't she beautiful? This was right outside here, right out there by the woods. She loved to play in the woods, her and the other one."

"Yes," Caleb says. "Her sister, Christine, is in the big hospital over there. She said they send you reports about her. How's she doing?"

The woman frowns, flipping through a couple pictures of people Caleb doesn't recognize. "Christine is a bad girl," she says dismissively. "Oh, now look at this. Here's my Annie at her First Communion. What a little peach pit! Her dress was so pretty. And here she is sleeping. . . ."

"Mrs. Zikry," Caleb says, "why do you say Christine's bad?"

"Here's Annie with her little swimsuit on, her little water wings . . . "

"Why is Christine bad? What did she do?"

"Oh, and here," says the witch, then, "oh, no, no, no," and she flips past that picture and the next. They look like more pictures of Annie, but Caleb figures they must be of Christine—who knows? You could never tell them apart. Mrs. Zikry stops flipping. "Here's Annie on her new bike."

"What did Christine do, Mrs. Zikry?"

The witch raises one trembling hand to her face and seems to stop breathing.

"Do you want a drink? You boys are too young to have a drink, but I'll have one, and you can have Cokes. Do you boys like Coke?" she asks, standing.

"We already have Cokes, Mrs. Zikry," says Caleb.

Mrs. Zikry takes a half-full whiskey bottle off the table and tips it vertical for a long moment before letting it fall sloppily to her side, exhaling sharply.

"Oh, here!" she says—like it's a great realization. "Here's Annie's school picture." She snatches a framed picture of a pretty little girl missing a tooth. It is the only item in the home not sheathed in dust.

"She was in second grade, do you believe that? What a grown-up. I pulled that tooth and she cried and cried," says Mrs. Zikry. "Cried and cried . . ."

"They never found her, did they?" asks Caleb.

The woman stares at the picture. The corners of her mouth are down-turned, her bottom lip trembles. She sighs deeply. "Never."

She emits a little sound—it might be a laugh, but it isn't—and raises the picture over her head as if to smash it on the table. Bean leans back and raises his arms to protect his face, but the woman brings the picture slowly back down again and cradles it tight to her chest.

"What about your other little girl?" Caleb asks. "What about Christine?"

"That little tramp," spits the witch, suddenly ferocious.

"What did she do?" Caleb says, his voice rising almost to her pitch.

"Nothin'," she says, like the word is venom. "She won't help. She won't tell me where my Annie is!"

"What makes you think she knows where Anna is?" asks Caleb.

The witch takes another pull off the whiskey. She's standing now, pacing back and forth and brushing the dream catchers above with one hand as she does, making them swing wildly.

"I tried everything, Billy. I got tarot cards, tea leaves, even bought me a set of pig bones, got me a Ouija board. I tried to learn the black arts," she says. "I sold my soul, lock, stock, and barrel. And they still won't talk."

Caleb has no idea what she's talking about, so he continues with the previous course of questioning.

"Why would Christine know where Anna is?"

"Because they talk to her!"

"Who talks to her?"

"The spirits!"

Caleb and Bean exchange a stunned glance.

"The spirits?" Caleb says. "Christine says she talks to spirits?"

"They talk to her all the time," says the witch, in disgust. "Never a word to me. To me, they won't say nothing. They'd rather talk to a damned lying little whoring bitch!"

"Maybe she's lying," Caleb says. "How do you know the spirits really talk to her?"

The witch is suddenly placid. "Oh, they talk to her alright. She knows things. Impossible things. Lying whore."

Silence, except for an electric snap as a fly-zapper in the corner claims a victim.

Caleb glances at Bean again, uncertain how to proceed. Bean only stares in rapt silence, the shadows of the swinging dream catchers playing strangely across his face.

"Where does Christine say Anna is?" Caleb resumes.

The witch swigs her whiskey. "Dead," she says; the word is almost a moan.

Caleb doesn't know what to say. He's hit a roadblock. A strange feeling floods through him; he pities this woman. He fears her, but he pities her more.

"Christine can't know everything," he says, trying to comfort her. "Maybe she's wrong about Anna."

She looks at him. "She knew you'd come."

To this, Caleb simply can't respond. Of course, Christine had sent him a letter, but to go so far as predicting that he'd actually come back to Hudsonville because of that bizarre piece of correspondence—that's another thing entirely.

The witch sits down in her recliner, leans back and pops the footrest up before taking another long pull off the bottle.

"Mrs. Zikry," says Caleb, "do you mind if I look at Christine's room?"

The woman gestures dismissively and hides her face with her hand. Caleb has a feeling now that she's curled up with her bottle, she won't be saying much else. He stands and glances at Bean.

"Don't look at me, I'm staying right here," says Bean.

Caleb figures Bean has just about reached his limit on drama for this vacation, so he sets off on his own, down the dark hallway leading to Christine's room.

He gropes for the switch and, finally finding it, snaps it to life. What he finds is the last thing he expected: a pretty normal room. The walls are plastered with posters of rock groups and pictures of half-naked men ripped out of Abercrombie & Fitch catalogs. There's a tall CD tower full of good music, an unmade bed with a hair-straightener sitting on it, a half-open closet stuffed with clothes, shoes, and hats. On a dresser he finds makeup and hairspray bottles, scattered specks of glitter, a couple stacked books: *Romeo and Juliet*, *To Kill a Mockingbird*, and *The Notebook* by Nicholas Sparks. Pictures line the smudged mirror; each features Christine with her arm around a friend or two. Some of her friends are guys, some are girls. In a few pictures, she's holding a beer and looks fairly trashed. He opens one of the top dresser drawers. Socks, a stocking cap, some old movie ticket stubs. Next drawer: underwear, some of it white cottony stuff, some of it more sexy. Next drawer, tank tops and T-shirts, next jeans. Over to the bedside table. There's a box. He opens it, and jumps back, startled as the tinkling tune bursts forth. A music box. He snaps it shut and looks down the hall to see if the sound disturbed the witch, but no one is coming. Good. He looks around again. Nothing weird at all. This is a normal room. The only slightly strange thing is that over in the corner, there's a small child's bed, neatly made, with a frilly, yellow comforter, stacked high with stuffed animals. Anna's bed. But that's only natural. They would have to keep something of hers. It would be heartless to throw it all out, or donate it to Goodwill—and Mrs. Zikry would never agree to that anyway. So Christine lived with it.

Strange, being here, he feels so close to her. And there's a feeling in his chest, oddly painful but also nice. Maybe it's because he smells her in here, just a little bit, and it's bringing back something from his childhood. Maybe it's just pure nostalgia; after all, he hadn't thought about her in months, probably even years, before the letter came, but now he suddenly realizes he missed his buddy Christine. His old best friend, his playmate. And it's kind of nice to know she's not that crazy, or at least she wasn't when she lived in this room.

The question is: how to help her? That's the tough one. He walks to the door, takes one last look around, and shuts off the light.

Then turns it back on.

Something caught his attention, just before the light went out— probably nothing, but there's a large, antique-looking wooden chest under the bedside table. He crosses to it and pulls it out, hoists it up (it's heavy), and sets it on the bed. He glances down the hallway again, full of the feeling that now he's about to delve into something very personal—but the hallway is still empty.

Of course, the chest will be locked, he thinks, perhaps hoping it will be, fearing what he'll find inside—but when he tries the lid it opens freely and lightly. It's so full that when he opens it, part of its contents spill out onto the comforter and even onto the floor. But it's not full of money or costume jewelry or severed dolls' heads or any of the other things he had imagined might be under the lid. It's just a bunch of folded-up papers. He picks one up off the floor, and opens it.

> *Dear Billy,*
>
> *School sucked so bad today. Mr. Phizer was having us find complementary angles in triangles. I don't know how anyone could actually think trigonometry is hard. . . .*

He folds the letter and puts it back in the box, then pulls another one out:

> *Dearest Billy,*
>
> *Hello, my love! I have missed you so, so, sooooooooooooo much!!!!! I can't wait until we get married and have babies and get the hell out of this town!!! Everybody here is evil!! I'm in English class right now, snooze. . . .*

He pulls out another:

> *Dear Billy,*
>
> *I've been thinking about you so much lately, I just can't help it. Every time I do I start touching myself and I get so wet. I can't wait to . . .*

He folds this one up quickly. He's about to toss it back into the box, then thinks twice and sticks it in his back pocket instead. He takes out a handful of letters:

Dear Billy,

There are so many voices screaming at me every moment, but Anna is the worst. I keep telling her to SHUT HER GODDAMNED DEAD FACE, but she WON'T . . .

Dear Billy-baby.

what's up? so I'm killing my mom. I haven't decided when or how, but the bitch must die. She is really, truly the most crazy and certifiably f-ed up woman ever to live. . . .

Billy,

i can't sleep, can u? I wish I couldn't hear them whisper to me, but I always can—when I'm sleeping, when I'm awake. It's gotten so much worse you wouldn't even believe it. I thought about stabbing my eardrums out with a pair of scissors today, then I thought what if I could still hear them, but I couldn't hear anything else?? It would be horrible with nothing to drown them out. I wish you were here. . . .

Billy, my Billy

June 19th
Forever
We are one.
Love, MEEE!! xoxoxoxoxoxoxoxo

Dear Billy,

Okay, so I was telling you about my friend Mariam,

right? Well, she was cheating on her boyfriend Will with this
guy Casey (don't worry, I'd never cheat on you, lover) . . .

Billy—Caleb—stops reading. This is enough. He stuffs a handful
of letters into the cargo pocket of his shorts, then shovels the rest
back into the chest, and claps the lid shut. With one last sidelong
glance down the shadowy hall for safety, he puts the chest back on
the floor and shoves it roughly under the nightstand. As he leaves the
room, he flicks the light off again.

"A lot of wisdom, a lot of laughing, a lot of happiness," says a
slurred voice.

"What about my lifeline?" asks Bean eagerly.

"Ah, can't see in this damned light," says the drunken witch. She's
hunched very close to Bean's outstretched palm.

Bean looks up at Caleb in the doorway.

"Hey, there, buddy," he says. "Sit down. Mrs. Zikry is reading my
palm. You're next."

"We should really get going," says Caleb.

"Ah, come on, party pooper," says Bean. "Don't you want to know
if you're going to be the editor of the *New York Times* someday?"

"Hmm, your lifeline—" begins the witch, smiling.

"Maybe next time," says Caleb. "Let's go."

Bean looks disappointed, but the witch just goes back to her bottle.

"My Annie was such a dancer!" she says, but whether she's talking
to herself or to them, Caleb can't tell.

"Let's go," he says again.

"Okay, okay," says Bean. "Thanks for the warm Coke, Mrs. Zikry.
Maybe next time I'll drink it."

"Thank you, Mrs. Zikry," says Caleb. "Hey, don't drink so much, okay? It's bad for you."

"My Annie was such a good, obedient girl!" she says, staring at the coffee table and taking a shallow swig of whiskey.

There's nothing else he can say, so Caleb follows Bean out the screen door, thinking that even the strange, heavy Southern air is like a mountain breeze compared to the rot of that trailer.

They cross the field of stars and step into the twisted paths of the forest.

It takes them almost twice as long to get home as Caleb thought it would. Almost every path he leads them down, he has to double back. Finally, the familiar wooden fence, now half fallen and peeled of all but a shred of its paint, ushers them into the Masons' backyard.

Only then do they speak, and only a few sentences.

Bean: "So what did you find in her room?"

Caleb: "Nothing." He wants to explain, but for some reason, he's ashamed for Christine and can't say it. "She's crazy, just like you said. She's crazy and her mom's even crazier. I'm sorry I dragged you here. We'll leave tomorrow."

"Sweet," says Bean.

And that's that.

TRANSCRIPT—Patient #62, SESSION #79

(In this session, the patient begins to show signs of progress.)

DIRECTOR: You're very quiet today.

(The patient doesn't respond.)

DIRECTOR: You had some visitors earlier. Tell me about them.

PATIENT #62: *It was Billy.*

DIRECTOR: *What was that? Speak up, I can't hear you.*

PATIENT #62: *It was Billy and his friend.*

DIRECTOR: *And who is Billy? Patient Sixty-two, please answer me. Who is Billy?*

PATIENT #62: *He's my best friend.*

DIRECTOR: *Well, that's nice. Did you enjoy seeing him? I thought it might be nice for you. Did you enjoy it?*

(The patient nods.)

DIRECTOR: *Were you ashamed for him to see you like this?*

(The patient nods.)

DIRECTOR: *What do you think he would say if you told him about all the voices you think you hear? Do you think he would believe you?*

PATIENT #62: *I guess not.*

DIRECTOR: *Patient Sixty-two, look at me. Did you think he was going to rescue you? Did you think this Billy was going to take you out of here?*

PATIENT #62: *I guess so.*

DIRECTOR: *Well, how long has it been since he came?*

PATIENT #62: *He came today.*

DIRECTOR: *No, he came three days ago. This is Thursday; he came on Monday.*

PATIENT #62: *I thought it was today . . .*

DIRECTOR: *Three days. Patient Sixty-two, I don't think he's coming back. Do you?*

(The patient is becoming agitated.)

PATIENT #62: *I don't know. I don't know.*

DIRECTOR: *Relax, relax, relax.*

(The director walks behind the patient and places his hands on her shoulders, then slips one down inside her nightgown.)

DIRECTOR: *What's wrong? Why are you crying?*
PATIENT #62: *Because.*
DIRECTOR: *Tell me why, I don't understand.*
PATIENT #62: *Director, please stop.*
DIRECTOR: *Stop what?*
PATIENT #62: *Please stop touching my breast.*
DIRECTOR: *I'm not. You're touching your own breast. Why are you doing that?*
PATIENT #62: *I'm not.*
DIRECTOR: *Why are you touching your breast, Patient Sixty-two? Does it feel good when you touch your breast like that?*

(The patient nods.)

DIRECTOR: *Then why are you crying?*
PATIENT #62: *Because I'm so confused. I know I'm not crazy, but . . . I just don't know anymore. . . .*
DIRECTOR: *You know what? I think we're ready for the next phase of our work together.*

(The patient begins crying loudly and shaking, but does not move.)
(The director bends close to Patient #62's ear.)

DIRECTOR: *{This portion is inaudible.}*

﹂ Chapter Six ﹄

PACK OF MARLBORO REDS. One left. He holds it in his good hand, sticks it in his lips. It dangles there until he digs a lighter out from under a crushed RC Cola can and pops a flame. Then he snaps the cigarette to attention, taut, and breathes all that mother-lovin', toxic shit into his lungs. He dumps it out in a sigh. Looks down at the crumpled map on the desk in front of him. Spreads it out with his good hand as if to smooth out all the wrinkles, an impossible task. He slouches in his chair and takes another drag. No revelation, nothing. One thing's for sure, he's no Sherlock Holmes. Praise God.

Not surprising. In middle-school gym class, he was no rope climber. At Markston High School he was no mathematician. No writer, either. Not much of a mechanic when he did that stint in his stepdad's shop, and the old bastard never missed a chance to remind him of it. Was never much good with women, so it made perfect sense that he was a lousy husband when he finally got the chance. Couldn't hold down that job keepin' books at the industrial sup-ply—morphine makes the numbers swim once you're on the third or fourth pull from the whiskey flask. Couldn't just keep his blessed mouth shut and swallow his pride enough to appreciate that job checkin' groceries at the Publix, even though they had health bene-fits and everything. And, of course, let's not ever forget the last fiasco, the crown of them all. After that one, anything is easy to swallow. So there's not a speck of surprise in the fact that he can't figure this out, a bona fide mystery. One thing, though, gotta be fair. One thing no one can deny, one thing they can scrawl on his gravestone: *Ron Bent was a good father.* At least there's that. Praise God.

He goes to fold up the map and gets ashes all over it: one more screwup to go in his ever growing screwup file. He brushes the map off and folds it up, against the folds. Seems like he's folding against the folds every time with this blessed map. Seems like there's no *right* way to fold the thing. The shiny star stickers—gold, red, blue, and the scrawled, nearly illegible "Ron writ," as he thinks of it, disappear in the folds until finally, miraculously, the part saying "The Florida Panhandle, by Rand McNally" faces up. He sets it neatly in front of him, thinking he might never unfold it again, now that it's actually put away right.

Maybe that would be best. He's been staring at the thing for over two years.

Three big steps and he's at the sink, tosses the cigarette in. It hisses and smokes, then shuts up. Squirts some Colgate on his finger (forgot his toothbrush at the last motel, go figure) and brushes. Looks at himself. Gaining weight? Check. Hair a little thinner? Check. Grayer? Hard to tell with this flickering fluorescent light, but it's safe to say—check. Spits, splashes water into his mouth, pulls the rubberband out of his ponytail. It pulls and hurts. Tosses it next to the sink, takes a leak, undresses to his skivvies, and sits down on the bed, feeling it strain and hearing it squeal under the weight of his body. What's the blessed box spring complaining about? He's the one who has to carry his heavy ass around all day, not it. He shoves his feet under the covers and clicks off the light next to his head. It's dark. A truck yells past on the highway, then another, then another. Hollow light seeps in between the curtains. Somebody's clomping up the steps outside, shaking the whole place. They walk by his door; he can hear them clearly:

"That's fine. Let's just worry about it in the morning. Jesus."

"I'm just saying . . . " This voice is a woman's—the other one was a man's.

"Goddamn, I've been driving all day, can we just—"

The words are cut to a dim muffle as the door to the room next to him thumps shut.

He closes his eyes.

This is the ritual. It never changes. Another night, another cheap motel, another shallow sleep with another restless day nipping at its heels. Now, one last thing before sleep: the prayer.

Hey, Lord.
Here we are again.
Bet you get tired of hearing from me.
Same old prayer as always.
Keep me alive, keep me breathin'.
Keep me believing.
Not much new, I guess, just another day
On the trail.
Keep Keisha well, Lord.
Hold her tight to you.
Keep her safe.
And if I can do her any good,
Bring me to her.
If I can't do her any good,
At least let me see her bones once
Before I put her in the ground
Before they put me in the ground.
And when they do, please bring us both home,

Lord.

Thanks for your blessings.

You know I'm your servant.

Always have been,

In my way,

Always just been waiting for your bidding.

Waiting for you to touch me.

Or to answer me at all.

Still waiting.

Anyway.

God, bless the sinners,

And the believers,

And bless my Keisha.

Amen.

Ron opens his eyes. All is still. A truck rumbles past again. The far wall starts shaking, a rhythmic hammering. A breathy moaning, animal grunts. Every cheap adornment in the cheap room rattles.

Before he knows it, Ron is stifling tears. Embarrassed, he blinks them away, pulls his lips together tight. The muscles of his face quiver with tension. He tries to remember the last time he cried. It's been a long time, he knows that much. Why now? Why here, finally?

Why anything?

The muscles of his face relax and his eyes stop blinking. He sits very still and stares at a picture on the wall in front of him across the darkened room. It's a print of an abstract painting, which is to say a picture of nothing. He's won the fight, knows he's not going to cry tonight. The emotion has ebbed and left him vacant, an empty sea-shell washed up on a deserted beach. Not surprising that's how he'd

READER/CUSTOMER CARE SURVEY

HEFG

We care about your opinions! Please take a moment to fill out our online Reader Survey at **http://survey.hcibooks.com**.

As a **"THANK YOU"** you will receive a **VALUABLE INSTANT COUPON** towards future book purchases

as well as a **SPECIAL GIFT** available only online! Or, you may mail this card back to us.

(PLEASE PRINT IN ALL CAPS)

First Name _____ MI. _____ Last Name _____

Address _____ Email _____

State _____ Zip _____ City _____

1. Gender
- ☐ Female   ☐ Male

2. Age
- ☐ 8 or younger
- ☐ 9-12   ☐ 13-16
- ☐ 17-20   ☐ 21-30
- ☐ 31+

3. Did you receive this book as a gift?
- ☐ Yes   ☐ No

4. Annual Household Income
- ☐ under $25,000
- ☐ $25,000 - $34,999
- ☐ $35,000 - $49,999
- ☐ $50,000 - $74,999
- ☐ over $75,000

5. What are the ages of the children living in your house?
- ☐ 0 - 14   ☐ 15+

6. Marital Status
- ☐ Single
- ☐ Married
- ☐ Divorced
- ☐ Widowed

7. How did you find out about the book?
(please choose one)
- ☐ Recommendation
- ☐ Store Display
- ☐ Online
- ☐ Catalog/Mailing
- ☐ Interview/Review

8. Where do you usually buy books?
(please choose one)
- ☐ Bookstore
- ☐ Online
- ☐ Book Club/Mail Order
- ☐ Price Club (Sam's Club, Costco's, etc.)
- ☐ Retail Store (Target, Wal-Mart, etc.)

9. What subject do you enjoy reading about the most?
(please choose one)
- ☐ Parenting/Family
- ☐ Relationships
- ☐ Recovery/Addictions
- ☐ Health/Nutrition
- ☐ Christianity
- ☐ Spirituality/Inspiration
- ☐ Business Self-help
- ☐ Women's Issues
- ☐ Sports

10. What attracts you most to a book?
(please choose one)
- ☐ Title
- ☐ Cover Design
- ☐ Author
- ☐ Content

TAPE IN MIDDLE; DO NOT STAPLE

NO POSTAGE
NECESSARY
IF MAILED
IN THE
UNITED STATES

BUSINESS REPLY MAIL
FIRST-CLASS MAIL PERMIT NO 45 DEERFIELD BEACH, FL

POSTAGE WILL BE PAID BY ADDRESSEE

Health Communications, Inc.
3201 SW 15th Street
Deerfield Beach FL 33442-9875

ııllıııllıılıılılıılıılıllılılıılııllıılılılıılılı

FOLD HERE

Comments

end up. He was never good for much anyway.

In five minutes, the screwing is over next door and his tears are forgotten. Another truck bellows past and Ron Bent falls asleep.

It's dark in the Mason house. The fire has burned away to smoke. Caleb blinks in the dark. He hears Bean breathing next to him in long, even breaths. Outside, the wind gusts and a tree branch whispers against the window. When the wind dies away, Caleb hears something. The noise is tiny, barely a scratch in the surface of silence, and he pushes up on one elbow and cocks his head to listen intently, to be sure. Something is ticking. His first impulse is to look at the mantle—there was always an antique clock there, and a memory races through Caleb's mind of his father winding it before bedtime with the slow, mechanical-sounding twist of a silver key. The clock is still on the mantle, its once-white face dark with dust, but even with no light Caleb can see that the pendulum is still. *Tick, tick, tick.* Caleb reaches for the flashlight—should be by his shoulder. His heart begins to feel tight with fear as his hand gropes the dirty rug, finding nothing. Then he finds it—it had only rolled a few feet away.

With a click, the light is on. Caleb glances over at Bean. There's a glint of drool at the corner of his mouth, but he lies still and his breathing stays steady. For a minute, Caleb considers waking his friend, then decides against it. *Tick, tick, tick.* After all, he's dragged Bean halfway across the country, and for what? To visit some crazy girl and squat in an abandoned building? Some vacation. Some friend. But at least he knows when to quit. They'll buy a plane ticket tomorrow and be back in LA by happy hour. *Tick, tick, tick.* Caleb looks at the ceiling. The sound is coming from upstairs.

He crosses the living room in slow, measured steps. His feet crackle across the grit-strewn marble floor of the foyer.

Suddenly, he freezes. He whips the beam of his flashlight around. It comes to rest on the obsidian surface of a window. Felt like somebody was watching him, but there's nothing there but homogenous darkness and the white oval of his reflected flashlight beam.

Up the steps, slow, one at a time, his eyes trained upward, toward the darkness crouching behind every doorway in the long, long, hallway. He reaches the top of the steps. This was the spare bedroom; that was a bathroom. He remembers when this carpet was new. His mom had dragged him all over three counties trying to find the perfect color to match the drapes. Now it's littered with little black seeds of mouse crap and stained from the mildew and the dust.

Tick, tick, tick.

He pushes open the door to his old room. There's a desk and a computer, a home-gym system against the far wall; nothing else. Not a single teddy bear or Matchbox car or old baseball poster; nothing to indicate that Caleb used to live there all. He shuts the door and walks on.

A sound. He stops, freezes. A scraping, faint. Then again. Something moving slowly, just behind the door right next to him.

With a crash, he elbows it open and the flashlight swoops in. His breath exhales in a hiss. Two glowing eyes stare back at him.

There's a raccoon in the bathtub.

He curses and shuts the door, angry at first, then laughing at himself. He shakes his head and continues down the hall. He's remembering back a few years when he was a kid, almost a teenager. He hadn't been living in California too long when he went to a Halloween party with some friends. He had always been a well-liked kid, but he was just becoming cognizant of the social implications of real popularity when he got invited to this party. There were five or six of the most popular kids in the school there, and they led him down to the basement. They all got some punch and were arguing about Pete Rose or something when Caleb wandered over to a coffin sitting in the corner of the room, ignored by everyone else. Inside was a mannequin, or an exquisite dummy, which looked just like the dead body of a beautiful girl. Caleb had leaned close, admiring the detail of the pale figure—even the eyelashes looked real—when it screamed. Caleb jumped back, yelled, and dumped his punch on his pants and had to go home. Turns out the woman in the coffin was the mother of Caleb's friend, an ex-Playboy model, who had set everything up for a little Halloween joke. Looking back, it was funny. It could have been anybody who walked up to the coffin and got the shit scared out of him. Caleb just wished it hadn't been him.

This is what he thinks to himself as he walks into his dad's old bedroom, where he used to sleep between his parents if he had nightmares. He's still almost smiling with embarrassment at the memory as he flashes the beam of light over the objects in the room. Some are familiar, the bed, the dresser—and some are new, like an ugly, African-looking statue in the corner. He walks to the nightstand and the ticking gets softer. As he rounds the foot of the bed, it gets louder again, and when he slowly opens the closet door, it becomes twice as distinct. As he looks up at the closet ceiling, Caleb stops smiling.

There's a square of plywood with a pull string hanging from it. Pull the string, and the staircase comes down. Climb the staircase, and you reach the attic.

Around the edges of the plywood, Caleb sees a light.

Tick-tick-tick-tick.

He reaches up with a trembling hand and pulls down hard. A dusting of particles drifts into his eyes, but he blinks them away, finishing the motion and pulling the staircase down as the light of one bare electric bulb, burning above, leaves him half-blinded. *But there's no electricity. So how . . . ?* His shoulders are tense, pulled almost up to his ears. He isn't breathing. The staircase moans as he puts his weight on it. He wants to look down to make sure he doesn't miss a step, but he can't take his eyes off the door above. Because somebody turned on this light.

Tick, Tick, Tick.

His head breaks the plain of the attic floor and he jerks it around, back and forth, looking for feet, looking for a figure, seeing only walls and rafters, layers of fluffy, dusty, pink insulation. Satisfied that he's alone, he pulls himself up, kneeling first, then standing halfway, as much as the pitch of the roof will allow. The light beam traces back and forth. Nothing but cobwebs and suspended dust. But here—over this way, a series of particleboard sheets bridge the insulation. Somebody put them there. That's the direction. *Tick, tick.* That's the way. He hears his footfalls on the boards, muted steps. He breathes shallowly. The air is heavy, almost too thick to breathe at all, and hot. The particleboard sheets tilt under him, but he walks on. Ahead, something reflects in the light. Something glass. As he comes toward it, a room emerges out of the darkness, walled off with plywood. He steps slowly through the uneven doorway, *ticktock,* and sees a clock, choked with dust. Its pendulum is still. The light beam drifts to . . . another clock. And another. And another. And another. And another, and another and another and anotherandanother.

And this one's still ticking.

"Bean!"

"Bean!"

Caleb hears himself screaming, but doesn't feel his mouth moving, doesn't remember making the words.

Floor to ceiling to floor, all around him.

"Bean!"

Ticktockticktockticktocktick.

Who would make a room of all clocks, just clocks?

"Bean!"

Then it came, faint. "Caleb? Jesus, where are you?"

"In the closet! In the attic! Up here!"

Caleb stands very still. His arms are wrapped tightly about himself, as if he were about to freeze to death, and his flashlight beam blazes into the clock, the one that still ticks, the one that somebody must've wound.

That's how Bean finds him.

"Jesus Christ, you okay, man? I thought I'd find you in a bloody pile."

"Look," says Caleb, and he lets his flashlight play across the faces of the many clocks.

"What the hell?" says Bean.

"I heard the ticking," says Caleb.

"What kind of nut-wagon has a room full of fifty clocks?"

"Sixteen," says Caleb. "There are sixteen of them. And somebody wound this one within the last couple of days."

They look around in a pregnant silence, then glance at one another with wide eyes, but neither of them speaks.

Caleb waits for Bean to make a joke. He doesn't. He says: "Let's get out of here, man," then whispers: "This is a haunted place."

They cross the attic bridge, climb down into the closet, trudge to the bottom of the steps, and wordlessly start packing up their stuff.

Finally, Bean starts ranting: "Somebody was here. Somebody wound that shit up. And whoever it was, I don't want to meet him. I just want to be back home. We can take a road trip up to Big Sur, do some surfing, play some video games. You know, I don't even care if my parents nag me about what to do with the rest of my life anymore. I don't care what I do with my life, as long as I'm not here, in this messed-up, crazy place. In fact, I'm glad we came. It's taught me a very important lesson; namely, no matter how bad anything is, we are some lucky bastards because we don't have to be *here*. We get to leave. Some people live in this town, and they're screwed, and I feel bad for them, but we live in a place where, despite the drive-by shootings, child drug use, and rampant bullshit, nobody is crazy enough to put sixteen clocks in one room. I'm just glad—"

"Bean?"

"Huh?"

"What did Christine say about clocks?"

"Ummm . . ."

"She said something about clocks."

"Uh . . . I don't remember."

Caleb is looking at his friend with fierce eyes. Suddenly, he covers his mouth with his hand.

"Bean," Caleb says, "we can't leave. She said *the clocks are ticking*."

"Maybe she snuck out, came over here and wound it," Beans says, sounding unconvinced.

"Maybe," Caleb says, "she isn't crazy at all."

Eyes open. There's no sound now, no traffic. Ron looks over at the green-burning numbers on the old alarm clock next to him. They say five-oh-four. He's never been so awake in his life. He rolls onto his back and looks at the ceiling. There's nothing to see. With nothing else to look at, he looks back on his life. He does this a lot. He's gotten good at it, so good that he no longer has to look at it piece by piece. Now he can see it all at once, like a big mosaic. It's better that way. Like a bed of nails: you lie down on one nail, you might puncture a lung; you lie down on ten thousand nails, no problem. You may never be very comfortable—hell, you'll never get a good night's sleep on a bed of nails, but it sure beats the alternative. Praise God.

Ron's life has been reduced to a movie montage. Sledding with his brother; cut to being slapped in the ear by his drunk mother; cut to the principal telling him "young men who get caught smoking marijuana on school grounds can't participate in the graduation ceremony"; cut to Nick Wilford appearing out from behind some foliage with a strange, electric look in his eyes and his intestines dangling down to his knees, asking if he can bum a smoke; cut to playing solitaire in the dark at the VA hospital, listening to the guy down the hall who hasn't quit screaming in three days; cut to hitchhiking through Montana—beautiful. Cut to running his tongue up the dark skin of Camilia's thigh, tasting her sweat, tasting her desire, the way she moved her hips; pan up, see her nipples poking hard through that thin, worn white tank top; cut to being slapped in the ear by Camilia, drunk; cut to Keisha, Keisha the day she gets her bike, the birthday bike he saved up for three months to buy her. Cut to Keisha sitting on his lap, listening to him read her *One Fish, Two Fish, Red Fish, Blue Fish*, her big brown eyes really watching him, her arms reaching up to really hug him. Close-up on Keisha. That's how the montage always ends. Close-up on his little girl.

Tap. The sound chokes off his thought. Tap. A drip. Must be the faucet. Tap. His tired old body doesn't want to move, but now his mind is running like a hamster on a wheel, and it'll never stop before sunup. Might as well get up, watch some early-morning TV, catch the weather, maybe. He grunts as he hoists himself up onto one elbow. Reaches over, fumbling, fumbling—where's the damned switch? Click. Light. He blinks, sits up, rubbing his eyes with the palms of his hands, hears himself sigh deep and thinks what a sad sound it is. Leaning with his elbows on his knees, exhausted but wired, the light's okay now, not blinding. He sees the map on the floor, half open. Must've fallen down last night during the sex earthquake. He gets to his feet slowly—slower every day, now—takes a couple of heavy steps to the table and braces against it with one hand and leans down, about to scoop the map up.

Tap.

On the map in front of him, a drip of water. He looks up. One of the pipes in the ceiling is going. Slow leak, but someone had better get up here before the water damage starts. He knows about water damage—he used to do some construction work. He wasn't much good at it, but he has enough experience with water damage to know it can be an expensive pain in the ass to take care of, especially if you let it go. He'll pack up, head down to the office and let them know, then hit the road. Reaches for the map.

Tap.

He stops midreach and leans down, squinting, his sight is still a little feeble in the dim light. The drips are landing on the little black dot of a town. He picks up the map, brings it close to his face to read the tiny letters. They're hard to make out. He needs to snap out of his denial about needing glasses, but he can still make out the name of the town: Hudsonville.

He's coughed up enough unanswered prayers to know that while God is great and God is good, he ain't much of a communicator. He doesn't seem to deal in signs much anymore. No burning bushes for us. And even if you come across what seems like a sign, chances are it's just a reflection of the desperation in your own mind, an expression of your own reckless need for meaning—and if you follow this supposed divine advice, you have about a 65 percent chance of wasting your time. *Still*, Ron thinks, *might not hurt to check out Hudsonville again.* Anything's worth a shot. Praise God.

The car rattles over train tracks. Ron flicks his cigarette out the window. Hudsonville. He's passing the downtown now, what there is of it. There's that diner, there's a gas station—not much here. Bunch of big, old trees, folks walking along the road looking at him with dark, sharp eyes. Not much here. He remembers where the sheriff's station is and turns in. Has to crank the wheel, 'cause the power-steering fluid is low—it's a pain in the ass with only one gripping hand, but he manages. That's one thing Ron does well: he manages. Always has. He stops the car in front of the white trailer. Birds are calling. Pine needles and sand. Out of the car, up the steps, and in the door.

The only one in the office is a woman. She's sitting in the whir of an old electric fan.

"How can I help you?" Her voice is a mechanical drawl. She looks up with her big hair, over the top of a *People* magazine. When she sees Ron she shuts the magazine and tosses it on the counter. "Well, hello," she says, then squints. "You ain't from around here, but I seen you before."

"I guess you probably did," says Ron. "I wondered if you had anymore information about a missing person, Keisha Bent? She'd be about fourteen. Her momma was black, so her skin is pretty dark. She's probably tall by now."

The woman's popping her gum. She leans up against the counter, looking at Ron hard. She juts out her enormous breasts and her lips bow up into a crimson smile on her saddlebag of a face.

"Yep. I remember you, alright. You was looking for that colored girl, 'bout a year back or something, right?"

Ron nods. "That's right. She went missing from the beach about thirteen miles away—Rabe Point State Park. It was two years ago, October twenty-seventh, around dusk."

"Well," the lady cop says, "she ain't turned up yet, but tell you what I'll do. I'll give you my phone number and maybe you can give me a call and check in with me from time to time, in case she does turn up. How long you in town for?"

"Not long," says Ron. "Any other children gone missing around here?"

The woman looks surprised, then laughs. "You really ain't from around here, are you?" She glances over her shoulder, then looks back at Ron, serious now. "There's a lot of people around here who don't turn up," she says.

Ron's heart flutters. He leans in. "Yeah? How many kidnapping cases do you have open right now?"

"None," she says. She greets Ron's confusion with another bout of laughter. "I never said anybody got kidnapped. I said a lot of people just don't turn up. Maybe they move someplace else to get better jobs. Some of them maybe ain't happy with their home situations so they hightail it outta here. There's lots of reasons to leave. Kids run away from their parents all the time."

Ron says: "My daughter didn't run away."

"I didn't say she did," says the woman. "My name is Janet. Deputy Janet to you."

"How many kids, or people, are missing right now?"

"None," Janet says, "but lots of people—maybe hundreds—might have left."

"You're telling me hundreds of people have disappeared in this area, and I haven't read it in any of the papers, I haven't seen it in the news, I haven't heard a word about it from anybody in the two years I've been combing this county looking for my little girl?"

"Ron—it's Ron, right?" she says. "There ain't no paper in this town. And nobody is going to go to Panama City or someplace and blab to their paper about it because if they do, then maybe they might be the next one to get lost. You get me? People are dumb, you know. They're superstitious. A lot of them think there's a witch stealing the kids."

"And what do you think? Haven't you done a little investigating, seeing as you're the law enforcement around here? Haven't you come up with some kind of evidence, some kind of theory?"

"Sure." She shrugs. "Sheriff says people move away. Kids run away from their parents. Husbands run off from their wives. There ain't no laws being broken."

"My daughter was stolen from me. There's no law against that?"

"Well, Ron, if you'd like to file a report, we'll be glad to—"

"I already filed a blessed report!"

"Then when something comes up, we'll be in touch." She smiles. "I'll give you my number, just in case."

She starts writing on a scrap of paper. Ron is livid. His face feels hot and flushed. The light in the room seems to be growing brighter, then dimmer, to the beat of the blood pulsing through his head. He puts his hand, his good hand, on the counter and presses it flat to steady its shaking. He's learned to watch all the trappings of his rage as a spectator, to distance himself from his own emotion. Otherwise things get ugly. It's amazing how well it works. There was a time when he'd have punched a hole in the wall by now.

Deputy Janet presents the slip of paper to him. "You feel free to call me if you need anything," she says.

Instead of taking the number with his good hand, he reaches up with "the hook," as he likes to think of it. It splits along its length, following the prompts of his readapted forearm muscles, and clamps down on the little slip of paper.

Janet frowns. The hook has that effect on people.

"Jeez," she says, "what happened to your hand?"

"It's missing," he says. "Maybe it ran away."

She laughs, but instead of a flirty laugh, it's an uncomfortable one.

Ron hears a click behind him. Light floods the entryway and a figure steps in the door. It's the brawny-looking sheriff with that Neanderthal forehead. He stands very erect, clearly an ex-military man, and clearly the boss around here, judging from Janet's reaction.

"Everything alright, sir?" asks the sheriff.

"No," says Ron. "I hear there are hundreds of people missing from this town, and nobody's doing anything about it. Well, I am going to do something about it, because one of the missing children is my daughter. What are you going to do to help me?"

The sheriff glances at Janet, then nods slowly, studying Ron. When he speaks, his words are slow. "Well, we can take a report, keep our eyes peeled."

"What if that's not good enough?" says Ron.

"Well," says the man, whose name tag reads Sheriff Johnson, "it'll have to be."

⊰ Chapter Seven ⊱

"SO LET ME GET THIS STRAIGHT," BEAN SAYS. "Based on this clichéd phrase that anyone might use, that in fact I have used on many occasions, namely: 'the clock is ticking—'"

"*Clocks* are ticking," Caleb corrects.

"Whatever. Based on this, we are going to break into an insane asylum and kidnap your emotionally unstable childhood girlfriend. That is what's going on, right?" Shadows race across Bean's face as they drive past the few streetlights that demarcate downtown Hudsonville.

"You can wait at the house," says Caleb. "I don't want you to do anything you don't want to do."

"Yeah, I'll just go ahead and wait for you at the abandoned house with the psycho living in the attic. You know, I'm going to write a letter to the Nobel Prize committee; I don't know how they overlooked you last year."

Caleb laughs in spite of himself. "Okay, maybe it's a coincidence that she said that. Maybe you're right. But I couldn't fly back to LA right now without knowing for sure what's going on here, or at least that she's okay, could you?"

Bean doesn't say anything. A moment passes, and the guys both laugh.

"You're a total jackass," says Caleb, and he cuts the car's headlights as they pull into the driveway of the Dream Center.

"Wait," says Bean, "back out. We should park along the street and walk up. Somebody might hear us."

Caleb smiles as he clicks the transmission into reverse. Bean is in.

They step out of the car into the balmy night. Just out of range of a streetlight, Caleb sees the silhouettes of little bats reeling in tight circles, darting and weaving like birds gone mad.

The two friends turn up the driveway. Neither of them says a word, and neither of them has to. They played Little League together—Bean was the catcher and Caleb played center field. They double-dated at their first high school dance, taking a couple of weird upperclassmen girls who Bean decided he didn't like at the last minute. So they took them out to dinner at Pizza Hut and ditched them after the dance in favor of video games and beer in a football players' guest house.

They rode bikes together and dreamed of owning cars.

They watched porn and dreamed of touching girls.

They crammed for tests and dreamed of outgrowing work.

They dreamed of being grown-up, and now, somehow, Caleb realizes suddenly, they are. As they creep down the shadow-barred driveway, both mindful to stay close to the tree line, both as silent and attentive as Indian braves, they have somehow, perhaps, found their way outside the realm of adolescence at last, and into the terrifyingly stark world of . . . what? Reality? Surreality? Caleb wonders when they crossed that threshold, and how he missed it when they did. Even now, right at this moment, they might be Christine's only hope. The thought makes him feel dizzy. And excited. And empowered. If he and Bean could steal Calabasas Christian's famous "warrior" statue on the night before the state championship, then they can do this. They can do anything.

The trees part and the Dream Center rears its massive flank, silver with moonlight. Bean stops. Caleb shivers. They both stare up.

"This is a bad place," Bean whispers.

Caleb looks over at his friend, startled by the sobriety of his statement. He doesn't see the sarcastic smirk he was looking for. Bean's face is stone.

Caleb gives him a slap on the back. "We can handle this," he says, but the tone of voice is utterly unconvincing.

Bean flashes a lopsided grin. "Sure we can," he says. "We just have to find a window without bars, give it a smash, wiggle in, find Christine, and wiggle out. Nothin' to it."

"No," Caleb says, "I have another way. Come on."

Shadows. Tree branches, dewy-moist and groping. Clinging webs of forest spiders as big as your fist. There's a lot of quiet in these woods, so when a branch snaps, it screams.

Caleb whispers as they go:

"We used to play here all the time.

As kids.

We knew every inch of the forest,

But we never went in the asylum.

That wasn't allowed.

But we heard stories about it all the time.

About why it was shut down.

Ghost stories, you know?

Kids in cages.

Some pregnant woman jumping off the roof,

Killing herself,

Or getting pushed,

However you like to tell it.

But there's one story that's true,

About a set of tunnels underneath

That lead into the forest.

They say the tunnels were built a long time ago,

In the Underground Railroad times,

Then when they built the asylum they kept them,

Cemented them, shored them up.

Some people say they used to take the bodies

Of abused patients out this way,

Once the shock treatments finally killed them

Or if a lobotomy went wrong.

They'd take them out the tunnel

And throw them into the pond behind the building

In the dead of night.

Those stories scared the crap out of me as a kid."

"Thanks for sharing," says Bean.

"I don't know if all the stories are true," Caleb says. "But I know there's a tunnel." And he stops and points. Bean squints at what seems to be a door, freestanding in the middle of the forest.

"What the hell?" Bean says.

They walk toward it slowly. It's steel, half obscured with vines and grime and rust-stain tears. Instead of a knob there's a wheel in the center, like one you would find on a submarine hatch.

Bean walks up to the door and places one hand on its face. He cranes his neck and sees that the door isn't freestanding after all. It's attached to a cinderblock structure in the shape of a triangle that could only hold a staircase descending into the ground.

"Wow," he whispers.

"Let's go," says Caleb, and he pulls on the hatch. Only it doesn't budge. He runs his fingers along the seam of the door. "It's open," he says. "I think the hinges are just rusted. Help me."

They grab the wheel and tug. Bean braces one foot against the block of the door frame, and finally, with a deep, throaty grunt of protest, the door swings open.

Caleb flicks a flashlight on and hands another one to Bean.

"Oh man," says Caleb.

A rusted, cockeyed steel staircase descends into the murk of what must be waist-deep water.

Caleb looks at his friend in despair.

"We came this far," says Bean, forcing a grin. "But you're buying me a beer once you get that fake ID."

Caleb looks down, taking a deep breath. Bean gives him a little shove, and gestures with mock graciousness. "Ladies first."

Caleb puts one careful foot on the first step. There's a metallic "gung" as one side of the staircase gives way, and the whole structure tilts a little. Caleb slips down a couple of steps, but manages to grab a handrail and catch himself, with his footing and his flashlight intact. Now the staircase seems stable enough again.

"Careful, Fred Astaire," says Bean from above.

As Caleb continues his descent, Bean decides it would be a good idea to close the door behind them, to cover their tracks. He tucks his flashlight in his belt and pulls the door toward him with both hands. The dark greenery of the forest begins disappearing behind the slab of steel, until only a sliver remains.

That's when Bean sees it. Or thinks he sees it.

A figure in a white gown, pale skin, steps out from behind a tree, then back behind another.

Bean freezes, eyes wide, hands shaking.

"Caleb . . . " he whispers.

"It's only waist deep," says Caleb from below. "It's not even that cold."

Then Bean sees the figure again. It's far away, but it looks like a man, young, with dark hair. The person pauses, turns his head slowly, slowly to face Bean, and begins walking toward him. Just then, the flashlight slips out of Bean's belt and clatters down a few steps. Bean fumbles, trying to catch it, finally groping and finding it. He stands up, shaking badly, and finds himself staring out into the night, at nothing. No white-gowned apparition. No one at all.

And he almost laughs at himself.

That guy couldn't have been real, must've been his imagination. Because the whole time the guy was walking, even when he turned his head, even when he was walking right toward Bean, his eyes were closed.

Bean shakes his head at the absurdity of his own imagination.

He starts to go down the staircase again, then pauses, thinking twice, and pulls the submarine door shut behind him, just in case.

The steps feel a little uncertain under him and shift once with a great metallic shriek, but they hold, bearing him down one foot at a time into the black, still water. It smells like an unwashed toilet full of tuna fish cans. The air is heavy, clingy, dead.

Bean makes a face as the water hits his balls, wondering what kind of disturbing microbes are tadpoling their way up his urethra.

He steps up next to Caleb, and the guys pause for a second, letting their flashlight beams crisscross down the length of the tunnel. It's a cement arch, simple and smooth, with a reinforced concrete buttress every ten yards or so. Some bear a burned-out lightbulb in a rusted steel cage. There is no terminus, only the place where their lights are too weak to shine.

Neither of them speaks. Caleb takes a deep breath and starts walking.

For the first twenty-five yards or so, they see graffiti:

RANDO RULES!!

(a fairly good depiction of Satan's head)

~SATAN'S DEN~

Tittie tittie bang-bang

METALLICA

Screw Mike Sanchez!
(a drawing of balls
and a penis)

(A big, creepy drawing of a red eye)

Do not enter, or you will die!!

Then the graffiti stops and is replaced by something even more disturbing: places where the concrete has fallen away, revealing rusted rebar. Every so often, one of the guys feels something brush against his leg in the murk, but neither of them says anything. Neither even looks down. Whatever's down there, they don't want to know.

There's a bang and a sound like a metallic cough.

Caleb stops.

Bean wheels around, flashing his light behind him. Vision is a joke. They've already gone too far to see the entrance.

"Did you hear that?"

"Yeah."

"What do you think it was?"

"I don't know. A rat."

"You think?"

"Yeah, what else would it be? Let's go." Caleb starts slogging on. Bean lingers, watching his flashlight beam dissolve into distant blackness.

Bean: "I thought I saw somebody when we came in."

Caleb is still walking. He calls back: "Yeah?"

Bean: "Yeah. But . . . it couldn't have been."

Caleb: "Why?"

"Because he was walking," says Bean. "But he had his eyes closed."

Caleb stops. He turns and splashes water at his friend.

"Hell, no!" says Bean. "Don't splash me with this piss water! We have no idea what's in here! There might be piranha or God knows what."

"Piranha would have eaten you ten minutes ago."

"Ebola, then. I don't care—just don't splash me with it."

"Don't try to scare me then, dickhead," says Caleb.

"I wasn't. Dude, I was dead serious."

"Shut up," says Caleb, laughing, and Bean does.

But he doesn't stop looking over his shoulder.

They trudge on. The tunnel seems interminable. The water slows them way down. It's almost too deep to walk in and the idea of sinking chest deep into it and swimming is far too scary. So they settle for this leg-aching, mind-numbing pace. It gets to be like a weird dream; they keep walking, but the tunnel never changes, the water never changes, and they never get anywhere. All that happens is their legs get tired and their minds turn to mashed potatoes. Once Bean thinks he hears a splash and turns his flashlight behind him—but there's nothing there.

It's then that finally something does change: the tunnel splits. Right, or left?

"Which way?" asks Bean.

"No idea," says Caleb. "As a kid, I never made it past the door."

"We'll flip a coin," says Bean. He pulls out a wheat penny (he sometimes carries them for luck) and flips it. It clacks off the roof and splooks back down into the water, almost hitting him in the head. He shines his flashlight into the dark, opaque water. Light won't even penetrate an inch down, much less to the penny at the bottom.

"Heads it is," Bean decides. "Let's go right."

They set out again. No more than thirty feet ahead, they reach another cross tunnel. They shine their lights first left, then right, but there's no end to the tunnel in either direction.

"How far do you think these tunnels go?" asks Bean.

Caleb just shakes his head. "I think the Dream Center is this way," he says. "As long as we keep going straight, we'll be fine." They haven't gone more than fifty feet when they reach the cave-in. It's a solid wall of sandy dirt, chunks of concrete, and jumbled rebar.

"Fubar," says Bean. "Stellar."

"Maybe we can go around," says Caleb. "Those other tunnels have to lead somewhere."

"I don't know," says Bean. "Maybe we should just head back."

"Think about Christine stuck in there," says Caleb, trudging back the way they came.

"Think about us stuck down here," says Bean. He splashes some water on the cement wall and follows.

Backtracking, they reach the place where the other tunnel crossed the one they had been following. They look both ways. The new tunnel looks identical to this one.

"Left, or right?" asks Caleb.

"Straight ahead and out?" says Bean with a hopeful smile. "Okay, left."

They head left and walk for about ten minutes. (Caleb thinks it must be ten minutes, anyway, but his watch is waterlogged and worthless by now. Lousy five-hundred-dollar watch dies in four feet of water when a twenty-dollar Timex would endure the apocalypse. . . .) The tunnel starts to curve left. At first, the change is slow and, because the walls are so smooth, almost impossible to detect. But Caleb does detect it, and so does Bean. They exchange a glance and walk on. The tunnel splits and they go left. It splits again and they pick left again. Then, they reach a cross tunnel. Straight ahead is a dead end, and to the left and right, the tunnel extends to the limit of their sight in both directions. They go right. They haven't uttered a word in a long time. They're tired, sore, numb. And the water is getting colder.

They reach another cross tunnel. Infinite tunnel straight ahead, infinite tunnel to the left, and to the right: A boy, about fourteen, dark hair, fine features, pale skin, wearing what looks like a nightgown, once white with a blue pattern, now stained a filthy brown. He stands very still.

And his eyes are closed.

"Hey," Caleb whispers to the boy, "are you okay?"

He doesn't move. No one moves.

"What's your name?"

The boy cocks his head slowly, like somebody shifting on their pillow in their sleep.

Then it snaps. His face contorts into a snarl, his limp hands seize up like claws, and he lurches forward and grabs Bean.

Bean screams, hitting the kid with his flashlight, creating a weird light show on the tunnel wall.

Caleb splashes up and tries to pull the kid-thing away. It fights like a dog; its teeth gnash and its mouth foams, its head tosses back and forth, finally striking Bean's forehead with a dull thud. He bites at Bean's face twice as Bean tries to push him off, and finally succeeds in sinking his teeth in. Bean screams.

Caleb is there now, and punches the kid in the temple twice, hard. Still clutching Bean, the sleeper lashes out at Caleb with one claw-like hand, scratching his face—but Caleb manages to punch him once more, and this third hit finally knocks him off Bean. The kid hits the water with a splash and disappears beneath it. Bean moves away fast, wailing, cursing, covering his face.

"Run!" says Caleb. "Come on!"

"Which way?" whimpers Bean, crying.

Caleb looks around and realizes he has no idea.

"Which way?!" cries Bean, louder this time.

The boy rises from the water, eyes still closed. His face is placid again, but hands are still taut and clawlike, and he begins taking slow steps toward them.

"Come on," says Caleb.

"You know where we're going?" asks Bean.

"Yes!" Caleb lies. He grabs his friend by the shirt, dragging him. "Come on!"

They run and paddle forward, battling the water at every step, looking back often and always seeing *him,* close behind.

"I think he got my eye, dude," says Bean. "Do I look okay?"

Caleb only has time for a glance, but a glance is enough. Even through the tendrils of blood, he can see the lopsided, deflated globe of his friend's right eye, now torn and useless, ringed by deep-gashed tooth marks, weeping blood.

"I think it's fine," Caleb lies again. "You just got blood in it."

"It doesn't feel fine," says Bean, tears betraying his voice.

"You'll be fine," says Caleb. "Just keep running."

No matter how fast they go, no matter which way they turn, the boy waits over Caleb's shoulder, blind, stalking.

Caleb wants to scream. This is like a scene from some dark surrealist painting, absurd. The faster they go, the faster the sleepwalker goes, and a horrifying thought bleeds into Caleb's mind: *he's waiting for us to get tired.*

Unending pathways to nothing, running slower and slower. Bean screams now at nothing, just screams.

"Is he still back there?" Bean's voice is shaky.

"Just keep running."

"Wake me up!" screams Bean. "Somebody wake me up!"

They turn a corner and pull up short.

It's another one.

Another sleepwalker; this one, a blond boy of no more than thirteen, walks toward them through the black water.

And Caleb says: "We *are* awake."

The blond boy melts into fury just as the first one did. He snarls and lunges forward. Caleb shoves his friend down the tunnel in the opposite direction and scans the barren walls for a weapon, anything. There's nothing. All he has is speed, and the water has stolen that. Still, he tries to run, following Bean.

"I can't run," says Bean. "I'm dizzy."

Caleb looks over his shoulder.

The two sleeping boys meet at the crossing of the tunnels, then turn toward him as one. They pause, standing together for an instant, looking peaceful, like a pair of sleeping twins in a nineteenth-century portrait, then they advance.

Caleb sees a tunnel splitting off to the right and takes it, dragging Bean with him.

They take one turn, then another, and their pursuers are lost from sight, at least for a moment.

Bean's breath is fast and shallow.

"I can't make it," says Bean. "I can't run."

"Come on," says Caleb, "you can do it."

"I can't, I really can't," Bean says, gasping for air.

Caleb looks hard at his friend, and realizes he's right. The entire right side of his face, his neck, his shirt, all are drenched with red. The light reflects on a bead of blood, which forms just above Bean's eye, then trickles down his check like a tear. A moment later, another bead follows, then another. They keep pumping out, one by one, from this particularly deep gash and from several others, and Bean is looking paler and paler by the moment. There's no way he can keep running.

Caleb looks over his shoulder. The echo of splashes is drawing close.

"I'll stay and fight—you go," says Bean in a raspy whisper.

"No," says Caleb. "I have another idea." He looks around. They're at a place where two tunnels cross, and probably still have a few moments until the sleepers navigate the turns and find them.

"Go down this tunnel," says Caleb, fast and feverish. "I'm pretty sure this is the way out. Be very quiet and keep your light off. I'll keep my light on and draw them off this way."

"No," says Bean. "I'm not leaving you. We'll stay and fight together."

"Bean, shut up. You can't run, you can't fight. You've lost too much blood, man. Now get your ass going. I'll get rid of them and double back. Just sneak back to the door, I'll be there. Keep your light off! Go!"

The sounds of frothing water is getting terrifyingly close. Caleb shoves his friend and takes off down the other tunnel. He propels himself through the water as fast as he can, exploding with his legs and paddling awkwardly with his one free hand, trying to put as much distance between himself and the place where the tunnels cross as he can so that the psychotic brothers don't realize there's only one of him. When he's gone about twenty feet, he glances back and is comforted to see that Bean has shut off his light. At least he has the sense to listen to Caleb now, when it really matters. He listens hard and doesn't hear the sound of pursuit—of course it could be that he's drowning it out with his own racket. He glances back again. Nothing. Gotta fight them off somehow. Go back, get Bean. Gotta wake up. Can't wake up. Not dreaming.

No one knows what real darkness is until they experience it. This isn't like a moonless night or a room with the door shut and all the lights out. In real life, there's always some kind of light—a crack in the curtain, a distant streetlight, even one solitary star. This isn't real life. But this is real darkness. It vibrates. It chases itself in circles. It wraps itself around you like a python. It lives. And it's terrifying.

Bean is very still, except for the violent shaking. His arms are wrapped tightly around himself for warmth (the water is terribly cold now) and his hand is clamped on his now-dead flashlight.

His face pulses in a constant rhythm. It even makes a sound, kind of like the deep bass line of the music they played at a rave he went to one time.

Bean listens as the sounds of Caleb's thrashing get fainter, fainter, and disappear.

Just vaguely sad.

He stands very still.

Maybe he should have gone a little farther down the corridor, but suddenly he can't move much. Legs feel hard and heavy, not right. He just sort of took a few floating steps out of the intersection and stopped.

He fantasizes about leaning against a wall, but can't bring himself to take a step and find it. Too cold.

Just wait for Caleb. Just wait here.

Sometimes, fear pricks through the sadness, and he listens hard, very hard, but once Caleb is gone there's nothing but the dripping all around. Not even a slosh.

He's just kind of sad.

For some reason, he thinks of a Christmas, the one before his mom split from her third husband, Rich. Rich was a good guy. Dressed up as Santa. Tried real hard. Got Bean a Louisville Slugger with his name on it. A real pro bat. Rich was always doing nice stuff like that. And his Mom was like, "Oh, Rich, stop being an ass. The boy knows Santa isn't real," and Rich got real quiet and didn't say much for the rest of the day. But Bean always loved him for trying. They must've split, what? A year after that? Six months? He never heard a word from old Rich again. Rich was a good guy.

Splash.

The flashlight fell.

The thought slices into Bean's brain, and he panics.

If it fell, the water will ruin it.

It'll always be dark.

There might never be light.

He might never get out.

And he lost his eye. Caleb said he didn't, but he knows he did.

He lost it.

He gropes for the light, but the water is too deep. To get it, he has to dunk himself all the way in. Going down. He tries to shut up his eyes and nose and ears, but he knows the water is getting in, black and unclean.

He lost his eye.

The floor is gritty and smooth.

Water is warm as blood now.

Gropes and gropes and finds the slippery shaft of the flashlight a few feet away. He pulls himself up, taking a big, shuddering breath.

Suddenly, he's so dizzy he isn't sure he's on earth anymore, isn't sure he's right-side up, isn't sure he's himself.

In a moment, reality comes back. He steps over to the left, finds the wall with a tentative hand, steadies himself.

Clicks the flashlight switch. It doesn't work.

Clicks the flashlight switch. It doesn't work.

Feels himself crying. It hurts his face, bad.

Shakes the light, clicks it on, it doesn't work.

Shakes it hard, clicks it on. It works.

And in the light, he sees—

Them.

Maybe twenty pale faces. White gowns.

Eyes closed.

Facing him.

Very still.

The flashlight paints them white against the wet, black cement.

Don't wake them up, he thinks.

Dreaming eyes snap back and forth beneath their lids.

Suddenly twenty faces contort into rage.

Bean hears his own scream, and it echoes and echoes and echoes, and all those hands grab him, and he fights and fails, and he doesn't know what's the water and what's his blood, and he wonders—if there is a God, does he know about this?

And all those hands tear him, deep.

→

The corridor is long, but the water's getting shallower. Caleb's legs burn, feels like his blood's battery acid, but he chugs on. Gotta put enough distance behind him. This is almost enough. He glances back. No sleepwalking faces. Good. Maybe he lost them in those turns. Maybe they gave up.

Maybe Bean's already made it to the door, or even back to the car, and the sleepwalkers have given up. Everything will be okay. It always is. It has to be.

Something ahead. A moon. A crescent moon, in the heart of the blackness. Closer; it's light! And the water is getting shallower, and—it's the door.

Caleb clatters up the lopsided steps, throws his weight on the door, and it grinds open. He smells the air.

The morning after a nightmare.

His cheeks tense up to cry.

But . . .

He pulls himself off the door, tears his eyes from the light.

Suddenly his stomach winds into a knot.

The way he sent Bean was supposed to lead to the exit, not this way. That means Bean is still in there, alone.

He listens. No splashing.

"Bean?"

No one behind him . . .

"Bean!"

. . . means the sleepwalkers didn't follow him.

He half falls down the steps, sloshes forward.

"Beeean!"

. . . Means they might have followed Bean instead.

A scream.

Echoing, it seems to amplify, wave upon wave, a tooth-gritting, blistering, piercing sound. *The sound of an animal dying.*

"Beeeean!"

The sound of a dying man.

Caleb battles through the water, blind with fury and tears. The echo dies away and his ears are starving for something more, for the slightest sound, and for a half an instant he thinks he hears a whimper, faint as the sound of a flower opening, then nothing. Nothing. His own flailing. His own howl of blind rage.

He finally reaches the crossing of the corridors, the place where he left his friend.

Blood in the water.

The tunnel ahead is empty. The tunnel to the left is bare. The tunnel to the right is vacant. Not even a ripple there.

"I'M HERE!" screams Caleb, veins beating, voice grating.

"I'M HERE!"

His voice echoes back to him, mocking.

He growls through his tears and punches the wall of the tunnel with all his force.

He hears a snap and doesn't care.

He cries harder.

"I'm right here!"

But there's no one to hear him call. Bean is gone.

⇥ Chapter Eight ⇤

THE SUN SHINES, BUT THE LIGHT FEELS HOLLOW.
Bob Dylan's on the radio, singing the story of the "Hurricane," and even though it should be as familiar as the voice of an old friend, the campfires and late-night talks and crisp, hungover mornings and late-night lovemaking sessions that Bob's tunes usually evoke in Ron Bent's memory are somehow missing. All he sees is a pine-hemmed stretch of two-lane highway and the whistle of the wind through the broken rearview mirror.

Ron feels like an eggshell today. Helpless, useless, fragile, empty. In another time, he'd be in jail right now. He'd have grabbed that damned smug pig's neck in the crook of his arm, grabbed his face with his hand, his good hand, and jerked his head to the side. Snapped his smug pig neck. He was a thick fella, it might have taken a couple of tries, but he'd have done it. Even to think of it gives him a shot of adrenaline, makes him smile around his cigarette. Then he'd have pulled the dead cop's gun, turned it on the woman, which probably would have made her wetter than a Seattle winter. Yeah, she'd have liked that. And he'd have made her spill her guts. He'd have made her get him into the police database, show him all the files, call in the families of the other missing kids, the lonely, the bereaved, and they could figure it out together, ride out like a posse from one of those Old West movies they always played on Sunday afternoons—and, of course, he'd be the leader, like a real-life John Wayne. The Duke. And they'd find Keisha. Get revenge with smoke and lead, as it should be.

And he'd take her home, his Keisha, and they'd make macaroni and cheese with hot dogs and she'd sit on his lap and put her arms around his neck and say, *"Thank you, Daddy, I knew you'd never give up."*

Except he *did* give up. Well, not exactly—but he sure hadn't snapped the cop's neck, that's for sure. He'd asked some questions, pressed them as much as he could, tried to make them at least *understand*. But in the end, he'd left as empty-handed as ever. Except with the knowledge of what she had said, what Deputy Janet had let slip, what he couldn't make her repeat or even acknowledge in front of the sheriff: *hundreds are missing.* Ron shivered.

Pine trees whooshed past and white clouds with bottoms of heavy gray hung motionless in the blue sky. Maybe it was for the best, the way he had shut up and walked away. It was easy to be rash when he was young and full of whiskey. Easy to be stupid and heroic. His heroism had earned him breakfast in jail on more than one occasion. Maybe it was a good thing to walk away sometimes, "know when to fold 'em," as Kenny Rogers once said. Or hell, maybe he was just getting old, getting soft, getting tired.

Now he drives that old stretch of road all over again, seeking what he looked for more and more nowadays. Not vengeance, but *communion,* with Keisha or with God. He doesn't really know which. It's hard to know the difference between the two sometimes. Times like these, he always goes to the spot of beach where he lost her, and that's where he's going now. Times like these, he sits on a driftwood log (his knees won't tolerate sitting Indian-style anymore) and he looks into the wind, into the sunset, and finds the will to search on.

As he drives, he prays:

> *Hey there, Lord.*
> *Here we are again.*

How many times have we talked
On this same stretch of highway?
On the way to the same empty beach?
I don't even know what to say anymore.
It's all been said.
Only thing new is a number, and it can't be real.
Hundreds, she said.
Hundreds of folks just went away.
Did you have the Rapture and forget to invite me?
I pray that's true because that means you took her,
You took my Keisha.
And if it's true and she's up in your kingdom,
Then praise you, Lord, thank you, Lord.
Take her and leave me behind,
An old man like me has seen too much anyway.
I wouldn't make much of an angel.
Think my wings might be dirty brown,
Not white like they ought to be.
But, Lord, if you would take any pity on me at all,
Just bless me with the truth,
Bless me with—

The engine stutters, then stutters again. Ron curses under his breath, knowing what's coming. This is really a stroke of crap luck. He leans forward and taps the fuel gauge. It says half-empty. If he were an optimist, it might say half-full. But Ron Bent isn't much of an optimist. He flicks the clear plastic of the fuel gauge and the needle falls down to empty. Damned, blessed, stinkin', car. He knew he should have had that gauge fixed. The car is shimmying now, shivering like a dog shaking off water. All Ron can do is ease it over to the side of the road and sit there, head pressed back against the headrest, eyes closed in frustration. It's gonna be a long walk to get a gas can.

He gets out of the car, wanders into the empty road.

For a minute, he's so pissed off he thinks of walking away from the car, just leaving it here—even though this hunk of crap is just about the only thing he has left—and pushing forth on foot. Maybe that's how it should be. He can spend the rest of his years wandering the earth, like Christ, a pauper and a pilgrim. Except he'd get pretty damned wet in those Florida rainstorms. Christ didn't live in a semi-tropical climate.

He looks up the road; as far as he can see, nothing but yellow lines and pavement and pine trees in sand. He sighs, looks down at his feet. Time to start walking.

Suddenly a sound: the snap of a twig. He turns his head and squints (his old eyes don't work like they did—seen too much, they have). Someone is there, in the woods, moving between trees. Ron watches. He sees a pink shirt, blue jeans. Whoever it is doesn't seem to see him. Ron stands still and watches the figure move in slow, limping steps, parallel to the roadway at first, then toward it, and finally breaking into the clear perhaps forty yards up ahead. Several times, Ron almost calls a greeting to the stranger, but something strangles his voice in his throat. Finally he speaks.

"Hey."

The figure, a young man, looks back at him, or maybe past him, then continues up the road in the opposite direction, unfazed. Ron almost turns and walks away, but he doesn't.

"Hey," he calls again, and when the teenager seems to pick up his limping pace, Ron jogs after him. Even with the pain in his knees sparking red like firecrackers at every step, he catches up to the kid in no time. When he does, he draws up short.

The kid's jeans are dripping wet and smeared with mud. His shirt, which had appeared a pinkish red from a distance, now appears to be a white T-shirt, soaking wet and stained with blood or something like it. He grips a flashlight in each hand so tight that his arms are shaking with tension.

"Hey," Ron says, touching the kid on the shoulder.

The boy, probably no older than eighteen, wheels around, raising both flashlight-wielding fists defensively.

"Who are you?" the kid says, his voice a rasping whisper.

"Name's Ron. Ron Bent," he says, trying to smile. "You okay? What are those flashlights for?"

Ron sees now that the kid is shaking. His face is covered with grime, except for two paths trailing down from his eyes, where tears must have washed it away. Four bloody scratch marks streak one cheek. Must have been a fight, and someone clawed his face. As Ron studies him, the kid's eyes begin welling up again, though he tries his best to sniff it away.

"My friend lost his light," he says, looking hard at one of the flashlights in his hand.

The kid tries to pull away, and Ron detains him as gently as possible.

"Wait a minute, wait," he says. "You don't look so good. What happened to your arm?"

The kid looks at his arm, uncomprehendingly.

His left wrist has swollen to almost the size of his fist, and it's blotched and streaked an angry, bruised shade of purple.

"Oh shit," the kid says.

"Maybe we should get you to a doctor."

"No, listen," the kid says, "he's lost down there. They took him away. There was nothing but blood in the water, then I found the flashlight. I looked and looked and he was gone. We have to go back. We have to find him."

"Wait," Ron says, "somebody kidnapped your friend?"

The kid nods, his eyes wild and haunted. He looks back over his shoulder.

"The door is back there. We have to go find him."

"Wait, slow down now. Who was it? Who kidnapped your friend?"

The kid is staring at the yellow line of the road, curving away at his feet. He has dark circles under his eyes. Ron wonders how long he's been wandering around like this.

"It was them," says the kid, as still as stone now. "It was the sleepwalkers."

Wasn't as far of a walk to the gas station as Ron had thought, praise God. He left the kid in the car, walked maybe half a mile down the road, and returned with two gas cans. One he emptied into the tank, the other he put in the trunk for the next time the fuel gauge crapped out on him.

The kid was pretty wet and pretty dirty, so Ron had pulled an old towel out of the trunk and covered the car seat. Now they're rolling. The kid sits on the towel, still gripping his flashlights, not moving. Ron glances over, hoping the kid won't notice the scrutiny. No worries there. The beleaguered youth leans back against the headrest, staring up at the treetops as they pass, his eyes looking glassy. Something about that kid's eyes . . .

Wide boy's eyes, narrowed to slits.

Ron hasn't seen eyes like that in a long time. Not since—

June, 1969. Huge drops of rain fall from the thick, green canopy above, tapping on his helmet, slipping down his face and away. Nobody's talking in the jungle today. There's nothing to say. They've been marching for a lot of days now. Everyone else keeps track of days, dates, holidays, birthdays, but not Private First Class Ron Bent. He'd rather not, thanks very much. He measures time in incidents. Today is three days since Pvt. James McPhereson, a handsome, quiet, probably secretly gay kid, was walking point and tripped a booby trap, lost his legs, and took six hours to bleed to death waiting for a lift that never came. Three weeks since they left Lai Khe *for Dodge City. Maybe four days since their squad of fifteen guys broke off from the rest of the company. Two days since they encountered heavy resistance trying to rejoin the platoon and realized they'd been cut off, with the goddamn radio crackling and hissing, some kind of malfunction, and no way to call a taxi for a ride out. One day since they ran out of food.*

Now, there's just the dripping of rain, the sloshing of mud—the mud isn't just at their feet, it's everywhere, under his fingernails, in his hair, caked in the moving parts of his M16, in his mouth, gritty and nauseating, even between the cheeks of his ass, God knows how. In the distance: the rumble of a mortar going off and the dry snap of gunfire.

Somebody stepped in shit. Maybe the rest of their long-lost platoon.

The man on point (it's hard to tell from the back, but he thinks it's Dirty) raises a fist and the men all stop, crouch, and listen, scanning the foliage around them for any sign of Charlie—as if that'll do any good; there could be a whole regiment of North Vietnamese regulars on the other side of the next leaf, and the only way to know would be to smell 'em, since they're so goddamn supernaturally quiet *and vision is so limited.*

"Charlie's so quiet," *for some reason, makes him think of playing hide-and-seek as a kid.* He would cover his eyes and Paul would hide and Ronnie Bent would count his little ass to one hundred as fast as his lips could move, and then he'd look around for his big brother, only Paul was gone. Impossibly, completely gone—not under the dining room table, not in the pantry—so impossibly gone that little Ronnie would look for him for hours and start to think maybe goblins snatched him away. (Paul would really make use of his vanishing abilities ten years later, when the draft came around. Then he vanished so completely that even his loving family never heard from him again.) Little Ronnie finally surmised that his brother probably snuck up the stairs, out his bedroom window onto the roof of the porch, climbed down the sycamore tree, and walked to the drug store for a soda. Or a root beer float. Probably laughing his smug ass off the whole way.

Private First Class Ronald Bent was still thinking about root beer floats when the first tracer round whistled past, maybe two inches in front of his face. He felt it more than anything, a puff of wind on his cheek. Then the guns were rattling off rounds, littering all that mud with piles of spent brass as the leaves around them danced a strange, flicking, bullet-induced jig.

Ron's gun was jammed. He tried to clear the round out of the chamber, but it was the mud, the goddamned drying, cracking mud that wound its way into everything and strangled his M16. He crouched lower. It was raining bullets now.

He heard "Corpsman up!" behind him, to the right, and there was Pvt. Jack Spagnoli, facedown in the mud.

Ashes to ashes, mud to mud.

Jack was funny and mad about cards. Texas hold'em and blackjack.

Red Jack was his game now, as blood from the gaping exit wound wicked into his fatigues, dark as Rorschach ink.

Jack was dead.

Ronnie pulled the M16 out of the already-stiffening hand that would never hold an ace again and turned it on the enemy. Spitting lead. Somebody was hit off to the left and was moaning. Somebody else kept telling the wounded guy to shut up. Finally, Ron saw Dirty (Dan Dawson, Dirty Danny) up ahead, frantically waving the men on.

They hightailed it out, those of them who could, through the slashing leaves of the jungle. They all knew they were running blind, but they followed Dan all the same, because to sit still when badly outnumbered meant death, just as running might mean death—you could run into a booby trap or a machine gun nest or worse. As fast as they ran, the machine gun fire still didn't abate; tracers kept whizzing past on either side, heavy pops of hand grenades burst not too far behind. Several times, he heard cries of pain behind him, or cursing, but he didn't look back. He had become like a jungle cat now. It was a primal thing: death was behind him and death was the enemy. He ran until his breath was a loud wheeze and his heart filled his head with throbbing, always staying a few steps behind Dan, Dirty Dan, who wound up to be from a town right near Ron's, a football rival, in fact.

When, at last, the rattle of gunfire had fallen off and the only sound was the slap and swish of leaves, Dan slowed and finally stopped, his hands on his knees. He looked at Ron and past him, then stood up straight.

It was then that Ron noticed it. Dan's eyes had changed. They were drawn into a tight squint, implacable as burnished steel. Nobody in northern Ohio had eyes like that, Ron thought, and Dan's hadn't been like that either—not before the war, not before today. Now they had changed—and it was frightening.

Ron followed Dan's gaze back over his shoulder, and he saw what Dan was looking at: nothing.

There was nobody behind them. None of their comrades had made it. There was only the rain.

All this flashes before Ron in an instant. The memory fills him up to the point of spilling over. He glances at the boy in the seat next to him, wanting to share the memory with him, wanting him to know that he isn't alone, that the feelings consuming him right now aren't insurmountable. They can be conquered. Ron wants to say a thousand things, but as so often happens, the words just won't come. Finally, he says:

"I lost my daughter. She was kidnapped too. I'll help you however I can, I promise."

The kid doesn't answer him.

Ron turns on the radio, an oldies station, and sighs.

In the sick-clean smell of Hudsonville's only doctor's office, Caleb sits staring at a children's toy. It has a flat board as a base and stiff metal wires protruding upward from it, four or five of them, each painted a different color. The wires twist and loop around each other like roller-coaster tracks. On them are brightly painted beads. There are yellow beads on the blue wire, blue beads on the green wire, red beads on the blue wire, purple beads on the orange wire . . . Caleb remembers these things from his childhood. They were always touted as a "game" or a "toy." And with the festive, eye-catching colors and the complex shapes, it looked pretty exciting; until you started playing with it and realized all you could do is push the beads to one side and back, and back again, and back again. It wasn't a game. It wasn't fun. It was something else. A distraction. It makes Caleb so angry he could smash it into the bland-papered wall of the waiting room, watch the beads explode and scatter . . .

And he wonders how many other things in his life have been nothing but distractions. Maybe everything.

"Caleb," a heavyset nurse in a white smock says.

Caleb rises, glancing at the old fella sitting next to him (Ron? Was that his name?)

The guy nods back. "I'll wait for you," he says.

"That's okay," Caleb says. "Thanks for the ride."

The old guy doesn't respond, and Caleb doesn't wait for him to. He follows the woman through the door and back down a long narrow hall.

The exam room is like all exam rooms. The nurse takes Caleb's temperature, takes his blood pressure, and looks at his arm.

She leaves.

He sits, as uncomfortable on that crinkly paper as a fish in the bottom of a boat.

But all doctor's visits are like that.

He waits for maybe ten minutes, his arm aching like hell, until finally the doctor shows up.

In the sterile light of the exam room the memory of the catacombs, the witch, the sleepwalkers, Bean's disappearance, all seem like the stuff of B horror films, so unbelievable as to be laughable. Here, there are no shadows, no eerie feelings, not even the ticking of a clock. Maybe that's why he doesn't see it coming.

→

Ron sets down his *National Geographic*. The "Lost Incan Cities" article was interesting enough, but when he started checking out the naked aborigine chicks, the shame just got to be too much.

Guess I'm a little hard up, he thinks.

Jesus and his Pops ain't gonna like that one. Course, that's why he isn't behind the pulpit anymore, isn't it? The place for him is out there, wherever "there" is. Not cooped up in some hallowed church but on the streets, on the hallowed highways.

Searching for Keisha, that's where he belongs. But he's beginning to think that reunion won't happen until he reaches the white gates. Even if he can just glimpse her through the bars before he heads down to *his* place in the spiritual fires, that'd be enough.

But this, today, almost gives him hope. It's something worth looking into, the fact that this kid's friend got abducted. And even though the kid is rattled, he was an eyewitness. He thinks he saw the abductor. Together, maybe they could find out what's going on and who's behind it all, and put a stop to it.

But all that's pie in the sky.

If there's one thing Ron Bent knows, it's when he's not wanted. His "no thanks" detector has been fine-tuned through years of rejection, God knows (of course he does—God knows everything). And this kid doesn't want his help. This kid wants to be left alone. And Ron can take a hint. So he gets up, adjusts his belt, and—

"Sir?"

The lilt of a woman's voice is coming from behind the counter. Ron steps over and sees the haggard face of a young girl, perhaps twenty-five years old.

"Yes?" says Ron.

"Is that young man your son?"

"No," says Ron.

"Do you know who his parents are? If they're looking for him, we should let them know."

"I dunno," Ron says with a shrug. "I just picked him up on the side of the road and figured he should have that arm looked at."

The girl nods and makes a note on her clipboard.

"So you don't have any idea if anyone's looking for him, who his parents are, anything?"

Ron shrugs. "No."

She makes another jot.

"And has he been showing any signs of mental instability? Combativeness, depression, anxiety?"

"Well, yeah," Ron says. "But he said he lost his friend, and I'm pretty sure that arm is busted, so I figure he deserves to be a little cranky."

The girl nods to herself. "Good," she says. "Good. And have you noticed any sleep disturbances, nightmares, insomnia?"

Ron looks at her. "In me, or in him?"

"In him," she says.

"Well I ain't sleepin' with him," says Ron. "What part of 'picked him up on the side of the road' don't you get? If you're askin' me, I'd say he doesn't look like he's had a good night's sleep in a while, but what do I know?"

"So you can't rule out sleep disturbances?" she persists.

"Well, no," says Ron. He sees her check a box marked 'yes.' She nods to herself.

Ron looks at the door. Something about this place is making him uneasy. Claustrophobic. Panic biting at its heels. Boy, just when you think you got something beat. He's craving a drink too. That thirst is whispering in his ear. He has to get out of here.

"That it?" he asks.

"That's it, thanks," the girl says to the clipboard.

Ron heads to the door, grabs the handle, and stops. He walks back to the counter.

"You know what?" he says. "I'm going to leave my cell number with you, just in case he needs it." he says.

She hands him a scrap of paper. He writes on it, then pushes it back to her.

"You'll make sure he gets this?" he asks.

She smiles, for the first time. "Of course," she says.

As Ron walks out to his car he has a strange feeling, like just after an argument when you remember everything you *should've* said. Only there's no argument, no "should've said," and no reason to have a strange feeling.

> *Please, Lord, don't let me get*
> *any stranger in my old age.*

Ron digs out his keys and drives away, without any idea of the terrible danger Caleb is in.

❧ Chapter Nine ❧

TRANSCRIPT—Patient #62, SESSION #85

(In this session, the doctor introduces "The Dream Viewer Machine.")

DIRECTOR: Well, Patient Sixty-two, you've been making excellent progress, don't you agree?

(The patient nods.)

DIRECTOR: Have you been enjoying the radio we put in your room for you?

(The patient nods.)

DIRECTOR: Good. Let's get started then. We're beginning a new mode of therapy today. Put on the helmet.
PATIENT #62: I don't want to.
DIRECTOR: And lie on the table.
PATIENT #62: It's cold . . . Something's poking me inside the helmet.
DIRECTOR: Those are cathodes. With this machine I will be able to watch your dreams, just like a film or television show. That's pretty exciting, isn't it?
PATIENT #62: It looks like a metal dish attached to an old TV by some wires.
DIRECTOR: You don't think it will work?

(The patient doesn't answer.)

DIRECTOR: Well?
PATIENT #62: I'm afraid to say.

DIRECTOR: *Then lie down on the table and we'll find out. Now relax.*

(The director plays the relaxation tape and begins talking the patient down into hypnosis.)

PATIENT #62: *Director, I have to ask you a question.*

DIRECTOR: *You're supposed to be embracing the hypnosis.*

PATIENT #62: *Please?*

DIRECTOR: *Yes, Patient Sixty-two, quickly.*

PATIENT #62: *Are you a real doctor?*

DIRECTOR: *Why yes, of course. I studied at the University of Heidelberg in Germany, among other places. Why do you ask—because my methods seem unconventional?*

PATIENT #62: *No.*

DIRECTOR: *Why then?*

PATIENT #62: *Because somebody told me you're not really a doctor at all.*

DIRECTOR: *And who was that, one of the other patients?*

PATIENT #62: *No.*

DIRECTOR: *Who then?*

PATIENT #62: *I'm afraid to say.*

DIRECTOR: *Why would you be afraid to tell me something? Have I ever hurt you?*

PATIENT #62: *Not yet, but . . .*

DIRECTOR: *But what?*

PATIENT #62: *But you will.*

DIRECTOR: *I thought we had dispelled all those silly fears. What did we decide together? About the hole in your head? About the dreams?*

PATIENT #62: *There is no hole in my head and there are no dreams. Having no dreams is just part of the healing process. But I did have a dream the other night.*

DIRECTOR: *And what did you dream?*

PATIENT #62: *That I was sleepwalking.*

DIRECTOR: *And what else?*

PATIENT #62: *Nothing else. That's all I remember.*

DIRECTOR: *You're an interesting case, Patient Sixty-two. Let's try the Dream Viewer, shall we? Please close your eyes.*

(The director urges the patient into a deep, hypnosis-induced sleep. He then observes the screen and speaks into his tape recorder.)

DIRECTOR: *It's difficult to make out what I'm seeing here. Okay, this is better. It's a girl, a younger version of the patient, I imagine. She's running through a labyrinth made of shrubbery. She's come upon a lake. She knows there's something in the water, alligators is the feeling, and now she's sliding, like a waterslide, however she's passed the surface of the water and is still going down. And the patient has landed in a pile of clothes. Clearly, we're picking up the smell of laundry detergent, and the clothes are warm, fresh out of the dryer, I gather. And she's poking her head out of the pile. She must be very small. The sun is very bright through the window. There's the silhouette of a woman laughing, and there's a girl in the basket next to her, also very small, I'm sure representing the twin sister. The sister whispers in her ear. I'm having trouble making out the whisper, but it sounds like bees buzzing, not words—like a big hive of angry hornets, kind of frightening, maybe causing some of the distress we're seeing. Okay, now it's changed. She's in a hallway; it's dark. There's a door with a light shining out of it. And she opens the door slowly, and sees—what am I seeing here? It's washed out from going from the dark hall then into the bright light. Okay, here we go. We have a girl lying on a ceramic table, very pale, dead maybe, something on her head. She's turning now, looking, sees a man sitting in front of a TV. It's me, or somebody very closely resembling me. How interesting. Okay, now she walks around the chair, looking over my shoulder. She looks at the TV—*

(Patient #62 then begins screaming. After some effort, the director is finally able to wake her.)

DIRECTOR: *Patient Sixty-two. Patient Sixty-two! Calm down now. Stop crying, or you'll be confined to your room for a week. There, that's better. Now tell me, what was it that made you so frightened?*
PATIENT #62: *I'm afraid to say.*
DIRECTOR: *You must say. If you ever want to make progress and live a normal life, you must cooperate with your therapy. What upset you?*
PATIENT #62: *I was dreaming. And I saw you and me, in this room, just like we are now. And you were looking at the TV, to see what I was dreaming. And . . .*
DIRECTOR: *And what?*
PATIENT #62: *And I saw the TV screen and . . .*
DIRECTOR: *And?*
PATIENT #62: *And . . . there was nothing there. It was blank.*

(The Director smiles.)

DIRECTOR: *And if the TV is blank, how was I able to see your dreams, do you think? That would be impossible.*

(The patient begins crying.)

DIRECTOR: *What? Why are you crying?*
PATIENT #62: *Look. The TV. It's not even plugged in.*
DIRECTOR: *Of course the machine works. If it didn't work, how would I know that you dreamt of playing in a basket of clothes with your twin sister when you were just a child?*

(The patient becomes distraught, crying, shaking her head.)

DIRECTOR: *How would I know that, Patient Sixty-two?*

PATIENT #62: *She says . . . she says the drowned ones tell you.*

DIRECTOR: *Who says that? I promise if you tell me, I won't get angry. Who's talking to you?*

PATIENT #62: *My sister.*

DIRECTOR: *And where is your sister? I'd very much like to meet her.*

PATIENT #62: *You can't.*

DIRECTOR: *Why.*

PATIENT #62: *Because she's dead. Stop, stop smiling at me! I want to go home now. Billy was supposed to take me home. I can't take this. I can't take this. The devil is coming, and you know it, and you know it, and you know it! I hear you, you sing his song at night, you—*

DIRECTOR: *I think we've accomplished enough for this session.*

Patient Sixty-two appears to have gotten a pen somewhere, and attacks the director with it, stabbing it into his forearm. The director strikes her, knocking her unconscious, then directs the orderlies to undress the patient and remove her into the basement. End of session.

DESPITE HIS DISCOMFORT, by the time the doctor walks in, Caleb is fast asleep.

The doctor clears his throat. "Young man?"

Caleb starts and sits up fast, gripping the crunchy exam-table paper hard with his unbroken hand.

The doctor backs up a step, blinking fast.

"You scared me," Caleb murmurs.

The doctor, "Doctor Rodgers," according to the embroidery on his white coat, smiles warmly, and Caleb likes him instantly. He has salt-and-pepper hair, overgrown eyebrows, and must be sixty years old or so. He's short of stature, round of body, and red of face.

"Well, don't worry about a thing," he says. "Nothing to be scared of here. We'll fix you right up. Now, I heard something about an arm."

Caleb presents the arm.

"Oh, ouch. That doesn't look too healthy, now does it? Okay, I'm going to touch you now, it might hurt a little. Tell me what hurts, okay. Does that hurt?"

Caleb nods.

"Okay, how 'bout now? Not really? Okay, what about this? Ouch, okay, sorry. That's it, then. Let me just feel around here for a minute. Okay. Well, we're going to have to X-ray it first, and then I'm going to set it, which is going to hurt a little bit, but we have to do it to make sure you heal right, okay? I'll just order the X-ray and my nurse will be in soon to take care of that for you."

Doctor Rodgers sits on the stool with wheels, puts on his glasses, and writes something in a file.

"I imagine that hurts a good deal, doesn't it? I'm going to order you something for pain as well. That might make setting the bone a little easier to take if the painkillers have set in."

Caleb hears all this from inside a black hole. He doesn't care if his arm is amputated. He doesn't care if his arm never heals again. The problem isn't that his arm is broken, it's that the world is broken.

For the first time, he notices that one of Dr. Rodgers's eyelids is violently twitching. Blink-blink-blink-blink-blink.

It's disconcerting. He wonders how Mrs. Rodgers, if there is a Mrs. Rodgers, can stand it.

" . . . Are there any medications you're allergic to?"

Caleb shakes his head.

"Are there any medical conditions we need to be aware of?"

"No."

"Have you ever experienced shortness of breath? Loss of vision? Dementia? Anmesia? Chest pains? Leg pains? Chronic headaches? Chronic joint pain? Nightmares? Back pain?"

"No."

"No?"

"Well, nightmares, yes, I guess, sometimes. All the rest, no."

"Alrighty!" Dr. Rodgers says, his left eye snapping open and closed like the wings of a dragonfly. He claps the folder shut and stands. "The nurse'll be right in."

The door closes behind the doctor and the room is silent.

Caleb marinates in his own confusion, disbelief, grief, even restless apathy. It's disbelief that wins out, though. He just can't believe in his own experiences. Reality seems as fragile as a spiderweb.

The nurse comes in. She doesn't say anything, just half smiles and sets something down on the counter, rolls up Caleb's sleeve and begins making a small, circular scrubbing motion with an alcohol swab on his shoulder.

"Dang, you're filthy," she says. "What you been doing, campin'?"

"Yeah," Caleb says absently.

"Uck. Look," she says, showing him the blackened alcohol swab. "You might shoulda jumped in the river for a swim," she says and tosses the swab into the wastebasket.

She gets out a syringe and a tiny bottle. Caleb watches her hold the bottle upside down, draw the clear medicine out from it, then pull the long needle free again.

"You from around here?" Caleb asks.

"Born and raised," she says.

"You ever know a pair of twin girls, Christine and Anna?"

"I did at one time," she says, flicking the syringe. "But one's dead or something and the other one's over at the Dream Center getting her head shrunk. That's who you meant, right?"

"Yeah," Caleb says.

"Well, maybe you'll see her there. Little prick now, honey." She sticks the needle in his arm, pushes hard, empties the syringe and pulls the needle out again fast, replacing it with a cotton ball.

"Hold that there," she says, turning away to dispose of the syringe. "Now," she says, "a handsome boy like you ain't from around here, I know. You got a girlfriend back home?"

One time, Bean had dared Caleb to ride a wildly spinning fair ride, the Gravitron, ten times in a row. Now Caleb feels just like he did getting off from that tenth ride.

"What did you give me?" he asks.

She raises her eyebrows sensually. "Sup'm that'll knock the pain right out of you, and then some."

Red panic is leaking into Caleb's brain. He can't feel his feet.

"What did you say a minute ago, about seeing Christine?"

"Well, I don't know as you'll see her, but you'll sure be neighbors."

"I've gotta go," Caleb says. He tries to get up, but his legs give out from under him. The nurse's quick hands are the only thing that saves his face from smashing on the tile floor.

"Hold on now," she says, "before you hurt yourself again. There's worse things than going to the Dream Center . . . like going there a virgin."

She smiles her sexiest smile, the one she practices in front of the mirror sometimes, but it's too late. The guy is already passed out on the floor, drooling.

No real point in getting his number anyway. Even though the

Dream Center is supposed to be a great place and all, she hasn't seen it cure anyone of bad dreams yet. Come to think of it, she hasn't heard of anyone being let out at all, cured or not.

→

Creedence Clearwater Revival. Let people call rock and roll the music of the devil all they want; some of it, not all but some, is divine. Like blades of sunlight cutting through treetops is divine, like ice cream is divine, like Keisha was—is, is—divine. Rock and roll. Beautiful.

Who knows how people miss the implicit meaning behind all these little miracles, but they do. And Ron knows he's no exception. He's lived in the dark for years, wandering the catacombs of disillusionment, looking for the stairway back up to faith. And today, for some reason, as he beats out the rhythm to the song with his "hook" on the steering wheel, he feels a little closer.

Bitter clouds litter the sky, fluffy white on top and heavy gray on the bottom, portending rain, but the sun is still out, the sky is still mostly blue, and Ron feels better than he has in a long time. More awake. More real. He continues tapping "the hook" on the steering wheel, and with his good hands hoists the last bite of a Whopper into his mouth, then takes a sip of iced tea. Hudsonville's only fast food restaurant, an outdated Burger King, is dead now, at eleven AM. Ron looks next door, through the drive-through, at the sign of the doctor's office next door. "Dr. Rodgers" is all it says. He eats some fries. The back lot where he sits is empty, save for a few stray burger wrappers skittered across by the wind. Some seagulls pick at stray fries by the Dumpster.

Ron tries to think of the next step, the road ahead.

Probably, he'll go back to Panama City. The next check from good old Uncle Sam should be arriving any time, and the wallet's getting a little thin.

Still, there's something here. Something going on, something happening. For the first time in years, the dismal still life of his world is churned up, like a shaken snow globe.

And Keisha might yet be near, yes she might.

But where to turn? Not to the sheriff. He's tried the police for years and all they seem good for is putting paper into files, drinking coffee, nodding, and looking at their watches. But where then? Maybe the FBI should step in. After all, they're the big dogs, the Saint Bernards of law enforcement. And maybe they could crack the whip on these lamebrained, limp-dick, small-town, Barney Fife pigs.

He takes a deep breath to calm himself. No use getting his piss boiling again. That wouldn't lead to anything but indigestion.

No, the FBI isn't the answer. He's tried them. He's written letters to the DA, to the governor (that worthless jackass), he's seen the FBI agents—Marley and Grovner were their names—take down his statements and stash them away in a nice, neat manila folder, never to be seen again. Never a call returned. Never a letter acknowledged.

Piss in the wind, Dirty Dan would've said.

Still, there's something going on here, all around him; he can feel it in the air, in the ground. Like getting near a big machine—even with the earplugs in, you feel the vibration. (Ron Bent knows about machines. He ran a printing press for almost three months in Dothan. Wasn't much good at that, though.)

The truth is all around him, and it's big, big as the miracle of life, big as God, and just as hard to see, praise him.

And that kid. If somebody took his friend, then at least there's an ally. Somebody on the same road, somebody else who maybe knows a piece of the truth.

Ron shovels a handful of fries into his mouth, and for the first time in years, maybe in his life, he wallows in the possibility that he's lonely. Really, desperately lonely. Because right now, the thought of a brother-in-arms is as tempting as a beer is to a drunk. And Ron Bent knows something about that. He was always a pretty good drunk.

There's only one problem, and that's the fact that the kid didn't seem too eager for a friend or too interested in the handicapped old bastard who had given him a ride to the doctor's. The kid had hardly uttered a word. And why should he? Why would somebody want to take up with a bitter, crotchety old screwup like Ron anyway?

Lord,
Grant me the humility to face myself
And the strength to walk my road alone,
Because that's the path you've laid out for me,
Hard as it may be,
And—

Ron freezes in the midst of his sip of iced tea.

He almost laughs—it's that strange a sight he sees through his windshield.

The pretty young nurse and a small, timid-looking doctor appear at the back door of the office, looking over their shoulders like a couple of spies in a pulp magazine, hauling a limp, heavy object to the waiting door of a silver Lincoln Town Car. And that object is a body. And that body—Ron knows without knowing, since it's too far to see for sure—is the kid he dropped off half an hour ago.

Ron is very still, staring. He breathes in slow, and as he does his mouthful of sweetened tea jets down the wrong pipe. By the time he stops choking, the town car is already pulling onto the street. But no amount of coughing or blurred, teary-eyed vision will stop Ron Bent, not now, and he slaps his car into gear and lurches forward, spilling some tea on his lap, not caring. As he pulls onto the road with a bottom-thunking "whack" and punches the throttle, he can almost hear little Keisha laughing, and sweet damn does it sound good.

Praise God.

He bubbles up into consciousness, like oil rising to the surface of water. Later, he'll remember that his name is Caleb, that he lettered in track for the last three years, and that his best friend was stolen by sleepwalking apparitions. Right now, though, all he knows is that his head is vibrating with poisonous agony. When he opens his eyes—it isn't for a few minutes—the world is blurred, like a sidewalk chalk drawing after a storm. This would be very frightening if he could formulate the thought of panic, but it seems his brain has shattered and the piece holding fear, along with the piece that focuses his eyes, is missing. Instead, the guy who'll soon realize he's Caleb lies still, listening. There's the rattle and hum of an electric fan. A bird sings far away, and a heavy door closes. Footsteps echo in a hollow place.

The guy who is Caleb tries to get up, but his legs are liquid, and a sizzling brand of pain slashes through his arm and he falls back. The clacking stops, and there's a voice, smooth and even and deep.

The guy who is Caleb remembers a wood-shop teacher he used to have, a really odd, skinny guy with buggy eyes, thick glasses, and a million bizarre quips. His main focus in life, it seemed, was getting pieces of wood very smooth. That was all that seemed to get the fella off. He'd rub the project, whatever it was, a cedar box, a pine cutting board in the shape of a pig, or a small stool, and shake his head, "Needs more sanding, needs more waxing." But when he was finally pleased, there was only one phrase he used without fail: "Slicker'n snot on a doorknob," he'd say.

And that is the only way to describe the voice that fills the guy's (Caleb's) head now.

Slicker'n snot on a doorknob.

"Relax, don't try to get up," the slick voice says. "You'll just injure yourself further. The doctor says you only have a mild fracture, but we wouldn't want to make it any worse."

He (Caleb) tries to see the face of the person talking to him, but all there is is a grotesque white blur that looks nothing like a person.

The voice must've read the look of concern on his face, because it says:

"The medication causes some blurring of vision. It's normal, don't worry. You might close your eyes for a while; sometimes the distortion can cause nausea."

(Caleb) does as the voice bids him. It continues:

"It will dull your pain, though, even render you unconscious in large doses, as I'm sure you observed. In some military circles, it's also used as a truth serum. Interesting, how as complex a thing as a human being is ruled by simple chemicals. And most of us fancy ourselves to be unsolvable riddles. But let's try an experiment, shall we? Just to see. Just to know if it works. Are you ready? Let's see, let's just start with your name. What is your name, although I already know? This is what, in science, is called a 'control question.'"

"Caleb," he says. He had forgotten he was Caleb, so it was strange to hear the word coming out of his mouth. It sounded a little foreign, a little distant, as if somebody else were saying it across a bad phone connection.

"And where are you from?"

"Hudsonville, Florida."

There's approval in the voice: "You see, that's interesting, because you could have just as easily said 'Malibu, California.' But you aligned yourself with your birthplace. How interesting. Let's make things even more interesting. What is your father's profession?"

"Attorney."

"Do you consider yourself an attractive person?"

"Yes."

"Do you have sexual fantasies about men or women?"

"Women."

"Do you believe in evil spirits?"

"No."

There's a smile in the voice. "Interesting. Where is the friend who came to town with you?"

"I don't know."

"Where did you see him last?"

"In the tunnel. In the dark."

"What happened to him?"

There's a hesitation.

"Answer. What happened to him?"

"I don't know."

"What do you think happened to him?"

"They took him."

"Who are they?"

"Pale and sleeping."

"That's interesting. Very interesting," says the voice. "Where is your father?"

"I don't know."

"Do you trust the witch, Christine Zikry's mother?"

"No."

"Why?"

"She's a drunk."

There's a long pause. Some talking, far away.

"Do you believe that you are the key to everything, that you have the power to set whole universes in motion and bring them to a halt?" asks the voice.

"No."

"Did you know that the dead sing of you?"

"No."

"Do you believe you have the power to bring about the end of the world?"

"No."

"Well, you do."

Pain is seeping back in for (Caleb), seething deep in his left wrist and melting through his head.

Feels like a cat is chasing a mouse inside his skull, knocking things over.

Tom and Jerry.

"Open your eyes," says the voice.

Caleb does. He blinks, then sees. He's in a small, sparely furnished office. There's a steel desk, a file cabinet, a floor lamp with a Tiffany glass shade, probably (but maybe not) a fake. Caleb is lying on an ancient, stained puke-green couch. There's an ACE bandage wrapped around his aching left wrist, wound from the knuckles of his hand three-quarters of the way to his elbow. And sitting on the desk in front of him is an old-fashioned-looking white intercom box.

"Well, good morning," says the voice, crackling a little now as it buzzes cheerfully from the slats in the box face. "My name is Barnett DeFranklin. I'm director here. You, young man, are at the Dream Center. Welcome. We've been expecting you."

⊰ Chapter Ten ⊱

R ON SITS IN HIS IDLING CAR, staring at the huge building in front of him. He has to lean forward to see the upper stories through his windshield. It reminds him of the old VA hospital he spent all those months in, and that thought alone freezes him in his seat. The bad memories come floating back, along with that black cloud of desolation that hung over him during those long days.

He remembers the phone call to his old buddy Casey, who called him a baby killer and hung up on him. He remembers calling his old girlfriend (Cheryl was her first name, but her last name? Funny, that year and a half in the jungle she had been his beacon, tinting his every waking thought with the promise of something better. Now he can't even remember her last name . . . Walters. Cheryl Walters. But that was a whole world ago). She hadn't even bothered with the "baby killer" justification, she had simply hung up, and the next time he called back, a man had answered and said Cheryl didn't want to see him anymore. In that big hospital full of echoes, some guys were quiet; they'd just sit there and stare at their oatmeal in the morning, and their hand's would shake just slightly as they brought the spoon to their mouths, and you knew there was a horror playing itself out behind their eyes. Some guys would talk up a storm, brag and joke, then at night you'd hear them crying, wailing like babies.

In the dark of that hospital, in the glow of an EXIT sign, Ron wakes up. He has to take a leak. He stands up and has to steady himself with one hand on the bed—the pain meds make him dizzy—and in that minute, that pause, he happens to glance over at the bed belonging to

151

Private Ned Felspauch. Ned's a good guy, tells funny stories at mess. He took shrapnel to the head, and his nose is messed up; otherwise he isn't that bad off. He's one of the loud ones, one of the braggers, one of the ones who's going to be okay, get a good job selling insurance or something like that and do well for himself. He's always writing letters to some blond back home with big hooters. In fact, she's one of the things he brags about most.

Looks like he fell asleep writing one of those letters tonight and the ink spilled out of his pen, because there's a big ink stain all over his sheets. Ron leans close in the dark. The exit light is red, and casts uncertain shadows, warps colors, but—

Ned's mouth is gaping, open and still. The stain on his sheets isn't from ink. The razor is still in his hand, shining red in the light. Ron sits back on his bed and stares. Another twenty-one-year-old, one who had seen less, might panic. He might yell, run for help, try CPR. But not Ron Bent. He's already seen enough to know a dead man when he sees one.

Ron didn't cry when he lost his hand—at least not that he remembers. He didn't cry when his number came up and he got shipped out; he just got drunk and packed a bag. He didn't even cry when Dirty got killed. But now, sitting on that bed in that big, dark hospital full of echoes, Ron's face gets hot, and the tears keep coming and coming and coming.

And it's not because he lost his hand.

And it's not because he hasn't had one visitor since he's been back in the States.

And it's not because Ned Felspauch is dead.

It's because Ned was supposed to be one of the ones who would be okay. And if Ned isn't okay, maybe nobody will be.

In the driveway of the Dream Center, Ron is already out of his car. He hates hospitals, hates his life, hates everything—but if God gives him wheat, he's gonna bake bread.

And if anybody thinks they're going to do anything bad to one more kid, they'll have to literally do it over his dead body.

He pulls back one of the heavy double doors and walks in. Smells like Pine-Sol, medicine, and something else . . . dust? Decay?

"Hello, sir," says a voice.

To his left, behind a counter, sits a man with a tweed jacket and a shaved head.

"Welcome to the Dream Center. How can I help you?"

"A boy was just brought in here," Ron says. "I need to see him right now. Bring him out."

"That's against our policy, I'm afraid," says the man behind to counter. "Only immediate family members are allowed to see the patients here, and then only on assigned visiting days."

"Okay, I'm his uncle. The kid's name is Caleb. Let me see him."

"Sir, today is not a visiting day. If you'd like to fill out a visitation request form, you might be able to see the patient on Wednesday."

"Goddammit," says Ron. "He is not a patient. He was just brought in here. I found him out in the woods, and I took him to the doctor because he was hurt. Now, I watched the doctor drag him out to the car, I followed the car here, and I watched them drag him inside through these doors. Now I ask you again, where is he?"

"Sir, only approved relatives may visit patients."

"He's not a patient, I just told you."

"You also said you were his uncle and then that you found him wandering in the woods. Did it ever occur to you, Uncle, that he could have been a patient here who escaped?"

Ron straightens up. In fact, that hadn't occurred to him.

"You're telling me that Caleb, the kid who just came through these doors, is a patient here."

"I'm telling you, sir, that we do not share information about patients unless it is with an approved relative."

Ron is paralyzed by the thought that perhaps the kid was here for some kind of therapy. After all, he had seemed pretty out of it, pretty disturbed. Maybe there was no lost friend, maybe it was just some psychosis in the kid's mind. But no. Ron doesn't think so. He believes the kid. And when a belief takes root deep inside him like that, he's inclined to think that it's God who planted the seed. So he puts his misgivings aside.

The man with the shaved head, apparently taking Ron's silence as acquiescence, has gone back to reading an issue of *Guns & Ammo* magazine. With shocking quickness, Ron reaches through the open window of the glass booth and snatches it out of his hands.

The man's eyes are huge.

"I'm going to have to ask you to leave," he says, once he's composed himself, and he slides the window down, separating himself from Ron.

"I'm not going to," says Ron. "Not until I see my nephew. And if I do not see him, I'm going to call every government agency, every private investigator, and every parent in the northern half of this state and come down on this place like a hammer."

Two big orderlies round a corner, one black and one white, each equally huge and menacing. They come with long, purposeful strides, clearly ready to take Ron apart, but before they can, the man with the shaved head stays them with a gesture.

"You say you're the boy's uncle?" he says. "Let's hope for your sake that that's the truth."

→

"What are you going to do to me?" Caleb asks.

The speaker box sitting on the desk crackles back: "What makes you think I'm going to do anything to you?"

Caleb doesn't know how to respond. His mind is clear now. He can vaguely remember answering some strange questions, but for some reason he can't seem to remember any of the questions or his answers to them.

The director seems to sense his confusion, and the box says: "You were found injured and dirty, and on top of the broken arm, which my good friend Dr. Rodgers was nice enough to patch up for you, you were diagnosed with a sleep disorder. So, he sent you here for a brief evaluation. Nothing to be alarmed about, I assure you. The sooner begun the sooner done I always say, so let's begin, shall we? You'll find a sheet of paper and a pencil in front of you."

Caleb looks down. For some reason he hadn't noticed it before, but there is indeed a paper and pencil in front of him.

"Pick it up. And begin."

Caleb picks the pencil up.

"Thank you," the box says.

Caleb stares ahead. The wall behind the speaker box is entirely dominated by a huge mirror. He stares at it, knowing it's staring back at him. He glances around the room, looking for something to defend himself with if he has to. There's nothing; the place is next to empty. But his gaze lingers on a hat rack by the door with a rope looped over it.

"What?" the box asks, "admiring my lasso, are you? I promise I'll tell you all about it—once you've taken the evaluation."

Caleb takes one more look around the room, then looks down at the paper and sees:

Patient name _____

Birthdate_____

City of origin _____

PATIENT EVALUATION
STANDARD FORM 1A

DIRECTIONS: Please select the most appropriate answer by filling in the corresponding circle.

	Agree	Not Sure	Disagree
1. I usually get a good night's sleep.	O	O	O
2. I wake up 1–3 times per night.	O	O	O
3. I wake up 3–5+ times per night.	O	O	O
4. I sometimes wake up because of nightmares.	O	O	O
5. I experience insomnia 2 or more times per month.	O	O	O
6. I sometimes find myself falling asleep during the day because I am unable to sleep at night.	O	O	O
7. People tell me I sometimes talk in my sleep.	O	O	O
8. In my dreams, I sometimes see people who have passed away.	O	O	O
9. In my dreams, deceased people sometimes appear and tell me about or show me events that later come to pass.	O	O	O
10. I sometimes wake up in strange places and do not know how I got there.	O	O	O
11. I sometimes dream of a little girl who disappeared many years ago.	O	O	O
12. Sometimes when I try to do something good, something bad actually happens.	O	O	O
13. My friend died because of me.	O	O	O
14. It is my destiny to bring about the end of the world, and no matter what I do, I cannot help it.	O	O	O
15. My father believed if you stand in a room with sixteen ticking clocks for one hour every day, the spirits will come.	O	O	O
16. Christine Zikry is mad.	O	O	O
17. My father was mad.	O	O	O
18. I am mad.	O	O	O
19. I am mad.	O	O	O
20. I am mad.	O	O	O
21. _____	O	O	O

When he's finished, he sets the pencil down. Already, he's forgotten how he answered each question, as if the test were a dream that he hardly remembers upon waking.

The box crackles to life:

"About the lasso. Before I became director here, many years ago, I was a rodeo clown. That was during some of my wandering years, although some would argue that all my years have been wandering ones.

Rodeoing is tough business. I saw one man break his back, and another was gored to death not three feet from me. It was unsettling. The man who broke his back was a cowboy, but the one who got gored, he was a clown, like me. It's funny, or rather not funny, because the clowns are taking on almost as much risk as the riders themselves, but, but, they get no respect, no fans. No love. But what nobody knew the whole time was that the man behind the makeup was actually faster and better than any of them, and could rope any living thing in the whole world. I always took pride in that."

"What are you talking about?" says Caleb, confused.

"It's just a little parable about making judgments before you fully understand things. And it happens to be a true story from my life."

"What's going on?" Caleb says. "How do you know all this about me? Did Christine tell you?"

The box crackles. "You'll see," it says.

"Look, you can keep me here, that's fine. Just let Christine out. She doesn't belong here. Take me instead."

From the box comes the sound of a phone ringing. "Yes," says the director's voice, " . . . his uncle, eh? Well, I don't know . . . Let me ask him. Caleb? What's your uncle's name?"

Caleb frowns, not wanting to say the wrong thing. Given the

paper on the desk, he figures if he lies, this man will know.

"I don't have one," he says. "Both of my parents are only children."

"Did you hear that?" The director laughs. "Looks like we have an impostor. Let's detain him and have our good friend, the sheriff, come and arrest him."

"Arrest who?" says Caleb.

The box hisses in silence for a moment. "The gentleman who took you to Doctor Rodgers, a mister Ron Bent, I believe, seems to be posing as your uncle. He seems concerned for your well-being, isn't that funny? He doesn't know you're safe and sound. Don't worry, we'll handle him."

"Please," says Caleb, "just let him go."

"No," the box says, "I don't think so. Karl, please call Sheriff Johnson. And as for you, Caleb, you're free to go. We don't want to detain you. You have work to do."

Caleb's many questions (What do you mean, work? Where's Christine? Why are you arresting that guy who helped me?) are left to wheel about in his brain, unanswered. The intercom box clicks off, and despite all Caleb's efforts at communication, it won't click on again.

Caleb just sits there for a moment, stung, staring at the piece of paper in front of him with his eyes half-closed, guarded.

When he finally gets up and approaches the door, he expects it to be locked. Instead, it opens right up, revealing an empty, darkened hallway. Caleb peers out into the hallway, and then glances over his shoulder, back at the office he had been sitting in. This might be the time to make a run for it, but his curiosity gets the better of him. He has to know what's happening. It's the budding journalist within him, he knows, the part that wants—needs—to make things coherent, to give them order, to put them together with a premise, support, a logical conclusion. Except he has no premise, only nonsense, a string of non sequiturs as far as the eye can see.

He closes the door leading to the hall and begins ransacking the office as quickly as he can. Instantly, disappointment envelops him.

The desk drawers: empty.

The filing cabinet: hundreds of folders, all empty.

The trash can: empty.

In fact, the only scrap of paper in the entire office is the "evaluation" the director had given him, and the only other object of any interest at all is the lasso, hanging on the hat rack.

The place is sterile.

There's a soft knock at the door. Caleb's heart races. He wants to run and hide, but there's nowhere to go. The window is frosted and barred. He looks for a weapon, but there's nothing, just the pencil and the coat rack, and he doesn't think either one will do him much good. So if he can't fight and he can't flee, all he can do is go along for the ride.

"Come in," he says, his voice sounding hoarse, his eyes locked on the door.

The man who opens the door is not the director.

At first, Caleb has trouble placing him (maybe because the drugs he was given are wearing off, maybe because his wrist is throbbing with pain again, so much that it's difficult to think). After a moment, he realizes it's the man from the front desk with the shaved head. Caleb surmises it might be Karl from the other end of the director's phone.

"Hi, Karl," he says.

"Hello, Mr. Mason," says Karl. "Please, come with me."

Karl is unarmed and seems as mild as milk. With no better option available, Caleb follows him.

They pass down a long hallway. Every other rectangle of fluorescent bulbs above is shut off, and the effect as they walk from light to darkness and into light again is a little painful to Caleb's still-woozy brain.

They pass many doors on either side, each made of heavy oak and each bearing a number. Now he's passing 333. There are sounds behind a few doors, a shuffling sound behind one, a sharp cough issuing from another, but mostly there is only silence. Finally, Karl leads Caleb to a lobby area with padded chairs and a fake flower arrangement on a big, laminated wood table. There is a bank of elevators, but Karl doesn't push a button. Instead, he opens a door that leads to a stairwell of steel railings and peeling paint. Caleb follows him as he winds his way down and down with only the echo of their footfalls to mark their progress. When Caleb is sure they must be several stories underground, the man, Karl, pushes open another door. He gestures to Caleb, you first.

"Where am I going?" Caleb asks as he warily passes Karl, stepping through the doorway.

"Wherever you like," Karl says, and Caleb, squinting, realizes that he has stepped into the light spilling through the front doors of the building. This is the main lobby.

"Thank you for visiting the Dream Center. We'll see you again soon," says Karl. He walks around the counter, sits down on a stool, and looks down at a magazine.

"I'm free to go?" asks Caleb.

"That's right," says Karl, without looking up. "The director saw no need to admit you."

Caleb just stands there, frowning. Trying to figure out what's going on right now makes his head hurt. He'd rather sort grains of sand on a beach. Finally, he decides to simply be direct.

"Karl, please tell me what's going on."

Karl looks up from his magazine, a little annoyed. "What do you mean? You can go," he says.

"I know that," says Caleb. "What I'm asking is what's going on in the grand scheme of things here? Kids in this town are missing, my friend was abducted by—I don't even know what, then all this. And Christine . . . Can you just please tell me what's happening? Please?"

Karl looks a little amused. "Look, kid, it's not my place to say. My job is the desk," he says, and he thumps the palm of his hand on the counter.

"So you don't know what's going on either?" Caleb asks.

"Oh, no," says Karl. "I know exactly what's going on. I've been here since the beginning."

"Then why won't you tell me?"

"Because asking me is like . . . like asking the wick of a candle what the flame is going to do. A flame burns whatever it wants, it doesn't give half a shit, excuse my French, what the wick thinks."

"And who—or what is the flame?" asks Caleb. He feels that he's close to something if this guy would just—

But Karl only laughs.

"You mean you really can't hear them, kid? They're all around you. Tune in," Karl says.

Karl's words hang in the air for a second, and "who are they?" hangs on Caleb's lips, but before the words can come out, the phone on the counter rings, and Karl snatches it up.

"Dream Center. . . . Of course, right away." He hangs up.

"Who?" Caleb asks. "Who's all around?"

But Karl is already disappearing out the door behind the desk. It slams shut, and Caleb is alone in the lobby.

His shadow stretches long at his feet from the light spilling in the doors, reflecting brightly off the polished floor. Somewhere far off, someone is yelling. Caleb shivers. He should be glad he can leave. Glad he's getting away. Christine isn't as lucky. He takes a slow step through the doorway and out into the hush of impending twilight. Should it be twilight now, or should it be morning? Time seems suddenly disjointed. He feels like he lost a day somewhere, but he's not sure where. He walks up the gravel driveway on soggy legs. The wrist is aching bad enough to set his teeth on edge, but his jaw is slack, his eyes are slack, and his mind is adrift.

He finds his way to the car, still parked where he and Bean left it a lifetime ago. It starts right up. The only problem is there's nowhere to go.

After what he's seen, no place can be home again.

⊰ Chapter Eleven ⊱

BEFORE DARKNESS SETTLES IN, Caleb kneels next to the car, parked in the driveway of his lost father's house, and pulls the laces of his running shoes tight. He stretches, first one leg, then the other, then both, feeling the burn run along his sinews. The sun is lost behind the trees, but the color of the sky above is still vibrant, and he figures he still has a good half an hour until darkness marches in. When night comes he doesn't know what he'll do. He walks to the end of the driveway, looking at the woods all around him, eyes scanning the ferns for moving shapes, glancing at the treetops for lurking apparitions, finding none. When he reaches the road, he kicks into motion. At first, his legs feel heavy. He doesn't know if it's the drugs the doctor gave him, the fatigue (when was the last time he slept?), or simply the fact that he hasn't run in a while, but for some reason, he's dog-tired. Soon, though, all of it melts away: the leaden legs, the slight cramping in the chest, the pain in his wrist that strikes with every step. His surroundings, his pain, and the world, they all thin into one line of motion and become simple. Which is why he loves running so much in the first place.

Running is what he always does when he needs to think about a really important problem. His mind is clear, his thoughts are sharp.

I can't get lost. Can't make any turns. I'll just go up and back.

I have to get out of this town. This place is—

I have to find Bean. But how? He's gone, taken. Or worse. . . .

And Christine, too.

I need help.

I have to get that guy out of jail, that—Ron—I'm pretty sure that was his name. He didn't know what trouble he was getting into, giving me a ride. Or maybe he did. He followed me to the Dream Center. No, the asylum, because that's still what it is, isn't it? How many others are locked up in there? Maybe my father even. But not me. Why?

Too many questions.

But then there's the other good thing about running: you can shut your mind off. That's what Caleb does now, and he kicks out harder. The soles of his shoes slap the pavement, his legs feel free like they're running on their own. The forest dissolves all around him and there's only the sound of his breath, the *simplicity* of his breath.

And he thinks of Bean and how he lost him.

And he thinks of Anna and how he lost her.

He thinks of how he might lose Christine.

And his father.

And he runs his ass off.

When he gets back to the house, the dark is just coiling itself around the world. He walks up the squeaking boards of the front steps and into the living room. He's dripping with sweat and his legs ache, but it's a good pain. His wrist aches too, and that's not so good, but he bites his lip and ignores it. A terrible thought comes to him, that there might be no hot water—after all, who pays the bill at an abandoned house? And of course, there's no electricity. But after rummaging through a broom closet and finding a match and some candles to light his way up the stairs, he finds a working bathtub; one mercifully void of raccoons. He sets the candles up on the basin and disrobes. The shower actually works, and once rust runs itself out, the water is clear enough. The shower curtain is hopelessly moldy, but he leans as far away from it as possible as he climbs his way in.

He finds an old, hard sliver of soap and makes do.

If somebody paid the water bill, they certainly forgot the gas, because the water is by no means hot. It isn't cold enough to make Caleb cry, though, so he bears it.

He keeps thinking he hears something and cranes his head around the shower curtain, but all he sees is the back of the closed bathroom door. As he scrubs himself down, growing numb with cold, he asks himself the hard questions:

Do I leave?

Christine is still locked up, and even though that director let me go, I know there's something wrong at that place. There always has been. And maybe Bean is still alive; maybe he's locked up there. It's too much to hope for, but still. If he's alive, I can't leave him. And either way, if I don't help Christine, then he suffered, probably died, for nothing. So I stay.

And do what?

. . . I don't know. I have no friggin' clue. Help that guy Ron get out of jail? How? Bail him out, I guess. Then what? Find my father. Where? In Atlanta? But I know he's not really in Atlanta. I don't know how I know that, but I do. He's probably locked up in the Dream Center too. He probably tried to fight it, probably sued or something. There are too many people who need rescuing.

So . . .

Bail out Ron, try to rescue Christine, find my dad, in that order. Not much of a plan, but . . . what the hell good are plans anyway? I'm supposed to be in Africa. Dealing with simple things like starvation and AIDS. I'd give anything if all I had to worry about was writing a crappy article about starvation and AIDS right now. God, this water's getting cold. . . .

Caleb climbs out and gets dressed. He keeps looking over his shoulder, half expecting a sleeping demon to appear out of the shadows and claw him to death, but none do.

Night is deepening and the air is still as Caleb walks out to the car, starts it up, and drives to the sheriff's station—or the "Trailer O'Justice," as it might more aptly be called. He cracks a tiny smile at his own wit, but when he dwells on the fact that his friend isn't there to share the joke with him, the smile on his face quickly melts into resolve. He has to focus. There is somebody he can save tonight. It might not be Bean, but at least it's somebody.

He goes over it in his mind the whole way there, the plan, everything he's going to say. He's going to tell them that Ron is his uncle, that he was under the influence of medication so he said the wrong thing. He'll tell them that the whole situation was just a misunderstanding and that he'll be glad to make a statement or even testify on Ron's behalf. And then he'll take his mother's credit card (just thinking of the shit storm that'll rain down on him when that credit card bill with "Calhoun County Sheriff, $500" written on it comes in the mail makes him wince). And then what? He'll cross that bridge when he comes to it. Maybe Ron will know—whoever Ron is.

But his plans are laid to waste, as most plans are, when he rolls into the police trailer driveway and finds the windows dark and the driveway empty. He gets out and knocks on the door, even waits for ten minutes for somebody to come, glancing over his shoulder the whole time, but in the end he simply walks back to the car. As he sits in the driver's seat, he sees a sign in the window that simply reads CLOSED. Apparently in Hudsonville no crimes are committed after six PM.

Up the street he stops at the only gas station in town and buys a couple of PowerBars and a cup of coffee from a polite (but not friendly), old black guy and drives back over the desolate, carless streets to his father's empty house. He goes into the living room, builds a fire, stares at it, and is lost.

After maybe half an hour letting the fire's light burn into his brain, listening to the tiny sounds of the house, he walks over to his duffel bag on the dusty, old couch, and takes out a small leather-bound book. He goes back to the fire, worms his way into his sleeping bag, then sits, staring at a blank page of his journal. He clicks his pen, clicks it again, and clicks it again.

Come on, he tells himself, *you're a journalist; one day you'll be a famous one. And here it is, the biggest, most horrifying, most important story you'll ever have the chance to write. Maybe you can get the FBI to come here. Maybe you can spark a national investigation. That Dream Center must be licensed; who oversees the licensing?*

But even as he thinks that thought, he's disgusted with himself. Who gives a crap about licensing or pointing fingers at some bureaucrat? This is about *lives.* Bean's life, Christine's. This is about evil, real evil like Caleb never imagined could exist. But it does exist. And the world has to know. So he takes his pen, and in the firelight he writes:

The children of Hudsonville, Florida, are missing.

He crosses it out. Below it, he writes:

Deep in the woods in the small town of Hudsonville, Florida, something horrible is happening: people are disappearing.

He goes to cross it out, but then he continues.

The police, those assigned with investigating the disappearance of these people, are interested in nothing but . . .

He stops and crosses it all out. It's hopeless. Even if he could write it, it would sound more like a Stephen King book than a *Newsweek* article. And he wonders if that's how all truly horrific acts come to pass: nobody can, or will, believe until it's too late. If somebody had come to him in Malibu and told him that there were sleepwalking ghosts in northern Florida who lived underground and kidnapped people, would he have believed it? Never.

Except maybe for the part of him that never stopped thinking about Anna Zikry. That part would believe it, whether he liked it or not.

He closes the book and lays it under his head like a pillow. He doesn't have enough facts yet to write this story, and even if he did, exhaustion is too near to let him get any work done tonight. He pushes his feet deeper down in the sleeping bag. This is still some-how like camping. But lonely. The house doesn't seem horrible any-more either. Just sad. And empty. He sighs. He's about to close his eyes, then thinks twice. He reaches over and grabs the poker out of the fireplace rack, making a thick "tung" sound, then closes his eyes with one hand wrapped around the wrought-iron handle. Better safe than sorry.

⊰ Chapter Twelve ⊱

THE CLATTER 'CROSS THE RAILROAD TRACKS MEANS two-thirty AM. Wakes Margie up and pisses her off every night without fail. 'Course this morning Margie hasn't even been to bed yet. Which is unusual. She normally goes to bed early, wakes up at two-thirty, closes her eyes again, and sleeps like a stone until the four-thirty freight goes by and rattles her kitties (thousands of tiny, ceramic cat figurines adorn every flat surface of her little house), then she wakes up, runs a brush through her hair, and walks the half a mile to the diner. *The plates won't wait,* she always tells herself. That's a funny little phrase she made up herself, and she's proud of it. The plates won't wait, and neither will the grouchy, old regulars like Red Delaney or the truckers passing through. Nobody has an ounce of patience anymore, or a sense of humor either. Maybe that's as it should be. Not much worth laughing about in Hudsonville these days.

In any case, when the train blazes past today, blowing its whistle as it sometimes does (just for spite, it seems to Margie), she is already dressed, sitting at her kitchen table, staring at the phone for no other reason than that it's right in front of her, hanging on the wall. Certainly, she isn't expecting it to ring. Time was when it might have, when certain truckers passing through would get an appetite for a mouthful of something besides eggs and grits, and they'd look to Margie for that. Hell, she was right good-looking in her time. Wouldn't say beautiful, nobody would say that, but she'd given her share of truckers a swell in their jeans, there was no denyin' that.

169

She looks over at the stove. Minute and a half left. She gets up and opens the oven, peers inside. Well, it's getting pretty brown, no need to keep it in longer. Might get too crisp. She pulls it out, sets it on the stove, and stares at it.

She wonders what's gotten into her, sitting up in the middle of the night like this, baking a pie of all things.

Her daddy, rest his soul, always used to say the best remedy for restlessness is hard work. Well, that's what waiting tables for twelve hours a day, six days a week amounts to, she imagines. Usually, she sleeps like the dead, wakes up as her duty calls, and nods off again the minute her head hits the pillow once her day's work is done.

But not tonight. Tonight sleep seemed to be passing her over completely.

Is it the guilt?

Did Lee's words bite her that deep?

Might be. Or might be she's just getting old. Age plays tricks on you, they say. And it's worse being a woman. Christ, first there's the bleeding along with what they call PMS, then you gotta bear the babies ('course, no babies for old Margie with her mixed-up pipes), then you get old and you get the hot flashes and all that. Now what? Insomnia?

She wants to think it's getting old to blame, but she's staring at the truth.

The pie is for Lee.

A few hours ago Margie was sittin' at the kitchen table, playin' solitaire, and she heard some sounds coming from over at Lee's place. Yellin', fighting, crashing sounds. That happened more and more these days, in the years since their son, Keith, disappeared. The absence is eroding both of their sanities, and Margie knows it better than anyone. Poor Lee. Poor Ralph. Time was, they were the happiest young couple in Hudsonville, and Margie secretly envied their good fortune. Look at them now. God sure can play some tricks.

She grabs the little apology note she scrawled for Lee and sticks it in her pocket, then picks up the pie with the oven mitts and carries it out onto the porch, still hot. She walks down the steps carefully, watching her every step. No sense wasting a perfectly good pie by tripping down the stoop.

Crickets are loud, and the dew soaks her feet as she treads through the long, unmowed grass of her yard, over toward Ralph and Lee's place. Stars peek at her through the dark spread of leaves above, haphazard specks of scattered light. Margie has crossed Lee's yard now, which is just about as unkempt as hers, and steps onto the tilted cement walkway leading up to the door. The lights are all on in the house, which is strange. Ralph has been out of work for a few months now, mostly drunk, and Lee has made do with selling her crafts over in Bristol. But Margie has never known her to be up at this hour makin' no crafts. Maybe the insomnia is catching.

She comes up the steps, one, two, three, and balances the pie in one hand, careful not to touch the still-scalding pan, (no sense in staying up all night just to burn yourself). She goes to set the pie on the little table by the door along with her note, then stops. A sound, a shuffling, and the wheezing of breath.

"Lee?"

There's no answer from inside. There's a creak of a floor for a minute, like somebody took a few steps and stopped, but that's it.

"Hey, Ralph, if you're there open up this door, I got a hot plate."

There's another shift from inside. Now Margie is getting pissed. It's not neighborly to leave somebody standing on the porch like that, not neighborly at all.

"Lee, I'm sorry about what I said. About Keith. I just . . . I just don't want no trouble. I'm too old for trouble."

No answer.

"Jumpin' Jesus," Margie mutters. "Alright, well I'm leaving this here pie on the porch, and if you decide to accept my apology, you just give me a holler."

She's trying to figure out how to take off the oven mitt so she can set the pan on it without scalding herself when she sees a shadow move inside.

Next, she sees the gun.

The screen door burst open and the gun barrel jams into her chest, so hard she thinks a rib broke. Her breath shoots out of her in a sharp rasp from shock and the impact.

The pie tumbles to the floor, a mess.

Margie tries to scream, but it comes out a mangled, sharp groan.

"Jesus Christ. Say that name. Jesus Christ." The voice is deep.

The man holding the gun steps back a step, pulling the stock in tight to his shoulder and sighting the gun with a squint. He has a huge, white, hairless gut hanging in front of him, white jowls hanging on either side of his face, and a matted mop of gray hair on his head.

"Jesus Christ, Ralph, it's me, Margie! Jesus Christ is right!" Margie says.

"Do you renounce the devil?"

"I'll renounce you if you don't get that goddamned gun out of my face. What's wrong with you?"

"Margie, I ain't playing. If you cannot say you renounce the devil, I will have no choice but to shoot you right now. Say it."

"I renounce the devil, Ralph. Jesus Christ, I renounce the devil!

Look, I just come over to give you a pie. Just let me go back home,"

"No," says Ralph. "You stay here. It ain't safe outside of this house."

"Why?" asks Margie.

"You mean, you didn't see nothing tonight?

Margie shakes her head. "Saw *Wheel of Fortune*, nothin' else. Why? What on earth is going on here? Where's Lee?"

The big man leans back against the door frame, his shotgun lowered to his side. His big belly starts jerking and gyrating, but it isn't until she hears the wet sniff that Margie knows he's crying.

"They took her," he says, the words barely audible through his tears. "Like a pack of dogs."

"Who? Lee? They took Lee? Who took her?"

The man is sobbing, now, covering his face with both hands.

"First Keith, first my boy, now my wife. Why couldn't they just take me?" He sobs for a moment, then: "I couldn't stop them. I cain't hold a job, I cain't protect my family. I ain't no kind of man."

He's weeping like a child.

"Here," he holds out the gun to her. "Shoot me."

"Ralph, no."

"Do it."

"No, Ralph. Why would I do that? Now where is Lee? Who took her?"

"Goddammit, I said shoot me!" Ralph turns the gun on Margie again.

The barrel is huge in her eyes, two holes big enough to spit cannonballs. And it enters her mind that there's a real chance he might shoot her. The thought fills her with fear, but not the kind of fear she had expected. It's not mortal, desperate terror, but more like fearful anticipation, like the moment before jumping into a cold pool. She doesn't know what to make of it. She doesn't know what to say.

"Shoot me!" Ralph says again.

Margie is looking at her feet. "I just came to bring you a pie, Ralph. It was rutabaga."

Ralph stands still for a moment, trembling, then lowers the gun.

"I'm sorry, Margie," he says, weeping again.

"It's alright," she says, dragging a breath into her reluctant (and now bruised) lungs. "Now speak a little sense if you can and tell me what happened to your wife."

"Lee went out back. I was . . . watching *Cops*, fixin' to go to bed, but she goes out into the backyard, you know how she was, with her queer ways, taking the laundry off the line at eleven o'clock at night. Who would do that? And I warned her not to, many a time, but she was never one to listen to me. And sure enough, they come out of the dark, out of the forest, and they grabbed her. I heard her screamin' too late to get my gun. All's I could do is grab my shovel off the back porch and come down swingin', but still—" and he starts weeping again. "There was too many of them. And they took her off and into the forest. I tried to follow, but some of them fought me and the rest was gone. And they took her."

"Who was it?" Margie asks. "A gang? Some kinda cult?"

"Demons," he says. He's stepped back into the light now, and Margie can see a shine creep into his eyes, an animation that she doesn't like, and she can smell the liquor on his breath.

"There ain't no such thing as demons and you know it," Margie says.

"There is," Ralph says. "Sure as you're born. Come see, if ya don't believe me. I got one locked in the shed right now and I'm fixing to burn it."

$$\rightarrow$$

Margie scrambles after Ralph Parsons through the dark. He has a gas can swinging in one hand, a lit cigarette in his mouth, and a shovel propped over his shoulder, stained black with blood. As Margie slides down the slick, grassy slope to the spot by the brook where the Parsons' old shed sits, thoughts blast through her head, livid and bright as fireworks.

Ralph's lost it.

He mighta killed Lee.

Might be fixin' to kill me.

Or demons. What if he's right, and there's really demons?

She's terrified, but follows anyway. If only she had gone to church more, she'd know the right way to handle a demon. Mrs. Scutt, her old neighbor, God rest her soul, used to say the way to fight the devil was with a cold shoulder and a righteous heart. She didn't suppose it would work like that against a pack of demons that could carry off a grown woman and fight off a big man with a shovel. 'Course, nothin' ever works out like it's supposed to, so far as she knows. She doesn't need no Bible to tell her that.

She realizes suddenly that Ralph has been talking, murmuring, half to himself:

" . . . The rest was fast, like hunting dogs, but this 'un was slower. Limping, like. After I hit it with the shovel, I drug it by the leg down here. It was knocked out, bleedin' from the head. I figure if it was a person, it'd be dead. Lost a lot of blood and all. But just before you came knockin', I heard it rattling the door from up at the house, and it was hollerin' and cursing and speakin' tongues."

The shed rises up now out of the gloom of the moonless night. Ralph brandishes an electric lamp in the shape of an old-fashioned lantern over his head, casting an eerie, halolike glow over the patch of barren, blood-speckled mud, and the door of the shed, which is made of heavy wood and padlocked shut.

"Ralph—"

"Hush, woman! If it knows we're here, it might call the others, and that's a sight you don't want to see, believe you me. Here."

He hands her the shovel.

"You stand over here." He puts a guiding hand on Margie's back and leads her over to a small, dirty window.

"This is the only way it can git out. You make sure if it busts through that window, you hit it with this shovel, and don't you quit until it stops moving. Understand?"

"Yes," says Margie, staring at the opaque window, shaking.

"Good," says Ralph. A sheen of sweat glitters on his forehead in the lamplight. He snatches up a gas can and starts unscrewing the cap. The smell of gasoline makes Margie's head reel (always has) as she watches Ralph douse the window with petrol, then work his way to the other side of the shed and disappear, jerking the gas can desperately with each splash.

Margie stares at the window, but all she can see is her own smudged reflection. Even though there's next to no light, she sees enough to know she's old, and for an instant she grieves. Even now, there's no rest. No ease, no retirement. All she had wanted was to make her neighbor a pie. Now this.

A stick cracks in the woods and she jerks her head around. A bird swoops out of a tree, probably an owl, and she gasps.

Bam.

Behind her, the shed!

She whirls back, and behind the window, she beholds the pale face of a ghost.

It bangs on the window softly, like it's knocking—which is somehow much more terrible than if it had slammed against the glass like a monster. It seems to be . . . pleading.

Margie takes a few steps back, holding the shovel in front of her like a spear.

And the face disappears.

Suddenly, the door starts rattling fiercely. It shakes so hard she thinks the shed might come off its foundation.

"Ralph!" she calls.

"It's awake!" he says, rushing around the corner of the shed to join her. The door is still shaking.

"Jesus, sweet Lord, save us!" he says. "Lemme get my matches."

He pats all his pockets. "Shit, I think I dropped them around the other side. Watch the window."

"Ralph . . . " she says, but it's too late; he's already disappeared again.

She grips the hard, gritty handle of the shovel tighter. *I can do this,* she tells herself. *I been fighting all my life.*

The face is back. Something is going around and around on the glass, probably the thing's hand, wiping off the window. She hears its voice, whining, shrill, like a sick child calling for its mother, and it makes her shiver. She can't make out what the voice is saying, and she's glad.

Its face. She sees it clearly now that the glass is wiped mostly clean. Big, dark eyes, pale skin framed in long, black hair. Its lips are working fast, and now that she can see them, she can no longer deny what her ears had heard all along. It's calling her name.

"Margie! Margie, it's me!"

"Found 'em," Ralph calls from the other side of the shed. "You watch that window!" And the next time Margie blinks, she sees flames creeping over the roof of the building, wrapping around the walls in a morbid embrace.

A muffled scream vibrates the glass of the window, as the demon-girl realizes her prison is about to burn.

And she screams.

And she screams.

Margie stands frozen, gripping the shovel handle, eyes stinging from the smoke.

Margie!

Ralph appears again, hurrying around the side of the shed, one eye on the flames and one on Margie.

" . . . This fire is Jesus," he declares, and she thinks he might have been talking the whole time, she just couldn't hear him. "This fire is justice."

He stops, stands next to Margie, his hands on his hips.

It's me!

"Jist look at it suffer," he says. "Damn, it's a beautiful sight."

And a window pane shatters, and a pale hand bursts through in a shower of glass. It's a small hand, not a demon's claw at all. The face reappears at the window.

The fire has crept up the walls, now, and dances, hissing, atop the roof. The wood screeches and pops.

The voice is clear: "Margie, help! It's me!"

And the face at the window isn't a demon at all; it's a person. It's a girl.

"It's me, from the diner! It's me, Christine!"

The realization fills Margie with horror.

"Ralph, we have to let her out," Margie cries.

"Never on your life—that there's a demon."

"It's the Zikry girl!" says Margie. "I know her! Open the door! Let her out!"

"MARGIE! PLEASE!"

"They take forms, don't ye be deceived!" he says, his eyes shining in the firelight. "That there's a demon, and that there demon's gonna die."

The heat is coming at Margie in waves.

Screams from inside.

"Margie! Help me! Margie! Mr. Parsons! I'm burning!"

The white hands are pounding through the glass, sending sparkling shards into the mud, but they can't break through the wood muntin bars that hold the glass in place.

"Let her out!" says Margie. "Now!"

Ralph wheels and faces her, and she realizes just how big he is: over six feet tall and very heavy.

"It's gonna burn," he says. "Now you give me that shovel."

Margie looks down. There's the shovel, forgotten in her trembling hands, still held in a defensive position, except now the demon it's holding at bay is Ralph Parsons.

He takes a quick step forward, grabbing at the shovel. Margie brings it back, out of his reach, then snaps it forward again with all the force her wiry little body can muster.

A dull ringing sound hangs in the air for an instant, and the shovel is still vibrating in Margie's hands when Ralph collapses face-first into the mud. She jumps over him as he falls.

"Look out, Christine," she yells. "I'm breaking you out!"

There's no sound from inside. The girl is dead, but Margie swings the shovel anyway, not to free the demon locked in the shed, but to vent her rage. Another Hudsonville child lost. How many can they forget?

The shovel splinters the window frame, and she jerks it back and forth, leaving a clean opening.

Margie almost screams, drops the shovel and slips in the mud when the girl, the demon, springs half out of the window frame. Her upper torso extends out of the window, but her legs are still inside.

"Help me, Margie!" she screams, and Margie does. She takes the girl's hands, pulls as hard as she can, and the next thing she knows they're lying in the mud together, watching the flames lash the night sky, watching the smoke writhe upward through the treetops.

She hears a trembling breath, looks over and sees the girl, the demon, is crying. Her face is streaked with dirt and soot. Grimy strings of hair hang in her face.

"It's okay," Margie says, and she pulls the Zikry girl close, feeling her frail frame shudder as she cries. Why, she can hardly weigh ninety pounds! How could Ralph Parsons have ever been scared of her? Then she thinks of his words: *they take forms; don't ye be deceived.*

She looks at Christine again, closer, but still all she sees is a scared little girl. She relaxes a little.

"It's okay, honey," she says. "You alright? You hurt?"

"I think . . ." the Zikry girl says. " . . . I think I got burned some, but I'm okay. And I cut my hands . . . on the glass."

Margie looks under what's left of what could only be a singed, tattered nightgown, and sees that there are some burns beginning to blister on the girl's already scarred legs.

"Yeah, you're burned alright," she says, "but nothing some salve and a few days of cold baths won't fix, I think."

The girl sniffs, puts her hair back behind her ears, and pulls herself up and into a ball.

Margie is reaching for the shovel.

"Now, Christine Zikry, I'm going to ask you a question, and you tell me the truth," Margie says. "What are you doing out here tonight?"

The girl wipes some snot off her nose and looks at Margie with big, dark eyes.

"I'm not here, Margie. I wish I was, but I'm not. I'm just dreaming."

Margie holds the girl's gaze and shivers. Her groping hand finds the shovel, and she grasps it and stands up slowly, backing away.

"I think we'd better have the sheriff decide whether you're awake or not, Christine, and whether or not you and your friends did something with Mrs. Parsons."

"What do you mean?" the girl asks, a perfect picture of innocence.

Margie keeps the shovel between them.

"Why are you holding the shovel like that?" the girl asks. "Are you scared of me?"

Margie is deciding how to answer when something distracts her. A stain seeps across the mud toward them, red and thick.

"Oh, Jesus Christ," says Margie, and she rushes over.

But there's nothing she can do.

Ralph Parsons is already dead.

The fire has burned almost to coals. It paints the room red and draws shadows thickly across the walls. Caleb Mason doesn't know what he was just dreaming, but he knows he's now wide awake. He sits up, looking wide-eyed around the still life surrounding him. Nothing has changed. Something has changed. There's no sound. There is something . . .

He stands up, fire poker in hand. He sticks his feet in his running shoes and slowly crosses the living room to the foyer, slowly mounts the staircase, slowly walks up the steps, down the hall, into his father's bedroom, up into the attic. The upstairs is dark as the deep sea at night, but he knows there will be a light on in the attic. And there is.

He walks among the rafters, step after step, into the little room where one clock ticks and seventeen are silent.

15. My father believed if you stand in a room with
    sixteen ticking clocks for one hour every day,
    the spirits will come.   O   O   O

Caleb Mason stands staring at the ticking clock. It says three forty-two, but he has no idea if it's accurate or not. Somehow, he thinks it is. He glances down, and sees a corner of the insulation is loose next to his right foot. He kneels and pulls it back. There are dusty lath boards beneath it, and sitting upon them is a very, very old key.

One by one, Caleb winds each of the clocks.

Maybe the answer to the Dream Center director's question is: *Agree.*

As Caleb kneels on the dusty particleboard floor, the dissonance of mistimed "ticks" washes over him, then seems to intensify. His arm hurts worse than ever, suddenly throbs so hard he feels nauseated and throws up on the insulation to his left. He wipes his mouth. The ticking is worse than he had imagined. His mind can't follow all the ticks at once, and the feeling is very uncomfortable, almost maddening. A torture. Suddenly he wants to smash all the clocks. He's still clutching the fire poker, after all. He doesn't care if these clocks are antiques or hand-carved—which they look like they are. He doesn't care if they belonged to his father, and his father is now dead.

17. My father was mad.   ○   ○   ○

No, that's impossible, because Dad was an attorney. Dad was respected, successful, rich, and . . . had sixteen clocks in his attic.

And when you listen to the ticking of sixteen clocks at once, it makes you . . . makes us a little . . . really makes you feel—

18. I am mad.   ○   ○   ○

He has to smash the clocks now, before they eat away at him anymore. The ticks tickle his brain, like sixteen ants running on his scalp, like sixteen mosquitoes buzzing in his ears, sixteen, sixteen— he closes his eyes and sees Anna Zikry lifted into darkness, that silent movie loop that plays over and over again, but he covers his ears, tries to keep the sound away, and has a horrible thought:

15. My father believed if you stand in a room with
    sixteen ticking clocks for one hour every day,
    the spirits will come.   ○   ○   ○

And he closes his eyes. And they do.

Caleb's eyes are wide, and he sits up. The fire is nothing but a few specks of red in a bed of ash, but there's still no hint of the sun. Without warning, the house shudders and Caleb gasps, only to realize an instant later that it's only the sound of thunder. Outside, the wind has picked up. He looks around, remembering everything: ascending the stairs, finding the key, winding the clocks—that horrible ticking. But he doesn't remember coming back downstairs. And he doesn't remember going back to sleep.

So was it a dream? No. Definitely not. As he looks around now, everything is the same but not the same. The windows are still closed, the furniture is still dusty, the—and then he sees it—the fire poker is back in the rack. And in his hand, instead, is his pen. He looks behind him, remembering that he had used his book as a pillow. It's not there. It's gone. It's not gone. It's on the coffee table, open. And he kicks out of his sleeping bag, crawls over and looks at the book, afraid to see, desperate to see if *<the spirits will come>*, if there's something there to read—but there's nothing, nothing but his own writing from earlier, his own lame attempt to make sense of this chaotic, unexplainable shit, only his own crappy handwriting saying:

~~Children of Hudsonville, Florida, are missing.~~

Below it:

Deep in the woods, in the small town of Hudsonville, Florida, something horrible is happening: people are disappearing. The police, those assigned with investigating the disappearance of these people, are interested in nothing but amamamamamamamamamamamamamamamamamamamama mamamamamamamamamamamamamamamamamamamamama mam-------------------------amamamamamamamamamamamama mamam

Caleb holds his breath. His mind churns desperately. What is this? He didn't write this. Did he?

Mama?

Amam?

Ama. Anna? Maybe. Or . . . or AM?

Like Christine said. Five thirty-five AM? He scrambles to his watch. It's only a few minutes after four. And upstairs, with the clocks, it had been only three-something AM, not five thirty-five. And in the tunnel, when the things had come for Bean, it was late, but not that late, not—

Lightning bleaches everything a frigid white and cracks with a dry fury that rattles the china in its cabinet and makes Caleb jump in spite of himself. And it must've caused a power surge, too, because the TV bursts on in the other room, and the foyer light snaps to life. In a panic, Caleb jumps over an armchair into the other room and shuts the TV off in the middle of some commercial for the Mega Juice Machine, then shuts off the foyer light, too. He doesn't know why a simple electrical surge should bother him so much, but it does.

Then he comes back into the family room and hears it. He turns.

There's a big, old wood-encased radio—his great-grandfather's from the 1930s. He stares at it. It hisses. The realization is there already, but he's afraid of it. Part of him, most of him, wants to find the power switch, to yank the plug from the wall, to kick the speaker in and end the scream of white noise. But when he steps up to the radio, instead of smashing it, his hand reaches for the dial and turns it slowly, slowly through crackles, past blaring oldies and bleating country ballads, past angry political rants and through a blizzard of hissing, toward five thirty-five on the AM dial.

The thunder rumbles low now, like far-off drums of war.

Caleb turns the dial very, very slowly. It's at five thirty-five exactly now. And he's so relieved to hear nothing but electric mumble of static that he almost cries.

With a sighed laugh, he looks for the cord to unplug it, and as he does he leans close to the speaker.

<BiLly>

He freezes. Did he hear it, really? That whisper? Or was it just part of the . . . the sound of nothing? His muscles cramp with tension as he listens. The next sound to distinguish itself is high and pinched. It's the voice of a little girl.

<buRn it>

Caleb hears. He can't deny he hears it.

"Who are you?"

<you watched me>

The voice falls back into the hissing sea.

"I can't hear you," Caleb says.

<you watched me go . . . >

There's a long break.

<into the dark>

"Anna . . . is that you?"

Something garbled comes back then:

< . . . dared me . . . into the asylum . . . BuRn it>

Tears are coming down Caleb's face now, but he doesn't know it. He's leaning heavily on his broken wrist, but he doesn't feel it.

Thunder cracks again. The house creaks with the wind's force.

"Anna, I'm so sorry," Caleb says. "What do you want me to do? I'll do anything."

<my sister . . . margie's . . . tRouble>

The voice keeps wavering in and out between coherence and distortion.

< needs yOuR . . . >

The little voice fades into something else, like when you're driving on a road trip and a new station starts coming in over the old one. This station is filled with horrible voices, chanting in harsh, inhuman tongues. Screams pierce through every few moments.

The voice of a man rises out of the cacophony, deep and distorted.

<we are . . . WAiTinG>

A chorus of a thousand screams rises out of the radio, so loud Caleb thinks the speaker or his ears will burst. Screams are all around him, so sharp they could tear him to shreds. He can almost feel the stale breath, gushing in agony from invisible lungs. The storm has changed too, somehow. Even the wind through the trees issues a scream. Without warning, a couple of windows by the fireplace shatter, showering Caleb with glass and blowing leaves from outside. The wind is cold as hell.

<we watch you> a female voice says. <always>

There's a rush of white noise. Caleb is huddled on the floor.

Then it's Anna again:

<help Christine . . . Margie . . . before you do it . . . you make it . . . the eNd of the world>

Thunder growls again. Only the static speaks now, and it says nothing.

Caleb doesn't move for a long time. Rain is blowing in from the jagged glass holes where the windows used to be, drenching his shirt, lashing his face, but still he doesn't move.

When he finally shuts the radio off, he doesn't feel the tears on his cheeks or the blood running down his head from the rain of broken glass. He grabs the poker by the fireplace and bolts out the door. He jumps down from the front porch and strides out to his car as the storm tears loose with huge drops of cold, stinging rain.

Caleb turns the key, slams the gas, and speeds into the mouth of the maelstrom.

⊰ Chapter Thirteen ⊱

FOUR AND TWENTY BLACK BIRDS, baked in a pie . . .

As Christine Zikry sits in the backseat of Margie's old station wagon, staring at the wash of gray behind the window, the nursery-rhyme line sizzles across her mind over and over, sometimes as a chant, sometimes as a song, a strange melody ascending the chromatic scale. She knows about music; she knows about scales. She wanted to be a singer once, in another life.

But that isn't really her anymore, is it? The girl who won blue ribbons the last two years in the solo and ensemble choir competition has passed away. The one who thought about fashion, kittens, college, the future—she fell off the bleachers at a high-school dance, never to be heard from again. This new girl remembers the former Christine with a mixture of emotions: pity, envy, contempt. Baked in a pie.

Someone new has emerged. This new Christine might be stronger, or she might already be too broken to survive. The new Christine has known greater horrors than losing a sister and watching a mother go mad.

This Christine lives in fear of something stealing her soul while she sleeps. This Christine knows the deafening silence of the House of White Rooms.

The truth is all she wants is to be safe, normal—maybe even happy. But this Christine knows better than to hope for that. She has seen far too much.

The wiper blades screech through her thoughts. Margie is talking again; or maybe she was talking the whole time.

"I want you to tell the deputy everything. I ain't ashamed of anything I did. But it's for Sheriff Johnson to decide, you hear? I have no fear of justice. A man dies, a man dies. There's no denying it. And you'll tell the sheriff what happened to Lee, too, won't you? Won't you?"

Christine thinks Margie must be crying, but she lacks the strength or the will to turn her head, look over, and make sure. For a moment, she thinks of sitting up, grabbing Margie by the shoulders and shaking her until she finally shuts up. Who cares if they crash into a tree? Who cares if they die? Right now, hell seems like a great vacation spot. Anywhere but here would be just fantastic. She can't take the chatter, the prattling. The voices. Margie is still talking:

"What happened to Lee, Christine? Don't think I won't tell your mammy that you had something to do with whatever happened to her. You teenagers don't respect nothin', I know that, but everybody in this county is a little bit afraid of your mammy, and I bet you are too, aren't you? Aren't you?"

"Four and twenty blackbirds, baked in a pie," says Christine. For some reason, it seems like the proper response to her, and she smiles to herself.

"I don't know whether you're mocking me or trying to enchant me with some black-magic voodoo your witch momma taught you, but it ain't gonna work on me, or on the sheriff neither."

Christine sits up so fast that Margie gasps and the wheel jerks. The station wagon fishtails, and Margie barely gets it back in control.

"Turn the radio," she says. "Turn it, turn it, turn it."

"Dammit, girl," says Margie. "You almost killed us! Sit back. Dwight Yoakam is good enough."

But Christine leans over the front seat.

Margie tries to push her back with an elbow, then gives up. Better to let this devil child fuss with the radio than have her sitting there cookin' up ways to get away. She's already manipulated Margie into killing poor Ralph. Margie knows she'll have the shadow of murder hanging over her soul for the rest of her life. And for what good? To save the life of this sarcastic little witch girl? For that, Margie will have to explain to her Maker the stain of blood on her hands.

The girl is pressing buttons. She switches the radio to AM, now she's turning the tuning dial, filling the car with blasting, flickering static. She stops on a nonstation, just some screeching and hissing. Margie bites her tongue. She's always been taught to pity the mad, and that's clearly what this girl is, but this—this is just too much. Margie's nerves are fried as it is.

"Christine," Margie says, "there's only two AM stations that come in around these parts, and this ain't—"

Either one is what she was going to say, but Christine reaches over and clamps a hand over her mouth. The touch makes Margie shiver, for Christine's hands are cold as a corpse's, but she makes no move to shy away or make a sound. She can feel the strength in the hand on her face, and knows she's no match for it. She glances at the girl out of the corner of her eye. Long strands of dark hair are plastered to her face. Her eyes are lit up by a streetlight. They're dark blue and look vibrant despite the rough shape their owner is clearly in. The Zikry girl's head is cocked, as if she's listening hard to something. Only there's nothing to hear but static.

"Turn the car around," says Christine suddenly. *"Turn the car around!* TURN THE CAR AROUND!"

Margie presses the brakes hard, bringing her car to a skittering, sliding stop on the side of the road so sharply that both passengers have to grab on to something to keep from catapulting into the windshield.

The car is stopped, and Margie's heart is racing.

"Margie, please, turn it around. I can't go to the sheriff."

"Why?" asks Margie. "We have to."

"Didn't you listen?" says Christine. "He's one of them."

Margie stares at the girl. She's terrified. "Listen to who?" she asks.

"Anna. That was Anna."

"What was her? When?"

"Just then. That was her, in the radio."

"You're in need of medicine, child. For your head." Margie's voice is filled with almost as much pity as fear. "I ain't heard talk like that since . . ."

The girl is looking over her shoulder now.

" . . . since the asylum shut its doors all those years ago and put all those crazy folks back on the street."

"He's coming," Christine says, still staring through the back window into the dark of the storm, "and he isn't alone. We have to go."

"You're scaring me, Christine. We're friends, right? Remember, I served you a piece of cake on every birthday you ever had—and I remember every one too."

"We have to go, Margie. We have to."

"Okay, honey. We'll go. I just want you to remember I'm your friend. I don't want you to forget that. I just want to help you. I just—"

Margie stops. She sees something in the rearview mirror. She thought she imagined it at first, but as she squints through the raindrops, the flashes of red become clearer. And she thanks God over and over. It's the sheriff.

Christine sees it too.

"Go, Margie! You have to go! They'll take me back!"

The police car comes to rest behind Margie's car with a little burp of the siren. Christine is getting frantic.

"Go, go, go, go, go!"

"Sheriff! Thank God!" Margie yells out the window. "Help!" She looks in the water-dappled side mirror, and in its distorted face she sees the sheriff get out and begin walking toward her. She doesn't notice the other three smaller figures that get out of the squad car too.

"Margie, please, please *go!*" Christine begs. Tears are running down the girl's cheeks now, but Margie ignores her. All she wants is for this girl, this daughter of a witch, to be safely locked away. She just wants to go back to the diner and clock in for work, to go home and fix dinner and watch TV and go to sleep. She just wants it all to be over.

"Sheriff," Margie calls out the window, "come quick."

"They're coming to take us into the dark," says Christine. She sees them coming, but realizes that for Margie their figures must be drowned out by the glare of the squad car's spotlight, which is trained on her rearview mirror. In a flurry of motion, Christine bounces from one side of the car to the other, locking all the doors.

"Keep them locked," she says. "Roll the window up!"

"It's just the sheriff," Margie says, trying to sound comforting, but only sounding afraid.

The sheriff's figure is coming close now through the blinding glare of the spotlight, moving with slow, crunching steps over the gravel shoulder and up to Margie's window.

"Don't open it," Christine whispers. "They're with him."

Just as she speaks, the sheriff is passing the back window, and he ducks his head down and looks in, blasting Christine's eyes with his flashlight. She blinks and squints, but doesn't dare take her eyes off him. She catches him leering at her as he stands up and approaches Margie's door.

"Margie, don't open it, Margie!"

Christine stares out the back window, watching the figures move slowly, two on one side and one on the other, toward the car. They are only white streaks in the rain-distorted world outside her windows, but she knows who they are. She has seen their kind in the dreams she never remembers. In those dreams, something tells her, they always appear in her mirror.

Because they're me, she thinks, *or I was one of them.*

And I could never see them. Because . . . Because . . .

Because my eyes were closed.

"Margie, don't open the door! Don't!"

The white shapes are close, passing the back of the station wagon. Surely, Margie must see them now.

"Don't open the door!"

"What seems to be the matter, Margie?" the sheriff asks.

"Margie . . . " says Christine, "don't! DON'T!"

And Margie unlocks the car door, opens it, and gets out.

Through the rain-soaked glass, Christine watches in horror as the figures from her forgotten nightmares lurch toward the open door. Quick as a cat, she leaps over the driver's seat, yanks the door shut and pounds the lock down with her fist. She backs away from the door, into the passenger's seat, and curls herself up into a little defensive ball. Her mind reels. She's surrounded.

The sheriff bends down and looks in at her, with the same leering grin as before, then his face disappears, and Christine watches Margie's torso as she gestures to him emphatically. Trying to tell the sheriff what's going on, of course. As if he doesn't already know.

Christine looks to the back of the station wagon and is relieved to find the white figures are gone.

Maybe they left, she tells herself, maybe they . . . *woke up?* For some reason that sounds right.

She watches the sheriff's torso ushering Margie's torso back toward the squad car before they disappear in both the downpour and the glare.

This is it, her chance. She pushes herself into the driver's seat, wincing as she brushes her burned legs on the car seat. She puts one dirty bare foot on the brake, one dirty, pale hand on the wheel, and reaches for the key to start the car, to make her escape, to leave this damned town and run and run and be happy—but instead of a key, she finds nothing. Because Margie took the keys with her.

How many times can luck leave one girl orphaned?

Suddenly the police car's floodlight and headlights go dead, leaving only the eerie red blink of the light bar and the darkness. Rain hammers on the roof of the car. This is the end. Unless . . . and Christine turns on the radio . . . unless Anna has some advice—of course, the radio won't work without the keys.

Only somehow it does.

A shush of static fills the car, but instead of little Anna's voice there are other voices, thousands of them, tormented, mad voices, screaming words of venom in languages Christine doesn't understand, and doesn't want to. The screams and shouts rise and rise. She tries to cover her ears, but the sound bores through her hands, through her flesh, into the core of her brain. Screams rupture her mind, ripping her ears from all sides. From the air all around her, from the car seats, from the glass of the windows, from her own goose-bumped flesh, from every strand of her hair, death-screams sing and slice her will into a thousand pieces.

And then it all stops, and only one thought remains. It might be whispered to her from the radio, or it might be coming from her own mind, but either way it is a horrible realization, and it means the end of her:

The cargo door in the back of the station wagon is unlocked.

And in that instant, certainty settles into her heart: there will not be time to climb back and lock it.

She looks back and sees two white shapes blinking with bursts of red, blurred by rain, standing at the back window. And the tailgate opens.

They're climbing over the backseat with impossible speed. Their eyes are closed, but they see Christine Zikry all too well. Their pale hands claw her face already as she fumbles desperately with the door handle.

The sound of her own gasping and wails of terror are eclipsed in an instant by dissonant laughter from the radio, which swells to an eerie blast, loud enough to make the windshield quiver. One sleep-walker has her by the hair now and is climbing over the seat; the other is two inches from her face, teeth bared in a snarl, ready to bite her cheek off like a starving dog. That, she'll remember later, is when the white light comes back and her hand finds the door handle.

The next instant, she's out in the night, drenched, growling in pain as she yanks her hair free from the hand of the thing in the car. She slams the door, hoping it will buy her a second or two.

As she turns to run, though, her heart plummets in despair.

There were three of them. Two are in the car. One is here.

And now it's upon her. Her body seizes up with pain as the thing, the sleeping thing, slams her back into the car door. For a second she thinks it snapped her spine, the pain is so debilitating, but she's still on her feet, still fighting, holding its clawing hands back, ducking away from its chomping, gnawing teeth (this thing is a fourteen-year-old boy, she realizes, nothing more. Just a boy. And he's *asleep*—but he's also a monster).

Its teeth are closing on her face now; she feels the tips pushing into her skin, and she knows in another instant it will be chewing her nose in its jaws, but the horrible laughing from the radio is a little quieter since she slammed the door, and the white light—must be the floodlight back on—is blazing again, and that's a better way to die.

The light grows.

The gnawing teeth are on her face and they hurt, but they can't puncture the skin yet because of the slickness of the rain or because of amazing luck, she doesn't know which. But the biting doesn't stop, and she knows it will never stop until she's in many pieces.

And the light grows, then roars—*thud!*—and rushes past.

Christine Zikry is on her knees in the mud. No pale creature is attacking her anymore because he's lying twenty feet away in a reddening mud puddle, his limbs all bent the wrong way.

She feels very dizzy as she sees this, and realizes it's because she's been holding her breath a very long time. Still, she can't breathe in; her lungs are frozen with fear.

She hears something, but her brain can't register the sound, *pop-pop-pop.*

The side-mirror just above her head leaps off the car and skitters across the muddy shoulder. She stares at it, dazed.

"Come on!" someone yells. "Get in!"

A car idles in front of her with the passenger door open. It must've struck the demon—the boy—who now lies dying.

"GET IN!" shouts a voice—seemingly issuing from the taillight Christine is staring at.

She's about to get up when the popping comes again, but this time it sounds sharper, louder, more frightening.

And suddenly she gets it. The sheriff is shooting at her. And she's in shock.

She tries to stand, not knowing if it will be possible, not knowing if she's hurt beyond repair, maybe broken like the kid, the sleeping demon, but she finds that she can stand. And when she tries to run, she finds that her legs work fine.

As her feet slap through the mud, she experiences everything very clearly, hears the station wagon door open behind her and hears the two pale things get out to chase her, feels the rush of air as a gunshot whistles past her cheek, sees the demon again, somehow horribly just a dead kid now, lying in a pool of streetlight and summer rain. Then she's in the car. The door is shut, the rain is gone, and the sound of an engine roars her away.

She still isn't breathing when she looks over to see who's driving the car, because it might be one of them, or (and this is what she really expects, what she fears the most) it might be the director, ready to take her back to the white, white room.

When she sees who it is, she still can't breathe.

"Are you okay?" the voice says, deep with concern.

She can only nod. Breath can come later.

For now, her Billy is enough.

⊰ Chapter Fourteen ⊱

FOR A WHILE THEY RIDE TOGETHER without saying a word, letting the engine and the thunder do all the talking. Caleb, Billy, concentrates on holding the car on the road through the slippery, wet corners while keeping the flashing red lights of the sheriff's cruiser as distant as possible.

Christine concentrates on Billy. She watches his face—very serious and very handsome—in the periodic ruby blink that reflects in the rearview mirror. After a while, she breaks the silence:

"How did you find me?"

Caleb is distracted, fighting a wind gust to keep the car on the road; then he answers. "Uh . . . Anna," he says. "Five thirty-five AM."

Christine smiles. "I knew you'd listen. I knew you wouldn't leave. Somebody had to believe I wasn't crazy. I'm glad it was you."

"What's going on at the Dream Center?" Caleb asks.

"I don't want to talk about it."

"You have to talk about it if we're going to help everyone else there. We have to let the world know what's happening."

She's looking over her shoulder out the back window.

"I think they're gaining on us."

"Put your seatbelt on," says Caleb.

Christine smiles again, then pulls the belt over herself and clicks it in place.

"How did you get out?" Caleb asks, and Christine tells him the story of going to sleep in the Dream Center and waking up in Ralph and Lee's shed with blood crusted all over her head and a five-alarm headache.

She tells him how Ralph kept saying she was a demon, how he tried to burn her alive, and how Margie had tried to stop him and killed him with a shovel.

"Wow," Caleb says.

"Yeah," she says. "Ralph was always nice guy too. Except for the whole 'trying to burn me alive' thing."

Rain is pounding on the windshield, and even with the wipers going full tilt and Caleb leaning forward as far as he can, he can still only barely make out the yellow line in the center of the road.

"This is bad," he says.

She looks back. "They're closer."

The rain speaks in its mumbling, liquid language and the digital clock on the dash switches numbers.

"So what made you come back, all the way from California?" Christine asks.

"Your letter," says Caleb. "I just graduated. I was going to go to Africa. Your letter made me come here instead."

"What letter?"

"The letter you sent me, saying you were in the Dream Center and needed help."

He looks at her. Her face is puzzled.

"Here," he says, and he pulls out the letter.

She stares at it.

"I didn't write this."

"What?"

"I didn't write it. I mean, I wrote letters to you all the time, but I never sent them. I never had your address. This is definitely something

I would have written, though. It even looks like my writing."

"Maybe you wrote it and don't remember."

"They didn't let me have pens."

"Why would somebody else send it?"

"Maybe, whoever it was . . . I don't know . . . maybe they wanted you to come."

This sinks in, but neither of them speaks.

She glances over her shoulder.

"They're a little farther back now."

They sit in silence for a moment.

"So why Africa?" asks Christine.

"I write. I want to be a journalist. I wanted to bring attention to the humanitarian crisis in Sudan, for one thing, but mainly I was going to write about the AIDS epidemic. Orphaned kids. There's a whole generation of children over there growing up without parents."

She smiles.

"What?" says Caleb.

"That's very noble of you," she says. "I hope somebody does something about it."

Caleb digests this for a moment.

"Of course they will. Once people really understand what's going on over there, the government will send more aid and medicine, and more international workers will come to educate the population about safe sex."

"Then you'll make a difference," she says. It's a tone that, to Caleb, seems patronizing.

"People will take action," he says, miffed. "What's going on is horrifying."

"People like to be horrified," Christine says, as the wipers screech across the windshield.

Caleb opens his mouth to say something, then shuts it and decides not to push the subject anymore.

"Caleb, STOP!"

He had been looking at her, and when he looks ahead again, he sees flashing red and blue lights up ahead. Two cop cars are parked lengthwise across the road, a roadblock. He slams on the brakes.

They both brace themselves against the doors, and Christine grabs the front of Caleb's T-shirt into a ball with her fist.

First they fishtail left, then right, then they overcorrect and begin spinning out of control. The flashing lights get closer and closer, racing past like a strobe on each rotation.

Now: the impact, a terrible sound of ripping metal.

Caleb grits his teeth.

And they stop. They've knocked the two squad cars onto the shoulder like bowling pins. The sheriff's car comes sliding in behind and skids to a halt just a few feet short of their bumper.

Caleb sits, stunned, staring at the rain in the headlights of one of the wrecked squad cars, but Christine is working, frantically turning the knobs of the radio.

"What do we do, Anna? What do we do?"

Static fills the car, and Anna's little voice comes through, wavering.

<Stay ill . . . play dead . . . run . . . the river . . . then look . . . hallway great>

"Play dead!" whispers Christine, and Caleb nods.

Through the dazzle of headlights, he sees the silhouette of a cop approaching Christine's window.

The cop knocks on the window with the barrel of his drawn gun.

He leans down and stares at Christine for a second (she sits completely still), then he straightens up and turns back to somebody and says:

"Hey, Merv. I think this one's cooked."

Caleb barely hears: "What's the other one look like?"

He takes that as his cue. He stares at the dashboard, staying very still, fighting not to blink even as the Maglite's blaze burns into his retinas. Finally, the light turns away, and he hears the cop call:

"Yep, we got a coupla fried eggs. Too bad," he laughs.

Caleb hears the other voice:

"Check the sheriff's car, make sure he's alright."

Caleb hears screaming. It's a woman.

Careful to move only his eyes, he looks in his side mirror and sees Margie fighting with the sheriff, then gesturing to the approaching cop.

He can barely make out the words: "Tried to kill her . . . just a girl . . ." over the sound of the rain.

Caleb hears the sound of footsteps on the pavement and looks forward. He sees the other cop approaching Christine's window and plays dead again. This time the flashlight scalds his eyes for so long, he's sure he'll blink. He has to blink, but the instant before he *does* blink the flashlight turns mercifully away. The new cop at the window calls:

"Hey, did you even check the pulse of these perps?"

But just then more screams pierce the rain, and in the side mirror Caleb sees Margie. She's running away up the center of the road. The sheriff and the first cop are chasing after her—and having some trouble on the slick pavement.

"Jesus Kee-rist," says the cop at the window, and he sticks his flashlight in his belt and jogs up the road after his comrades.

Maybe twenty seconds pass, and all is still—so still, in fact, that Caleb's afraid Christine might have gotten hurt after all and passed out. Paralyzing ice seeps into his heart at the thought that she might actually be dead.

But just then she jerks to life. She shoves her door open, hisses, "Come on!" and sprints toward the shoulder of the road.

Caleb lettered in track three years in a row, and it's all he can do to keep up.

She's not as weak as she looks, he thinks, and the thought gives him comfort—because although he still doesn't know what they're up against exactly, he knows they'll need a lot more strength than he has on his own.

He watches her break into the woods ahead of him like a tailback through a defensive line. She doesn't slow as the branches gouge her skin and break against her rush. She doesn't slow as her bare feet pound over slick, sharp rocks and roots. And to Caleb's great alarm, she doesn't slow as she reaches the steep, almost sheer slope leading thirty feet down to the river below. Instead, she jumps, lands, slides, then jumps again and again until a final landing—*ploosh*—puts her knee-deep in a racing stream.

Caleb almost loses it twice trying to follow her. Once he slips and descends on his ass for a few feet, then he almost twists his ankle when a rock rolls out from under him.

One more jump and he lands next to Christine, grimacing at the sickly feeling as his running shoes fill with water, their soles oozing slowly into the mud of the riverbed.

"Come on!" Christine whispers.

She grabs Caleb's wrist and leads him under the bridge, into the deep shadows. Fifty feet away the shadow of the bridge ends and the river runs away in the blue of the moonlight, but here he can see nothing. There could be an army of sleepwalkers right next to him and he'd never know until it was too late.

But again, Christine does not slow. She pulls Caleb behind her at a relentless pace, weaving around what he can only guess must be rocks with perfect grace and precision. How can she see so well? Are her eyes that adjusted to the dark? Did they deprive her of light in that place, that asylum?

She leads on. They're only a few feet from the end of the dark, from the place where they'll step into the moonlight and out from under the bridge, when a flashlight beam slices down from above, cutting through the gloom just a few feet ahead of them. They both pull up short.

Two voices drift down from above.

" . . . see anything?"

"I can see enough to know they didn't jump down into that gully. Prob'ly they took to the woods."

"We could get the dogs."

"I don't know. Sheriff said the girl was from the Dream Center. That means no shoes, unless she got some someplace, and no shoes means no woods."

"She still coulda gone in the woods without shoes."

"Yeah, and she'd a poked her foot on a stick or gotten a sand burr and we'da heard her boo-hooin' by now."

Under the bridge, Christine frowns and wrinkles her nose at this assessment of her character.

Caleb smiles at her.

"Where'd they go then?" the voices continue. "Maybe they took off down the street?"

A new voice enters the conversation now, this one deeper. Caleb thinks this is the sheriff, but he can't be sure:

"They're under this here bridge."

It's a statement of dead certainty. Caleb's heart sinks.

"I dunno . . . "

"That's right, ya don't," says the sheriff, "but I do."

"Maybe we should call and ask *him*."

The voices are silent for a minute. Caleb and Christine look at each other. Even though the night is warm, she's shivering. Caleb puts his arms around her and pulls her to him. She keeps shivering, however, as the voices resume.

"He doesn't much like to be disturbed."

"He won't like that we lost them either."

"Yer right there."

"Shut up now and let me think," the deep voice says.

A moment passes, then one of the other voices says: "Look at those rocks down there. No way they'd have jumped. That's a sure way to bust an ankle."

"Shut up," the deep voice repeats. The other two comply.

Caleb is getting antsy. Panic grips him. If they don't get out soon, they might not get out at all. The certainty of that thought almost knocks the wind out of him. He looks at Christine. She nods. She knows it too.

From above, there are voices too quiet to be heard, then:

"Shine your light on that side. You shine yours under there. They come out either side, you shoot. Got it?"

Grumbles of reply, and a ray of light reappears just in front of Caleb and Christine along with a twin at the far end of the bridge's shadow.

They look at each other, and Christine's eyes say:

This isn't good. What do we do?

There's a scrambling sound at the far side of the bridge, and suddenly it's too late to make a plan, too late to escape.

First one sleepwalker leaps down to the riverbed from above, landing as gracefully as a puma. Another follows, then another. They walk abreast, slowly. Because there's no hurry. If Caleb and Christine step out from under the bridge, they'll be shot. If not, the sleepwalkers will have them.

"Caleb . . . " whispers Christine.

"I'm thinking."

What do we do . . . ? Maybe the cops aren't great shots, he thinks. *Maybe we make a break for it.*

The deep voice from above comes booming:

"I'm three-time national shooting champion with the .38 revolver, kids, just in case yer wondering."

As if Caleb had spoken aloud.

The sleepwalkers come.

Caleb yanks Christine to him by the arm, so hard she nearly falls over, cups his hand to her ear, and whispers. "What I'm about to say, we have to do now. No arguments, no second thoughts. You run past the sleepers to the right. I'll hold them back for as long as I can. There's only one cop on that side of the bridge, I'm pretty sure the sheriff and the other one are over here. Come out from under the bridge like you're one of them, slowly. When you've gone like fifteen steps, sprint down the riverbed, and I'll have your back. Go!"

He gives her a little push.

"But," she says, her eyes pleading.

"GO!" he says, and she does.

It's a play right out of backyard football, and not a very inventive one either. Christine streaks to the river's edge, where dry sand pokes up in enough places to allow real running, and she takes off toward the far side of the bridge. Caleb runs along next to her as her blocker.

Though their eyes are closed, the sleepers turn toward them like plants to sunlight, all three at once. The nearest one springs at them, but is caught up in the deeper water and slows just enough to allow them past. The second one finds footing on a dry rock and makes a much more effective lunge. Just as it leaps, Caleb sees a piece of driftwood protruding from the water so close it's almost in his hand. He snatches it up and swings it all in one motion. If the stick were stuck in the mud, things might have worked out quite differently, but as it happens, Caleb pulls it free at just in time and catches the creature (this one a handsome boy of about seventeen) just under the left side of his jaw. The stick snaps, but the force knocks the sleepwalker off balance and back into the water. Caleb looks up and sees Christine. She's made it almost to the far side of the bridge.

A voice from above: "What's going on down there?"

Someone answers, but Caleb can't tell who.

The final sleepwalker has made it onto a sandbar and is racing across it, straight for Christine. Caleb feels sick to his stomach suddenly. She's not going to make it. Caleb's bogged down in water, and as hard as he pushes his legs, his speed is no match for the preternatural thing now that it's running on dry land.

And then he sees it. Maybe his eyes finally adjust to the dark or maybe it's something else, but he finally sees the path and he goes. He springs ahead on a series of dry rocks, and then he's on a sandbar of his own. It intersects with the sandbar on which the sleepwalker runs, fast approaching Christine.

If he can just make it . . .

His legs pump ferociously, but he knows he can't possibly get there in time; the thing is still too fast.

But somehow, he finds a burst of speed, and just as Christine reaches the line where the river runs into the moonlight, Caleb tackles the sleepwalker from behind with all his force. He clearly hears the crunch as one of the thing's bones breaks, and they both tumble into the water.

In the next instant, Caleb is on his feet, desperate to rejoin the world from the half death of submersion. For a terrifying instant, he can't hear, he can't see. And then he can, and he smiles at the sight:

Christine is walking out the other side of the bridge slowly, like a sleepwalker, like one of them.

"What's happening on your side?" a voice comes from the far side of the bridge, and from the near side, the one Christine is walking out from, he hears:

"Nothing, all I can see is one of ours."

Caleb smiles. It's working.

His smile abruptly fades, however, because the other two sleepers are coming for him, and they look pissed.

He widens his stance. They may take him, but they won't catch her. He'll make sure of that; or die trying.

Both sleepwalkers are on the sandbar now, walking, creeping, slowly. One is the handsome one. The other is shorter. Something about him looks familiar, but under the dark of the bridge . . .

Suddenly, he glances over, afraid that the third one might be pursuing Christine. Instead, he sees it floating in the water in a halo of blood. Head must've struck a rock on the way down. Caleb bites his lip. That one was a girl.

Now, the others are on him. The closer of the two lunges and grabs his injured arm. Suddenly Caleb's whole body feels hot as his fractured wrist is wrenched in the tight grip. He punches the thing with all his might with the other hand, and manages to open a gash on its face. But the blows don't slow it at all. If the demon even registers pain, it's going to take a lot more than that to phase it. And speaking of pain—now it twists his arm even harder. Tears come to Caleb's eyes despite his effort to squelch them, and he's forced to his knees.

The other one brushes past Caleb to pursue Christine, but he manages to free himself just enough to kick its legs out from under it. The boy/monster turns back to him, silhouetted against the moonlit creek, and grabs him by the neck with a grip of steel. The other one grabs both his arms and pulls them behind him so hard he knows for sure that his shoulder tendons are ripping. He fights his best, but they slowly drag him into deeper water. He knows this is the end, but his only thoughts are of Christine.

A loud splashing then the sound of swift footfalls means she's making her break. *God, help her.*

Voices above: "Shit, I thought this one was one of ours, but I think it was the girl."

"Then shoot it, ya imbecile, shoot!"

And gunfire does ring out, but Caleb is able to see out of the corner of his eye that the shots are just harmless blips in the water, all falling short.

Run, he thinks, *run fast.*

Then he's under.

Water rushing past, cold, pulling him downstream toward Christine. The cold is wicking his will to fight, but he still does, and his foot finds a rock to push against on the muddy, slippery bottom, and for a second he surfaces, and the moonlight is just right for him to see what he had missed before, or denied before, the familiar one, the one who's killing him is—

"Bean?"

The sleeping face is a mask of stillness, but hands are busy pushing him back under.

Into the pull of the current. Into the dark.

And this time there's nothing to push up against. His feet rake helplessly against the slick, black mud. The water steals his breath.

This really is the end.

He jerks his head back and forth, fights with his whole body to wriggle out of those hands.

And somehow, he does.

He surfaces.

"BEAN!" he screams with his only breath, his last breath, before he's under again.

And now he barely fights, because he can't. All his effort has been consolidated into one primal scream in the center of his brain. A silent scream. The one that comes from gaping mouths in hospital beds. The last scream, the one that nobody hears but God. Then the scream spreads, and it's coming from every cell in his body.

I'm dying.

I'm dying.

I'm dying.

And with the last trickle of breath in his lungs, the breath that might have kept him alive an instant longer, he sighs the word:

"Bean."

But the sound is just a gurgle.

Now there's just the cold.

But something's different. Something's changed.

In the all-encompassing, maddening tingling of his body, the sense of touch is a foreign language. But he can feel enough to know that the hands aren't on him anymore.

And he pushes against the mud bottom with quivering arms, into the world of sound, into the world of light. And in that world, against the backdrop of the moonlit river, he sees two gowned figures, struggling. One has the other pinned to the ground, and as Caleb fights to get to his feet, he sees the figure on top groping with one free hand. The free hand finds a large rock. The figure rears back. The rock hangs in the air for an instant, held aloft, then comes down like a hammer. And the struggle is over.

Caleb approaches. His whole body is quivering. He doesn't know how close he came to dying, but he knows if he has to fight again, he will fail. He skirts the figure, the victor—for the other is now limp, and even in the scant light Caleb can see the crater where his face used to be. He walks around until the moonlight falls right, illuminating the victorious sleepwalker's face, so he can be certain.

"Bean," he says, his voice tremulous.

Bean smiles big, and lets out a laugh that turns into a rattling cough.

"I was having the nicest dream, before you woke me up a minute ago. I was back home, and . . . surfing. At sunset. Nobody else was out there, just me and the seagulls."

Bean rises from the body of the sleepwalker on which he was kneeling, blinking tears away from his good eye, and lets the rock fall out of his hand.

"Come here," he says.

Caleb does.

Bean reaches over and touches his face. "I'm not gay or anything,"

he says. "I just want to make sure it's really you. I'm blind as a freakin'
bat, man."

"It's me," says Caleb.

Bean nods. "Now take off your shirt."

"What?" Caleb says.

"Take it off, you homophobic bastard. We don't have time. Take
it off."

Caleb does.

"Give it to me."

Bean puts the shirt on over his robe.

"Look, Caleb," he says, "one thing I wanted to tell you. I don't
really think your idea of going to Africa is stupid. I think it's . . . it's
pretty cool of you."

"Thanks," says Caleb, but his mind is on other things, like why
Bean wanted his shirt, like what's going on, "What—?"

"Now point me toward the side of the bridge. Not the way Christine went, the other way."

"Why?" says Caleb. "And if you were just dreaming, how do you
know Christine is here? And if you're blind—"

"There's no time to explain, man," says Bean, with a small, sad
shake of his head. "I'm handicapped now, you gotta do what I say,
now point me."

Caleb does.

"Now go help Christine," Bean says, and he takes off running.

"What?" says Caleb. Maybe the near drowning deprived his brain
of oxygen because he has no idea what's going on.

"GO!" yells Bean over his shoulder. He trips over a rock, going ass-
over-teakettle into the water, then he's back on his feet, still sprinting
recklessly.

Grudgingly, Caleb obeys. He jogs in the opposite direction, in the direction Christine disappeared, but he keeps looking back at Bean. He's about to cross into the moonlight when the first shots ring out.

The deep voice above: "The boy's on this side. Forget the girl, we'll get her later."

Caleb looks over his shoulder.

He sees a nightscape, black shadow with blue water and rocks, and beyond the bridge he sees Bean take the first shot and keep running for a few yards until the second one hits him, then the third, then the fourth.

Caleb stops dead in his tracks. He can't leave Bean again! He has to help him, has to do something.

Shots sound again and again. Bean is on his knees. Bean is dying, again.

Caleb takes two splashing steps toward his fallen friend, horror and sadness lashing through his heart.

But it's already too late to help him, and Caleb knows it. Bean is dying, and if Caleb doesn't get away, he'll have died for nothing.

He knows what he has to do. Now he's running, but not toward Bean. He breaks into the moonlight on a sandy part of the bank and runs at full stride, not looking back, not slowing, just flying.

If Bean dies, it won't be for nothing, he swears it.

After a while the gunshots stop, but the pounding of his footfalls beats on.

⊰ Chapter Fifteen ⊱

IN A THICK PATCH OF FOREST perhaps fifty feet behind the trailer that serves as Hudsonville's sheriff's office sits a squat, cinderblock building. There is no sign on the door and there are no windows. The exterior was painted a nauseating green color once, but the paint has all but peeled off by now, exposing the dreary gray of the block beneath. Inside, Janet Faris, the deputy with the big hair, is watching *Wheel of Fortune*. She likes *Wheel of Fortune* because it makes her feel smart. Right now, she's way smarter than this jackass on the screen, some accountant from Utah.

"Don't judge a book by its cover!" Janet shouts. "Don't judge a book by its cover! Don't judge a—"

And the smattering of pixels on the TV says: "Uh, I'd like to buy a vowel."

"Aaaw, you're stupid! He is so stupid, isn't he? I *had* that one! I had it! It's going to be 'Don't judge a book by its cover,' you just wait and see."

"I bet you're right," says Ron Bent from where he's pacing behind the steel bars.

Getting himself behind bars is one of the few things he seems to be very good at indeed.

"You're a smart gal, Janet, no doubt about it," he says. "Almost as smart as you are pretty."

Janet turns to him, batting her eyelashes. "Flattery will get you everywhere, Ron. You ever heard that?"

"I guess I have."

"Never a truer word spoken," she says.

The building is lit by a single flickering neon light. The only other illumination is the uncertain glow of the television. Maybe it's something about the shifting light, or the smell of the place—or maybe it's something else altogether, but Ron's stomach is in a knot. He could puke at any second. And Ron Bent is prone to a lot of things, but getting sick isn't one of them. He has to get out of here. Now.

Lord,
I feel you calling me;
I feel it so much it hurts.
I don't know what I can do
For that boy they kidnapped,
But I know I should be doing something.
I've always felt I should be doing something,
And I know we're getting close
To the secret,
And to Keisha.
Use me.
Wield me like a sword if that's your will.
I want to be worth something to you,
Finally.
I want to do something right.
Work through me.
Get me out.
Show me the way,
And I'll follow.

"Awww," bawls Janet. "I should be on this show! You hear all these nincompoops! I'm smarter than all of them combined!"

"I noticed that right off," Ron says.

He looks at Janet sitting there a few yards away squinting at Pat Sajak and wonders how many hours this relic of a woman has spent just like that: reclined in that chair, talking to the TV all by herself, alone, forgotten. And maybe, just maybe, he sees a path. It's not a glorious path, not at all, but it just might lead out of here.

"Forgive me for saying so, but I don't think that old boss of yours knows just how smart you are either."

"You're damned right about that," she says, watching a commercial for hairspray. "I been working here for seven years, and he only lets me answer phones and guard the prisoners. That's it. I went through training. I could be doing a lot of crimnal investigations."

"Sure, that's what I'm talking about. I can see you got a good head on yer shoulders."

"Sure I do."

"And a pretty one too, if you don't mind my saying so."

This turns Janet away from the TV to face Ron.

"You, sir, are making me blush!" she says and cackles like a crow. Ron smiles a little.

"You oughta tell my husband that," she says.

"You're married?" Ron asks, doing his best to sound surprised.

Janet looks hurt, then mad. "What, you didn't think I'd be a spinster, did ya? I had more than a few men after me in my time."

"I'm only saying," says Ron, "if you were my wife, I wouldn't let you out of the house, if you don't mind me sayin' so."

"What, you're some kind of a bigamist, or what?"

Here is the crossroads. Ron knows if he pushes on down this road, it might lead to a dead end, or to disaster. Still, there's a chance it might work.

He takes a breath, then lets it out in a slow, measured stream.

Ron Bent was never much good at taking risks, but for some reason he's feeling lucky today, praise God. So he decides to go for it.

"No," he says, "I'm no bigamist, and no controlling husband either. But if you were my wife, I think we'd be too busy to leave the house, if you know what I mean."

Janet's mouth drops open. She spins all the way around in her chair and her face turns bright red.

Ron holds his breath. Yes, this is the crossroads, and she chooses which way they go from here. She holds his fate just like she's holding her breath right now.

And Janet says: "Is that right? Well . . . maybe you ought to tell my husband that. He don't . . . well, let's just say, he ain't of the same way of thinking that you are. And even if he was, he wouldn't be able to . . . put his money where his mouth is."

Ron is sweating. The air in here feels like poison and his head is pounding. There's no time for subtlety. He has to get out. He can feel it.

"If I were him, I'd have my mouth where your money is all day," Ron says, almost smiling. That's a pretty good line for him. He was never any good at coming up with lines.

Janet stands up. "Is that right?" Her voice is confrontational but tremulous, and her cheeks are still glowing.

"You know what I think?" Ron says. "I think that's what you want too."

"Is that right?"

"Only I don't think you want it from your husband anymore," he says. "I think you want it from me."

"You are a bold man," she says. Her lipstick looks garish, even ghoulish in the strange light, her lips contorted into a prurient smile.

"I bet you tend to get what you want," he says.

"You bet I do," she says, moving forward. Still, she remains at least an arm's length back from the bars.

"So how about you tell me what you want and how you want it," Ron says.

"Yeah?" she says, her voice breathy now. She unbuttons the top button on her shirt. "You like this? You want this? Then why don't you come on over here and get it?"

He can see her chest rise and fall in trembling breaths. This is good, this is—

"But I can't open the door, Ron," she says.

Ron represses a sigh, blinks, regroups.

"That's a shame," he says. "Guess you'll be missing out then," and he takes the biggest risk of all—acting uninterested, he walks away from her, over to the cot on the far side of the cell and sits down.

"Ooh!" she says, stomping a foot in frustration. She looks back at the door. She stands there for a moment, thinking hard.

"Alright," she says. She takes out her gun and sets it on the table, still well out of Ron's reach. "You'd better make it quick, though. I don't want to get caught." She walks toward Ron, swaying her copious hips as she comes. She unbuckles her pants and starts to pull them down, pressing her wide ass up against the bars.

The horrible thing is that Ron actually feels a grain of attraction beneath the revulsion. *God,* he thinks, *I must be pretty hard up.*

But there's no time to contemplate his miserable love life.

He steps up to her, passes the arm with "the hook" on the end of it through the bars and wraps it tightly around her waist, feeling her gasp with excitement as he does.

With the other hand, he reaches through and grasps the metal buckle of her belt.

"Come on," she says, "quick, now."

And Ron is quick. He yanks the belt out of her belt loops with his good hand, holding her to the bars with his other arm. Then he passes the belt around her neck, as fast as he can, and before Janet Faris knows what's going on, she's strapped by her neck to the bars. When she tries to pull at the leather, Ron reaches through the bars with "the hook" and restrains her.

"Okay, Janet," he says, "where are the keys to the cell?"

All that escapes Janet's mouth is a dusty-sounding wheeze. Ron jerks the belt for a second, a dog's choke collar.

"Where are they? Point."

She points down and makes a pathetic gagging sound.

Ron rummages through her pockets. He finds several Tootsie Roll wrappers, some change, and finally a fairly large, almost cartoonish-looking key.

Now he's getting somewhere. Gripping the belt with the hook now, (and hoping its squeezing force will be enough to keep Janet pinned in place), he reaches the key toward the lock on his cell door. But it's too far. And from this angle he's not able to keep the pressure on Janet's neck. He looks back and sees her fingers already creeping under the strap of her belt. In another second, she'll be free. He has to make a split-second decision and hope it's the right one. Instantly, he lets go of the belt and steps over to the lock. Fumbling, fumbling, now the key is in.

On the other side of the bars, Deputy Faris is coughing herself into a frenzy—now trying to run for her gun on the table, now stumbling with her pants around her ankles.

And Ron is turning the key, turning it more, finally hearing the click of release resonate through the whole steel frame of the door. He's sliding the bars out of the way and stepping into freedom.

And into the path of Janet's waiting gun barrel.

Her face is now redder than ever, fueled not by libido but by fury. In one fist she holds the bunched-up front of her pants, which are thankfully now pulled back up where they belong, and in the other trembling fist she holds a .38 revolver.

"Well, you are one sick criminal, mister, trying to take advantage of a woman like that," she spits.

Ron doesn't put his hands up; he just stands there.

"I need to get out of here," he says, trying to calm her, to lead her on the long road back to reason. "That boy they took into the Dream Center, I think he's in trouble. I think there might be a lot of kids endangered by what's going on at that place."

"There's a lot of folks endangered right here in this room, mister," she growls.

Didn't Shakespeare say something like "hell hath no fury like a woman scorned"? Looks like the old codger was right.

"Janet," Ron says.

"No," she says. "Get back in there!"

And she waves the gun barrel toward the open cell door.

"I can't, I have to go," Ron says. "You can shoot me if you have to."

Saliva glistens on her chin now, and Ron watches her finger tense on the trigger.

"You can go one of two places," she says. "Back into that cell, or to hell."

Just then, there's a sound outside. The door opens. The sheriff's wide, lax face balloons into view.

"Janet, come on, we have to—" and he stops. "What in the—?"

Janet turns to look at the sheriff, and that's all the opportunity Ron needs. In one step, he's struggling for Janet's gun. It discharges one shot straight up, shattering the last dying fluorescent bulb before he wrestles it away from her.

"Ned, help!" Janet screams.

The sheriff charges into the pitch blackness, gun drawn, and promptly runs right into a heavy wood table and almost falls on his face. By the time he rights himself and skirts the obstruction, Janet has found her Maglite and turned it on. It strobes around the room. Here's the desk, the TV, the table, the blinking sheriff, the open door.

But there is no Ron Bent.

Outside, Ron races up to the sheriff's office and past it. There are no pains in his joints now; the adrenaline pumping through his veins has calmed their throbbing ache.

As he passes the squad car, he glances in the window and sees the keys still in the ignition. By the time the sheriff rounds the corner of his trailer, he can only get off one shot at the car as it speeds away. One taillight shatters, and Ron Bent is free.

And it looks like his luck might finally be changing. Praise God.

Christine crouches in a stand of cypress trees, listening to the murmur of insects. Sometimes, something disturbs the water nearby and she stops breathing, listening hard. It's at such times when she can hear her sister's voice. At first, she could only hear it in the electric rustle of the radio station, AM five thirty-five. Now she can hear it whispering all the time, especially at times like this when all else is silent. And her sister's voice isn't the only one, not by a long shot. There are thousands of voices, maybe millions, and they never stop. Some whisper sadly, some scream in vengeful madness. Some are so, so lucid. One such voice is speaking now, from the boughs of the cypress.

<I can see from here, Sugar, sure as you're born. The boy is on his knees and the lead is pumping through him, piece after hot piece. His guts are popping open all over from them holes; I can see it from here. And now he's face-first in the water, Sugar, just a-floating downstream like the rest of us!>

And the laughter starts, the laughter of thousands.

Christine knows the dead. All they want is company.

"Shut up, you dead hag," she whispers. She fights to disbelieve what the voice told her, but in her mind all she can see is Billy, floating facedown in a slick of his own blood.

She heard the gunshots maybe five minutes ago, a whole volley of them, but she won't let herself believe any of those bullets found her Billy. She doesn't believe it because she *can't* believe it. Because if Billy is dead, then her hope is dead.

And besides, the voices can be tricky.

<it's okay, Billy . . . alive>

Anna's voice is tiny and far away. It's instantly shrieked down by a dissonant chorus.

Christine hears a cracking sound above, and barely steps out of the way in time as a huge, ancient limb crashes down and pounds the black earth where she was just standing. If it had hit her, she would probably have been knocked out, fallen face-first into the water, and drowned.

All they want is company.

And they don't like being called hags, or especially being reminded that they're dead.

The darkness seems to deepen. Bats flick past above, though Christine can't actually see them.

"Anna," she whispers, "where is Billy? Should I look for him? Is he okay?"

A moment passes, then the silence answers back: <wait>

Christine does.

She looks up, through the life-woven canopy of leaves above and spies the North Star. Did runaway slaves see the same sight, running up this river two centuries ago?

<yes-a-ma'am> says the silence <an' some a dem didn't run as fast as dem hound dogs and made the river red, sho did. An' otha ones made it alla way North, walkin' many a long, long night to freedom, hallelujah.>

<A lotta niggers tried it and swung too.> cackles the dark.

And the voices become murky again, a cacophony of laughs and screams and whispered mumblings, and Christine can't stand to hear it anymore, but it's getting harder and harder to unhear it. So instead, she decides to drown it out, and sings an old hymn she learned as a child:

> Mine eyes have seen the glory
> Of the coming of the Lord,
> He was stamping out the vintage
> Where the grapes of wrath are stored
> Something, something, something . . .
> With his high and mighty sword,
> His truth is marching on . . . Billy?

The sound of something moving in the water is more distinct than before, and it's more than just the "blip" of a frog or a fish. The sound comes closer, and Christine stiffens with fear.

"Don't stop singing." He comes around the trunk of a cypress. His chest rises and falls, fast. Even in the dark, she can see his face is streaked with sweat, dirt, and tears.

"Please, don't stop," Caleb says again, almost pleading.

"I thought you were dead," she says.

"I thought you were crazy."

She smiles sadly. "I might be. I honestly don't know."

"It wasn't me they shot," says Caleb. "It was my friend."

"The dead will be glad to have him," she says. "They like humor."

"What do you mean?"

"There's no time. Let's go."

Already, she can hear the distant scratch of the sheriff's radio, and the chorus of whispers saying:

<maybe the guns will fell them>

<maybe they'll trip and drown>

<yes, we'll have two more young ones among us>

<how nice to have two more around>

Hand in hand, Billy and Christine run along the riverbank. When the rocks hurt her bare feet, he carries her piggyback, and when the sun finally cracks open the darkness and the whispering shadows give way to the birdsong of morning, they are still among the living and are grateful.

As the heat of the day rises, painting the forest with rich greens and browns, the witch (for so even she thinks of herself) hums a song. She doesn't know the words, or can't remember them. She doesn't remember much, nowadays.

Except Anna, dear Anna.

Made a piece of clay in kindergarten, Anna did, put her tiny fingers in the mud and by the magic of science the teachers made the mud hard, made it immortal, and now they sit on the counter, Anna's hands. Or the empty places where her little hands once were. Hateful, empty places.

That makes her think "The Thought" again, and The Thought makes her bite her lip hard and close her eyes and think of Christine, hateful Christine, the bad, bad girl who put the seed of The Thought into her head.

Even though she's a powerful witch, no spell will banish the thoughts. She knows; she's tried.

Now she's holding a hoe, standing in a patch of sandy dirt and wearing only her socks, a long skirt, and a baseball cap; no shirt. She doesn't wear a shirt much these days. There are no eyes to see her except those belonging to The Forest, and he likes her skin just as it is. She lifts the hoe and hacks at the unyielding earth. She must make an herb garden. She bought the seeds a year—no, no, two years ago—but so far has been unable to plant them, because every time she tries, the shakes start up so bad she can't grip the hoe. Because of Christine, hateful bitch-child.

The sun feels good on her breasts and the handle of the hoe feels good in her hand, hard and sure. But as she strikes the earth again, tearing up a big clod of dirt this time, The Thought streaks across her mind again, big as a billboard, horrible and certain.

She cries out and throws the hoe to the ground. It lands with an unsatisfying "pit" sound. (Shouldn't she be able to make it explode? Shouldn't she be able to make the earth tremble with her rage? She is a grand witch, after all.) She walks away from the hoe with her hands over her ears, shaking her head back and forth.

The song is in her head still, she realizes suddenly. It's an old song, she knows that much, and the melody is sure and strong in her head, but the words elude her, all but:

"glory of the coming . . . "

The phrase thrills her, spreads goose bumps all over her body.

The coming. But whose? Who can bring Anna back? Who can banish these thoughts, *The Thought*, from her mind?

She thinks she knows who.

She heads up to the trailer and reaches for the screen door. When The Thought comes, there's only one answer, and that's the bottle. It isn't a final answer, but it is a potent magic. It has the power to derail time, even do away with it altogether sometimes. And in time is where The Thought lives.

Anna's in the dark.

The witch, all powerful, she screams, slams the screen door shut again. Curse The Thought to hell!

Anna is dead.

She tries to think of something else. She should check the cellar. Never go outside without checking the cellar door.

She lets the screen door go, heads back down the steps, and walks around the side of the trailer, not looking at the hoe, especially not looking at the shadow of the trailer making a sharp, black "V" at her feet as she turns the corner.

Anna is empty with dark, and I will be too, when it takes me.

The witch walks faster.

The cellar door is locked and still. Safe. It hasn't moved in a long time. Years. Good.

She spins back toward the screen door, toward home, toward safety, and in doing so almost loses her balance. She has to put one hand on the rotting side of the trailer to steady herself. She hates to step into the trailer's shadow—it makes her shiver to do so—but otherwise she'd have pitched forward onto the grass.

Once the vertigo subsides she walks on. It seems darker out now, but the sunlight is more biting too. The sun is a pale, burning, seeing eye—and she hurries inside, out of its unnerving gaze.

She looks around first when she comes in—to make sure it's really her living room, really her trailer.

Reality is a reflection on a pond, she's known that for a while, ever since she was young and pretty and the tits that now hang almost to her waist like empty plastic grocery sacks were ripe and plump and made men do wild things. Reality is a reflection on a pond, and you never know what might be swimming underneath.

Today, though, her living room is her living room. She looks up at the dream catchers hanging from the ceiling, and is comforted to know not a single one is out of place.

She sits down heavily, not noticing the waft of dust that rises up from the cushion of her chair as she whops down into its embrace.

And she picks up the bottle, so smooth and hard, so nice-feeling with the little white tatters of the torn-off label as soft as goose down against the palm of her hand. So real. She unscrews the cap slowly, teasing herself.

She glances at the window. Did a shadow move behind the blinds? Did it? Did it?

Now, an instant later, she's forgotten about the blinds, about the shadow, about everything.

She takes the magic of the bottle inside her, feeling the burn, and the burn is good, because the opposite of the burn is The Thought, is the <nothing>.

First, the spinning in her head steadies, then it feels like she's doing great wide backflips—except she's still sitting in her favorite orange and brown plaid armchair, watching the bottle drain <empty> into her insatiable, drooling mouth. And the beam of sunlight coming through the window first doubles, then blurs, then becomes a cat's cradle of light, and the throbbing in her head that she didn't even realize was there slows into a brick of pleasurable pain as her eyes go slack, then shut. The Thought loses and the magic of the bottle wins out again—for now.

→

There's a wind in the trees, and all the birds are flying away. Caleb and Christine walk very close together along the sandy bank of the stream, in and out of light beams filtering through the boughs of the forest. They've walked out of the night and into the morning. Sometimes they would think they heard a sound behind them, a footstep or the rattle of a bush, and they'd sneak into the woods, away from the water, and watch. But their pursuers never appeared, neither the cops nor the sleepwalkers.

Christine has wanted desperately to talk, to gush all her feelings and fears and the experiences of her imprisonment to Billy, but every time she takes a breath to speak, fear seizes her jaw and thrusts it shut again. Whether it's being heard by her pursuers or being alone with Billy that scares her more, she doesn't know. But for the last hour or so, since the sun has evaporated much of the previous night's horror and sorrow, she has been marshalling her will to break the silence. Finally, she does.

"Thank you for coming. Even though I don't remember sending you that letter, I did think of you. I dreamed of you rescuing me. Even though it was completely far-fetched, part of me knew you would."

"Really? How, after you hadn't seen me in so long?"

She smiles. "I don't know, I just knew. Besides—when we would play—you, me, and Anna—you were always the hero. I guess I figured you always would be. You were always a pretty lucky knight, having two damsels in distress."

Caleb musters a small, sad laugh. "Yeah."

"Are you sorry you came?"

"No," he says. "No. When I read your letter, I knew I had to come. I didn't know what was going on, but I knew I had to do something . . . I'm just sorry Bean came."

"Don't be sorry," she says.

From the look he shoots her, she's afraid she's pissed him off big-time. But when she takes his hand, he doesn't resist.

"How can you say that?" he says. "It's my fault he's dead."

"He's with Anna now," she says, "making her laugh. Soon, we'll be able to hear him too on the radio."

"How is that possible?"

"The clocks, I think."

"But how does it work?"

She shrugs, as if to say "it doesn't matter."

"It just does," she says.

"And you listened to the clocks too?"

"Yes."

"When? Why?"

"The director made me listen to them at the Dream Center. But I could hear them—the voices—before that. I always could, but only really faintly. Since the clocks and the surgery, I hear them everywhere. But I hear them most clearly on the radio, especially 535 AM"

"Wait, you mean you can hear them right now?"

"Yes, but . . . " she hesitates.

"What do they say?"

"It's hard to hear. They all talk at once."

"How many are there?"

She spreads her hands, looking up at the emerald treetops.

"Many," she whispers.

"And what are they saying right now?"

"Nothing, just . . . "

"What?"

"One is saying 'time to reap the field.' They're happy because their work is almost done. And the end is near. And they're happy because . . . "

"Because of what?"

She looks at him hard, then just shakes her head. "It's hard to hear," she mumbles.

"What are they talking about?"

"Who knows?" she says. "Something's been going on here for a long time. Anna was one of the first to disappear, I think, but there've been a lot more. Some folks even called a meeting at town hall when it started. Mom and I were there, and she spoke. She was a lot more 'together' back then."

"What happened?"

She looks down at her feet, then at the swirling water of the river, and sighs to her core.

"Some wanted to fight, but nobody knew who the enemy was. The kids just disappeared. Other people wanted to call in the authorities. They made the mistake of expecting the mayor and the sheriff to take care of that. Others, just . . . "

"What?"

"Said nothing." She smiles sadly.

"So what happened?"

"The mayor didn't go for any outside help for a long time. When he did, it was too late."

"What do you mean, too late?"

"The people who he went to for help betrayed him, as far as we could guess. Then he disappeared. He's in the dark now. The rest of those who still had the will to fight formed a militia. Some of them had seen who took their children, and they didn't think they were human—not really, anyway—but they were willing to stand and fight all the same. The militia would patrol, even had a phone line for emergencies. But they couldn't hold guns all the time. They had to sleep and eat, and one by one they disappeared. The few folks left who had a mind to fight changed their tune fast. They shut their mouths and locked their doors at night, and there were no more town meetings."

"What about the sheriff?"

"He played everyone along for quite a while, but now everyone— or the few of us left, anyway—know he's part of it, whatever it is. He never lifted a finger to find one missing child."

"And what about the Dream Center?"

"That came along not long after it all started. I guess the only way the problems 'round here showed up anyplace on official records was in the suicide rate or something, because pretty soon trucks just appeared out of nowhere, rattling up the driveway to the old asylum, and in no time the place was rebuilt. Doc Rodgers knew the director, he said, and he referred almost all his patients over there because they pretty much all had sleeping problems of one kind or another— all of us did with everything going on: babies stolen out of their cribs, kids grabbed off their bikes and never seen again . . ."

"And my father?"

"Just disappeared. I'm sorry, Billy. Around the same time I went into the Dream Center. Some people said he had something to do with what was going on. I think they didn't trust him because he was educated or something. Other people said he tried to fight it. Either way, he just vanished."

"So it wasn't just Anna . . . "

"She was only the beginning. The tip of the iceberg."

"And your mother? I met her. She wasn't doing too well."

"She was sure magic was the answer. She mixed all kinds of potions and started learning all sorts of crazy spells. She got so far out there people started thinking she had something to do with all the stuff going on. She just missed Anna, I guess, and that was her way of doing something. It was sad. People stopped talking to her. Then they stopped talking to me too. She really wanted to believe that the magic would work, but it was too late: Anna was gone. I knew it, and the more I tried to explain it to her, the more she started to hate me. And then I think she started to believe me because that's when she started really drinking."

"I'm sorry I wasn't here."

"It's okay. You didn't know."

"I should have been here anyway."

"You weren't supposed to be, Billy. But you're supposed to be here now."

"To do what?" Caleb asks. "What can we do?"

Christine grins strangely. "The ghosts know," she says, "but all they'll say about it is 'charku, charku,' over and over."

"What does that mean?"

"It's in a tongue that the living no longer speak. It means 'bringer of death.'"

Caleb stares off to the horizon, toward the spot where the river disappears, taking in Christine's words.

"What—or who—is the 'charku'?" He finally asks.

"Billy," she says, giving him a surprised look, "it's you."

⊰ Chapter Sixteen ⊱

THESE ARE THE DREAMS OF THE WITCH:

They are fraught with the unsettling faces of strangers. All are watching her. All are judging. She grasps them, claws at them, screams in their ears:

"Where is my daughter? Where is she?"

But every face she sees turns to stone.

These are the dreams of the witch:

The earth is made of sliding sand, with each grain falling, falling as if through an hourglass. It gives way under her feet. She knows she mustn't be caught, mustn't go *down* because down is dark and in the *dark* she isn't alone. The dark is filled with invisible stone faces that watch and judge and laugh, hands that take and take, and quiet that smothers.

These are the dreams of the witch:

She mounts the steps of her childhood house, the yellow one with the blue trim on County Road 67. She stands on the porch and looks around, and the leaves on the trees are golden with fall, the grass is crisp and healthy green, the corn is dying in the straight, straight rows her father broke his back to make. All is as it should be. Then the porch swing falls, the windows shatter, the corn plants crack and bow as if genuflecting to some terrible god. And she looks out far over the plain and sees it, a thing that has haunted her dreams ever since her little daughters learned about it in science class and explained it to her. It's a trap for light. It's a cancer in the skin of the universe. They call it a black hole. And in that instant, everything melts upward, falling into the gaping mouth of Nothing, and is gone.

These are the dreams of the witch:

Inside that nothing, she meets a little girl named Anna. Anna lives in the dark, and Anna is alone.

"Mommy?"

The witch stirs, whimpers. The stench of alcohol and vomit fouls the air. The puke has run down between her dust-bag tits, but a hand is cleaning it up. The witch feels the brush of a towel on her chest. It's arousing, and a confusing sensation in this dark place. And then, all at once, she's in the light.

And Anna is there. And she's alive!

The witch blinks in uncomprehending joy.

"It's me," Anna says, "Christine."

"Hateful, hateful little—" the witch begins, realizing she's been fooled. She looks for a weapon and finds one. Snatching the now-empty gin bottle off the table in front of her, she stands up, full of fury and power, cocks back to strike her traitor-child into bleeding, whimpering silence—but the other one, the one she didn't notice, the little neighbor boy, Billy, now somehow a man, grabs her wrist and snatches her weapon from her hand.

"Awww!" she screams in childish frustration.

"Sit down, Mother," says Christine.

"You scrawny little whore," says the witch, drawing herself up in indignation. "You shouldn't have been born, you traitor; it should have just been Anna, my Anna."

The witch is almost spitting fire. Caleb takes a step back, alarmed in spite of himself, but Christine stands her ground.

"You slut," the witch hisses. "You little bitch, you—"

Quickly, without warning, Christine cocks back and swings her small fist. It catches her mother's face, hard, making a low, sharp "thump" sound.

The great witch falls back into her armchair, staring at her daughter with a dazed, quizzical look as a ribbon of blood slithers from her nose and down over her lips.

"I loved her as much as you did, Mother," says Christine. "It's not my fault she's gone." She rubs her fist gingerly and sighs. To herself, she says: "I should have done that a long time ago."

Christine pauses, perhaps waiting for a response. When she doesn't get one, she tosses the towel she had used to sop up the puke to her mother.

"Cover yourself. For Christ's sake, Mom, have some dignity."

Again, Mrs. Zikry's only response is a bleary-eyed stare, but she does cover her breasts with the puke-wet towel.

Caleb speaks: "We shouldn't stay here long. They must know we'll be either here or at my old place."

"We're safe here until night, I think," says Christine. "The sleepwalkers won't be out during the day."

"Who are they? The sleepwalkers?"

She just shakes her head, still staring at her mother. "Ones like me," she says. "All I know is what I've figured, and what Anna told me. They're kids from the Dream Center, like I was, and they do the work the ghosts want done. Under the bridge I could hear the spirits urging them—or more like cheering them—on."

"So what's the plan?" asks Caleb. He's clearly antsy, glancing at the door. He doesn't want to be here—but would they really feel safe anyplace else, either?

"First, I have to clean my mother up," says Christine. "Come on, Mom, you're getting in the shower."

She offers a hand to the great witch of Hudsonville, who now seems very old and frail.

"What do we do when night comes?" asks Caleb. "Do we run?"

"Well, we have two choices. We could run," Chrsitine says, gently guiding her mother through the living room and into the bathroom, "or we could stay and fight."

And she disappears into the room and pulls the door shut behind her.

"Yeah, let's fight," mutters Caleb, alone now, surveying the hundreds of hanging dream catchers with contempt. "They've only taken over the whole town."

In the other room the shower springs to life. Apparently, the witch somehow got her interior plumbing fixed.

Caleb paces around the small house, still wearing a sarcastic smirk, still dwelling on how stupid it is to risk your life to fix something that the cops *should* have taken care of a long time ago, something that *should*, theoretically, not even be happening in the first place.

But then he thinks of Bean, Christine, his father, Anna, even Mrs. Zikry: all those who've suffered because of what's happened in Hudsonville. And he thinks that maybe they should fight after all; because if they don't, who will?

It's maybe twenty minutes later. Caleb sits on the couch, half dozed off, having finally convinced himself to ignore the filthy upholstery and make himself comfortable. He only sort of hears the shower click off and the sound of water fade to an indistinct drip. He thinks he hears the far-off sound of moaning, like that of the distant wind. It almost seems like it's coming from the trailer itself, from the floor—

but it might just as easily be coming from just beyond his conscious mind, where sleep is stalking him relentlessly.

The moaning sound fades as he falls out of consciousness. Fantasies flash through his head: he sees himself drinking the last swig of alcohol from the bottle on the table. He sees himself in the heat of battle, cutting down attacking demons like a swashbuckler in a black-and-white movie. He sees Amber in his head—this is the first time he's thought of her in days—she's wearing a sexy little pair of underwear and a bra, but despite that fact, his mind discards the image. He's outgrown Amber. He's outgrown a lot of things. Next he sees his father. It's an image Caleb has long since forgotten—or at least it sunk to his deep subconscious for many years before being dredged up today.

His father, with his ever-present beard, sits Indian-style in the foyer of the Hudsonville house, wearing a ten-gallon hat, the kind cowboys wear. A child, hardly more than a toddler, runs around the room, yipping and yelling, riding one of those toy horses that's really a broomstick with a stuffed, plush horse head attached to it. Little plastic six-shooters in plastic holsters bob at his waist. A little cowboy hat is cocked back on his head. The child is a little Caleb—or a little Billy, as he would have been called in those days. Little Billy dashes around the love seat, laughing as his father, usually a somber man, calls out to him:

"You'd better ride, boy! You gotta rope that steer! Catch those Indians! Ride, or that bull is gonna get you!"

Little equestrian Billy gallops around his father as if he were the barrel in a riding competition.

He's never seen his dad so excited as he was that Christmas when he gave him that cowboy getup. Of course, the excitement kind of waned when his mother got pissed off about the toy guns. But while it lasted, Billy and Dad had a real good time.

As Caleb sees all this, he's transported instantly back to that lost day. He smells the gingerbread cooking. He knows his mother is out at the store, having forgotten some important ingredient for Christmas dinner, and left him with his father for some rare alone time. And Caleb thinks he knows why this memory stuck. Because his father would never have been this silly, this carefree, in front of his mother. Maybe their relationship had already deteriorated too far for fun to exist between them. Maybe there was some other reason, one Caleb would never know; but this is the only time he can remember having this much fun with his father. He lingers here, savoring the memory, studying the child's laughing face, listening to his beaming father:

Ride, boy! Ride!

Then his father looks up, distracted. It's hard to see, from his infant's perspective, as he rides out from behind an armchair: what's his dad looking at? Might be the fireplace. Might be the Christmas tree. Might be the clock on the mantle.

A hammering sound snaps Caleb's reverie.

Back in the trailer.

He's on his feet instantly.

The pounding comes again. He sees the front door rattle on its hinges.

"Christine," he calls, uncertain of what else to do. "We've got company!"

He looks around for a weapon. Finally, he runs into the kitchen and grabs a flimsy steak knife off the counter. It doesn't do much to assuage his fears, but it's all he can find.

The pounding again.

"Who is it?" he barks.

"Margie from the restaurant. And the sheriff ain't with me."

Caleb is so relieved he almost laughs. He reaches out to unlock the door, then stops. Maybe the sheriff is with her. Maybe he has a gun to her head making her pretend she's alone. Or maybe she was on his side all along.

Caleb sneaks over to the window and peeks out from behind the curtain. He sees Margie, all right, but she's not alone. A large man is standing next to her. The man's build is very close to that of the sheriff, although he isn't wearing the sheriff's usual wide-brimmed hat. Caleb moves around as much as he can, but he can't get a good look at the man's face.

"Who's with you?" he yells.

"Man who picked me up and helped me when I was hiding from the sheriff. Says he knows you too," Margie says. There's a slight pause. "Says his name is Ron."

Caleb reaches to unlock the door, then stops again. His first inclination was to trust this Ron guy, but maybe he should rethink that. Look where that got him last time. Ron took him to that creepy quack doctor, and he wound up at the Dream Center.

The House of White Rooms, he thinks, though he doesn't know where the phrase came from. Was that what Christine called it?

"Let me talk to Ron," he says.

"It's me," says a man's voice.

"Why should I trust you?" says Caleb. "You took me to that doctor."

"I also followed you to where he took you and got arrested trying to help get you out," says Ron.

That's certainly what the director wanted me to believe, Caleb thinks.

"Why are you trying to help me?"

"I have a daughter," he says. "Her name is Keisha. She was abducted a few miles from here, years ago. I been trying to find her ever since."

"And you think the people who took my friend took her, too. Is that it?"

"I don't know," he says, "but it's the only thing I've got to go on."

Caleb's hand is on the lock, but he's still not ready to turn it, not yet.

"Margie," he says, "why are *you* here?"

There's silence on the other side of the door, and for a moment he thinks they've gone. Then he hears Margie clear her throat.

"I thought maybe we could trust the sheriff, until I saw him shooting at poor Christine. Now I know there's no one to trust. No one but us. A lotta kids've turned up gone. Good kids. There ain't but a few of us in Hudsonville left to do anything about it, and I reckoned I might be one of them. Besides," she says, her voice muffled from behind the wood, "they say some folks'll burn when Judgment comes around and some won't. Might be too late now, but I'd like to be one of the ones that don't. If I can help it."

"It isn't too late," Ron says quietly to Margie. "Never think it is."

Caleb thinks of Bean and Christine's skepticism about anyone helping the people in Africa. Hundreds of people are missing in Hudsonville, and who's left to stand for them? Only these five people, out of hundreds. Maybe that's how it always happens.

He turns the lock and opens the door. Ron smiles amicably.

"How's the pitching arm, slugger?" Ron says.

Caleb smiles in spite of himself and looks down at the dirty ace bandage on his left arm.

"Fine, as long as I don't move it or shake it or breathe," Caleb says.

"Little Billy, you really have grown up so handsome, I declare!" says Margie, and she gives him a big hug.

Caleb is desperate to free himself, because the wide-open door is terrifying him. He makes himself abide the hug, then shoves the door shut and twists it locked.

Ron picks up on his discomfort. "Nobody followed us," he says, "I made Margie look behind us the whole way."

"How did you find us?" Caleb asks.

Ron shakes his head, "I don't know," he says darkly.

"Someone told him," Christine says. Caleb hadn't noticed her come in from the hallway. She's washed her face, brushed her hair and traded her filthy hospital gown in for jeans and a tank top. To Caleb, she somehow looks both completely normal and fantastically beautiful.

Despite the ominous connotations her statement might hold, she's smiling.

"What do you mean?" Ron asks. "Nobody told me, really, I just figured . . . I thought . . . I don't know how I knew," he concludes finally, frowning.

"Somebody did tell you, whether you knew it or not," Christine repeats. "Somebody good. My sister." She looks over at Caleb, who stares back at her.

The witch appears from the hallway on bare, tentative feet, her gray hair dark with moisture and hanging in her face. But she looks better already, Caleb thinks, healthier. The heat of the shower has made her cheeks ruddy, and she wears a timid smile on her face and a white terrycloth robe over her body.

"Margie, you remember my mother," Christine says.

Margie nods at the witch and flashes a guarded smile.

"And this is—what's your name?" Christine says.

"Ron."

" . . . Ron."

The witch nods, her eyes trained on the floor. "Welcome, all," she says. "Make yourselves at home."

Everybody stands silently for a moment. Here they are, brought together somehow in the most godforsaken town, in the most god-forsaken trailer imaginable, five strangers. Margie looks wired and edgy, Mrs. Zikry gazes at the floor, Ron looks from person to person, stoic but expectant. And Caleb suddenly realizes he's staring at Christine. And Christine is smiling.

"We should all rest while we have the daylight," she says. "Some of you folks haven't slept in a while. I know I haven't. This isn't the most inviting place to sleep, but if we work together maybe we can clean things up enough to find a place for everybody to get some rest. Sound good?"

Everybody murmurs in assent.

"Who's hungry?" she continues. "I'll make some food."

There are some nods.

"Billy," she says, "will you help me in the kitchen?"

"Sure," Caleb says.

"I'll help out too." Margie says, "I'm a little whipped right now, but this wouldn't be the first time I pulled a double shift, I'll tell you that."

"Thanks, Margie," says Christine. "Maybe you can help my mom clean things up so everybody has a place to sleep."

"I wouldn't mind at all," Margie says.

Everybody sets to work. Margie throws the bed sheets in a rusty washing machine on the back porch. Ron digs into a closet and pulls out a vacuum that could use vacuuming itself it's so dusty. Mrs. Zikry putters around, picking up, tidying up. At first, her pace is slow, but soon she is accomplishing as much as everyone else.

In the kitchen, Christine and Caleb find a frozen lasagna that seems like it might feed everybody, and they put it in the oven and go to work on the massive pile of dirty dishes composting in the sink. Those plates that can't be salvaged get tossed into a big, black plastic trash bag; the others, Christine washes and Caleb dries.

"You handled your mom pretty well," Caleb offers.

"I'm used to it," Christine says. "Since Anna, she's been like this on and off. The next few days, if she can't sneak a drink someplace, she'll be in bed with the DTs."

"DTs?"

"Delirium tremens. The shakes. Alkies get it when they're going through withdrawal. It's a pretty common cycle around this household, unfortunately."

"I'm sorry," Caleb says.

"It's okay," Christine says with a little smile. "I'm just glad she's okay. Without me around to keep her off the bottle, I figured . . . When I was locked up in that place, I kept expecting to get a letter or something saying she died. I stopped her from killing herself, like, fifty times. I figured without me there to stop her, she'd go pretty fast. And then I'd be in that place forever. But she's strong, I guess. She surprised me."

There's a long silence.

"I'm sorry," Caleb says, "about Anna."

"That was a long time ago," Christine says.

"No," Caleb says. "I mean I'm sorry I dared her to go into that place. It was my fault she went in there."

Christine sets down the plate she's washing and looks him full in the face.

"Don't tell me you've beat yourself up about that all these years."

He shrugs.

"That wasn't your fault. You loved Anna as much as I did."

Caleb doesn't say anything.

"Anna forgives you," she says. "And so do I."

He looks down at the sink.

She takes a handful of suds and slowly, solemnly places them on his nose—then laughs. He looks over at her, trying to keep some of his dignity, then finally breaks down and laughs with her.

He scoops the suds off his nose and puts them on her head. She just laughs harder.

Caleb is still smiling but suddenly sighs, serious again.

"How did you do it all these years? Knowing your sister was dead, taking care of your mother, seeing other kids disappearing? I feel like my life has been so . . . easy."

She shrugs. "Everyone does what they have to do. It's nothing special," she says.

"Well, I kind of disagree," says Caleb.

"Are you saying you think I'm special?" Christine says, batting her eyelashes jokingly.

"Maybe."

"Special Olympics special, or prom-queen special?"

"A little of both."

Christine gapes in mock shock.

She scoops some suds out of the sink and tosses them at Caleb. He grabs her from behind and tickles her. She laughs and turns to retaliate, and before either of them know it, their lips and bodies are pressed together tight. They emerge, breathing hard, staring at each other.

Caleb takes a trembling breath and blinks, breaking their eye contact to stare at a can opener on the counter.

"I should have told you, I'm kind of seeing somebody," he says.

The light in Christine's eyes goes out, and in that instant Caleb thinks he would give anything in the world to take back the words he just spoke.

Except they're true. Aren't they?

Christine just smiles sadly. "Then that kiss'll have to be enough," she says, and goes back to washing the dishes.

Caleb picks his half-soggy drying towel up off the counter and they finish their work in a silence that neither of them seems able to break.

Caleb replays Christine's last words in his mind, over and over. *Then that kiss'll have to be enough.* It isn't just the guilt that sets that awful auditory loop in motion, nor is it only regret.

He's trying to decide if the undertone he heard in her voice was sorrow, or well-concealed malice. After all, she was a sleepwalker too.

Candles are lit on the dinner table, and the fake flowers in the centerpiece almost look real. The trailer has undergone a miraculous transformation in only an hour. The trash, old whiskey bottles, and slowly rotting food have been bagged up and taken out. The carpet, once gray with dust, has been vacuumed and revacuumed. Margie found some incense among Mrs. Zikry's magic supplies and managed to exorcise the stench that permeated the little place. Now everyone sits around an old, round table. Patches of its laminated surface have peeled away like the skin of a leper, revealing bits of particleboard beneath. Lepers make Ron Bent think of Jesus, and so when they all sit down at the table, staring at the still-bubbling lasagna in the foil pan, the first thing he does is offer to lead the prayer.

"I was a preacher once, in another life," he says. "Not a very good one, maybe, but good enough to string together a quick blessing, if y'all don't object."

Nobody does.

"Let's all join hands."

Ron looks around the table before he begins. At the far end, the kids, Caleb and Christine, sit next to one another. They sit close, but neither will look at the other one. It's a big departure from the way they had behaved together when they stepped into the kitchen an hour ago. *That's love,* Ron thinks, watching them, *never sane.* He smiles. Next he looks at Margie. Her wary eye is drifting to the witch. Margie doesn't trust her. This isn't Ron being astute—he knows he isn't much good at being astute—Margie flat out told him as much while they were taking the trash out.

"Not too many people might know it, but she was in that asylum once upon a time, and not because she worked there, I'll tell you that much. She's got secrets," Margie had declared. "They fly around her as plain as a swarm of hornets."

Maybe so, but right now the "witch" sits very quiet and still, staring at her own lap. Hard to imagine what horrible secrets a woman like that might have. She's more like a parishioner at his old church than a servant of the devil. Still, you never know about people. . . .

Looking around the table, Ron smiles. Five strangers were brought together here, and despite the distrust, the uncertainty, the unfamiliarity, right here in this moment they might be a family. They might be the only family he'll ever have again. And he prays:

Lord,
You have brought us here in fellowship together,
And we thank you.

We do not pretend to know
What your will holds for us,
But we know we are thankful for this food
And for each other,
And for the chance to follow
The path you're leading us down.
May we stay on that path,
Wherever it takes us,
And may it lead us always to you.
Please bless Keisha,
Bless Caleb's friend—

"Bean," Caleb murmurs.

"And Anna," says Christine.

"And Ralph and Lee Parsons," says Margie.

"And my father," says Caleb.

Bless them all, Lord,
And those whose names we don't know,
And be with us,
As we do your will,
'Til the end.
Amen.

All, even the witch, say amen.

"I think you might've been a better preacher than you give your-self credit for, Mister Bent," says Margie.

And they start eating.

In the paranoia of his mind, Caleb thinks he hears a far-off moan and a clacking sound, so soft it isn't real at all. It's the wind through the eves and the rustle of leaves, he tells himself; nothing more. And he forgets about it.

They eat and are full. The place is full of warm energy, of together-ness and anticipation. Christine finally looks at Caleb, and he catches her eye and they smile. He squeezes her hand under the table. Just like that, they've made peace.

In Caleb's frantically churning mind, his plans of a life with Amber are dissipating like an approaching mirage. The question is, when they're gone what will take their place? For the moment at least, he has no answer. Too many things have turned out to be mirages over the last few days, and he's having trouble figuring out what *is* real.

"This is delicious," Ron says.

"My Anna loves lasagna. Wherever she is, I bet she's fat and healthy and eating it right now," Mrs. Zikry says, then adds: "She ran away."

Everybody nods. Christine seems like she's about to speak, but doesn't.

"A lot of children've run away," Margie says, "and pretty soon, maybe we'll find some of them and bring them home."

"Or die trying," says Caleb. It was meant to be a joke, but the smile turns sour and dies on his lips.

Instead of laughter, the clink of forks on plates fills the silence.

After a few minutes the eating is done, but nobody moves to pick up the plates.

The witch begins weeping.

Everyone watches her. They look at one another, but nobody com-forts her. Christine just stares at her plate, in another world. Finally, Ron speaks.

"My wife," he says, "she was a strong woman. Way stronger than me. If I came in and tried to steal a piece of bacon before breakfast was done, she'd slap me so hard with her spatula that the welt would still be there after lunch. My brother made some racist comment one time about me being married to a black woman, and she threw a cup of beer in his face before I even knew what was happening. She was a hard worker, too. Started working at the age of twelve, 'cause her daddy made her. At sixteen she was out on her own and had her daddy locked up for beating her mother. She took care of her mom after that and her three little sisters; worked three jobs and went without new socks and underwear most of the time to keep them fed. When I met her, her sisters were grown and she only had two jobs. Her mother was blind with diabetes, and she took care of her. She worked nights at a truck stop and days at a plastics factory. I was driving trucks then, long hauls through South Dakota and Montana and Idaho, from Seattle to Chicago, then sometimes down to Atlanta. Her mother died the week we met and she went on the road with me. Nine months later, we were on the road, in South Dakota near Rapid City, in the Badlands, when our baby came. We had no doctors, no medicine, no nothing. She laid in the sleeper bunk and had that baby. It took all afternoon and all night. We sat all alone on the side of this lonely road in the middle of the night with the wind howling and dust blowing, and had that baby. And I swear to God, she never she cried once.

"I retired from trucking after the baby came. We got a little house, and I got a little job. Then Keisha, my daughter, disappeared. My wife started drinking. She started taking painkillers. More and more. She started looking through me instead of at me. Then she started looking through everything.

"On October twenty-ninth, four years ago, I came home from work and she was on the bed with the covers up to her chin, just like she was sleeping, as tucked in and comfy as could be. Except there was vomit all over. And her eyes weren't shut; they were open. She was the strongest person I ever knew. But not strong enough."

His words hang in the air, touching everything with their weight.

Nobody says anything or moves for a long time.

Finally, without turning her tear-filled eyes from her plate, Margie says, "Mr. Bent, why did you tell us all that?"

Ron looks around the table. A small, wistful smile hangs on his lips.

"Because all of us, we're still here."

Everyone looks at one another. A few heads nod.

"We should get some rest," says Christine. "We'll have to wake before dark."

⊰ Chapter Seventeen ⊱

SEE THE SLEEPING HOUSE:

The door is locked, the windows shut tight. The afternoon sun that made warm squares of light on the carpet has waned to nothing. It is a silent place. See the master bedroom. Here, two middle-aged women sleep far from one another, each wrapped in her own troubled dreams. See the other bedroom, the room of a teenage girl, with its perfume and posters and books. Here, a young man sleeps. His LA Dodgers cap is tilted down over his eyes. He dreams of a man in chains, whispering *"help me,"* and the dream makes him frown and mumble in his sleep. Now, look down the hall. See the living room. Here sleeps a man who some would call middle-aged, but who would call himself old. He snores softly. He is supposed to be awake, watching, but even the coffee, even the danger couldn't hold him. He tried pacing, tried watching TV (but found there was no TV to watch), even tried biting his lip. But in the end, the weight of his eyelids was insurmountable. He swore he would only rest his eyes for a few minutes, only for the time it takes to count to one hundred. But by forty, the numbers bled into silence, and the silence became everything.

Now, hear the creak of the floor. Hear the shuffling tread of slow, tender steps crossing the carpet, crossing the stained linoleum of the kitchen. Hear the breathing. It is deep and slow, but there is the faintest hiss as breath passes teeth. The footsteps stop. Hear the brush of a hand on the counter. Hear a metallic rasping sound, followed by a soft, momentary ringing of steel. Watch, as the figure crosses the kitchen and advances, slow and certain. See her eyelids, closed tight as coffins, the eyes behind them thrashing back and forth as if trying to get out. Watch her cross into the living room. Watch as her footsteps stop at the couch where the old man sleeps. Watch as the girl, the sleepwalking girl, suddenly makes a hideous, rage-warped face and jerks back the long, long carving knife.

Listen very, very closely, and in the bedroom, in the boy's dream, you might hear the man in chains screaming *"wake up!"*

And Caleb does, and rolls over.

And in the living room, Ron Bent opens his eyes just in time to see the mercurial streak as the knife blade speeds toward his face.

He snatches her tiny wrist in his hand.

The killing point of the blade quivers an inch above his left eye.

"Christine!" screams Caleb, just entering the room. "Wake up!"

She only snarls, jerks free of Ron, and raises the knife again.

Ron can hardly believe her strength, can hardly digest the nightmare image hovering over him. Shocked, he doesn't utter a sound. When the knife comes down a second time, he doesn't know if he'll be able to stop it.

"Christine!" Caleb yells again, as behind the apparition of a girl, Margie and Mrs. Zikry rush into the room and stand in the doorway, still groggy with sleep. Christine snarls again, and the knife blade falls, bringing death on its tip.

Ron knows his reaction is too slow, and waits for the sound of the blade ripping his skin, popping the lining of his stomach, biting into his spine.

Instead, at the last instant Christine is jerked sideways, tackled by Caleb, and Ron deflects the knife.

Now Christine is on the ground, under Caleb, eyes still closed, mouth still folded into a quivering, evil grimace.

Ron glances at the knife, now jutting from the arm of the couch only a few inches from his head. Then he rises, takes a deep breath to clear his head, and stoops to help Caleb restrain Christine.

"WAKE UP!" Caleb shouts, his face close to hers, his hands clamped on her wrists. "WAKE UP!"

And she does.

"What's going on?" Mrs. Zikry says.

Caleb doesn't say anything. He's staring at Christine and struggling to regain his breath.

Ron watches, utterly still.

Margie, stepping into the room, pipes up: "She tried to kill him, that's what's happening."

"She's a bad girl . . . " says the witch next to Margie.

"No," says Christine, "I didn't mean to."

"Don't just stand there," Margie says, nudging Ron. "We have to do something with her, or she's going to kill us all!"

"No!" says Christine, still pinned to the ground, tears filling her eyes. "I'm so sorry, Billy. I swear I wasn't trying to hurt him. I would never hurt him, I swear! You believe me, right?"

Caleb looks around, at a loss for words.

"Right? Ron? I'm sorry, I would never . . . "

"You had a knife, Christine," Caleb says finally. "We all saw what you tried to do."

"I wasn't me!" says Christine. "You have to believe me! It's whatever he put in my head! It makes them come."

"Makes who come, sweetie?" says Ron.

"Them!" she says. "The ghosts."

Caleb rolls off Christine, and they sit up, both shaking.

"Why do the ghosts want you to kill me?" Ron presses.

"They want to kill all of us," she says. "Because they think we'll stop them from waking the devil from where he sleeps in the dark. And the director wants the end of the world. But Anna says . . . "

Christine leans against the couch now and her head drops into her shaking hands.

"What does Anna say?" Caleb asks.

"She says it's already too late."

And from just outside the window comes a low voice filled with poisonous mirth: "Five little blackbirds, baked in a pie. . . ."

Caleb spins around and slaps the curtains back from the window.

No one is there—only the black outlines of trees against the deep blue of twilight.

"It is too late," says Christine. "We should have run away. We should have left town during the daylight, when we had the chance. Now they're all around us."

A pounding begins at the front door. Then there's a pounding at the wall of the room behind Christine, then on the wall next to Margie.

"Sweet Jesus Christ," she says.

Now there is pounding on every wall. The entire trailer is shaking.

The witch leans against the door frame, covering her ears and moaning. Finally, she steps over to the nearest wall and starts pounding back.

"Stop!" she screams. "Stop, stop, stop!"

"Do we have any weapons?" Ron asks.

"Only the knives in the kitchen," says Christine. "But they won't do us any good."

"Let's get one for each of us," Ron says. "I have a gun in the car," he adds. "But I doubt if they'll let me run out and get it."

And suddenly the pounding stops.

The five look at each other.

"Let's get those knives," says Ron.

"We ain't giving that girl a knife," says Margie. "I'll tell you that much. She's one of them, I don't know how much clearer it can be."

"I'm not one of them," says Christine, and she turns to Caleb. "Tell her, Billy!"

He looks at her for a moment, eyes veiled with conflicting emotion.

"Maybe we shouldn't give you one," he says finally, "just in case whatever they did to you comes back."

"It's only when I sleep," she says. Then, appealing to her mother: "Mom?"

The witch is scuttling back and forth, eyeing the walls warily. For a second, her mouth almost twitches into a smile.

"Christine is a bad girl," she says. "My Anna was always the sweet one."

Christine tries one more look at Caleb, but he won't meet her gaze.

She storms down the hall toward her room. A door slams shut.

Ron hands out the knives, one for each of them. "God be with us all," he says.

From Christine's room, a great hissing sound erupts.

Margie gives Caleb a look.

"I'll check on her," he says.

As he leaves, he hears Margie whispering to Ron: "I don't trust that witch none either. You shouldn'ta given her no weapon . . . "

Caleb tucks the knife into his belt and steps into Christine's room. She sits Indian-style on the floor in front of a bookshelf stereo.

"Anna," she says, "talk to me, please. What's going on? Anna?"

And the static forms a reply, deep as thunder.

<anna is gone>

The voice is loud enough to make the picture on the walls rattle.

"Who are you?" says Christine.

<we are . . . coming>

"What did you do with Anna?" she says.

At first, there's only the hiss of nothing, then:

<COME OUT!>

The sound shakes everything in the room, knocks two pictures off the wall, and blows out the speakers. Only a soft, electric buzz remains.

From the living room, they hear Margie:

"There's somebody out there!"

Christine and Caleb look at one another, then she gets up and starts to go down the hall. He grabs her arm and turns her toward him.

"I know you didn't mean to hurt Ron," he says. "Alright?"

"Billy," she says, "you've always been my favorite person of all, and if Ron helped you like you said, I would never hurt him. I would never hurt anyone. I thought you of all people would know that."

He can see the hurt in her eyes as she pulls away and disappears down the hall. He sighs, then follows.

In the living room, Ron is peering out the curtains. Margie and the witch seem to have taken up a defensive position behind the kitchen counter.

"The sheriff's out there," Ron says. "And . . . what the hell?"

Caleb and Christine look out. In the half-light they can see the sheriff with his brown hat and uniform, and next to him . . . Next to him stands an inhuman-looking, white-faced figure with large, strange eyes, wearing a black suit. In his hand: what appears to be a length of rope.

"Who's the other guy?" asks Ron.

"It's the director," says Caleb, but he doesn't know how he knows it.

The sheriff pulls out a megaphone.

"THERE'S TWO WAYS TO DO THIS," he says. "THE EASY WAY, OR THE FUN WAY."

And in the director's hands, a torch flares to life.

"WE WANT TO SEE ALL OF YOU OUT ON THE LAWN, NOW. YOU DON'T WANT TO COME OUT, THAT'S FINE. WE'LL BURN YOU OUT."

The director leans over and appears to say something to him.

The megaphone belches to life again. "UH . . . THIS IS JUST A TÊTE-À-TÊTE, THERE'S NO NEED TO BE AFRAID. THE FIGHT COMES LATER."

And the man with the torch, the director, starts walking toward them.

"What should we do?" Caleb asks. "Jump through the back window and make a break for the woods?"

"Uh, Billy," Christine says, staring out the back window, "look at this."

Out the back window, Caleb sees only an empty forest, at first. Then in the deep shadow he glimpses one white-gowned figure. Then another. Then another.

"We're surrounded."

"IF NOBODY COMES OUT BY THE TIME HE REACHES THE HOUSE, HE'S GONNA LIGHT IT UP."

"I'll go out," Christine says. "They already had me once. I'm not scared."

But her lips tremble as if with cold as she says the words.

"No," Caleb says. "I'll go."

"I'll go too," says Ron.

"Don't leave me in here!" says Margie, gesturing to the two Zikry women with her eyes.

"Believe me," says the witch, smiling, "you got bigger things to worry about than us."

For some reason, that makes everybody laugh, and the humor gives them all the courage they need.

Caleb steps over to Christine.

"I just wanted to let you know that I've missed you," he says softly, "and that you were always one of my favorite people too. It's just—"

"It's okay," she says, putting one shushing finger gently on his lips.

"He's getting close," says Ron.

"Lock the door behind us," Caleb says. He kisses Christine on the cheek, turns, and steps out the screeching screen door behind Ron.

They both stop short at the top of the cement steps. The director stands only ten feet away—but he never should have been able to cover that distance in so little time. And beside him are two sleepwalkers that weren't there before. Each of them holds a pistol aimed at the sky, like a couple of duelers.

The director smiles and brings the torch up a little. In the flickering illumination, Caleb sees why his face looked so strange before. He's wearing clown makeup. His skin is smooth and white, with black stars around his eyes and livid red paint emblazoned on his lips.

"Hello," says the director, "hello, hello. This is a festive day. Do you know why?"

Ron and Caleb shake their heads.

"Today," says the director, "the world ends. Or begins to end, anyway. And both of you have a wonderful part to play. That's exciting, isn't it?"

"We aren't helping you," says Caleb. He tries to sound defiant, but his voice wavers.

The director leans forward and whispers in a mock-confiding tone, "You're helping me right now."

Caleb can't tell whether he's really laughing, or whether the makeup just makes him look that way.

"Would you like me to explain, or should it be a surprise?"

"Explain," says Ron.

"Well," the director says, "I only need a few more souls in my little soul soup, and then my work here is done. So, I'm taking two of you. But *not* this one."

He points to Caleb.

"Why not me?" says Caleb.

"Because," says the director, "you have to be the hero. That's how you will help me. *He*," he points to Ron, "will help me by dying."

"What if I don't cooperate?" says Ron.

"Ron, have you ever watched a bullfight? The funny thing about a bullfight is the bull only thinks it's fighting. Really, it's just taking part in an elaborate, entertaining ritual culminating in its death. This is kind of like a bullfight."

Ron remains still, silent.

"Now, Ron. Thinking of going for your knife?" the director gestures to the gowned figures on either side of him. "Just because their eyes aren't open, do you think they can't see?"

The sleepwalkers jerk their arms toward the dark sky and twin shots crack. An instant later, two bats fall at the foot of the stoop, shot out of the sky.

The director smiles. "That was well done. Even I'm impressed. But precious time is ticking past us. I'll need the others to come out now."

"What if they don't?" says Caleb.

The director sighs. "Please, little Billy. You already know the answer. They will shoot each of you, then I will light the trailer on fire. Your friends will either run out and be caught, or they will sizzle inside. Now quit stalling. COME OUT!" he roars.

Caleb and Ron exchange helpless looks.

"Don't come out!" Caleb yells over his shoulder.

"Oh, Billy," sighs the director, "always the fighter. Tell me, have you read the paper these last few days? Do you know about the big earthquake in China? The tsunami in Indonesia? That probably breaks your big ol' heart, doesn't it? Over five hundred thousand people are already corpses. And the dead are still washing up on the beaches. I bet you wish you could go help those people, don't you? Just like you wanted to help those millions of poor colored folks dying by the truckload in Africa?"

"How did you know I was going to do that?"

"I know everything," says the director. "From beginning to end, I know it all. Here's a lesson: when you die, things are revealed. The dead tell me many things because I help them. And in turn, they help me. As you can see." He gestures to the sleepwalkers.

"But my initial question regarding the mass carnage in South Asia is this: if you believe there is a heaven, then aren't these people actually better off? Their suffering is relieved, their poverty and disease have been cleansed from them. It's hypocritical to believe that good people who die go to heaven and yet still mourn death. Death is divine release. In the words of Shakespeare, 'Tis a consummation devoutly to be wished.'"

"Every human life is precious," says Ron. "We can rejoice when a spirit rejoins God, but when people are taken before their time, it is a tragedy."

"Ah, words from the preacher who lost his faith. Bravo. But you have it wrong. It is life which is the tragedy. And it is the transcendence of life which should be celebrated. Therefore, you should rejoice in the opportunity to help two of your friends reunite with God in heaven. Now, SEND THEM OUT so the celebration can begin!"

The director is fidgeting with the loop of rope in his hand. His eyes, behind all that black makeup, appear dazzling, almost hypnotic, almost familiar.

"Your words wear a mask that looks like the truth. As the devil's words often do," says Ron. "And I didn't lost my faith. I just misplaced it."

The director smiles.

"My dear Mr. Bent, I am not the devil. The devil is sleeping now. But he's rolling over in his sleep. He's . . . stirring. You'll hear his words for yourself soon enough, I assure you. When the sixty-six are sleeping in the cold with him, then you'll hear his words like a trumpet. But for now, I ask once more that you BRING OUT YOUR FRIENDS."

Ron shakes his head.

The clown face smiles.

All Caleb sees is a flick of the director's wrist and a streak of brown, and the lasso is around Ron's neck. The director snaps his end of the rope back as fast as a cobra striking, and Ron is yanked forward. His knees hit the steps hard and he slides down and lands face-first in the grass with a "thud" that shakes Caleb where he stands. The director keeps the rope taut and pulls Ron across the grass toward him. Ron arches his back and raises his head. His face is already a deep red and strings of spit hang from his mouth as he grabs at the rope, trying to relieve the pressure on his throat, trying to catch a breath. The director just jerks again, dragging him ahead faster now, dragging him across the grass on his belly, and Ron's fingers slip off the lasso uselessly.

Caleb is leaping off the step, knife in hand, ready to cut Ron free, but before his feet even hit the ground, one of the sleepers strikes him in midair, slamming him in the head with the butt of its pistol. Caleb falls back on the steps. Before he can rise, the other sleepwalker is on him too. They each grab one of his arms. He tries to break free, but no matter how much he struggles, he can't move even an inch. They pull his arms behind his back and pain shoots through his shoulders and his injured wrist. He winces, dizzy and out of breath. Out of the corner of his eye, he sees the director working fast. In the next instant, he's bound Ron's hands with the same rope that's looped around his neck, so that if Ron struggles with his arms, it automatically applies choking pressure on his throat.

From the edge of the woods comes the sound of applause, many hands clapping. The megaphone says: "THAT WAS FAN-TASTIC ROPIN', COWPOKE. I'D LIKE TO SEE THAT ONE AGAIN IN SLO-MO."

The director gives a gracious wave.

"That," he says, "was the fun way. Now . . . " He looks at the trailer's darkened window.

"I know my beautiful little friend Christine is in there. Come out and bring your friends with you or—"

And the sleepers put their pistols to both Caleb's temples. The director pulls on the length of rope running between Ron's wrists and his throat, pulling it so tight he can't even make a gurgling sound. His eyes are red with burst blood vessels.

"The easy way or the fun way, Christine. Everybody has to go sometime; all you can do is choose how. I want all three of you out here—now."

And the door opens. Christine steps out, followed by the witch, followed by a reluctant Margie, who hangs back in the doorway.

"My sweet Christine," says the director. "I've missed you ever so much."

Over the director's shoulder, Christine watches in horror as the sleepwalkers emerge from the line of trees. When she was in the hospital, it was impossible to gauge how many patients were there. They were all kept apart, fed in their rooms and let out only for therapy. Now she sees there are hundreds of them, filling the woods on all sides of the trailer. And they're coming.

"I have one sacrifice here, this miserable wretch of a man, Mr. Ron Bent, so the good news is I only need one more," says the director, smiling. Ron expels a spray of spit and gasps a rasping breath before the director jerks the rope taut again.

"So now it's up to you, sweet Christine. Who do we take? Mommy? The old bag of a waitress? Or sweet little you?"

"I ain't going nowhere," murmurs Margie.

"Sweet little me," says Christine. "You already took Anna, didn't you? Why not take both sisters and have a matching set?"

"Yes, I did take Anna. She was the first. She was . . . a necessary ingredient in our little soul pie. And it's very noble to offer yourself as the last. I'm proud of you." He turns to the sleepers with their guns on Caleb's head. "Shall we?"

The guns snap toward the steps in perfect unison.

"CHRISTINE," yells Caleb, but his arms are still held in the sleepers' iron grips.

Both guns bark together.

Christine closes her eyes. She hears the gunshots as they come, hears the giddy murmur of the dead all around her. But no pain comes. When her eyes open, she already knows what's happened but still turns her head to see for herself:

On the steps behind her, Margie's kneecaps have exploded. The waitress pitches sideways off the steps, hitting the ground headfirst. She doesn't scream; the only sound she utters is a breathy groan. Sleepwalkers surround her in an instant, like a pack of dogs. Christine looks on in horror, expecting them to tear Margie apart, but instead they pick her up gently and bear her up over their heads.

More come and pick up Ron the same way. One holds the rope, always keeping the pressure on Ron's throat.

The director just looks at Christine and smiles.

"It's not your time to choke yet," he says. "But it's coming."

One by one, each of the army of pale, sleeping teenagers and children falls in step and disappears into the woods.

The witch stands looking on, utterly expressionless. Christine wrenches the knife from her mother's grip but remains there, standing on steps, her chest heaving big, furious breaths, with no idea in the world what to do.

"No! Take me!" she shouts.

The director cocks his head.

"Patience," he says.

At the foot of the steps, the sleepers release Caleb and simply walk away. Caleb rises and goes for his knife.

The director gives him a bemused look.

"Stabbing me now? *Et tu,* Billy? If only it were that easy." He turns away. "I'll see you both soon," he calls over his shoulder.

"You're not getting away with this!" Christine screams, and she charges the director with her knife.

The director wheels, another lasso already swinging in his grip.

He flicks his wrist and the rope almost seems to have a mind of its own as it flits through the air and jerks the knife out of Christine's hand. He whips the rope around over his head, then swings it back at Christine. The knife, caught in the loop of the lasso, whips toward her with incredible speed. It makes a tiny "tick" sound as it passes her face, and that's all. She falls to her knees.

Caleb takes a step forward to go to her but is cut off by three lingering sleepers, who hiss at him fearsomely.

When the director flicks his wrist again, the knife jerks into his left hand and the lasso winds itself into a neat loop in his right.

"Not now, my sweet Christine. Soon. We'll all be together again soon—you, me, and Billy. I promise." He blows her a kiss, and flanked by sleepwalkers, turns and disappears into the woods.

In an instant, Caleb is kneeling in front of Christine.

His heart is throbbing. He doesn't know what he's going to see when he looks at her face, what hideous disfigurement or fatal wound he will find there, but he's trembling just thinking of the possibilities.

"Are you okay?" he asks as he arrives at her side, breathless.

"No," she says, through tears.

And he looks at her frantically. First at her eyes—both there, both dark and beautiful and intact—then her throat; it's unblemished by blood.

He squints in the dark. "What's wrong?"

"Can't you see?" she says. "It's horrible."

He keeps looking, seeing nothing.

"What?" he asks desperately. "What?"

"He cut off a bunch of my hair," she says, clearly in shock from the sight she just witnessed.

Caleb looks closer. A chunk of her long, dark hair has indeed been chopped off—and her only other injury is a tiny scratch just in front of her ear, which oozes one huge tear of blood.

Caleb laughs and pulls her to him and hugs her tight.

"Do I look horrible?" she asks, sounding numb.

Laughing with relief, he says, "You look gorgeous."

She pulls away from him.

"We have to get Margie and Ron back," she says.

He takes her hands in his and squeezes them. "We will. I swear."

On the porch, the witch is on her hands and knees, scrubbing Margie's blood and tiny, shattered bits of kneecap off the steps, and humming.

⊰ Chapter Eighteen ⊱

KNEELING IN A FIELD OF STARS, this might be the night the world was made. Crickets chirp, the night breeze rustles leaves overhead, and all else holds its breath. In the dark, two childhood friends embrace. This might be Adam and Eve in the Garden. This might be the beginning of the world instead of the end of it.

"We'll fix all this," says Caleb, only half believing his own words. Then: "What is it?"

Christine stares hard at nothing. Finally, she says: "The voices—I can't hear them anymore."

"They're gone?" he asks.

"No. Still here, but . . . quiet. Like they're waiting for something. For the end."

"Then let's finish it."

They help each other off the dew-soaked ground. The Spanish moss hanging from ancient, dying oak trees, the strangling kudzu, the serpentine tendrils of mist creeping from the forest all around them: everything is a shroud. Hiding the truth. Hiding the future. Hiding any chance they might have had at a pleasant life full of denial and the appearance of happiness, a normal life. Now, even if they perform a miracle and somehow make it out of this ghost town alive, they'll be forever haunted. Maybe figuratively, maybe literally.

They listen to the squeal of bats overhead. They enter the circle of light cast from the windows of the squat little trailer, mount the steps—still splattered here and there with blood and bits of bone. They open the screen door. And Caleb freezes, listening.

There is a moaning sound, so soft it could be the creak of a tree trunk in the wind. Except it's not.

He grabs Christine's arm. "Do you hear it?"

She's still for a moment.

"I think we should go inside," she says. "It's not safe out here."

But Caleb is already ignoring her, already heading down the steps, around the corner, to the dark side of the trailer where the moonlight won't even go.

And he stops in front of the cellar door.

"It's coming from in here," he says.

"Don't open it, Caleb. I'm serious. I have a really bad feeling. The dead are screaming not to open it." Pain is in her voice, and she has her hands clamped to her ears—but Caleb is deaf to her, his eyes transfixed by the door. From its latch, a big, rusting padlock hangs.

He turns, looking for something, anything that might help him break the lock, then sees it. A hatchet waits, stuck in a log on the far side of the lawn, framed in moonlight, and Caleb brushes past Christine. Now he's running to the hatchet, yanking it free, now shrugging off Christine's restraining hand.

And chopping at the lock on the door.

"Billy, no!" Christine says. "It has to stay locked."

Why should I trust her? he thinks suddenly. She, who just tried to kill Ron. This could be a trick, a ploy. His father could be locked up in there.

"Everyone calls me Caleb now," Billy says.

And he chops.

"The voices say the devil is in there! They say you'll set him free!"

Caleb growls, eyes narrowed: "The voices make people disappear, Christine. You think we can trust them?"

"They also saved our lives," she says.

Caleb is chopping.

He says: "And can you tell the difference between the ones that want to help and the ones that hurt? What if they're lying to you? You ever think of that?"

"They said you'd say that," she says, backing away from him one step. "They predicted all of this. They said you'd betray us!"

Caleb stays his hand for a moment, looks at her.

"Who's down in this basement? Do you know?"

She just stares at him.

"Why are you trying to stop me? Your mother locked somebody in here. Who?"

"I don't know."

"Then we have to find out. It could be anybody. Could be a kid, for Christ's sake!"

"That's not what the voices say."

"It could be my dad!"

Caleb starts hacking at the lock again.

"Billy," Christine says, "they all say you'll help him bring about the end. They say you're the one who'll make it happen."

"I would never do that, Christine."

"Maybe you already are."

Silence settles between them, one more black shroud.

Sparks fall, and the hammering blows of the hatchet fill the forest. The moon passes behind a cloud, the lock falls, and Christine walks away.

Caleb doesn't notice her leave. He's pulling on the rusted handle, pulling back the peeling wood cellar door, smelling the rot and must behind it.

Inside, an abyss.

He's terrified to look into the blackness, terrified to look away. He has no light. But something makes him take the first step down into the dank cellar. Something makes him take the second. And he wonders suddenly if he's being drawn down by his own will, or the will of a thousand malevolent demons. The urge to run fills him suddenly with the urgency of vomit rising in the throat.

But he will not run.

It's too late, anyway. He's in the dark now.

The wet, sickly smell of decay surrounds him, making him shiver. He reaches the bottom of the stairs and steps into liquid up to his ankles. Something is brushing his face. He keeps swatting it away, but it keeps coming back; cobwebs, or something worse. He's suddenly about to cry; he just wants to leave, just wants to wake up from this nightmare that somewhere took a wrong turn and became real. And . . .

And he isn't alone.

Amongst the rustle of chains comes a dry, sharp whisper.

"If you've come to kill me, you're wasting your time," it says. "I'm already dead."

There's no way of telling where the voice comes from. It echoes from all around him.

Caleb opens his mouth, but terror has robbed him of his breath.

"Are you the devil?" he asks finally.

The laugh comes like the crackle of dry leaves.

"Well, I'm sure not God."

Caleb doesn't know what to say.

"You think you're a very brave boy, don't you?" says the devil.

Outside, a storm is blowing in. Rain begins pattering and builds until even from underground. Caleb can hear the drops pounding relentlessly.

"You wanted to save the world . . ."

"Who are you?" says Caleb, "If you're my father, then say so. And if you're really the devil . . . " He wants to finish, but doesn't know how. "You can't have me," he says finally.

The laughter cracks. "Certainty is like a straitjacket, kid, and you need both hands. Now stop asking questions and listen; our time is short."

Caleb shivers. Glancing over his shoulder, he sees nothing. All around him the darkness is total. He might be in outer space or the Mariana Trench. He might not be at all. He can't see the cellar door. He can't see anything.

"Listen, if you would undo what's been done here, I'm going to tell you the story of Jonathan Morle. This is the first and the last time anyone will tell it, so pay close attention."

Caleb does.

"Morle grew up in Boston. He was a sad kid, tried killing himself several times before he was even fifteen. Maybe that's what happens to the son of a Harvard professor and a whore.

"After his mother died of syphilis, he broke into his father's house. He found him in his study asleep and strangled him, then hung him from a rafter. Next, he found the old professor's wife and two grand-children, killed them with a fire poker and hung them up as well. Most of the police thought it was a murder-suicide, that the professor did it, that it was the work of a brilliant but slightly insane intellectual. But not all of the cops were convinced. And one of the detectives came after Jonathan.

"With no money and no means to flee, Morle joined the merchant marines, boarded a freight ship, and departed immediately for the farthest ports this world offered. He went around the globe, from

Amsterdam to Cape Town, Bangkok to Sydney.

"His shipmates described him as a quiet man with a beautiful singing voice. He didn't drink alcohol, didn't care much for prostitutes, stayed away from fights. But at every port he landed, a family was found dead, hung from the rafters of their house. Nobody on his ship knew about that. It didn't even hit the local papers until they had weighed anchor and left port. The only strange thing about Jonathan Morle, his shipmates said, was that he seemed to collect a clock at every stop.

"Morle finally landed in San Francisco where he was accepted at the University of California, Berkeley. Fellow students characterized him as handsome, pale, distracted, articulate, and punctual. He was three years into a degree in psychology when the law once again caught up with him. This time, since the sea no longer seemed safe for him, he chose the most desolate place he could think of within the United States. He moved to a small town a hundred miles west of Tulsa, Oklahoma, and took the only job he could find working as a rodeo clown."

"The director," says Caleb.

The voice continues: "He lived there for three years. Locals didn't say much about him, except that he read a lot of books and kept to himself. He rented an abandoned trailer on the outskirts of town and never seemed to leave except on rodeo days. That went on for almost two years, until one day he was gored in the head by a bull and nearly killed.

"After that, he disappeared. He didn't surface again for a long time. Most of the police who had been pursuing him had long since given up the chase by now. But not one. Finally, that detective's persistence paid off. Morle turned up in Chicago, this time under an assumed name. He had received a law degree from the University of Chicago. But just as he began his first job with one of Chicago's top law firms, friends began to see a change in him. Maybe it was due to head trauma from the rodeo days and maybe something else, but Morle— though they knew him by another name—became more and more reclusive. Soon he wouldn't leave his apartment. He would simply sit in his room, surrounded with his collection of clocks, and not move for days. Following a suicide attempt, he was institutionalized. It was just after he was released that he learned the detective was on his trail again, closer than ever. So he fled to Florida and checked himself into a mental hospital in a small town called Hudsonville, again under an assumed name. It was there the detective finally caught up to him. But by then it was too late."

Thunder rolls suddenly, like great, terrible drums shaking the ground under Caleb's feet.

"The detective infiltrated the asylum, posing as another inmate, hoping to befriend Morle, hoping to coax a confession out of him. What that detective didn't know was what a powerful manipulator Morle was. You see, he already had everyone in the asylum under his control. He had taught them his little secret with the clocks, how they could tune your ear to the voices of the dead. And when the dead spoke, do you know what they said? They said 'you'd better help John Morle.' And that's what everyone did. What they didn't know was that even Morle was a slave to the spirits, and the spirits, they were slaves to something else.

"Strange, all Morle really wanted was to die. He wanted the suffering of his life to end, according to his doctors. He tried to kill himself fifteen times at the asylum. Every time he failed. I guess some weeds are just impossible to kill. And the detective never got his confession."

"You were the detective," says Caleb.

The laugh sounds mechanical, fake. "Once upon a time."

The voice is silent for a moment. All Caleb hears is a strange crackling sound, then the gentle clang of chains, way too close. When the voice returns, it sounds strangely garbled, as if the speaker, this devil in the basement, were choking. The first words Caleb understands are:

"—the asylum closed, the inmates scattered to the wind or hid their identities, and so did John Morle. But they came back to town a few years ago. Hell, a lot of them never even left. One became a doctor, one became the sheriff, one became the mayor of the town. And they came back to finish what they had started. To help Morle, as the spirits commanded them."

"What does he want?"

"Sixty-six souls, according to Morle, and his pact with the devil is finished. The end comes. The devil awakens."

"What do I do to stop him?"

The clangor of chains alone makes its reply.

"And what happened to you after the asylum closed and you were set free?" Caleb asks. "How long have you been here?"

Thunder pounds and wind howls above, but here in the dark there's only silence.

"I know who you are . . . Dad? You were the detective once, right? Then you became a lawyer, so you could put people like Morle behind bars, right? And they killed you for it."

Thunder breaks, hard enough to crack the world in half. Caleb takes a step forward, his hand outstretched.

"Dad?"

And lightning floods through the cellar door in one flash-frame instant, blazing away every ounce of shadow with eerie white fire.

There, in front of Caleb's outstretched hand, hang four chains, and bound in those chains are the four wilted limbs of a long-dead corpse. One bloated, rotting hand almost touches Caleb's fingers before he jerks his hand back. The mouth hangs open, the eyes stare into a black puddle below. On a table next to the corpse, an old, dusty radio crackles.

Caleb tries to scream, but nothing comes out.

In the next instant, the lightning is gone and he's back in darkness.

He wheels and takes off for where the light came from, where the door must be, but the voice, that electric, fake, dead voice follows him.

"Aw, Billy, don't run away—"

Caleb trips, falls on his face. Dark, stagnant water splashes into his eyes, into his mouth. The stench yanks at his gut muscles, almost jerking them into vomiting. Caleb's hand slips on the slimy cement, but he manages to get to his feet and runs on, blindly. Then he sees a little light come through the door—a glimpse of the moon or more lightning, he doesn't know which—and he's pounding up the steps and into the open, with that maniacal voice following him from the radio, from the basement, screaming:

"Kid, what you don't know could fill a warehouse! You'd better listen! You'd better not—"

And Caleb slams the basement door shut and leans on it, his face in his hands.

→

"Caleb?" It's Christine; she's there. "What's wrong?" She comes forward through the rain, reaching out to Caleb, seeing his distress, but draws up when she glimpses the hatchet still clutched in his hand. He looks down at its sharp, curved edge. He had completely forgotten about it. By now Christine's hesitation has passed. She puts her arms around his neck and squeezes him tight. Caleb hugs her back, but he holds on to the hatchet, too.

"What was down there?" asks Christine.

"Nothing," he replies.

Inside, when they step out of the rain, they find the witch staring out the window with a burning cigarette in one hand and burning sage in the other.

"Aw, Mom," says Christine, "we just cleaned the floor. You're getting ashes all over it." She goes to the linen closet and gets a towel for herself and one for Caleb. As he towels off his hair, he confronts her.

"Christine, did you know who was down there?"

She stops drying herself and gives him a quizzical look. "I never went down there before. It was always locked up. Mom said she didn't have the key. Why? What did you find?"

Caleb turns to the witch. "Mrs. Zikry?"

She sings under her breath: *"Mine eyes have seen the glory of the coming of the morn . . ."*

"Mrs. Zikry!" he says louder.

"From the deep and darkest water great Lucifer is born. When six and sixty souls are dead he'll blow his mighty horn . . ."

"Hey!" says Caleb, grabbing her shoulder and spinning her toward him. "What did you do to my father?"

Her face is a grin full of gray, crooked teeth. *". . . and hell is marching on!"* she finishes with raucous laughter.

He throws her down on the couch with one hand and grips the hatchet tighter with the other.

"Billy!" Christine says. "Don't! She's just crazy."

"That was my father down there, Christine! He's dead! He was chained up like a dog." Tears are hot on his cheeks now; it's too late to try to stop them, too late to be ashamed.

He turns back to the witch.

"Why?" he screams, "You'd better answer me! Why did you do it?"

The witch just laughs and hums to herself. She takes a bottle out from under a couch cushion and takes a swig.

"You'll pay for what you did," he says flatly.

"Billy, don't hurt her," says Christine. She's close behind him now, with a gentle hand on his shoulder.

"Don't hurt her. She isn't well, you can see that. I never told you this, I never told anyone, but she was in the asylum once. I found some papers in her dresser one time. She isn't well."

"Ticktock, ticktock," says the witch.

"She was in the asylum?" says Caleb.

"Yes," says Christine. "I never told you because—"

But he's already turned on the witch again.

"You!" he says. "Put down that bottle and look at me, or I swear to God I'll chop you in half!"

The witch raises the bottle to her eye and looks at him through it, laughing soundlessly.

"Why did you lock him up down there?" he says, trying to appear calm now. "Just tell me and I won't hurt you."

She drops the bottle and looks at Caleb squarely.

"He told me to."

"Who?"

"You know who," she says. "Johnny."

"Jonathan Morle?" Caleb asks.

She ignores him.

"Why did Morle tell you to do that?" he presses.

"That detective was always sneaky," she says, gesturing to the cellar. Then changing the subject: "The spirits won't talk to me . . . " she says sadly, then pauses and stares down into the whiskey bottle as if it were full of tea leaves. "But Johnny talks to me."

"And you knew him in the asylum?"

"Of course."

"And you followed his orders?"

"Of course."

"Why?"

"Why, why, why, why? Four and twenty blackbirds, baked in a pie!" says the witch with a repulsive, childish giggle.

"And what about Anna? Did you let him take her? Or did you kill her yourself?"

"ANNA IS ALIVE!" screams the witch, and suddenly she's on her feet. Her ritual knife has appeared from nowhere, and it's at Caleb's throat.

He thinks he could take her with the hatchet if he's fast enough, even though he can already feel the sharp edge of her knife breaking the skin in tiny places. His muscles tense to strike.

"Mom, no!" yells Christine, jumping between them.

"You bad, bad, bad girl!" spits the witch. "Get back."

"Mom! Caleb! Both of you, please, let's just figure out how to save Mr. Bent and Margie and the other kids, if we can, and get the hell out of this town. Please," says Christine.

Caleb and the witch exchange an icy look. She isn't laughing anymore.

"Maybe we should wait until morning," says Caleb.

"By morning it'll be all over," says the witch.

"What?" says Caleb sarcastically, "the end of the world?"

The witch just smiles a slow smile and plays her fingers across the blade of her knife.

"She's right," says Christine. "They'll be dead before morning, if they aren't already."

"We could just leave," says Caleb. "Get as far away as we can as fast as we can. There's no way the world is really going to end. That guy might be able to talk to ghosts, but that doesn't mean he knows what's really going to happen. Maybe everything will be okay."

The witch smiles big. "Tick, tock, tick."

Christine shakes her head. "The dead are guiding his actions," she says. "Maybe you're right; maybe he's just crazy. But can we really take that chance? What if it's true? We have to stop him."

"If the devil walked among us, if the world ended, everybody would suffer and die . . . And we would have turned our backs on trying to stop it," says Caleb with a sigh. He makes up his mind. "Do we have any weapons? Besides this stupid hatchet?"

Christine shakes her head. "Just the cooking knives."

"Wait," says the witch. She disappears into the bedroom.

Christine and Caleb exchange a look.

"Billy," Christine says, "I'm sorry—" Tears swell in her eyes and her voice cuts off, then comes back. "I'm sorry about your dad. I swear to God I didn't know. I wouldn't blame you if you killed my mom; it's just . . . she raised me. She tried. She's just . . . broken. I'm sorry, Billy." She puts a hand on his arm.

He sloughs it off. "Everyone calls me Caleb now," he says.

The witch reappears from the hallway, carrying a dusty little cardboard box. She sets it on the coffee table then looks at them expectantly.

Christine leans over and looks in the box. She reaches into it and pulls out a small, dust-covered revolver. It's so old its chrome plating has worn off in places.

"Was this Dad's?" she asks.

The witch nods.

"Why are you giving us this?" asks Caleb. "I thought you were on Morle's side."

The witch shrugs.

"We should go," says Christine.

"No," says Caleb. "I want to know why she'd give us this if she really wants Morle to win. It's probably a trick. It doesn't make any sense."

He turns back to the witch. "Well?"

She smiles again, shrugs. "Johnny's gonna win," she says. "No matter what."

"Caleb," Christine says, "we should go."

Caleb's stare lingers on the witch as he tries to plumb the depth of her insanity. Finally, he gives up and follows Christine to the door, gun in hand.

At the door he stops, turns back to the witch.

She's already busied herself lighting candles and humming.

"My father was a great man," says Caleb. "He won't be forgotten."

The witch pauses in her humming and looks at Caleb.

"Yes, Billy," she says pleasantly. "I know."

As Caleb steps out through the screech of the screen door, he hears her singing behind him:

"Mine eyes have seen the glory of the coming of the morn . . . "

And he and Christine cross the field of stars for the last time.

Awareness comes in patches, like glimpses though a dense fog.

Ron feels many hands on him, the burn of the rope on his throat; he hears the crackling of leaves and sticks under bare white feet somewhere below. When his eyes flutter open he sees tree branches dissecting the night sky. Once he sees a star, a bright one. Might be the North Star, but he can't tell. Then he falls back under, to a place even below dreams, a place of uneasy silence.

When he opens his eyes again, all he sees are green blades of grass. He sneezes and realizes some of them are tickling his nostrils. Must be what woke him. He also realizes the rope on his neck has gone slack. He raises his face slowly from the dewy grass, wincing as the muscles of his neck knot up sharply. His skin burns from the rope, and when he looks down at the grass, he sees little dots of his own blood.

At first everything is blurry. All his eyes can make out is shadow upon shadow. As a moment passes, though, the shades of darkness differentiate. He sees trees arching grandly above him, forming the roof of a great, natural cathedral. A few feet in front of him is the utterly placid surface of what looks like a pond, reflecting the blackness of the sky like a great, dark mirror. Except it reflects no stars, and the moon, which hangs just over the treetops, is nowhere to be seen on its surface.

Now he sees white shapes. They form a ring surrounding the pond. The shapes become figures, young people, wearing white nightgowns. Their eyes are closed and their faces are as still and calm as the surface of the water they encircle.

Ron hears a voice and looks up. Next to him a man stands, his arms stretched wide. Bizarre, inhuman sounds emanate from his lips and fill the little clearing with chattering, bellowing, screaming, hissing. The old Ron, the one who was a preacher once in Mississippi, the one who was run out of town by his own congregation, would know these sounds for what they are: the man, the director, is speaking in tongues.

In one of his outstretched hands he holds the end of a rope. The other end is still looped around Ron's neck.

Ron takes a deep breath, fighting to think clearly. He sees the sleepwalkers, the director, and the sheriff at his side, all facing the pond. All have left their backs to him, apparently thinking his lights would be out for quite a while. If he has a chance at all, this is it. He glances over and sees Margie next to him. She's on her back. Her lips move as if she's speaking, except no sound comes out. Her eyes are rolled back in her head with only the whites showing. She's deep in shock. Her legs look like they belong in a butcher's shop, and the puddle of blood she's lying in must be an inch and a half deep. Her face is very pale; her breathing is so shallow Ron can't see her chest moving. In another fifteen minutes, she'll be dead. Whatever he's going to do, he'll have to do it alone.

Just as he thinks this, the babbling ceases and in a booming voice the director proclaims, "Bring forth the sacrifices!"

"John," says the sheriff, so quietly Ron can barely make out what he's saying. "One of them—that lady, Lee—got away while we were dealing with the ones at the trailer. We're going to have to get one more to make sixty-six."

The director, still in his clown makeup, steps up to the sheriff, a much larger man, and slaps him in the face as if he were a snotty child. He smiles.

"Never fear, the spirits will pick a replacement," he says. "Maybe . . . even . . . you!"

He steps away from the sheriff and opens his arms wide again, addressing the eerie assembly.

"Who will go?" he says.

Ron knows this is his chance. He slips the rope off over his head slowly, carefully, trying not to put any tension on the line and alert the director. There's a moment of terror when the rope catches on his hook, but he's able to pull it loose without too much wrangling.

Finally, he's free.

He glances once more at Margie, wishing he could help her, knowing he can't, and looks up again. One of the gowned figures has stepped forward, a slender black kid with cornrows in her hair. The director looks at the kid and begins speaking tongues again.

Then Ron is on his feet running.

The edge of the clearing is only maybe ten feet away, and he's shocked to see the Dream Center rising up just about twenty feet beyond that. From where he was lying, he was unable to see it. Now every perception comes to him with amazing clarity. He must dart between these two small trees, slip around that oak, then make it around the corner of the Dream Center. If he can make it that far without their noticing, he should be able to escape. His knees don't hurt him now. He feels strong. He feels utterly free, as the ground races past him, and here come those trees. This is the victory he's waited for his whole life. They won't take him, no way, not Ron Bent. They'll turn around and he'll be gone. He'll find Caleb and Christine, get some guns, come back and burn this old hospital into the dust. Here come those trees, and he's shooting between them—now just pass the oak, get around the corner, and—

First, his mouth snaps shut so hard he feels his teeth shatter. Then he sees his legs; they've miraculously shot out in front of him and hang suspended in the air for an instant. He hears something snap in his windpipe. Then he's on the ground with a devastating thud. Trees spin around him like he's on a carnival ride. And maybe that's all this is, maybe that's all life ever is; he suddenly thinks. After all, here's a clown, looking down at him, snarling. There are some teenagers, hanging out. Of course, the teenagers' eyes are shut and the clown is holding the end of the noose that's choking Ron's life away.

These thoughts, these sights, spin around him. And he realizes in a flash that he was just jerked into the air, like a dog who chases after a kid on a bike, forgetting that it's tied to a tree, and almost breaks its neck when he reaches the end of its chain. Except instead of a chain, it was the director's lasso that got him. And unlike those tough, ol' dogs, Ron thinks, he might've actually broken his neck. He tastes blood in his mouth. His tongue sifts through shards of broken teeth. This head sings a one-note, droning song. And hands carry him to the water's edge.

He watches out of the corner of his eye (turning his head would hurt too much) as the end of the rope around his neck is tied to a big cement weight. The sheriff loops some rope around Margie's neck and ties her to a weight as well.

Margie is utterly still. Ron tries to find the words to pray for her soul, but can't. All he can think of is the one-note ringing in his head. He can't even hear the babbling of the director anymore.

And it's kind of peaceful.

Several sleepwalkers come forward and put Margie and him into a rowboat. The black kid climbs in the boat as well, also with a weight and a rope around the neck.

The sheriff pushes off the shore and steps into the boat. There's a little rocking motion as they get going. It's kind of nice.

For some reason, it comes into Ron's head that this might be the start of a good joke . . . an old preacher, a sheriff, a waitress, and a black kid all get in a boat. . . The punch line eludes him. Still, if he could smile, he would. As it is, all he can do is watch the stars sitting so still way up there in the sky. Clouds race past them, but the stars always reappear, faint but eternal. He doesn't hear the singing from the shore as all the sleeping possessed ones join the mad rodeo clown in chorus. Instead, he thinks back on his life. Ron Bent was never much for paying attention, even when things were really serious, like now.

He remembers Camilia's sweet potatoes with the brown sugar on top, the same color brown as her skin as they made love in the back of his Challenger on their wedding night. He remembers lighting up a smoke and breathing it deep in the cold, cold of morning before getting on a bus to God knows where. He remembers holding a stranger's hand during prayer at church, not knowing who the man was, and loving him anyway. And he remembers Keisha. Keisha, trying to teach him how to double Dutch, begging for money for the ice-cream truck, Keisha, with the same beautiful, caramel-colored skin her mother had. Keisha, loving him no matter how many times he'd messed up and disappointed everyone else.

God, why are you taking me now?
I thought I had a bigger part to play.

He was never much good at accepting his lousy luck.

More stars go by. He realizes his clothes are wet. Did a storm come through while he was unconscious? If so, it's cleared up now.

The boat is slowing. Just then, feeling begins to trickle back into his fingers and toes, and the cold metal of the boat bottom finally registers against his body. He wiggles his fingers.

Maybe Ron Bent isn't completely broken yet.

Sheriff's leg moves next to Ron as he rows. There's a gun on his hip.

Ron, his face pressed awkwardly against the aluminum bench of the rowboat, smiles.

A gentle rain starts falling again.

This is it. Ron tenses and strikes.

He yanks the sheriff's gun from its holster and shoots him in the head. Bang. In one second it's over.

The chorus on the shore of the pond chokes to silence.

As Sheriff Johnson topples overboard, the boat pitches. Nobody makes a sound; the sheriff's mouth is gone, Margie is passed out— or dead, and the girl with the cornrows is peacefully sleeping, possessed. Only Ron yells, tumbling into the water as the boat capsizes.

The water is freezing. Ron pulls to the surface and takes a breath, sees the ring of sleeping faces, the makeup masked director, the big, round moon wreathed in clouds. This is it. This is where he'll pull Margie and the sleeping girl to safety. And he'll kick the director's ass. And he'll, he'll—

But now, suddenly, he's rushing down, away from the moonlight into the dark.

He panics at first, not realizing what's happening. Then he understands. The weight dropped when the boat tipped over, pulling the rope taut around his neck. When it ran out of slack, he was pulled under. And now he's being dragged down fast.

Despite the speed, the descent seems like it'll never end. His ears pop painfully over and over. The pressure makes his head ache. Already the cold of the water has numbed his fingers and toes.

He's still falling headfirst into oblivion.

He glances over and sees the outline of somebody else falling next to him, but whether it's the sleepwalker girl or Margie he can't tell.

He flails his arms, trying with all his strength to pull himself and the weight to the surface, but his effort doesn't even slow his descent. He tries to get his fingers under the rope, to loosen it enough to pull his head out, but the noose is so tight he thinks it might have actually cut into his neck. So he falls.

The blackness mixes into a dizzy delirium. He's going to die. He tries to make his life flash before his eyes, but he can't. Maybe he already did that too much anyway.

Figures, he was never good at much. Why should dying be any different?

He's falling.

Maybe he passes out for an instant and dreams, or maybe he just thinks he does. Anyway, he's back in the jungle.

Ron sits with Dirty Dan in an old, blown-out foxhole. They're up to their knees in brown rainwater, and it's still coming down. Another forty-eight hours and they'll be able to swim back to Lai Khe, Dan jokes in a whisper. Ron can't bring himself to laugh. They've been in the hole for two days, ever since Ron turned around and found that his few remaining companions had disappeared, sleeping beneath the emerald canopy of leaves somewhere behind him, full of lead. He wonders: have the others found them yet, put them in a box and shipped 'em stateside? Or are they still out there in this rain, being eaten day by day by roaches and lizards? Would he even recognize them anymore?

For two days, Ron and Dan have sat in the hole, watching the water creep up around them. By now they'll both probably have to have their feet amputated from jungle rot. But there's no way they can leave. Somehow they wandered into Charlie's backyard. Hardly an hour goes by without their hearing footsteps pass above, or hearing the coarse, evil-sounding chattering of the North Vietnamese from amongst the nearby trees.

Yesterday a group stopped so close Ron could smell the piss as one of them relieved himself.

Usually when they hear the enemy approach, Ron and Dan submerge themselves as much as possible and try not come up for air if they can help it. If the enemy sneaks up on them, they'll just sit very still, holding their fingers on the triggers of their rifles until they tremble with cramping, waiting to be discovered, waiting to die.

Moments like that, Ron and Dan will just stare at each other. They were never really friends before. The friends each of them hung around with most are still lying in the jungle somewhere. But in those wordless moments when death is only a blink away, they share more with one another than Ron has ever shared with another human being in his life.

Now he's staring at the little rings the raindrops make in the water all around him. He reaches absently into his pocket and takes out a lighter. It should have run out of fluid days ago, that or the rain should've killed it, but like the Hanukkah miracle, somehow it still works. Ron can't remember for sure, but that might be the first thing he ever thanked God for. He takes out a soggy cigarette and starts to light it. It takes a few flicks, but finally a flame pops up. Ron inhales deep and puffs out a big batch of smoke. It's only then that he sees Dan, staring at him with wide, wild eyes. Dan jerks his head to the mouth of the hole.

And then Ron hears it, though it's too late now. Voices, chopped and harsh, and the click of a bullet filling a chamber. Ron drops his cigarette and swallows hard. He puts his finger on the trigger of this rifle, and his eyes dart back and forth around the rim of the hole.

Dan sees it first, and he turns fast and faces the mud wall of the hole, pressing his body and face against the muck for protection.

Then Ron sees it. A hissing Chicom grenade seems to drift through the sky like a kite before dropping into the water just at Dan's feet.

Half the time it seems like Charlie's grenades are duds, but the other half they blow you to pieces. Ron won't take that chance with Dan. He drops his gun, jumps over, and thrusts his hand into the brown murk at Dan's feet. All he gets is a handful of mud, then more mud, then finally the grenade. He pulls it out—surely this thing must be a dud; it should have gone off by now, plus it's drenched—and he cocks back sidearm to throw it out of the hole, and there's a sound, just like a firework.

All Ron can think of is the Fourth of July when he told his mother he wasn't going to Canada; he would stay and fight and be a hero, and his mother shrugged and lit another cigarette and popped another beer.

When Ron wakes up, it's later. He'll never know how much later. All he knows is he's on a stretcher. Somebody's passing him out of the hole. He looks down over his left shoulder and sees Dirty Dan. His helmet is missing and the side of his head is gone. His lips are blue. The eyes that had confessed so much are crawling with bugs. And Ron hears the thunder and rush of a chopper and blacks out.

When he wakes up, there's nothing but a pus-soaked bandage where his left hand used to be.

And the only thought that goes through his head for days is "so much for being a hero."

For some reason, that thought goes through Ron's head again now. But this time it's not steeped in bitterness. It's just a thought. An acceptance. So much for being a hero. He wonders where Keisha is.

Still falling. His ears pop again, and the pain is catastrophic. He thinks his head might actually rupture.

Still falling.

This must be a natural spring; some of them are hundreds of feet deep. This one seems like thousands.

Way too far to swim back up now. Even if he could get free, he doesn't have nearly enough air or strength to make it.

So he prays.

Lord,
I know you can hear me,
Even way down here.
I'm scared,
But I feel you.
I just wish I had been able to accomplish something.
One big, world-changing thing.
But I guess old Ron Bent never had what it takes
To change the world.

His thoughts are interrupted. The falling has stopped. He hangs upside down in strange weightlessness. His eyes have adjusted to the darkness, and he's surprised to see that the moonlight permeates this deep. He can make out shapes around him, black, shadowlike shapes floating like jellyfish. He strains to make them out in the half light.

Then he realizes what they are: bodies. He can't tell how many, but he thinks there must be at least fifty. Bodies, floating upside down in eerie blue suspension, just like him.

A big bubble escapes his mouth. He has a horrible cramp in his stomach.

Maybe one of these is Keisha.
Maybe we're finally together again.
I hope she ain't too disappointed I couldn't save her,
Praise God.

His air is completely gone; his thoughts fragment and dissolve. He blinks fast and claws at the rope, at his face. He flails his arms and expends the last of his energy in panic before joining the sixty-five bodies floating around him in utter stillness.

And Ron Bent dies.

Amen.

⊰ Chapter Nineteen ⊱

CALEB IS DRIVING. Christine watches him. The radio crackles at AM five thirty-five, but for now the dead are silent.

"The world is strange," says Christine.

The rain had started falling gently at first, but it's picking up fast. Caleb leans forward, squinting out the glass, looking for the driveway that leads to the Dream Center.

"I always thought I'd run away sooner or later. I'd find you, we'd love each other, and everything would be different. We'd have kids and stuff. That's all I ever wanted. Now it's like . . . " she shakes her head.

"They say if you want to make God laugh, make a plan," says Caleb. He tries to smile, but his stomach is tied up so tight he winces instead. All he can think of is the sight of Margie's blown-out kneecaps and the way everything would smell if the world actually ended and everything burned.

They both know that no matter how things work out, they're bound to end up dead. They're up against an army of fearless demons, a sheriff with a gun, a ruthless madman, and a host of evil spirits. Maybe even the devil himself.

And the word on the street is that Caleb is the one who's going to make the end of Creation happen. Word on the street is it's inevitable.

"What are you thinking?" asks Christine.

Caleb sighs.

She puts her hand on his hand on the car's automatic shifter.

"It's going to be okay," she says. "We're together."

He looks in her eyes and finds sincerity, even hope. It surprises him.

"I still don't know if you're crazy or not," he admits. "I don't know if you helped hold my father prisoner. I don't know anything. I was supposed to be in Africa, writing, making a difference. Going to Stanford, winning the Pulitzer Prize. What happens if it all just disappears?"

She shrugs. "You want to make God laugh, make a plan," she teases.

They pass the driveway. It looks like a tunnel leading to nothing. Caleb pulls the car over just past it, shutting off the headlights. They both sit in the quiet for a second, listening to the sound of rain on the roof. Behind the trees to their right they can already see the shape of the Dream Center, huge, dark, and imposing.

Christine offers Caleb the gun. He shakes his head.

"You take that," he says. "I have this."

He holds up the hatchet.

"We should try not to kill any of the kids if we can help it," he says. "But if it comes down to it and a few of them have to die to save the world, then I guess . . ."

She nods. "So what's the plan?"

Caleb stares at the steering wheel. They took Ron's car, hoping it'd be less easily recognized. It smells of stale cigarettes. "Yeah," says Caleb, "the plan . . . I've been trying to figure that out. There's a gas can in the trunk. It's only about half full, but it's something. We might be able to burn them out."

Christine frowns. "Everybody might be trapped in there," she says. "The spirits won't let them leave. They'll all burn."

"Maybe we can bluff the director with it then," says Caleb. "We should take it just in case. We'll try not to use it."

"I got this from the house," says Christine, holding up a little radio

Walkman. "I don't even know if it still works—it was Mom's. But if the battery's still good, Anna might be able to communicate with us. I don't know why she doesn't talk to us now when we need her the most." She glances at the car radio, but only static replies.

"Maybe the others won't let her," Caleb says. "Where do you think Margie and Ron would be?"

Christine thinks for a second. "I don't know. I never saw any prisoners except the other patients, and when we kidnapped people I was always sleeping. I can't remember what we did with them."

"We'll just have to go room by room, stick together, and hope we find them," Caleb says.

Christine nods. They look at each other for a long time. Caleb sees Christine looking at his lips. He wants to kiss her too—so bad his chest hurts. Then he thinks of Amber and his life, and he's frozen. He pulls back.

A hurt look crosses Christine's face.

"Let's go, Caleb," she says. "We can do this." She musters a smile.

As she opens the door a rush of rain and wind comes in. Caleb grabs her hand, pulls her back.

He opens his mouth to speak, then doesn't. He squeezes her hand.

They look at each other one more time, each wanting to say something more, but the rain picks up outside, pounding even harder, drumming on the hood of the car and the windshield, and they both know the moment has come.

They step out of the car, into the deluge. The raindrops are so huge and heavy it hurts when they hit their skin. Caleb takes the gas can out of the trunk and they head toward the Dream Center, hand in hand.

The canopy of trees over the long driveway undulates, their branches writhing in the ferocious wind like a million interlaced snakes. The driveway is mostly flooded from all the rain, and they walk ankle-deep in freezing water. The gale at their back pushes them forward, threatening to knock them off their feet with its power.

They can feel it all around them, a thousand unseen hands at work.

"The spirits are all here," yells Christine through the torrent.

"Trying to stop us?" Caleb yells.

She shakes her head, a strange, terrified look in her eye. "Pushing us on."

The trees open up in front of them, and through the stinging haze of rain they see the Dream Center, the old, abandoned, forbidden place of their childhood, waiting for them.

"There aren't any lights on," Caleb says.

"They're there," says Christine. "The director is in his office on the sixth floor. They're all there. Waiting for us."

"How do you know?"

"I just do."

"Are they alive? Margie and Ron?"

Christine just shakes her head. She can't tell.

She hurries forward first, around the big, circular driveway, past the fountain and straight for the nearest window. Caleb follows. They check all the windows on the first floor. They're all locked, barred, and dark. Caleb keeps glancing at the woods, expecting to see sleep-walkers in the shadows. But all he sees are the shadows themselves, watching him back.

They reach the basement door, the one that Anna disappeared into once upon a time, and the wind picks up a little. Caleb half expects them to find the door unlocked and waiting for them, but when Christine jerks on the handle it won't budge. By now they're soaked to the bone. The rain is cold, biting, almost sleet. Lightning fractures the dark above, illuminating what might be faces in the forest, clawing hands in the branches of the trees all around them.

They pass the old pond Caleb remembers from his childhood. Little Billy, Anna, and Christine used to splash each other there in those cold, clear, spring-fed waters. Now it sits still and black as the eye of a dead fish. Swollen with rainwater, it's flooded so much that one leg of its surface reaches nearly to the foundation of the Dream Center. He was always a little scared of that swimming hole as a kid. He eyes it distrustfully now as they skirt it and walk on. Caleb shivers and glances over his shoulder once, but there is no disturbance on the pond's obsidian surface except the pocking of raindrops.

They check another window, round the corner, and walk on.

There was a rusted old fire escape on this side of the building when they were kids, but the director—John Morle—must've had it torn off during the renovation. Now its skeleton rusts in the weeds by the edge of the woods. More locked windows. Christine is rubbing her hands together. The chill of the rain deadens every extremity.

They round another corner, and they're back at the front again.

"Did you see any places to climb up?" asks Caleb, keeping a wary eye on the towering building.

She shakes her head.

"Me neither," he says.

She's looking away from him at the front door. He grabs her arm.

"We can't just go in the front door," he says. Then he feels like an idiot; what other option do they have?

"He knows we're coming," she says. "Everything knows we're coming. The dead are singing about it. The wind is full of them."

"What are they saying?"

"You don't want to know."

"At least let me go first," he says. He readjusts the hatchet in his hand, as if it will do him any good against an army of restless dead, and walks up the steps to the big double doors.

He grips one of the big brass handles. It's freezing cold. He glances back at Christine. She's holding the old pistol casually, like a cowboy ready to shoot from the hip. Rain-soaked pieces of hair frame her big, shining eyes. Drops of water stand on the white, smooth surface of her skin and run down her slender neck. She's just looking back at him, waiting. She's beautiful. And she is his best friend, even if he hasn't seen her in ten years. And he loves her. And he needs her to live through this day.

"You don't have to come in," he says.

"Open the door, Caleb."

"Please, you don't have to—"

"Open it."

And he does.

The door opens freely, almost effortlessly.

They step into the lobby of the Dream Center, dripping. The lights are dimmed. Christine swings the door shut again, sealing away some of the sounds of the storm outside. All that seems to permeate the thick concrete walls is the eerie, distant wailing of the wind. At least, Christine hopes it's the wind.

The minute she steps inside, every muscle in her body clamps up. She can hardly breathe. Goose bumps break out all over her despite the almost impossible heat that hangs in the air.

With one backward glance at her and a feigned cocky grin, Billy—Caleb—is leading them forward, the hatchet hovering next to his head ready to strike. The halls are empty. There is no sound, no movement except for the flicker of the few fluorescent lights that are working. The place looks utterly desolate, but Christine isn't fooled. She can feel them, the dead. They grasp at her with every step. The energy of their malice makes the air everywhere vibrate, pulse, seethe. They reach an intersection with another long hallway full of doors, and Caleb looks back at her. Which way?

She nods to the left, hoping he won't see the hopeless terror in her eyes.

"Staircase is at the end of the hall," she whispers. "We have to go all the way up."

"You don't think we should check the doors down here?"

She shakes her head quickly.

"I guess you're right," he whispers. "He wouldn't put them on the first floor and leave the front door wide open."

They walk on.

Christine reaches out and grasps his forearm as she walks. She feels the strength there and it makes her feel a little better, but not much. The gun is still shaking in her hand. She knows even if a miracle happened and the old thing actually fired, she couldn't steady herself enough to hit an elephant.

They pass doors and doors and doors. Like in a nightmare, the hallway is endless.

Ahead, they see a set of double doors with round, porthole-like windows in their centers. They squeak in protest as Caleb pushes them wide. As they enter the new room Caleb looks for attackers, his head snapping back and forth, but there are no sleeping demons here, only old cobweb-covered toys.

Here, no lights are on. The only illumination comes from the crackle of lightning through dirty windows.

They move cautiously forward. Apparently this room was never renovated. There's a rocking horse in front of them, its paint peeling off. To the left is a model train half off the tracks, so covered in dust it looks almost white. There's a mural on the wall, smiling children swinging on swings under a jolly, smiling sun. A big, happy owl looks on. Some vandal (or Morle himself maybe) has spray-painted out the children's eyes. Red paint runs down their faces like blood tears. Against the wall to their right, time has reduced a pile of stuffed animals to fur, sawdust, and glass eyes. Against the other wall sits a huge, rusty cage draped in cobwebs. Christine locks her mind against wondering what that cage was used for so many years ago. Surely it wasn't to restrain the children who played with these toys. . . .

The air is so thick in here she can't breathe. She literally feels underwater. A tear runs down her cheek, and she doesn't know why. She lets go of Caleb's arm as he continues ahead of her, weaving through the wasteland of dead toys. She fumbles in her pocket before finally finding what she's looking for and pulling the little radio free. Trembling, she puts the headphones on. She adjusts the dial. Five thirty-five AM. Up ahead Billy, Caleb, has reached the double doors at the other end of the room.

"It's the staircase," she hears him say.

And she flips the switch and turns the radio on.

Caleb has the doors open now and looks in on a forgotten staircase strewn with plaster debris and dust. He's about to step into the stairwell when he realizes Christine isn't behind him. He turns back and finds her, and his heart stops.

She stands in the middle of the room shaking. Tears run in slick lines down both her cheeks. Her eyes dart back and forth. Her body is drawn up, tense and quivering, but her feet remain rooted in place.

"Christine? Christine!"

The second time she hears her name and looks at him. Her voice is a tiny squeak.

"They're all around us."

And it happens: the wooden horse begins rocking insanely; the pile of dismembered stuffed animals begins rolling toward her. The wail of the wind somehow becomes high, horrible laughter. The dust in the room comes to life, whipping up in blinding, swirling gusts.

Christine is screaming.

The door of the cage is slamming and slamming and slamming. Thunder shakes everything.

Through the storm of debris, Caleb rushes to her. Her eyes are squeezed tightly shut and her scream has becomes a rasping gurgle. He stuffs the hatchet in his belt and grabs her arm, still gripping the gas can in his other hand, and yanks her into motion.

"Come on!"

He drags her toward the stairwell. They slam through the double doors.

In here they are cut off from the dying fluorescent lights of the hallway, and darkness is deeper, so deep you could swim in it. And things *are* swimming in it. Caleb sees them all around now, contorted faces, hands, claws, eyes, ethereal but real.

"I'm getting you out of here. If we go down we should be able to find the back door," Caleb yells.

Christine is biting her nails, cradling the gun against her chest like a baby doll.

"It's a trap," she whispers.

"Come on," he says, tugging her arm.

"IT'S A TRAP," she screams.

And then he hears it.

It's distant at first: a pounding. It could almost be war drums. It could almost be thunder.

"It's all a trap," she says, another tear falling.

And then he knows. He looks over the railing, down the stairwell. The pounding is footfalls.

The sleepwalkers are coming.

There must be hundreds of them. They jam the stairwell, a rising, living tide.

They claw each other and fight their way ahead like a swarm of rats fleeing a flood.

"Up," says Caleb. "GO!"

He shoves Christine ahead of him up the stairwell.

She seems to snap back into reality and scrambles up one flight, then another, then another.

Caleb is just behind her, guiding her forward with one hand and gripping the hatchet with the other. On every landing they try the door. On every landing the door is locked tight.

Christine was right. This is a trap.

Caleb runs with one eye over the banister, watching in choking horror as, step by step, the throng of possessed ones gains on them. By the time he's reached the next landing he's made up his mind. He unscrews the gas can and stops, dousing the stairs below him.

"Billy!"

Caleb looks up and sees Christine leaning over the banister one flight above him.

"Go!" he says. "Keep running!"

"You're burning them?"

"Go!" he says. "I won't let them get you. I'll catch up."

By now the sleepwalkers are so close he can smell the sickness in their sweat. They're three stairwells down, now two, now one—there's no time to empty the last bit of gas; they're almost on him. He fumbles in the pocket of his soaked jeans for the lighter, finally pulling it out, trying to light it. And it clicks, and clicks, and clicks. Nothing.

Now they're at the landing just below him. Now their feet are slipping on the stairs a few feet away. Their claws, human hands filled with inhuman power, grope at the steps beneath him.

And the lighter clicks and clicks.

And now they're on him.

Caleb swings the gas can to fend them off. Gas splashes on them. The can thuds hollowly on a possessed girl's head, and it's too late. The lighter falls from his hand. A hundred hands grab him with impossible strength. He cries out as some of the fingers puncture his skin, worming into his muscle. He feels teeth bite deep into the flesh of his side and hears the sound as they tear a small piece away. His own scream is piercing in his ears.

And so is the clap and echo of the gunshot. He looks up and sees Christine's face over the railing above him, illuminated by the spark of fire from the barrel.

Then he feels the heat all around him, and knows the gas is going up. Firelight flashes across the walls. There's a collective shriek, and the hands that were tearing into his flesh fall away. Caleb tumbles down the stairwell into the flames, into a tangle of thrashing limbs. He smells his own hair burning, hears his screams mingle with those of the sleepwalkers.

In the next instant he's scrambling upward, out of the conflagration. He reaches the next landing, rolling, burning, rubbing his body feverishly, then looks down at himself, expecting to see his body wrapped in flames. Instead, his clothes are steaming, but he's fine. Then he realizes: his wet clothes, soaked by the rain, saved him.

But the sleepwalkers are burning alive.

Two of them break through the flames, flailing and hissing. Caleb yanks the hatchet out of his belt and swings only twice. Each of them drops with a hollow thud and keeps burning.

The rest of them are already burned black.

The smell of them makes Caleb puke as he runs. Vomit comes out of his nose and burns and makes him puke more, but still he runs, onward, upward.

The fire follows him, moving fast, almost burning his heels.

"Come on!" he hears Christine's voice echo from the landing above. "The door up here is unlocked!"

He runs hard, the fire licking his feet. He's already slick with sweat from the heat.

The way the fire is spreading the whole place will burn.

"Come on!"

Caleb rounds the corner and sees Christine at the top of the next flight of stairs, looking beautiful in the firelight.

Funny how things come around.

Funny how just when you've grown up and you think you're finally safe from your nightmares, you realize they were real after all.

There's Christine on the landing only a few feet away. Behind her, a door.

Caleb sees this all very clearly.

He sees it even before it happens, because he's seen it a thousand times before. It's more than *déjà vu*.

The door behind Christine opens, reveals a rectangle of black.

And before Caleb's foot hits the next step, Christine is jerked back into the dark.

Gone.

"CHRISTINE!" On the landing now, he slams himself against the door.

Locked.

"CHRISTINE!" He hits the steel door with the hatchet again and again and again and again and again.

Behind it the faintest scream fades into silence.

Caleb doesn't stop pounding on the door, doesn't stop until the flames are all around him and he can smell himself burning again.

The door won't budge. He looks up. Only two more floors until the top. If both of these doors are locked then that's the end of him.

On the steps, just out of the blaze, he sees Christine's radio. Must've fallen there.

He snatches it up and runs, coughing now, blinded by smoke and tears, dizzy. Tries the next door. Locked. One more flight to go.

The smoke is so thick he sees nothing. He knows where he is only by the feel of his hand on the railing. He reaches the landing, gropes and finds the door. The heat is almost unbearable now. He reels and almost falls, almost blacks out, but fights his way out of it. He finds the doorknob.

And it turns. He steps into the coolness and slams the door on the swirling flames behind him.

In the blackness, there is no sound but the ticking of clocks.

Caleb steps into the room, blind.

The only light is a bar of orange coming from beneath the closed door at his back.

He steps forward, gripping the hatchet tightly.

The sound of ticking is all around him, maddening as the buzzing of a million mosquitoes. He reaches out, groping in oblivion.

"I don't need to see you," says a deep voice. "They will tell me where you are."

Caleb jerks his head in the direction of the sound, but echoes jumble his perception, and he just winds up spinning around, lost.

There's laughter. He knows it's the voice of the director, Morle, but in the shadows he can almost hear hundreds of other voices laughing too.

"I could snap your neck at any moment. This is what surrender feels like."

"I'm not scared of you," Caleb lies.

There's no answer, not even the laughter Caleb expected. Then there's the sound of something whipping through the air, and the hatchet disappears, yanked from his hand.

The lasso.

"Now do you believe me?" says the voice.

Caleb tries to catch his breath. His mind is racing. "What do you want from me?"

"Nothing you won't give freely."

"I won't help you make the world end."

"That's exactly what you've come here to do."

He can't tell if he's imagining it or not, but the ticking seems to speed up. The heat is maddening. Sweat runs into his eyes.

Then he gets an idea. He reaches into his pocket and pulls out the little radio. He puts on the headphones. At first only white noise greets his ears.

Please, Anna. Come on. Be there.

The only sound is the rush of nothing and the ticking of the clocks.

"You should be enjoying these moments. The spirits of a million dead are chanting your name, do you hear it?" the voice says. It seems to be coming from everywhere at once. "For decades, witches, sorcerers, Satanists, a few enlightened Druids, have all ached for this moment."

Caleb's throat is so dry he can barely croak a reply. "Why?"

He can hear the fire crackling behind the door now, hear the door bowing in its frame from the heat.

"Because the followers of Lucifer have no place in heaven. But once they've awakened their master, they'll be able to create their own place here, on earth."

"What about the rest of us?"

"Those who survive will be enslaved. The rest will simply be gone."

"And you expect me to help you?"

"Aren't you listening? You already are. We couldn't do it without you, Billy."

Caleb is lost in the dark. He simply keeps spinning around, trying to pinpoint the source of the voice.

Come on, Anna, talk to me! Help me save your sister!

Only static answers his plea.

"Where's Christine?" Caleb barks.

"You will be reunited soon, rest assured."

"And what do you get? What's your reward for all this? You get to be the devil's right-hand man, or what?"

"No, no. Not me. I never wanted such glory. I don't even know if I believe in the devil, frankly. All I'm telling you is what the spirits told me. When the end comes, I'll finally get to sleep. They've promised me. The end of the world, to me, is rest. Escape. But first, I must finish my work. And we must hurry, tick, tick, tick."

The ticking has grown now, not only in speed, but in volume. Caleb grits his teeth against the onslaught of noise. He turns the static in the headphones up to drown it out. And in the sea of rushing silence he hears a tiny child's voice.

<Caleb> it says *<He's . . . your left.>*

Caleb turns and faces the darkness to his left. Now he can feel the presence there, almost smell the stale breath.

"Well, what if I don't help? What if I run back through that door and burn myself alive?"

"You can't," says the voice.

"Wanna bet?" says Caleb, and he's sprinting for the bar of orange he knows is the door. He grabs the handle but recoils instantly. The knob is scalding.

<duck!> says Anna.

Caleb drops to his knees and hears the lasso whip above his head. If his neck were caught in that loop, he's sure the director could snap it easily.

<turn left, walk two steps. Now feel on the wall—there's a light switch.>

Caleb does as Anna instructs, and two lamps on the far side of the room spring to life. But the director is already gone, the door on the far wall swinging shut behind him. Caleb runs toward it. Hundreds of clocks line the room. He knocks a few down as he barrels through, just for spite.

<the hatchet!>

On the floor in the corner of the room, he sees it. He snatches it up and shoves through the door. The next room or hallway—Caleb can't tell which—is utterly without light. He enters tentatively.

<no time! run! I'll show you!>

He does as he's instructed, running carefully yet clumsily at first, then at an all-out sprint.

<careful, a little left, now run! Fast! . . . slow down, slow down. There's a turn, right, now. good, now run; the hallway is empty, run!>

For all Caleb can tell, he could be running in outer space. The feeling of sprinting through darkness is the feeling of immortality.

<drop!>

He does, and the lasso whips over his head again, closer this time.

<he's running again—go!>

And Caleb does.

Through the hiss of static, Caleb can barely hear Johnny Morle's footfalls as he runs through the darkness ahead.

Finally, after traversing a complex series of blind turns and going through several sets of doors, Anna tells him to stop at one last heavy door. He heaves it open.

When he steps through, he's surprised to feel rain on his face.

He looks up. High above him rain pours through a broken-out skylight. Leading up to it, a ladder.

<go up> says Anna.

"Up there? He could just push the ladder down," he says aloud.

<Christine is up there. go now>

So Caleb tucks the hatchet in his belt and goes.

The rungs are slippery, and more than once his foot slips and he almost falls. Finally, tentatively, he peeks out and scans the rooftop, trying to see through the rainy darkness.

<he's over there>

Somehow, Caleb knows she means he's behind a large, green-house-like structure almost a hundred yards away.

He climbs up and steps onto the gravel of the roof.

He pulls out the hatchet as he strides toward the greenhouse.

"This isn't what he wanted, is it? I'm not helping him, am I?"

<this is the only way>

Caleb walks faster now. There is a strength, a purpose in his step he's never known before.

<hurry>

He breaks into a jog, then a run.

"If I don't make it, Anna," he says between breaths, "I wanted to say I'm sorry for daring you to go in the asylum that day. I never meant for you to get hurt."

<it was . . . the oNLY way>

The emptiness, the utter lack of emotion in her voice, chills him and fills him with foreboding, even fear, but he runs on.

In several places, fire has broken through the roof and is spreading fast across the tar and gravel surface.

He runs faster.

The fire seems to be running with him, following him, chasing him. It flares up on either side of him, then in front of him. He almost thinks he sees faces in the flames. He almost thinks they're calling his name.

The fire shouldn't be spreading this fast, not in this rain.

Unless . . . that smell. . . .

<yes>

Anna answers his question before he thinks to ask it. Morle soaked the roof with gasoline. Somehow, Morle knew this would happen. He knew everything.

Caleb has reached the greenhouse. Its broken-out windows are black holes. The remaining panes are too dingy to reflect the livid red glow of the firelight. They don't reflect it. They trap it.

Everything has been a trap.

As he rounds the corner of the greenhouse, he's more nervous than he's ever been in his life. He feels like a million souls are watching him. And they are. Every angel and every demon watches him right now, waiting to see his performance, his choice. Somehow, everything hangs on the next moment, and he knows it. Except he has no idea what the test is, what he's supposed to do, what—

And then he sees. He takes it all in, in an instant, all of it.

Morle is there, his white clown makeup streaked and almost completely washed away by the rain. In his hands he holds a rope. The rope runs up and over a broken, bent-down flag pole. The other end of the rope is around Christine's neck. She hangs over the edge of the building, her feet flailing in the air. Her face is purple. Her eyes are bulging and bloodshot. Spit glistens on her chin.

"You made it," says Morle.

This is the test. A test without an answer. Without a solution. If he kills Morle, the maniac lets go of the rope and Christine falls to her death. If he does nothing, she chokes to death. There is no answer. There is no "right."

"What do you want?" Caleb says quickly.

"It isn't what *I* want," Morle says. "It's what *they* want. Listen to them."

The fire is in a ring around him now. There's no running away even if he wanted to. The world is burning.

"Anna?" he whispers desperately. "God? Anyone?"

There is no answer, only static.

He takes a few steps toward Morle.

"Just let her go," he says. "Let her go and tell me where Ron and Margie are, and everything can be okay."

Morle laughs. "Ron and Margie are in the dark, my boy! Two of the sixty-six glorious sacrifices. Dead."

A wave of grief swells in Caleb's soul, but his concern now is for Christine. "Just let Christine go and I'll help you. I'll do whatever you want."

"I know you will," Morle says, smiling. But he doesn't move.

Caleb raises the hatchet. "I'll kill you if you make me, I swear to God. If she has to die, I'm making sure you go with her."

Morle just smiles back at him. With the makeup almost completely gone now, his grin looks less lurid and more—familiar. As Caleb's brain races to come up with an impossible solution, something threatens to click, some horrible revelation.

Caleb feels the fire at his back now, prodding him forward. The noose of flame is closing in on him. He takes another step toward Morle. And he sees. He sees it all. He looks so different now, without the beard, with the streaked makeup on his face, but those eyes . . .

It can't be. It must be . . .

Nausea cuts through his stomach. His head spins. It's awful, impossible. . . .

" . . . Dad?"

The rain on the director's face is mixed with tears so he can't tell that the man in front of him is crying until he takes another step closer. Finally, the clown speaks.

"I am so proud of you," he says.

"But you were dead! I saw you in the basement. I saw your corpse."

"No," the man with the rope says. "You saw the corpse of that obsessed detective. But your loving dad is not the rotting, dead cop. The loser. No, your father is the man he hunted: the lawyer, psychiatrist, rodeo man, friend of the spirits, and Bringer of the End. The winner. I am the one they called Michael Mason, who your pretty friend here knew as the director, though in the beginning and the end I shall always be Johnny Morle—and now, my dear son, we're together one last time. And I'm so proud."

Caleb's mind races to understand. At the end of the rope, Christine is moving less and less.

"Dad, why are you doing this?"

"To die," he says simply.

"Why?"

"Because it's all I've ever wanted. BECAUSE I CAN'T TAKE THIS WORLD!" he says. "I mean look at this: I have a beautiful son, and now he's going to die in fire. Everyone's going to die."

"If you want to die so bad, then kill yourself, Dad, but leave Christine alone! Look at her!"

"I tried to kill myself over and over and over, and I lived! The spirits said there was only one way . . . "

"What? WHAT WAY, DAD? Look at her—we don't have time!"

Fire is all around, everything burns.

"They said only my son could kill me," he says softly, "and if I helped them, they would make sure he did."

Christine isn't moving.

Smoke billows between father and son. The roof groans under their feet, about to give way.

"And with sixty-six souls in the darkest hole, the devil's work is done."

"Let her go, Dad. Everything can change. Everything can be okay—just let her go." Billy is crying now, his teardrops falling as hard as the rain.

Behind the smoke, the man shakes his head.

"I love you, son," he says, through tears, smiling. "Help me. Help me die."

"Dad, let her go. Now. NOW!"

Christine's face is almost blue.

And then comes the moment that, for the rest of his life, will teach Caleb the true definition of "nightmare." This moment he will always remember. He knows what he has to do. He can't let Christine die. There is no other way.

"I love you too, Dad," he whispers.

And he throws the hatchet.

It all happens so fast:

The sound is dull, hollow, but it echoes, and when it's finished, the hatchet is still quivering in his father's head.

Morle takes ones step back, as if about to turn and walk away, then falls backward off the roof.

Caleb is already moving. He sees everything so clearly that he'll remember every fiber of the rope for the rest of his life. It slips through John Morle's fingers as he falls, dead, from the rooftop, and Caleb throws himself over the edge and grabs it in midair.

At first, he's sure the wet rope, still attached to the flagpole, will slip through its fingers. It doesn't. His broken wrist explodes with pain, but his grip holds as he swings out off the edge of the building then back, and finds himself standing on the rooftop again. He wraps the rope around his hand twice to keep it from slipping, and reaches over, grabbing Christine's foot with his free hand. He pulls her to him as far as he can back onto the rooftop, then lets go of the rope. There's an instant when he loses his balance and thinks both of them will tumble down and fall seven stories to their deaths. But miraculously, he's able to steady himself. He eases Christine down. Everything is bright with fire now. In another minute, everything will have burned.

He pulls the rope off her neck and looks at her closely.

"Christine! Wake up, please!"

There's no movement, no glimmer of breath. Her eye sockets are a deep purple from all the broken blood vessels. Her lips are dark blue.

He sniffs hard, sucking up all his tears instantly, plugs her nose, puts his lips to hers and pushes his breath into her. He tries desperately to remember all the CPR he ever learned, but it all eludes him, so he breathes into her again, and again. He presses on the center of her chest where he knows her heart is. He presses hard, and there's a cracking sound there, and he starts crying again, knowing he's hurt her, broken a rib maybe. Her lips are still blue, hopeless. He breathes into her again.

Nothing. He's failed. He's failed everything. The world *has* ended.

"Please, please, please, God, please," he begs.

And he breathes into her again.

And the flames are about to turn them to ash.

And then, she breathes back.

Caleb smiles and cries, "Christine, come on. Please."

Her eyelids flutter. Her eyes are rolled back into her head.

"Come on, please, there's no time!" Caleb says.

And then, her eyes open. They look around at nothing, then finally focus on Caleb.

"Billy . . . you okay?" she asks.

He smiles. "Fine. But we gotta go."

He helps her up, and she can barely stand. They only have a tiny corner of the roof left; flames have claimed the rest. Caleb looks around. There's no way down. There are some treetops, but they're too far to jump to.

Christine slumps, about to collapse.

"No, no. Come on, you have to stay awake, just for now," he says.

"Okay," she mumbles.

Caleb sees the rope sitting nearby, limp and forgotten, and grabs it, snatching it away from the flames, pulling it free of the bent-over flagpole. In another ten seconds it would have been burned up. He coils it in his hands, eyeing the distance to the stub of a broken-off branch on a pine tree that should be big enough to support their weight. It's about fifteen feet away.

Christine is slumping again.

"Come on! Hey!" he says, gently shaking her. But it's no use; her eyelids are rolling back again. This isn't going to work. She can't hold on to him. He takes the end of the rope and ties it around her waist. He ransacks his brain for a single Boy Scout knot, but finds nothing. He settles on a double knot and a prayer. He takes the loop in his hand, gauges the distance, then hears a thunderous sound.

He looks over his shoulder to see the far end of the building collapse. No time.

He cocks back and tosses the lasso. At first, he's sure the throw is short—and there's no time for another; the sparks are burning little holes in his jeans as it is—but somehow, the loop catches on the branch. He pulls the rope taut. It doesn't seem as secure as he had hoped it would be, but no time to worry now. Christine's eyes flutter open again as he helps her steady herself and pats out a little spark on her shirt. He grabs the rope.

"Ready? We're going to swing," he whispers frantically. One, two, three."

Before there's time for a second thought, they jump.

The initial downswing is terrifying, and Caleb is pretty sure they're through. He feels like he's flying through the air at a hundred miles per hour when he clips the trunk of the big pine tree with his rib cage. It knocks the wind out of him, and he nearly loses his grip. He probably would have fallen and died, except for the fact that there was a small branch under his feet to release himself onto. The first thing he does when he's secure is look for Christine.

He's relieved to find her safe and even semiconscious, clambering onto a big branch maybe five feet below him, one end of the rope still secured around her waist.

There's another crash and a rain of sparks as a roof support nearby gives way.

Caleb hugs the tree trunk, his ribs and wrist aching. "You okay?" he calls down.

"My head's killing me. And this pine sap stinks," says Christine weakly. "You?"

"Well, we're still here. And the world's still here."

"I noticed," she says faintly.

They sit in silence for a moment, watching the show of flames and sparks play itself out for them.

"Christine," he says.

He looks down at her.

"I missed you all these years."

She looks up at him.

"I missed you too."

Half an hour later the sun is coming up. The rain clouds paint themselves in cool pinks and blues of sunrise and drift away.

The Dream Center continues to burn. Still perched in the tree together, Billy and Christine watch it fall.

Mostly, the minutes pass in silence; Christine sits with her head on Billy's shoulder, his arm around her, their chests rising and falling together in breath after grateful breath. When they do talk, it's about silly stuff, like building a tree house and living there forever.

Except somehow childish ideas don't seem so childish anymore.

⊰ Chapter Twenty ⊱

IN THE WHITE HOSPITAL ROOM IN PANAMA CITY, the flowers on the table by the window have already wilted a little. Sunlight pours in.

On the television, a local news anchor stands in front of the charred remains of a building, talking into his microphone and gesturing.

In the hospital bed, Christine doesn't hear a word of it. She has the volume turned all the way down. She's staring out the window, watching how fast the clouds go by. Maybe she never looked before, but she never noticed they went by so fast.

"Knock, knock," says a voice. It's Caleb. He has a stuffed monkey in his hand and a notebook tucked under his arm. His other arm is in a sling.

He presents the monkey to Christine.

"I told you not to get me anything else," she says. "Bribery won't make me heal any faster. But thank you. Did you have a good walk?" She nods at the notebook. "How's the article coming?"

Caleb smiles and shakes his head. "I couldn't even figure out where to begin. I wrote a poem instead. It's called 'And the World Remained.' Kinda cheesy, actually."

"A poet, how sexy. Let's hear it."

Caleb blushes a little and shakes his head. "The whole poetry thing's a little new right now. But I promise I'll let you read it sometime. So, did the doctors come back? What'd they say?"

She shrugs. "Just a cracked rib, minor burns, and a really, really bruised neck."

Caleb winces. "I'm so sorry."

"Shut up," she says. "You saved my life."

"And your head? What about the CAT scan?"

Her eyes darken. "Like we thought. He, uh . . . he took out part of my brain."

"What does that mean? I mean, is it going to affect you? Memory, coordination, stuff like that?"

"No. The doctors think it's an unused section of brain tissue. I think it has to be like a filter, you know? To keep the spirits out. Like a lock on the door to our minds. Without it, they can come in and possess you any time. Or at least during sleep. And it also makes the voices easier to hear, I think."

"I'm sorry," says Caleb again.

"It's okay. That's how it had to be, I guess."

Caleb looks at her. "That's what your sister kept saying."

She looks at the stuffed monkey absently.

He clears his throat. "They still pulling bodies out of the Dream Center?"

She nods. "Forty-seven now, I think, but they said there are more in there. I stopped watching."

"We should probably leave soon. Morle—my dad—had a lot of friends who might be pretty pissed off right now. Like that doctor. I keep thinking he's going to walk in here. It's creeping me out. I think we should take off soon, just get as far away as we can."

"Yeah," she says to the monkey, "but there's one thing we need to do first."

→

Trees shoot past outside the car windows.

"We gotta make it fast. This might not be safe for us at all."

As they pull in the driveway even the air feels different. The Dream Center is gone, and sunlight now shines on the front lawn where its shadow would have fallen. But there's something else, Christine thinks. Even with the sun shining right on them, it still seems a little . . . dim.

They park beside a Channel 13 news van and get out. Christine glances at Caleb. His brow is furrowed; his eyes are fixed on nothing. He's been like that for most of the trip.

"Penny for your thoughts," she says.

He smiles halfheartedly over the roof of the car.

"Nothing," he says.

"Okay, two dollars."

"You drive a hard bargain," he says. "But really, it's nothing."

"Thirty million dollars!" she jokes, and pounds her fist on the car roof.

He sighs. "I'm just thinking that . . . I have the blood of a psychopath in my veins, you know? The thought that my dad was somebody capable of . . . what he was capable of is . . . It scares me."

She nods. "Hey, if genetics are any indicator, we're both screwed," she says. "But they're not. Caleb, the world is still here. You didn't end it. You did what you had to do. What can I say? You're not your father: you're you. And, well, you're hot."

Caleb laughs.

"So turn that frown upside down, sweet cakes," she says. "You and me are going to drive away from here together and start again."

"I know. I can't wait for that," Caleb says. "But I still can't help feeling like . . . I don't know . . . like something's wrong."

"Shush!" she says.

And he does. He comes around to her side of the car and takes her hand.

The smell of smoke still hangs faintly in the air.

The old asylum is nothing now but a field of black ash and shattered glass. A few twisted steel girders jut up like lightning-struck trees, but aside from that the place is leveled.

They walk slowly toward the wreckage, watching for anything dangerous. Caleb feels the cold steel of the gun in the waistband of his pants, concealed by his T-shirt, and he's glad they brought it.

"Hey, where you guys going?"

It's a tall guy with a red goatee. A camera hangs around his neck.

"Just wanted to drop some flowers by," Christine says. She holds up the bouquet in her hand. "It's so horrible what happened."

"No shit, Sherlock," says the guy. "Smoke?" He shakes one loose from his pack and holds it out to them, while lighting his own.

They shake their heads.

"You know," the guy says, "you aren't supposed to be around here. Only search and rescue and press are allowed. And the cops, naturally. I'm taking some pictures for the *Miami Herald*, then getting the hell out of here and going to Waffle House. I'm freakin' starving."

He takes a big drag off his cigarette, squinting at them.

"You're just here to drop some flowers by?" he asks.

They nod earnestly.

He looks around. "Alright. I'll take you guys in, but only because this one is such a hottie."

He nods toward Christine, who blushes, embarrassed.

"I have a press pass; they won't question it. Just don't get me in trouble. Come on."

Caleb wonders where the hell the *Miami Herald* was when all the kids started going missing, but Christine catches his eye and smiles at him, cheering him up.

The photographer leads them through a chain-link fence and flashes his press pass to the cop posted there. Caleb and Christine walk quickly behind him.

The photographer talks without taking the cigarette out of his mouth while simultaneously fiddling with his camera.

"The death toll of this thing is ridiculous. Eighty-one barbecued bodies in the place so far. That doesn't even count the ones who got incinerated completely. . . . "

A wave of nausea comes over Caleb. He did that. He killed those people. But he reminds himself it was all for the good.

The guy continues talking as they round the corner and come into sight of the pond. Still swollen from the rain, its waters reach almost all the way up to the ruined Dream Center's foundation. "You want to hear something really messed up, though? They haven't even broken this story yet; it airs tonight and won't make the papers until tomorrow."

Caleb looks up. He sees a diver in the water, pulling something behind him.

"They found bodies in the water too. And these didn't die from the fire, no way. They were put down there. Anchored to the bottom. I talked to the coroner; he said he's pretty sure some of them were drowned alive. And I'm not talking about just a few of them either. A lot of them were preserved because the water's almost freezing from the spring down below. The divers said there's a huge cave system down there too."

Christine has stopped. She stares at the photographer with eyes that suddenly look haunted.

"How many bodies?" she asks.

"Sixty . . . something . . ." and the guy digs a note pad out of the pocket of his denim shorts and flips a couple of pages. "Sixty . . . five. Hey, you alright, honey? You look like you're gonna puke."

"They've counted all the bodies?" she asks.

"Yeah, they scoured the bottom. The official report said they pulled up sixty-five bodies."

Caleb grabs the guy's arm. "Listen, this is really important. Are you sure there were only sixty-five? Not sixty-six?"

"Yeah," the guy says. "I got a quote from the head diver. He said they checked the whole spring, cleaned it out, and found sixty-five. Why? Are you kids on drugs or what? You look completely tweaked out."

Caleb and Christine exchange a look.

"I think we're going to be alright," Caleb says to the reporter, to Christine, to himself. And he laughs hard, releasing some of the tension that had knotted in his stomach.

Christine laughs too and hugs him.

"Damn," mutters the photographer around his cigarette. "I want some of whatever you kids got."

He walks away, snapping pictures of the diver as he emerges from the pond.

"I'm sorry I didn't come back sooner and help you. I'm sorry I didn't believe you. I'm sorry my father did all this. I'm sorry I had to kill all those kids. I'm so sorry," Caleb says.

Christine smiles, tears welling in her eyes.

"You did your best," she says, "and it was more than good enough. It was amazing."

She kisses him.

For an instant he holds back, thinking of his life back home, his direction, his plan, and he throws them all out and kisses her back, hard.

Maybe she *is* crazy, but he's a mass murderer.

And if this is what it's like living in insanity, he wouldn't mind doing it forever.

"Are either of you guys with the Red Cross?" asks somebody.

Caleb and Christine turn to find a tall, beautiful black girl of about fifteen years old. She's wearing a muddy, white nightgown with a blanket wrapped around her shoulders.

"They're supposed to take me back to their office so we can try and get a hold of my folks," she says.

"No," says Christine, "I don't know where they are. Are you alright? What happened?"

She shakes her head. "All I can say is this," she says, "it's too much of an ordeal to go into all of it. I was locked up in there since just about as long as I can remember, and I didn't belong there, 'cause wasn't nothing wrong with me. I don't even remember how I got there, that's how long it was. And they did bad stuff in that place, too, let me tell you. And then last night I wake up and I'm in that pond over there and I got a weight around my neck." You can tell she's fighting the urge to cry. "Don't even know how I got there. I wake up and I'm in the water, and I grab the edge of this boat that must've turned over. Somebody put a rope with a weight on the end of it around my neck, but I was able to get out of it, praise God, otherwise I'd have drowned."

"She'd have been the sixty-sixth," whispers Christine.

"I'm sorry you had to go through all that," says Caleb. "But thank God you made it."

"Yeah," she says, "I just kept prayin' like my daddy always taught me, and everything was okay." A tear sneaks out and she quickly flicks it away with one finger.

"I'm Caleb," he says, reaching to shake her hand.

"And I'm Christine."

An inhuman scream pierces the quiet. They all turn.

From the darkness of the woods, a figure approaches. Gray tangles of hair fall over unblinking eyes. A tattered skirt hangs to her feet. Blood, like war paint, adorns her cheeks. It's the witch.

She's gotten inside the police perimeter somehow and is cursing at an officer who tries to subdue her and get her out of the area.

"Ma'am, please," he says. "Ma'am . . ."

"TICK, TICK, TICK," she says. "YOU'RE ALL BLACKBIRDS! You're all baking! You're all BURNING, BURNING, BURNING, BURNING!"

The police officer grabs her and begins dragging her away as gently as he can.

"Look at the sun!" she says. "Already wilting, already dying! The morning of darkness is coming! The trumpet of silence is blowing! Johnny Morle got his wish!"

Then she looks over at Christine and Caleb. Her gaze seems to clamp on them like an invisible vice. She will not turn her head away.

Christine looks for a place to hide, panicked, but it's too late.

Suddenly the witch lashes out.

It happens so fast, it hardly even registers in anyone's mind when the officer falls, unmoving. Stabbed into his eye: a knife.

The witch runs with inhuman speed. Before Caleb and Christine can react she's there. She grabs Christine by the hair, pulling her face-to-face.

Whispering, singing: *"Johnny Morle got his wish, Johnny Morle got his wish, Johnny Morle got his wish!"*

"No, he didn't," says Caleb, pushing himself between the mother and daughter. "I killed him."

The witch still ignores him, whispering instead to Christine. "Dying was his wish, it was. That's the end of the world for him. And dying would never work for him unless his son would do him in!"

"But that's it," says Caleb. "It's over now. The world isn't ending. Right?"

The girl wrapped in the blanket is looking on in disbelief. "This is freaking me out. What is going on?"

Christine just stares at her mother intensely.

"Christine was always the bad one," says the witch, "but my sweet Anna would always help me and Johnny."

"I killed John Morle," Caleb says firmly. "The world isn't ending."

The witch smiles. *"Six and sixty souls,"* she says, *"drowned in the dark."*

"There are only sixty-five, Mother."

"Count again, my daughter dear. The devil is awake."

And the witch lets Christine go, and as fast as she had come, she is gone, running away like a puma, melting into the shadows of the woods and disappearing.

The police haven't even noticed their comrade yet, lying dead amongst the weeds at the edge of the forest.

"She's crazy," Caleb says. "She can't be right."

"That was your mom?" the girl in the blanket says. "Dang. . . ."

Caleb is looking all around, noticing what he had somehow missed before. Things look fake, fragile, wrong. The sun is hollow. He can stare right at it.

"My name's Keisha," says the girl. She puts a comforting arm around Christine, who still stares at the place where her mother disappeared into the forest. "Look, honey, it's going to be alright."

"Wait," Christine says. "Your name is Keisha? Keisha Bent?"

"Whoa. How did you know my last name?"

The reporter with the red goatee is walking back by, taking the last drag of his cigarette and looking at the ground. He rolls the burning filter between his fingers. As he approaches, Caleb notices something over his shoulder sticking out of the surface of the water.

"Hey," Caleb says, stopping him. The guy looks up. "What's that in the water? That stake?"

The reporter turns around, shading his eyes, "Uhhh . . . oh, that's where they found another body. Foul play for sure. That one got whacked in the face with an axe or something. They think he mighta fallen off the roof."

Caleb's face is very still. His mouth barely moves. His voice is barely even a whisper. "And he landed there, in the water?"

"Yep," says the reporter.

"Is he one of the sixty-five you were talking about earlier?"

"Ah, no. Those were the ones in the deep part of the water with the ropes around their necks. If you count that poor bastard with the axe in his head as one of the pond bodies, that makes . . . uh," he glances at his notepad, " . . . sixty-six."

Christine looks at Caleb. Neither of them can breathe.

At that moment Caleb feels closer to her than he ever has to another human being.

"Let's get the hell out of here," he says.

Christine nods frantically.

"Can y'all give me a ride?" asks Keisha. "I'm sick of waitin.'"

"Yeah," says Christine. "Definitely."

"Look," says Keisha, "I don't know what y'all are freaking out about, but my daddy was a great man, and he always said no matter what you believe, whether you worship Allah or Buddha or Jesus or whatever, if you surrender to God can't nobody stop you. So whatever's goin' on, y'all are gonna overcome it."

"I hope he was right," says Christine.

"'Course he's right. My daddy's a great man."

"We know," says Caleb.

"What do you mean? Y'all know my dad?" asks Keisha, following them toward the car. "Is that how you know my name? Why are y'all walking so fast?"

Caleb glances back over his shoulder. A few large bubbles break on the surface of the pond. It's probably just a diver bringing up another body . . . Probably.

"Everything will be explained," says Caleb, "sooner or later."

That answer seems to satisfy Keisha, and she doesn't speak again for a while.

As the three of them walk up the driveway, leaving the old asylum for the last time, Caleb tries to pretend he's confronted all his old, silly childhood fears and won. He imagines waking up and realizing this was all just another dream, the random firing of neurons, the stuff of campfire stories. He almost succeeds.

The wind through the trees is eerily steady. There are no gusts. The air is just moving, slow and heavy, bending the tall pines with its weight.

The clouds are moving a little too fast.

The birds are all flying away.

"Everything's going to be okay," Keisha says, maybe to herself, maybe not.